ALSO BY A. E. OSWORTH

We Are Watching Eliza Bright

AWAKENED

AWAKENED

a novel

A. E. OSWORTH

GCP

GRAND
CENTRAL

New York   Boston

Grand Central Publishing
Hachette Book Group
1290 Avenue of the Americas, New York, NY 10104
grandcentralpublishing.com
@grandcentralpub

First Edition: April 2025

Grand Central Publishing is a division of Hachette Book Group, Inc. The Grand Central Publishing name and logo is a registered trademark of Hachette Book Group, Inc.

The publisher is not responsible for websites (or their content) that are not owned by the publisher.

Grand Central Publishing books may be purchased in bulk for business, educational, or promotional use. For information, please contact your local bookseller or the Hachette Book Group Special Markets Department at special.markets@hbgusa.com.

Print book interior design by Taylor Navis

Library of Congress Cataloging-in-Publication Data
Names: Osworth, A. E., author.
Title: Awakened : a novel / A.E. Osworth.
Description: First edition. | New York ; Boston : GCP, 2025.
Identifiers: LCCN 2024045647 | ISBN 9781538757697 (hardcover) | ISBN
    9781538757727 (ebook)
Subjects: LCSH: Artificial intelligence—Fiction | LCGFT: Fantasy fiction.
    | Novels.
Classification: LCC PS3615.S93 A95 2025 | DDC 813/.6—dc23/eng/20240927
LC record available at https://lccn.loc.gov/2024045647

ISBNs: 9781538757697 (hardcover), 9781538757727 (ebook)

Printed in the United States of America

LSC-C

Printing 1, 2025

For everyone who feels betrayed by J. K. Rowling

The Sun, Reversed

Pay attention. Something amazing is about to happen.

It is a chilly Maine morning, which, when the morning is in Maine, might be a large variety of mornings, given that many mornings in Maine could be considered chilly. Perhaps it is early spring. Or maybe fall is blooming red on the mountain. Heck, it could even be a winter morning, warm compared to all the other mornings huddled in around it. Regardless, it is Maine and the house is set very far from the road—the driveway wends through a wood for perhaps half a mile before the house, the exterior a happy yellow in the process of being repainted a lady bird brown, peeks out from behind the trees. Eventually, sometime in the future (though who knows exactly when), this shy house will smile from behind its mothers' skirts to greet a packed car inching its way up the driveway. But that is not the amazing thing about to happen. Presently, no such car exists. The house says hello to no one. The sun itself is just cresting the tops of the trees, the only witness and still sleepy. It is early, even for a morning.

The yard is strewn with ladders and buckets and tarps, which makes sense given the apparent renovation. Next to the fuse box, just inside the garage, stands a woman whose wild hair curls from under a knit beanie, static shock in the crisp air. She is blessed with a prominent nose (no delicacy here) and a neck that's dancing grace (all delicacy here), which is, at present, wrapped within a scarf. She closes her eyes and inhales deeply. Woodsmoke on the air. The wind gives her goose bumps.

She holds a drill, squeezes the trigger to test the battery, the electric whir cutting into the sound of a woods waking up. "Okay," she says, as though she is gearing up to do something difficult. "Okay." She opens the fuse box and shuts off the master switch, the red lever at the very top. She can hear the crackle as the power leaves the lines along her roof; everything is still for a moment as she stares up, listening, making sure she can't hear any more power. Only birdsong.

Now, one might expect her to operate the drill on some part of the house, given all the contextual clues. But her face changes, tentative to hard. She puts the drill down and walks through the interior garage door, stopping at a workbench along the way to interface with a coffee can full of batteries, some of them old and crusty and some of them brand-new, shining like jewels from un-use. She hauls the vessel onto her hip as she enters the house, conspicuously door-alarm-less. Her gaze flicks to every battery-supported piece of technology as she checks things off the list in her mind.

She can't think of anything else. She's gotten it all. She lets out a breath she doesn't realize she's been holding, deflating with relief only for a second before squaring her shoulders and facing the rest of her house.

She tears it apart. She begins a honey badger search for any device that one might consider "smart": she rips a thermostat off the wall, hauls a television outside, adds her laptop and phone to the careful pile, lovingly crafted of expensive technology and split firewood. When it becomes apparent she needs more fuel, she grabs a dining room chair from her set of six and breaks the legs off it with her bare hands, popping each rung from between the top rail and the bottom with a delicious snap, a smile creeping across her face: relief, as though crack-ing her knuckles.

When the pile is complete, her house stripped bare of anything that can connect to the internet, she pours herself the peatiest Scotch she has. She grabs a respirator and a can of gasoline and tucks a box of long hearth matches under her arm. Woodsmoke. Woodsmoke on the air. A portent. And after she drenches the pile, each motherboard and solid-state drive and display cable soaked well beyond recoverable function and smelling noxious; after looking once more to the fresh morning sky and giving a toast to the errant cloud above; after taking a decadent sip of expensive alcohol and fastening her respirator securely over her nose and mouth, she, calmly and deliberately, sets it all on fire.

PART ONE
The Magician

Four of Cups

On the morning of their half birthday in their thirty-first year around the sun, Wilder wakes in possession of Magic.

One might contend that things don't happen that way, that adults do not simply wake to Power. But one might consider this: adults often wake up to terrible things, like they have thrown their back out while *sleeping* or they have cancer or someone they know has perished in the night. Why shouldn't it be something nice for a fucking change?

When Wilder pictures themself, they see only their conscious thought, a cascade of pure blue light, a being created of twisted, rain-heavy cloud made solid and brought to earth. But outwardly, they do live in a meat sack. They are pale, not quite so luminously white as linen sheets, but not far from it, with freckles that stand out against their skin like they've been drawn on. Their hair is naturally orange and sits atop their head in a wild, gnomish fashion. Like a Troll Doll. They have the crooked teeth of someone whose parents never dreamed of incurring dental fees. They have breasts they never think about, which are currently cocooned under a quilt made of old T-shirts and topped with a cat, her long fur just as marmalade as Wilder's coiffure.

It is early for Wilder, which means it is a normal morning time for everyone else. They have six shitty gigs, and they squint at their cracked phone trying to decide which combination of them will net the most money today. Will it be Taskrabbit? Instacart shopping? It is very cold out; should they hop on Fiverr and try to get eight hours' worth of transcription? Or copywriting? That way, they won't have to leave.

Wilder loves not leaving their apartment. They are a rock in the middle of a river—everything rushes around them while they stay still. Or one might even think of them as the river. Ever-flowing, slow but impermanent and, therefore, aloof. At least that is what they tell themself when they try to narrativize why it is they have no friends, no family they speak to. The truth is, of course, much simpler and far harsher: they see other people only as rivals. Everyone is vying for the same limited resources, and resources are always limited. It is a very lonely existence, actually.

Their cat, the Lady Anastasia, makes biscuits on their chest, which gets them out of bed fast. They scoop food into her bowl and stretch their arms out to their sides. When they do this, they can put their palms flat on each wall. It is both depressing and comforting. Wilder likes a cave; their room certainly is one. Everything in their apartment is thin and long, railroad style. They have a twin bed shoved in a corner, a stack of library books next to it topped with a cold mug of tea from the night before. A wire rack of clothes. A small closet that can't open all the way, its door impeded by the steam heater. Legally, this counts as a bedroom.

Something about the day (they do not yet know what) quivers with possibility; they hope it is some good omen that they are about to make a lot of money. They charge the most for research tasks and their bank account has fifty-two dollars in it because they just paid rent. So it is time, they think, for Taskrabbit above all else. They accept a "research" booking, which is personal assistant stuff, never truly interesting. Their task today: plan a vacation for two people with a budget of ten thousand dollars.

It turns out it is extremely demoralizing to plan a vacation for two when the budget is what takes them nearly a third of a year to make. They have never seen this number in their bank account balance, not ever, not once. They decide to fortify themself with coffee. Wilder jams their glasses, taped at the hinge, onto their face, wraps their quilt around themself, and steps into the cold kitchen-dining-living-room-foyer. The floor is freezing and the zing on their toes wakes them up enough to make it across to the kitchen in a pre-caffeinated state. On their way, they pass a tired man in a janitorial uniform—their room-mate. He is eating cereal. They grunt "hey" at each other.

Wilder scoops coffee into a shitty percolator; their roommate watches Netflix on his phone and chews loudly. Wilder's roommate is a gentle, quiet dude named Andy who works as a night janitor at New York University; he is just getting home now, and Wilder presumes he's about to go to sleep. His phone rings while Wilder silently chugs a glass of water. Their roommate is as taciturn as Wilder is, as content (if one can call it contentment) to be alone, so when his phone rings and interrupts a confectionary war of some kind, it is the reasonable assumption that he will begin speaking in Spanish to his parents or his sister, the only people he regularly talks to, perhaps ever talks to. Indeed, he picks up the phone and says, "Hey, Mama." His mother is a loud talker. Wilder can always hear her clearly, though the phone is never on speaker.

As they pour nearly expired milk into their coffee cup, the vol-ume makes eavesdropping on the exchange unavoidable, which is less a conversation and more their roommate's answering to rapid-fire grilling—how is the school, do you think you'll ever go to the school, why is the school so expensive—in an exhausted tone that suggests this is, perhaps, the hundred and twelfth time he's had this "conversation" with his mother. Something nags at Wilder, but they still fix their coffee, take one sip, and trot back to their room. They are so pre-exhausted by the day that Wilder has forgotten they do not speak Spanish, have never even studied it. Uneasy without explanation (or rather, with the usual explanation of "capitalism"), they close the door and set about planning a vacation to a place they will never visit.

Two of Wands, Reversed

Aside from not knowing they woke up bilingual, Wilder also doesn't know they're being watched. Doesn't know they've been flickering, showing signs of Magic for days, doesn't know that on someone else's radar—someone with already Awakened Power—they've just lit up like a Coney Island Ferris wheel. Doesn't know that there is, at this very moment, a calming presence being dispatched, albeit a little later than he would prefer, given a set of unforeseen circumstances.

Quibble is wending his way toward Wilder's apartment the quickest way he knows how. He is a solid, steady man with sparkly brown eyes and generous lashes. He's a gentleman of alto experience, now a buzzy bass, slow and deliberate in his words. But quick in his mind; everything he says is clever. A real juxtaposition. He has a nose like someone played Pin the Tail on the Donkey with a scalene triangle, stuck it wherever, and called it a day. The nose umbrellas over a lopsided smile. He dumps out onto Wilder's street and intends to knock on their front door, introduce himself. Maybe take them out for coffee. Anything to ease the shock of what's just happened. This is his first time intervening with someone newly Awakened, but he is confident he can improve the process. Make it more believable, less traumatizing. Make it kinder.

A. E. OSWORTH

He remembers his own Awakening. It ripped through him like a stomach virus; he did vomit, actually. But that could've been the external circumstances. His parents had just died. Suddenly. A plane crash. He was seventeen, all alone. When his Power Awakened, no one came for him. For a decade, he thought he was the only one in the world. That he was crazy or a mutated freak or both.

His body begins to react to his flashback with a yawning void sensation, the floor dropping from under his feet until he buries the feeling. He notes that he has done it—something "maladaptive" his therapist is adamant he begin to mark—and he knows that later the feeling will poke its gnarled hand back up, undead, because one can never bury a live feeling without suffering the zombie repercussion. For right now, however, he has a job to do.

The building he faces is sad. Drab, with streaks of mold-esque black organic matter running down its block-concrete face. Quibble itches to power wash it, to watch the dirt run off the rough surface. He hopes it's not mold, just the hot breath of the city marking the façade with grit. A dumpster in front of the building overflows. Baby fussing floats from a window. He speculates about who he's going to meet—Artemis says this one is queer, trans. She's always right about that. But is the baby theirs? Hers? His? What do they look like? What does their Awakened Power feel like—what does it do without them trying, if anything, or do they have to actively use it? And what does it feel like to cast with them?

He texts Artemis. anything else i should know?

Well. We missed them. They're out

fuck.

AWAKENED

Yeah

can you see where they went?

I'm working on it. Right now I can just
See they're not where you are

Quibble wonders if he'll be able to clock this person. If, as a trans person himself, he would be able to tell who they were if he wandered around for a while. Immediately, he feels like a bad person for thinking he'd be able to use some kind of fucked-up trans radar—based on what sort of problematic clues, exactly? Based on who looks out of place? Who looks a little bit uncomfortable? Some kind of homogenized queer signaling? Then the internal (but not quite internalized) voice of his therapist says that's all very human of him. And then the voice muses about how sometimes, for him, it feels good to be clocked. That it's about intention, about who's doing the seeing. He types to Artemis, again, laughing at himself.

i'm gonna go for a walk, i guess? it'll
be scary if they come home and i'm
lurking outside their door.

Whatever else this is or winds up being, Quibble doesn't want it to be scary (though it will be, despite his best efforts). Softness is the whole point.

Wilder is also taking a walk. A walk with purpose, the purpose being the library. Because they couldn't shake the feeling that something was irrevocably weird, they couldn't focus on their work. They decided to change their scenery even though the whole point of taking this job was to not go out in the cold.

They cut through the weekday smattering of pedestrians at speed, past the low-slung bakery that always smells of rising bread, of the butter melting in baking croissants. The woman on the corner selling tamales—Wilder can understand her, too, as she speaks with a customer in a suit, and yet they still do not notice (come on, guy). They round the corner to the elevated metro platform, the tracks aboveground this far out into Queens. At the base of the platform's stairs, they see a very lost Japanese family speaking to each other, two adults arguing as the two kids helpfully point at the upside-down subway map in their hands, ignored by their parents. They argue about which way to take the train for Manhattan. They must be tourists. A strange time to come, February—New York City has a good six weeks on either end of summer where it doesn't induce depression. The father (Wilder assumes this is the father) pulls aside someone and says, "Pardon me" in the careful way of someone who does not speak English but for a few phrases they learned on Duolingo. The someone that the father pulls aside: a man with lines on his face so pronounced that he may as well *be* the subway map. Wilder watches the ultra-concentrated look of someone who knows six phrases of English being confronted by one of those phrases in English spoken by someone else who also knows six phrases in English. It is a familiar look in this borough. In this man's case the look is a stare of both fierce attention and resigned politeness.

Wilder does not generally speak to people. In fact, they generally go out of their way to avoid it. But something about the children, about the cute, stupid way they're holding the map the wrong side up, that they have a paper map at all, and something, also, about the way the other stranger looks so pained, torn between the desire to be helpful and the shyness manufactured by linguistic distance, makes Wilder at least think about stopping (and today is different from every other day they've ever had, not that they've realized it, so why not do something a little bit out of character?). It is so against their nature that their body tries to walk past. The crosswalk lights up with a blinking orange hand and they nearly run to catch it, have to think about pausing instead.

First, they speak to the lone lined man. "Don't worry," they say. Their voice is crackly, husky with disuse. They have only grunted one word this morning. This is normal. Many days their voice never wakes up. They clear their throat and try again. "I've got this." They—oh Christ—they still do not notice. Their mouth is making different shapes than it would normally make, their coffee has made them alert, they're outside in the suck-the-breath-out-their-lungs cold, their cheeks turning red, their mind on their actual face and the air flowing in and out through their nose, all the parts where the words come from and yet they haven't figured it out. What will it take? What will it take for them to notice that their life is forever different?

Then they turn to the family, who all turn toward Wilder, a bland politeness wiping their features clean of confusion. The mother looks like she is holding her breath. Wilder figures they better get to the point. "Manhattan is that way," they say. "The entrance across the street. Over there." They point and everyone, including the lone lined man, including Wilder, takes a second to turn and look at the opposing stairs, packed with people on their way into work.

Then the family turns back. The children's reactions are what Wilder would expect: one of the children smiles a small, smug victory—she'd been correct about which train to take. The other hides his mouth from their parents, like he is whispering, as he sticks his tongue out.

The parents, however—their mouths open so wide they look like they are about to receive a train into them. They both quickly close and cover their pie holes, the father with the back of his hand and the mother with the tips of her fingers. Wilder's brows furrow—had these two perhaps heard that New Yorkers were rude, that they would not receive help if they needed it? In Wilder's estimation, it was far ruder to do what they had just done—interrupt someone, approach them. The rule of New York, they figure, is to pretend that everyone has privacy in public. Or—is this a gender thing? Now Wilder's face echoes that same bland politeness, which isn't politeness at all but rather the armor of expected microaggression (or, to be perfectly fair, macroaggression). If they just paid closer attention, they would realize neither of these options is the correct answer. If they looked at the lone lined man, a New Yorker, perhaps they would be helped along by a few more context clues. Or perhaps not, as it seems as though, this morning at least, Wilder is a fucking idiot.

The mother recovers first, closes her mouth but keeps the tips of her fingers over it and smiles from behind them, genuinely this time. "Thank you," she says, and Wilder's face relaxes. "Forgive my surprise, it's just"—she gestures to them—"you're American."

"Uh," Wilder responds, not understanding what social territory they are now in and worrying that they don't understand precisely because they are "American" (white). "Yeah?" is all they manage to say, already wondering how to disengage and run away.

"Sorry," the mother says, registering Wilder's extreme confusion. "We just don't expect Americans to speak Japanese so fluently. How long did you live in Japan?"

"I don't speak Japanese," says Wilder, in Japanese. And as the family's mouths all drop open once again, Wilder notices. (Finally!) They notice the bend in their mouth that they've never had before, their tongue flattening to make a different set of glottal caverns. What they are hearing with their actual ears, the sounds pressing against their actual eardrums, slams into some new territory, an instant double consciousness that immediately gives them a headache. Sound pulses from ear to ear around them, like wearing bad headphones at the library. They unintentionally tilt their head to one side, trying to expel water that isn't there.

"Uh," they say, suddenly deeply aware of the pastiche of languages around them, the way they now innately understand the entire world as they argue, cajole, compliment, screech, whisper, rant, plead, cheer, ask, update, impress, answer, invent, predict, worry, and echo, echo, echo—it's too much. "I meant to say I have never lived in Japan." They say it very, very fast.

"Oh—well—your Japanese is very good."

An awkward pause, which would usually make Wilder want to perish. But what Wilder is feeling now is so, so much worse than merely wishing for death. The mother saves them by saying, "Thank you!" The family turns around and heads in the correct direction.

There is just the lined man left. Wilder stares at him. He stares back. Normally, the lined man would just grunt and move on with his day—not because he isn't cheerful. He actually is. Has a reputation in his family for being too nice, in fact, nice to stray dogs and strangers, chatty in queues even for unpleasant chores, but this country isn't like back home and not everyone can understand him when he talks. It is precisely because Wilder spoke in Urdu that the lone lined man—who isn't really lone at all, not really, not in the rest of his life—smiles warmly and asks, "How many languages do you speak?"

Instead of saying anything at all, Wilder's hands fly to their mouth and they run. If Wilder were a cartoon, the ground underneath their feet would fold like fabric and their departure would make a gunshot sound. But they are not a cartoon. They are extremely real. And that is why this is not possible, they think. That is why they are absolutely one hundred percent going clinically insane. Except, they think, if they were going insane, no one else would be able to understand them, and these people do understand them. They are interrupted by the idea that maybe they are sleeping and, therefore, imagining the people, so they kick a trash can to be sure, the result of their extremely scientific experiment being that their foot hurts and they scatter garbage across the sidewalk.

"What the fuck?" they hear the woman selling tamales in front of the bakery say in Spanish, another language that Wilder doesn't speak, and they scream—a quiet scream, high-pitched, and all the closest dogs begin to bark.

It's Magic, of course, but they haven't gotten there yet, which is hilarious because Wilder has spent so much of their childhood—all that time they should have been learning any of these other languages—reading fantasy novels, subconsciously preparing for this moment. Or perhaps *unconsciously* is the better word. They have packed so many narratives of magical discovery into their own head and the average of all the reactions is seated somewhere inside them, stuck in their rib cage and silently unfolding.

There is the doubt reaction, ranging from mild to hostile. Perhaps the first stage of magical discovery is denial. There is the patented and frequent but-I'm-not-special, and its opposite, the I-secretly-knew-I-was-special. There is awe, wonder. There is rocking back and forth, doubting sanity. There is joy at a crazier, happier world, the classic child-like acceptance of new circumstance. Protagonists have all sorts of reactions to being told they possess magic.

Alas, the average of all these reactions unfolding in their rib cage in the nonfictional world all at the same time is a panic attack.

Rarely are they surprised by panic attacks the way they used to be. Back when they were very small and had no language to describe gender dysphoria, their body would, instead, manifest a matrix of anxiety to house the dissonance. They never stopped getting panic attacks; they simply became expert in having them. Medication? Out of the question. Wilder didn't grow up as a person with health insurance and they didn't grow into one either, and even in the era of "universal" "health" "care," being a person with insurance isn't a quality one simply manifests overnight (like Magic). But what Wilder can do is breathe deep into their belly when they feel one coming. Count the number of things they can see, the number of smells they can smell. Pick at their cuticles until they feel the everyday manageable pain calling them to step from the undulating ocean of tooth-splitting worry back to shore. They can always mark the sensation of impending alarm. A swell like a tide in their stomach-chest. A hollow feeling in their bottom teeth. A shortening of attention span; a turning inward, unable to watch anything but their own sea-horizon.

So, just as none of the neat, received narratives fit the way they felt their body move through the world in a gender-sense, none of the neat, received narratives fit exactly the experience of discovering their own Power Awakened. But *more*. More extreme, more sudden, more alone—for who ever heard of magic really, actually happening? Plenty of trans people exist—you can throw a stone in any direction, really, and hit a trans person in the shins. But Magicians? Alone, alone, alone. And so. A volcano of dread-fluster-hysteria-cold-sweat-fight-flight-freeze explodes. Their hands shake with it, with the effort of seeming normal as they speedwalk, keeping themself as low to the ground as a slinking cat. The sounds around them become muffled and they struggle to breathe. Their face is numb. Their thoughts are light. They scream again, absent any trigger, and people cross the street to avoid them.

They finally reach their building's front door. They do not notice a man across the street, watching them.

But there's Quibble, squinting, watching them do a Monty Python walk because they are sick with worry-dread, not to mention a hurt foot from the trash can punt. Quibble texts, well i think we have a winner to his dispatcher.

Wilder claws at their keys with helium-filled fingers. They make their way to their bedroom, and Quibble can see them sit on their bed through the barred window. First floor. Easy enough, he thinks, if they don't answer the door. Certainly easier than it was to get all the way here.

Wilder stares at nothing, all their coping mechanisms forgotten. Or perhaps the better way to say it: their coping mechanisms do not quite address this, the sudden return to smallness, the dropping away of agency and understanding. They fling their hands around, try to feel something in them, shake them awake. They breathe shallow. They rock side to side. They hear a wet ripping sound immediately to their right, bouncing loudly off their too-close walls, and this is not a symptom of anxiety they're familiar with. And that's because the sound is real.

Wilder jumps off the bed, backs up, trips back onto it. They grab their T-shirt quilt and hold it up in front of them as if it were a shield. They mean to hide their eyes with it, but they can't look away. A—portal? Is that what they'd call it?—opens slowly, suckingly, in the middle of their limited floor space. It grows from penny-sized to human-sized in a matter of seconds, torn open like the air is cheap fabric instead of nothing. A man steps through, smiling crookedly under a large nose, holding his hands out and up. He opens his mouth, ready to speak some sort of words, but he is drowned out by the sound of screaming. Wilder does not realize they are screaming. They are enveloped by screaming. Only screaming.

Then *flick*. Dark.

Quibble catches them as they slide off the bed to the ground. He looks down at the body before him. He is unsure if he should be chastising himself for displaying Power before having the chance to talk about it. It may have been the wrong call. The thing is, though—what exactly is the right one? He and Artemis have been trying to figure it out for ages; they have gotten it "right" exactly zero times.

Quibble wonders if there isn't a right way, never has been and never will be. That this is never a conversation that feels good or sane or fair. The other person will always react however it is they're going to react, regardless. Still. He sought to be a comfort and he failed. He feels a way about that, even as he acknowledges the following: how else would he get inside their house? His knocks had gone unanswered.

Sometimes all one can do is make the next best decision in the moment, given all the givens. And not everyone can See the future. Quibble certainly can't. He kneels. He does not yet know Wilder's name. He thinks of them only as "this witch." Their face is somehow both flushed and paper-white, the standard pallor of the recently fainted. Their lips stand out plum against their panic-boiled skin. Their cheeks are heavy, round with sudden onset muscle relaxation. Their mouth lolls open slightly. Their eyelashes, hard to see given how light red-blond they are, flutter. Quibble can see Wilder's trying-to-swim-up-ness.

He can hear stirring in the next room. A roommate. Shit. Of course they don't live alone. Nearly no one lives alone, except for him. He forgets sometimes. He tries to be thoughtful, but the sharing of space isn't a mother tongue. Impossible to keep at the front of mind even at the most neutral of times, and this isn't the most neutral of times.

He feels strange, grabbing their face. He doesn't know them at all. But it would be ruder, he feels, to grab their Meta-Face with the internal Hands made of his own Awakened Power and yank. That is so much more personal than a mere body. So he touches them as gently as he can manage, tentative. He puts his palms to their cheeks. Taps. Strokes. "Hey—" Not knowing their name is awkward, and he draws the *e* and the *y* sounds out long. He tries to stay quiet. "Hey, buddy—"

He hears a muffled, sleepy "Wilder?" from beyond the wall. "What the fuck was that noise?"

"Hey, Wilder," Quibble whispers, thankful for the name supplied. "Come on, bud. Up time." The new witch, Wilder, stirs and Quibble eyes the closet. It is so small—will he be able to fit in there? Bouncing from the room will make the sound again. While the Unawakened will usually do anything not to notice Awakened Power, he doubts the roommate will be able to rationalize such a thing away, not when it happens in his own home. Twice.

Quibble spots a lock on the door and rocks back on his heels, clicking it quietly into place. He returns to Wilder. "All righty, let's—up. I'm going to get you onto the bed." He grabs them under their arms, can feel their ribs, their shallow breathing returning to something deeper. A short-circuit. A reset. Good. Perhaps they need it to readjust their world. Their head rolls on their neck and Quibble reaches out to support it with his hand as he struggles their no-help-weight up three feet, spilling them onto the bed as kindly as he can. He grunts. It's a low sound, an almost-growl.

"What? Who— Wilder, are you okay?" The roommate raps at the door, polite but firm. "Wilder?"

The new witch's face flinches at each sharp knock, which, ultimately, gets them to open their eyes. When they do, Quibble's face swims into view. His eyes are doe-like and worried. A set of three small wrinkles sits between his eyebrows and they relax as Wilder wakes. Awakens.

Wilder shoots backward, sits up and pulls their quilt back around them. They do not yet know Quibble's name. But he is handsome, and Wilder is surprised by the faraway small part of themself that wants to trust someone because they are beautiful. Then they remember with the weight of a falling anvil how he came to be in their bedroom. They open their mouth again, a sharp intake of air, ready to scream once more. But Quibble puts his finger to his lips and, for a reason Wilder can't quite acknowledge, they shut their mouth around the sound they were about to loose. Both turn their heads toward the closed door and back to each other.

Quibble's whisper is so quiet as to be almost entirely inaudible, merely a breath with syllables, an ASMR video. Wilder has to lean in to hear.

"Listen," the man says, and Wilder clocks the buzz. They don't have a lot of friends—any friends—but they're not stupid. They've watched enough trans YouTube to understand Quibble is a trans man. "I know what you've been through this morning. It is very confusing. I am very sorry. Get us—" The knocks begin again and Quibble speaks even more quietly, a feat Wilder hadn't considered possible. "Get us some privacy and we'll talk about it."

Wilder nods once, their movements restrained. They feel hungover and their head rings like a bell. They wince as they get off the bed, dragging the quilt with them, and Quibble plops down, sitting on the edge. Wilder clicks the lock open and cracks the door. "Andy—hi. Everything's, um. Fine."

Roommate Andy raises an eyebrow, then breaks into a wide grin of the shit-eating variety. "Ah," he says.

"What?" Wilder responds, confused, as they look over their shoulder where Andy's looking. "Oh, uh. I'm—um."

"Nah, man, I get it, totally—wow, you've never had anyone in here before and I wouldn't have guessed you liked the D." Wilder can feel themselves light up red and they hear the soft *whump* of a whole face being buried straight into rumpled sheets from behind them. "Listen, I'm tryna sleep, though. Could you two be a little quieter?"

"Andy, it's not—"

"No shame in it, bro! No shame in it! No need to deny it! Just quieter, okay?" His eyes twinkle as he pulls the door shut, and both witches can hear his low chuckle as he shuffles his way back to bed.

Wilder whirls toward Quibble, who is still face down in the bed. "What the *fuck* is going on?"

Quibble stands, and Wilder's body tries to do two things at once: back away from him and shake his outstretched hand. Quibble's eye-corners crinkle at Wilder's gawky weirdo dance. Wilder is struck by how completely he smiles. His whole face cheers and a knot they hadn't noticed between their shoulder blades loosens just a little bit.

"Hello to you, too. You're Wilder, seems like. I'm Quibble. And this morning, you became a witch. Congratulations!"

"I'm not a woman," they respond.

"I didn't say you were?"

"I— Sorry—you said 'witch.' I thought witches were—"

"Yeah? Witches are—?"

Wilder drops it. Instead they ask, "Why are you in my room? *How* are you in my room?"

"Magic," says Quibble, "is the answer to both of those questions."

Wilder deploys the voice of every adult their child-self heard right before whatever book they were reading at the time was ripped from their hands: "Magic doesn't exist."

Quibble raises his eyebrows. "Then what the fuck is going on with your day?"

In response, Wilder moves to open their mouth to argue, but they close it. Because Quibble has a point. The first thing they do with all this confirmation is touch their own still-hurting betrashcanned foot, pinching their a-little-bit-swollen pinky toe to make sure they are not still out cold. Just in case. But no, it hurts and Quibble pretends not to notice as he bends down and says, "Who ish dish? Who is dish pretty kitty?"

"The Lady Anastasia," Wilder says while their cat shamelessly requests pets from a terrifying magic stranger. Then: a not small silence in which Wilder thinks. They feel like they are going to puke.

"Okay," Wilder says. "So let's say magic exists, then, just for now. I haven't really decided yet." They pause to take a beer-sized gulp of air. "Do I get a book about it? Go to a school? All the stories say I get a toad or a letter or a broomstick. None of them mention getting a terrifying trespasser instead."

"I'm not a trespasser!"

"You broke into my apartment. I'm—still not quite sure how."

Quibble shakes his head. "It's Magic, pal. How else would you explain this, exactly?"

They close their open mouth because every single retort feels contrived, like they've seen it somewhere before. Except for one. One shining kernel of light that, if they know what is good for them, they should put their internal Hands around and cup gently; they should nurture this thought-feeling, the one that whispers triumphantly, *I knew it.* The one that is passion, excitement: *I knew this was the way the world worked. I knew that underneath everything there was magic.* But it is very difficult to choose that thought-feeling, even on the best of days, even for people who have a lot of practice doing so.

So instead: "Do I get an admissions letter? A syllabus? What about a massive safe full of gold guarded by goblins and a dragon? I wouldn't say no to that." And the hope in their voice sours into biting sarcasm as they try to make sure Quibble absolutely cannot see the kernel of light in their head, cannot hear longing, the hope that all the ways reality has broken their heart might be reversed.

Quibble isn't perceptive in a Magic way, but neither is he a complete ninny. He has been here before, after all, in the place where everything seems possible and impossible at once. "Sorry, bud," he says, and his smile is so kind Wilder hurts with it. Internally, they withdraw even further. This is not something Quibble notices; it's not something anyone would notice, unless they could hear thoughts. Wilder's face doesn't change; they do not flinch—and it's sadder, because this is just the way they are, the sediment layers of thirty-one and a half years of letdowns, disappointments, hostilities. Their face is an undisturbed pool of water, glassy, so neutral as to reflect back only what is put in.

Quibble continues: "No witch bank full of treasure. No such thing as a school for this. Never seen a book on it myself, not this exactly, not one that isn't fiction. And no one I know flies around on a broomstick. Unless—that's what you woke up being able to do today?" Quibble's face betrays his excitement at this absurd imagining, the thrill of the literal.

Wilder shakes their head; they think that they would have an easier time not feeling insane if they could demonstrably fly. They're brought out of their own imagining because Quibble is asking them a question: "What *can* you do, actually?"

"Uh—mostly I'm a freelance copywriter."

"No, I mean what can you do with the Power?"

"Oh! I um—" Their voice is warbly with post-panic-pass-out fatigue, which isn't only physical exhaustion, but also embarrassment. They sound so, so stupid. "I think I can understand a bunch of languages? Maybe all of them? I don't know. Spanish, Urdu, and Japanese so far—and I spoke Japanese without noticing."

"Oh *hell* yeah, that's just fucking useful. Passive. Doesn't draw much attention to you at all. You can just be a man who speaks a lot of languages—"

"I'm not a man."

"Ah, sorry, noted. You can use it whenever. No one will notice. You could work at the UN— Oh, bud, your hands. They're shaking. Let's get you some water. Can you walk?"

Wilder nods and they manage to wobble out to the kitchen. Their normal movements are languid, slow. They move through the world trying to cause the least amount of friction. Quibble moves up behind them and puts his hand on their back. "You can sit. I can see the sink. I can find the glasses."

As Wilder watches Quibble, a man they have just met, open all their cabinets with a look of open and honest concern, two things wash over them—a thought they're aware of and a feeling they're not.

The thought they're aware of: they can't tell anyone else why they're so freaked out right now, not the truth. Because no one will believe them. They didn't have friends before today, and now, if they were to go out and make an effort—or even try being a little more friendly with Roommate Andy—there will forevermore be a Thing. A thing that no one else can know about them but that is formative, that comprises a large part of how they move through the world, that literally shapes what they see and hear. They spent long enough in various closets to know that a secret of this magnitude means no one will ever actually *know* them. This stranger who can rip through the air like it's shitty exercise pants is their actual last shot at having anyone in their life.

The feeling that they are unaware of: unmitigated rage. Wilder is not the first to respond to change with anger and they certainly will not be the last. But they are not terribly self-aware when it comes down to it and they wouldn't be able to make the sentence "I am responding to change with unmitigated rage," not for a trust fund and a pound of weed; so instead, as Quibble returns to the kitchen table with a glass of water, Wilder's spoken "thanks" turns sour in their mouth, comes out short and sharp.

"Yeah," Quibble says. "That's—about right. That's how I felt, too. But I didn't—"

The rage has burned out all Wilder's shakes. They don't drink even the tiny sips of someone who's going to puke; they simply set the glass on the table and stand. "Well," they say, and their mouth is tight. "If there's no school or book or anything, why are you here?"

"Artemis sent me. She's like—" Quibble snorts, interrupting himself. "It sounds so cheesy to say—like, the head bitch in charge of our small coven. See, I don't even like calling it a coven. It makes it sound like we're Tumblr baby try-hards. It's— We're family. She looks out for me, I look out for her. We try to look out for others as best we can. She's—difficult to describe. She's also Awakened."

"Excuse me?"

"When she casts spells, it does real shit. It's not just thoughts and prayers. It's what you are, too. *Awakened*." Quibble perches on the stool opposite Wilder; Wilder wants to push him off the stool and watch him fall on his ass, watch his stupid face register shock. "She finds 'em, the Awakened ones. I round 'em up. Well, that's the new plan, anyhow. She's not exactly—gentle. A bit scary, if I'm honest."

Wilder's mouth gets so tight that if one popped a piece of coal in there, it'd be a diamond within a week. "Round me up?"

"Oh, I mean that casually. I'm not going to make you come with me or anything. I'm not here to kidnap you, nah."

"No, not kidnap me. Just break into my apartment."

It's at this point Quibble begins to suspect he's in territory he doesn't understand. He is gentle, thoughtful—but this is an erratic time, and Quibble, well. He tends to assume people like him, which means he isn't equipped to foresee Wilder's response. Plus, he has a speech prepared. He's thought about this hard and long. So Quibble soldiers on. "And the truth is we probably won't be all that helpful. We'll probably just ask you a bunch of questions. Everyone's Awakened Power is so different. Magic isn't structured. It happens to you one day, mostly when you're older. And then there is no wizard school, no manual, no self-help book that can save you. And people deal with it mostly how they deal with all other forms of adulthood, like personal finance or handling emergencies or asserting their own boundaries: they move forward and pretend they know what they're doing."

Wilder thinks about their roommate, who once lit a toaster on fire because he left a plastic bag too close to it. And rather than calling the fire department or using the fire extinguisher (which was right there next to him), he picked up the flaming toaster and threw it out the open window into the street. They think about that guy, but with magic. Magic and no user manual. Their anger shakes with fear. "That's terrifying," they say.

"Yup," Quibble replies.

"I think you're full of shit," Wilder says.

Quibble is now sure he's in territory he doesn't understand; his next word sounds defensive, the question mark a shield rather than a true invitation. "What?"

"How is the world not one giant smoking crater if people wake up with powers and there's not really a pedagogical system for dealing with that?" they ask.

Quibble shrugs, trying not to get thorny. He succeeds a little; he fails a little. "Same way economists are shocked there isn't, like, a lot more murder than there already is."

Wilder's eyebrows shoot up and they wonder if they're about to get killed. "Excuse me?"

"Some economists say that the practical barrier for killing another human is not really at all insurmountable. Most people who commit major crimes don't get caught and people are generally assholes in all other facets of life, so economists are like, well, why doesn't everyone do a murder when they get angry if they'll probably get away with it? And their best answer is: we're tryna have a society here. So it's probably like that. Everyone is sort of subconsciously aware we're tryna have a society here so not even the freshest baby Awakened explodes anyone by accident." He pauses. "Do you want to be?"

"What? Exploded?"

"No, rounded up. We're not teachers. But coming from someone who didn't have this, it sure beats trying to figure it out alone."

Wilder pauses. Not because they're not sure what they're going to say, but because they want to wind up before they verbally punch. "No."

"Wait—no?"

"No. No, I do not want to be rounded up."

Quibble blinks a few times in genuine surprise. "Why not?"

"Because I'm not some charity case," Wilder says, and it comes from the deep part of them that was treated like a charity case over and over as a child, the recipient of everyone's pity rather than anyone's true interest or desire for connection. "You said that you all are family. You don't know me. You don't know me at all."

And Quibble can't argue with that. He doesn't know Wilder. At all.

Wilder continues: "You also said you probably wouldn't be that helpful anyhow. So, like, why? Why do any of this, except to feel like you're saving someone?" Wilder sneers and a very-interior part of their consciousness recognizes the shape of their father's mouth come to rest on their own face. Word for word, their father bursts from them: "What even is the point of you?"

Quibble had been prepared for a variety of reactions, even anger. But the insistence that a person needs to have a point at all? He doesn't know how to respond. This Wilder is supposed to be queer! Queer people should know better!

Except, of course, that's not true, is it? Being a member of the same community doesn't mean that Wilder cannot look at Quibble and try to figure out where the softest parts are, what bruises will hurt the most when poked.

It so happens, however, they have it wrong. Because Quibble grew up rich. Like, really fucking rich. And he's still really fucking rich. So the service impulse they're assuming is a part of most queer people's personalities based on the idealization of community support absent systemic support? That doesn't exist here either. Quibble and Wilder misunderstand each other so badly that Quibble hurts Wilder when he doesn't mean to, and Wilder can't hurt Quibble when they do mean to. So what comes of it? Quibble's bemused reply:

"Bro, what?" Accompanied by a very inappropriate grin. The kind of grin that doesn't come from deep, wounded feelings but from confusion and discomfort, a face muscle spasm of what-the-fuck.

But unless one is on the inside of that grin, one just sees a grin, a disrespectful one, and Wilder is upset they haven't gutted this stranger, so they snap, "Get out."

"Wait, hold on—" Quibble tries to reason with Wilder, but they are already standing, already on their way to the door.

"I guess it doesn't mean much, kicking you out," Wilder says, shaking with rage, tears erupting, a long-buried hot spring finding daylight for the first time in forever, burbling into their voice, and they sniff. "You could always just—come back in."

"I wouldn't—if you want me out, you want me out, fine, I'm going." Quibble's hands are up above his shoulders, palms out, in surrender. "I just think—"

"I don't care. Leave."

And he is on the street, the door shot shut behind him, a crack so loud that he turns around expecting some part of the frame to be broken, the hinges buckled, something. But he sees only a very, very closed door. He sighs; he texts Artemis.

well that was shit

King of Wands

Artemis is at work, and she is not happy. She would not be happy at work any other day, it is true, given that she's pretty antiwork, but she is especially displeased on this day, the day Wilder Awakens to their Power for the first time, because she is experiencing what she can only call "light pollution." She notices it first on her phone, whenever she drops it to her side after using it: a sparkle, a wink, like the screen staying on just a touch longer than it usually would. She makes a mental note to take the Magpie to task for doing something to her damn technology again. But she quickly realizes: the pollution is everywhere. In every bar she goes to, she sees it blinking in the cash registers, except for the old, musty one with the vintage equipment, where the point of sale has heavy circular buttons and a shrill *ding*. In every cell phone, tablet, smart watch on the wrists of patrons and passersby.

At first, she takes it as a glare, digs her dollar store sunglasses from her bag, two white hearts with cheap pink lenses, and puts them on. It is a glaring day, both under the sky and through windows; the stark, cold sunlight of Brooklyn in February, gray but piercingly overbright in its cranked-up exposure. Rather than it dissipating, however, she is plagued further with these wisps of light and she understands now that it's not light she can see with her physical eyes. It's light that she can See with her Eyes. The internal Eyes that allow her to See Awakened Power that have absolutely nothing to do with cones and rods and retinas and electricity. Though perhaps it is still electricity; Artemis is maybe the most familiar with the stuff of Magic, yet even she can't venture a guess as to what Magic is made of.

She twitches as she does her job, empties the boxes of cash dues paid to the billiards league by which she is employed. A daytime bartender notices and offers her something for her headache. She doesn't even realize she has one until he asks.

Despite her deepness of thought, and thus her dissociation in this moment, Artemis does indeed have a body, like Wilder, like Quibble. So far, everyone in this group does. She is tall and dark, but she is not handsome. A Black woman, a trans woman. She is in possession of long hair and a soft, feminine beard, her graceful curls maintained meticulously. She glitters it, loving the way it becomes a disco ball refracting the afternoon sun, always a party even when she doesn't feel like dancing. She wears thick, warm leggings and a pink faux fur coat. Her beloved thrift-store-hot-find boots, which extend nearly all the way to the knee, are laced with ribbon, pink and white. Her eyes are lined heavily in black and she has a tattoo of an arrow on her right arm—whichever way she's pointing is true north. She holds heat in her like a lizard; all sun, all fire, no nonsense. In short, a badass body with a badass aesthetic. Entirely on the outside who she is within, and if anyone tries to give her shit about it? Well, people have tried. And Artemis is a witch, after all.

She's been so distracted by these annoying will-o'-the-wisps that she nearly misses that homo one borough over Awakening into their Power. She would have dispatched Quibble quicker if she'd been more on the ball. She wonders if the lights are related to the new queer, to the new Awakening. She supposes, if Quibble comes back with them, she'll soon find out. She doesn't know that their talk is in the process of going very poorly (though, to be honest, not the poorest it could go—there's a version of the present where Wilder punches Quibble; another where they run naked into the street and get arrested by a passing cop. ACAB.).

Artemis notes all the sparks at the edge of her vision. When she turns her head to look, they poof from existence. Slippery motherfuckers. She wonders if they're conscious, trying to hide, or if they're simply the barest traces of Magic, latent in the device, weak because they're weak and not because they have the capacity to try to *be* anything at all. She wonders if it's something to do with Quibble, actually, because the wisps look at least a little familiar, like the confetti lights all strung together when he rips the world apart, walks through whatever that pocket dimension is to his destination.

"Any issues?" she asks the next bartender, who shakes her head. Artemis half expects there to be some problem since every point-of-sale computer is blinking in her periphery. Oh glorious day, the bartender slides her a popcorn, on the house as usual, and she shoves a handful in her mouth as she steps back out onto the street, back into the different wall of sound that is Brooklyn, so ubiquitous as to be silent in her ears. She slips in her earbuds and walks like she is listening to metal; she listens to NPR. She stomps around in her boots because that is the only way Artemis walks. Like she owns the whole city and everything in it.

She wonders if the new one will believe Quibble—he is much more socially graceful than she is. He always gets better service. At restaurants, on the phone, doesn't matter, people love Quibble and they want to make him happy. That or he's so very clearly a man and Artemis's gender is illegible to most folks outside the community; femininity is something everyone loves to hate. As a team, they've only intervened on an Awakened Power once before, and that was the Magpie. It was a journey, that's for certain. Artemis handed the reins over to Quibs on this particular task so as not to repeat avoidable mistakes. She does not pretend she knows it all; hell, she does not pretend she knows anything.

Artemis's phone buzzes and she flinches as she raises it to look, a twinkle of light just barely out of reach, appearing a hair too soon, right before the screen opens its eye to her. well that was shit, she reads.

Shit how? she texts back.

The familiar ripping sound and Quibble walks beside her, having stepped clear out of the air. Anyone but Artemis would be nearly levitating (a man where there wasn't one before! No one likes a surprise man!), but not her.

"Shit, like," he says, "they wouldn't come. They kicked me out."

"That was always a possibility. They can say no. Anyone can say no." Artemis repeats what she's said over and over again, when she and Quibble decided to start intervening, at least in the lives of other trans people as they Awakened. And how did they decide only trans people? To make it manageable, was the first and honest answer. After all, they were only two witches. They couldn't help everyone, so they decided to focus their efforts within their community, and maybe when there were more of them, they could expand.

The second answer was one Artemis had come up with—to keep it as safe as possible. And lo, Wilder has, in fact, responded in a pretty *emotionally* unsafe way—which Quibble explains. "They tried to, like, humiliate me? Shame me? I think is what they were going for." But case in point: it didn't work, did it? Quibble isn't going to process this until the sun dies. Quibble probably won't even remember it in a year, especially if that's the last he sees of Wilder. So everyone is okay and it wasn't unsafe, was it?

No, the kind of safety Artemis had been thinking of, back when they outlined their parameters, was physical. She was not about to ring a cis man's doorbell as part of a "Congrats, You're Magic" welcome wagon only to get extremely murdered. She had better things to do with her time and with her death (she hoped it was both peaceful and full of drama, like a Wes Anderson movie; sepia, symmetrical, whimsical, purposeful). No, murdered by someone she was trying to help would have made her a statistic, and it would be embarrassing for a Sighted witch not to see that one coming. Trans people only.

"That's that, then," she says.

"That's that?"

"Yup. The new witch"—and here, she almost says *kid* but she catches herself in time—"said no. We respect a no. On to the next."

"Artemis, I'm not sure I one hundred percent agree—like, of course we respect a no, of course we do, that's not what I'm saying." He rushes his words in response to Artemis's terrifying arched eyebrow. "No, but isn't it a bit more complicated than that? Like, we respect an informed decline, but can this decline be truly informed? They woke up speaking every language."

Artemis grunts. That power is cool as fuck.

"Like, can anyone make a decision after that?"

"Anyone can say no before, during, and after anything. They don't want help. They'll have to figure it out on their own."

Two of Swords

Wilder is trying to YouTube their problem away, as if they're trying to reset a mousetrap or patch a hole Andy accidentally made in the wall. They Google *Learn Japanese instantly*, which nets them a good many ads for Rosetta Stone. *Wake up speaking Japanese* gets them the same. They have no idea what search terms to try. Everything they type seems too far-fetched.

They're embarrassed to even spell the real thing—is it a real thing? Andy saw Quibble, too, and Wilder is not close enough with Andy to share a hallucination. Wilder is not even close enough with Andy to share a half gallon of milk. Which brings them back to the feeling they had before, the one that says having made no friends before today they're now doomed to no friends forever.

They Google *solitary witches*.

Books on books, one by someone with a very stupid name, another about casting spells while staying at home without any friends. They click, but in this case "spell" means some kind of physical prayer that's popular, they think, with queer people who, deep down, miss church.

"What to do if you have magic." An article about how the best magical power is being kind to yourself. Fourteen ways to have a magical life. A teenager who wrote all about how to know if you have "magic in your blood" and appears to believe every single word of it in earnest.

Wilder clicks on that one, hoping, but it's just about feeling really chummy with the moon and liking animals, mostly the cute ones. This they do not understand. Where are the really intense snake people? This seems like a community for the really intense snake people.

Witch Tumblr—oh no, it's worse. Art witches, kitchen witches, financial witches that call money to themselves and their clients magically (Wilder wishes this were real), and, in one memorable case, a tie-dye witch.

Witch Reddit. This is—well, not more like it. But also not Tumblr. A thirteen-year-old asking if they need to be a lesbian or a woman or older to be a witch. And people are—actually nice? Actually helpful? Someone asking ChatGPT to make a prosperity spell and the AI chatbot declining. "I'm just a language model," it says. "I can't create spells or give spiritual advice." So many of these are questions. Question: "Is my neighbor practicing witchcraft on me? We see him lurking outside our door through the peephole." Question: "My friend accidentally gave a vial of his own blood to a witch."

Wilder pauses. They look at the clock. They've been Googling all morning and the sun is well into its downward swing. They could go to the library, they think, and they could try that before resorting to their own desperate Reddit question. They pull up the New York Public Library website, which yields mostly children's books about women with large warty noses. One book about herbs, academic analyses of different folk tales, research about burning people in Massachusetts. They pause again. Flip back to the Reddit tab.

Question: Woke Up With Magic Powers

Hi everyone, long time listener, first time caller. Well, not long time listener really. I just found this today because today's the only day I've needed it. I woke up with magic powers. Like real magic. Not like herbs or crystals or whatever, like real, honest to god magic. What do I do?

Post.

Wilder curls up for a nap. They feel impossibly exhausted. This will not change.

* * *

Wilder wakes sometime later. It is dark, but it is winter, so that doesn't mean shit about time. They reach for their phone meaning to check, but whatever arbitrary clock number they see with their eyes dissolves before it reaches their brain. They feel compelled to immediately tap Reddit. To see if their question got answers.

It had. So many.

what do you mean *real* magic? our magic *is* real
this man is coming in here and shaming us for our intuition,
but we are teh daughters of the witches who wouldn't burn
fuck you.

Wilder doesn't have any coping mechanisms to deal with disappointment like this. Or rather, so much of their life until this point would have been a disappointment if Wilder had ever allowed themself to want anything. The way they'd handled it until right now was to simply never desire, never wish, excise all their longing with the grapefruit spoon of first-world poverty. But today—not even God's own melon baller could scoop the want out. There is not one person in the world who they could ask to hug them, and they need a hug.

They see the red number one next to their SMS app. No one texts them; it could only be one person.

come on, bud, we have better answers than Reddit. They read Quibble's response and the friendless sorrow they slept on is immediately hip-checked by anger doing the cha-cha.

No, they type back. How did you get this number?

google.

Wilder is horrified. Please stop texting me.

it was better than, like, waiting at your
window. i could do that instead if you
want, i'm chilling in the neighborhood,
i just figured that would be creepy.
why are you doing this?

Doing what?

refusing help. like very obvious help.

Because I don't WANT help. That's what Wilder types, but what they actually mean is: because you are now the only person with whom I can achieve any kind of earnest intimacy, you are now immediately terrifying because I both crave and am repulsed by the kind of mutual witness that creates friendship because then you will discover that I'm a horrible person or you will use what you know about me to hurt me on purpose, one of the two, and then I will be even sadder and angrier than I am at present.

okay. well. i'll leave the ball in yr court.
don't ask me what kind of ball or court,
i don't understand sports. but if you
feel like hitting the soccer puck into
the endzone or whatever, we're very
easy to find.

                    Shouldn't witches be secret?

you asked about real magic on Reddit

As much as they don't want to admit it, Wilder figures Quibble has a good point.

we're not easy to find because we're
witches. we're easy to find because we
have a regular hangout spot. Cowboy
Jacqueline's.

                                    What?

don't tell me you've never been to
Cowboy Jacqueline's. it's the last good
queer bar on the whole ass planet.

Wilder forgets they are mad for exactly the length of time it takes to type, do I look like I have beer money? And they are mad again because it should be obvious; they can't have queer community because they can't go out because they are poor and "outside" costs a minimum of two hundred dollars.

if you meet me at Cowboy Jacqueline's,
i will buy you whatever drink you want.
not just beer.

Wilder considers a free drink. Or at least, that's what they consider on the surface. What they're actually considering, though they wouldn't be able to tell anyone, is the longing for a friend, any friend. You're there all the time? they type back.

In response, Quibble's face appears at their window, which is high enough off the ground that, even though he is tall, Wilder can only see his eyeballs. "Yeah, man. We're gay."

Seven of Wands

Cowboy Jacqueline's is, indeed, the last good queer bar on the whole-ass planet, if you don't count every other queer bar on the whole-ass planet—all of them are good for the people who they are good for. This one is lightly saloon flavored. Lightly, thank goodness, because it is in Brooklyn, and anything more cowboy-seasoned would be disingenuous. The proprietor, who is (obviously) named Jacqueline, had no great love for the Wild West aesthetic but wanted to open a queer bar and, when she rented the space, had to contend with a pair of saloon doors. Jacqueline is queer classic—older, silver in the high-and-tight haircut—and she eventually bought the place, which is why it's still a queer bar in a city of luxury dog hotels and whole apartment buildings that landlords keep empty on purpose. At that point, she could've torn out the doors and rebranded, but she was already in too far.

Instead, the doors are just the beginning, the literal entry point. On the first Wednesday of every month, there is queer square-dancing night. The glory holes in the gender-neutral bathrooms have tiny cowboy hats painted above them and tiny mustaches painted below (it would be too much to call it "tongue in cheek," would it not?). One wall—neon cacti of different heights and suggestive shapes, real neon with the *zzzzz* sound and everything, extremely expensive, or they would've been if they weren't bent by a nonbinary artist who gave Jacqueline the family discount as long as they could write up an artist statement and call it an installation, as long as their business cards were always available up front. The air inside is always hazy even though smoking isn't allowed, something about the pheromones that mimics cigarettes. Invariably there is a table in the corner, round, at which queers sit playing cards. A picture of a cowboy good time until you look closely and realize they're playing cribbage rather than poker. And at the bar, a patron in a crop top and low jeans demos a vibrator that she plays like a theremin—it vibrates faster and harder the closer her fingers get to the receiver. She made it herself and imp-grins while someone writes their phone number on her exposed hip bone in Sharpie.

Behind the bar stands Jacqueline. She is wearing a cowboy hat with the word *HOLE* embroidered on the brim (a custom job). She is also wearing an N95 mask, one of the real sturdy ones, because "I'm not getting sick at work. If I get COVID, it'll be at an orgy."

And on the bar, by the register, a sign. In big letters at the top: "Cowboy as in Assless* Chaps, Not Cowboy as in Manifest Destiny: this queer space occupies Lenapehoking, in particular the ancestral home of the Minsi clan. Most of the Lenape live in Oklahoma and Canada now, which is fucked up and private property is a total scam, I just can't figure out how to exist in this burning hellscape without it. I welcome any suggestions. —Jacqueline *PS, all chaps are assless."

Quibble and Artemis are—well, not *always* here. But good money says they're here during hours that one might reasonably be at a bar. They're here enough that when Jacqueline was thinking about putting in a pool table, Artemis begged her not to. Literally anything else, which is how the bar wound up with darts, giant Jenga, and crokinole, all off-theme for sure, but who cares, really, when Jacqueline is always in a pair of the loudest cowboy boots she can find?

Besides, the queers don't come primarily for the theme, though it is true that queers do love a theme. They come for the burlesque drag.

Technically, Artemis and Quibble come for the drag, too, or for one really specific drag king.

Rico.

Rico, who tried to pick a drag name and failed, just uses his name; he had enough naming energy in him for exactly one renaming, he jokes, and it was too important to waste on coming up with some clever smart-ass-ness like David Bro-y or Juan Nightstand. When pressed, he uses Rico Ricardo, but he resists, preferring to be known by one name and one name only, like Madonna. He has, however, done a whole Lucille Ball(s) act and he pulls that one out (pun intended) for special occasions.

Rico, who Artemis is in love with but she never says so.

Rico, who is in love with Artemis and he says so often.

Rico, Rico, Rico, who isn't a witch and who makes it in, somehow, to the coven when all is said and done (though Artemis continues to hold him at arm's length). Rico, who isn't performing this evening but is having a meeting with the troupe (called the Smoking Guns, run by Bootleg Jean the Cowboy Queen) in the back-room performance space, which is massive for a bar but small for a stage. The group has gotten popular, with a write-up in *Time Out* and a low-budget but beautiful documentary making the film circuit; they are trying to figure out how to fit more chairs on the floor while Jacqueline warns them about fire codes, says that unlike a good many regulations, these ones do, actually, matter in a community safety sense and therefore she does, actually, want to follow them. They are also trying to figure out how to discourage the straight people from showing up (and they have been showing up). Jacqueline is agreeing to post homo-aggressive signage about the glory holes.

And of course, with an increase in positive attention, there is the occasional threat that has become rather less occasional. There are threats about groomers, drag queen story hour (which this is not, this is extremely for adults), faggots and dykes and trannies and takeovers and corrupting teens and corrupting traditional family values and corrupting religion and corrupting woman's exalted place in the world. Through all of this, Rico wonders, if he's so corrosive, why can't he properly de-scale his shower? Artemis is too practical for such cutesy worrying. And Quibble has money so he's more or less untouched, but he's mad anyhow, and offering to hire Jacqueline some security, which she will not do, because "no cops."

"I'm not suggesting cops," Quibble says. "I'm suggesting you pay, like, two mama bears to stand out front in lipstick and muscle tanks."

"I am not turning my precious mama bears into cops," Jacqueline replies, wiping a spill off the bar and high-fiving theremin-vibrator-girl when she comes up for air, as she's now making out with Sharpie-wielder.

Rico comes out of his meeting, a wig to rival Marie Antoinette's piled on top of his head, a pouf of pink rococo cotton candy skyscrapering him into Artemis's height bracket (he's usually a head and a half shorter). His shirt is unbuttoned deep into his chest hair, his single top surgery scar stretching through the V like a smile. He carries a stack of large felt fig leaves and sits down at the bar, picks the top one up, and squints at where his last stitched veins left off. The adorable foliage is for the Smoking Guns' "Adam and Steve" show, which is an exploration and intentional perversion of Christian myth. They haven't made an antagonistic choice on purpose; they've been cooking up this show for a while and have just made the decision not to pivot, regardless of threats. Bootleg Jean, Polly Amorous, Rico, Miss Ree Markable, Glamazon Package Delivery, Boy Howdy, and Johnny Whoops all look each other in their determined faces and agree to take the risk.

"I wish I could know the future," Rico grumbles over his sour as he sticks his tiny wire glasses on his nose and unclicks his multilevel toolbox, which contains lipstick, several compartments full to the top of rhinestones, an awl and a hammer, a hot glue gun, pepper spray disguised as Zicam nasal spray, and, finally, embroidery thread and a needle, carefully wound around a sweet wooden bobbin and labeled with its color-number. And then it occurs to him. "Wait, can I know the future?"

Artemis snorts. "I don't know, can you?" She sips her pink wine.

Rather than feeling any way about it, Rico grins stupid under his mask—he loves when Artemis gets prickly, which is nearly always. He loves her difficult. "You know what I mean," he says. "Can you tell me? If that conversation we all just had about emergency scenarios was *for* something? If we're actually going to have to use anything we came up with? I would love to be able to breathe."

Artemis sets a wineglass on the bar and swivels toward him, laying her hand on his knee before she thinks better of it. She is already in a shit mood—the tech is winking light here, too. Jacqueline's point-of-sale iPad. Rico's jacked-up Android with the very cracked screen. Even the theremin vibrator (nothing is sacred). But his grin is so stupid and good even if it's presently obscured and he looks like a sweet bespectacled badger in a fairy tale, so she lets herself have this small touch. "I see what's in front of me," she tells him. "All in the present. But extra. I don't do the future. Most folks don't. It's too chaotic."

"Is there anyone who does the future?" Rico asks.

Quibble is about to answer, to say, *Yes there is*, and point Rico to exactly where. In the world where Quibble gets this information out quick, Rico takes a bus there the next day. But they aren't in that version of events. Artemis cuts Quibble off with "You don't want their help, trust me." If Quibble were a slightly different person, he would roll his eyes. Instead, he turns his head to sip his beer and laughs a bubble directly into it.

"Artemis," he says, and he nudges her ankle with his heel.

"Mmm?" Artemis's eyes reluctantly leave Rico's pretty, dumb face and land on Quibble's, who gestures with both his beer and his chin toward the saloon doors. Above the harp curves, Quibble can see a pair of eyes and some troll-esque red curls. Someone else pushes the door open and Quibble laughs harder at the complete image: Wilder's anger mouth in a thin line, the intense stare that they are trying to pretend isn't happening even though it's on their own face, their hands jammed into their peacoat pockets. An Allie Brosh cartoon made manifest. Everyone stares at each other for the duration of a door swing.

Quibble's eyebrows are the smiling kind, the laughing kind, but he keeps his face mostly steady. "Wanna come in, bud?"

"Don't call me bud," Wilder says as they push the door open.

"Okay, pal."

"I'm not here with you," Wilder says, and they don't take their coat off at the bar even as they slip their own mask on. They stand a good three feet from Artemis, Quibble, and Rico. "I'm just here. And you are also here. And that's it."

Rico's eyebrows are raised well above his glasses. "Can I still talk m-a-g—"

"They can spell, Rico. They're an adult." Artemis takes another sip and blinks, her eyes watering because the recently Awakened are so fucking bright. "Also yes."

Rico laughs at himself as he stitches. It's one of the things Artemis (privately) loves about him. When he does something himbo-y, he delights in both himself and the witness of it. He never feels stupid. He's so loose and free.

"You must be Wilder," Artemis says as she stands up and holds her hand out. Wilder is, of course, still mad and they don't want to shake her hand. But they also don't want to be rude and are also slightly terrified as Artemis looms over them. These three impulses dance-battling within them result in the weirdest, limpest handshake that's ever existed. Artemis smirks as she sits back down.

Jacqueline, meanwhile, serves Wilder, who, recovering from the horrible handshake, grunts and points at the Pabst Blue Ribbon, which is three dollars. Quibble catches Jacqueline's eye and, as quietly as anyone can gesture, points at himself. Jacqueline barely nods, so used to this is she. Quibble always pays. Sometimes for people he doesn't know. Most of the time they do not notice and just think that Jacqueline is either kind or forgetful. This time, though, Wilder notices because they are in a state of hypervigilance. They turn their head so fast that actual whiplash seems possible.

"No," they say, even though they'd considered free drink a plus in the "come" column. In the moment, it makes them uncomfortable.

"Okay," Quibble says.

And Wilder immediately wishes they hadn't noticed, even though it is only three dollars. Four, when they count the tip. But they do not wish they hadn't said no. Saying no feels good, powerful. Especially as they are starting to get a little nauseous: a couple at the table closest to the window is speaking Portuguese. Their mouths bend bows, lips smile long to the corners, each word is bitten and chewed and swallowed and takes up wider space in the cheeks than Wilder is used to. Everything twangs and they can hear both-and, the words they know and the words they don't and they wonder how their nose isn't bleeding yet, how the bartender can't smell burning as their gray matter catches fire.

They turn their head away, trying to limit their perception to the one language they are used to speaking and catch sight of three people signing to each other by the bathroom. It is *very* spicy, what they are saying they are about to do in that bathroom, and as each finger grasps a concept, fluid and slang and slut-hot, Wilder hears—hears? What is the word for a voice inside a person, rattling around in their head's hollow spaces, bouncing on their eardrums from the inside out? Because that is where they "hear" the words. Overwhelmed, they clamp down. Clench teeth. Grip diaphragm, stomach tight. Their eyes water from the overstimulation and they put the kibosh on it because if they don't control this dam break, it might give way to actual crying.

Rico barely looks up from his stitching when he says, "I actually do want to talk to the person who can tell the future."

"What?" Artemis replies, her narrowed eyes snapping quick to her—lover's? No, Artemis would rather shit in her own hands and clap than use the word *lover*. Boyfriend? Absolutely not, that stinks of commitment—her Rico, then, whatever he is.

"You said I didn't want their help. I actually do want their help. Jean is practically laying an egg over whether to perform—one of the threats seems pretty specific, and I would do nearly anything to give her the guidance she wants. So I just want to be clear, I do want their help and it's you who doesn't." The words in any other mouth could sound so aggressive. In Rico's, they sound gentle, matter-of-fact. This is the only person in Artemis's life who can talk to her like this.

Artemis sips her wine slow. Now that she's gotten over Wilder's brightness, the twinkling has returned. She's nearly as twitchy as

Wilder is. The truth is she's been wishing to see the future herself, and then squashing the thought dead with her Doc Marten. "If we talk to a future teller—"

"*The* future teller," Quibble mutters into his own beer, so quietly Wilder is the only one who can hear him. Is it just that they're on alert, or is their hearing getting more acute? It's so much harder to block out language. Whispered purrs in Spanish at the giant Jenga; cussing in French by the neon; loud moans coming from the bathroom in three distinct pitches.

"—it won't actually *be* help," Artemis continues. "Not the kind you're looking for, not the sure kind. Because they will tell you, ah, yes, nothing happens. But they might See Jean choosing to cancel the show and not tell you that part."

Quibble's brow furrows because he knows that this is not exactly true. It might be what Artemis believes to be true, he thinks (and it is; she isn't lying; she just has a different experience of the future teller than Quibble does). But the person she's talking about—they're generally quite specific. Sometimes painfully so.

Rico sighs. "Ah, well. That makes sense." And the look on his face is such that when Jacqueline passes by him, she reaches out and grabs his wrist, gives it a squeeze. Without thinking, Artemis slides one finger into one of his back belt loops, her thumb on his hip. He smiles small, wrinkles his nose up, and Artemis bursts with love that she still will not talk about. Everyone sits in long enough silence for Wilder to hear that there are now four different registers of sex noise emanating from the bathroom.

Rico, who wants to kiss Artemis and doesn't, speaks first. "Can you—you know—" He wiggles three of his fingers a little bit, being careful to keep the embroidery needle caught between his forefinger and thumb.

Artemis pulls her hand from Rico's belt loop. "You can say 'cast a spell.' Let's be perfectly real here—no one in this bar is going to think anything of it. Every one of these girlies got crystals. And yes, I can. But I'm not—I don't know exactly what you're looking for me to do. I'm a Seer, of a sort. I can't, like, put a force field up around you or Jean."

"The threat isn't about Jean," Rico says, "or about me. Not the very specific one, at least." His eyes flick to Polly, who is playing darts and drinking, perhaps more than she otherwise would be.

Artemis doesn't touch Rico this time; she wishes he would touch her, because what he means is obvious—it's about the trans women. "I can't stop a bullet," she says, quiet. "I don't know anyone who can." Rico's eyebrows furrow again, confused about what magic is for and what it isn't.

"There are things we can just—do," Quibble pipes in to explain, seeing an opportunity to offer not just some information to Rico, but to Wilder as well. And Quibble can see Wilder is clearly struggling. Cowboy Jaqueline's has gotten louder, more crowded. "For Artemis, it's Seeing magic, all kinds. For me, I can, uh—"

"Teleport?" Rico offers. "When Artemis talks about it, it sounds like teleportation."

"Not—exactly." Quibble sips his beer. "But, uh. Close, yeah. And Wilder—"

"Don't talk about me," Wilder interjects, snappy and more than a bit nauseously.

"Cool, okay." Quibble drops it. "So there are things we just can do. And then there's stuff we have to reach for. Spells we can cast. And they work, they do, it's just—not quite a guarantee. How they work is going to be a bit of a surprise. It looks more like praying from the outside, but it's way more than some vibes. And it's really different from that on the inside—how do I explain this? Most spells take more Power than each of us has by ourselves. So we all kinda— You remember the kids book called *Stone Soup?*" It's an abrupt topic change but Rico nods nonetheless. And Quibble's plan is working: Wilder is listening, osmosing some things about the way the world works. Quibble continues. "A bunch of witches can cast the same spell at the same time, and they all put magic into it, put their own spin on it, like when everyone in that book puts an ingredient into the pot. But it's also way more intimate than that." And Quibble turns a bit red, which Rico notices and Wilder doesn't because Wilder is on the verge of having a meltdown.

"So could you cast a protection spell?" Rico honestly does want to know; he also honestly wants to know what's so intimate about casting spells, but safety first and also Rico is used to dealing with Artemis, who is a show-upper in every other kind of relationship and extremely avoidant in romance, so he's used to providing an option to defuse intensity.

"We could," Artemis says. "But—what is protection? It's too vague. Without a clear idea of what we're actually asking for, we might make it too psychically difficult for anyone to show up and you won't have any audience at all, as an example. It's a lot less predictable."

Wilder, who looks positively green, interrupts: "Cast a love spell."

Everyone looks at Wilder.

"What?" Artemis asks.

"A love spell, cast a love spell. Make everyone love the place." Wilder both doesn't know and knows how good an idea this is. For even through the fog of their acute discomfort, they can see how easy it is to love Cowboy Jacqueline's. They yearn to be a part of it even as they stand separate. They long and they wish and it would be so easy to put those feelings in the metaphorical spell pot, to have them flavor whatever comes out. "They won't shoot it up if they just—love it."

"And everyone here already does love it," Quibble jumps in. "They might not even feel a difference. And if they do, they'll just chalk it up to a really good night. That's brilliant, bud." And Wilder even forgets to chastise Quibble for calling them bud; they feel the slight flip in their stomach at the compliment and a very small part of them is proud for being good at something.

Artemis sips her wine. "It's not bad." And that is the closest to a compliment that Artemis will give anyone.

Rico smiles with his eyes, glancing up from his half-done fig leaf. As is usual with the witch stuff, he isn't entirely sure what he's looking at, though he's got the gist, but with human stuff, the queer stuff, he can see through Wilder like cellophane. And Rico wears all that knowledge face-forward, so Wilder can see they've been made. "So," Rico says. "A love spell. Gonna cast it right now?"

Wilder turns red. "I—" They swallow. "I have to go." And as quickly as they blew into Cowboy Jaqueline's, they leave, the saloon doors nearly squealing on their hinges with the speed.

Quibble frowns deep. "Man, I thought we had them."

Rico snorts. "I knew you didn't."

Artemis just shrugs and takes Wilder's half-finished PBR from the bar. She makes to take a sip and Rico stops her. She smirks. "It's okay, they don't go anywhere." This time she gets the can to her lips, sips, makes a face at the shitty beer smell. "No thank you," she says as she pulls Rico's mask down and holds the can to his lips. Reassured, he sips without hesitation or follow-up question. He has a cute eleven between his eyebrows, two parallel wrinkles that appear when he is concentrating—in this case, concentrating on not spilling shitty beer onto his pristine fig leaf. Artemis feels herself get hard, but only a little, and hidden enough to maintain her plausible deniability.

"It would be better if they cast it with us," Quibble says. "It was their idea."

Artemis shrugs again, but her attention is only half in the room for two reasons. The first is, of course, the constant aggravating light-spots. The second: she has just spotted a familiar triangle of hair passing by the window, a saunter she knows all too well, and on the arm of some guy who isn't worth her time. On a school night, too. This concretizes her persistent headache into something far more solid, like anvil-solid, and she narrows her eyes at Mary Margaret, who is very much about to get caught. "We should cast it night of show, anyway." She says it fast. "Stronger that way. I have to go. I have a teenager to wrangle."

Two of Swords (Again)

Quibble buys a stack of Terry Pratchett novels because they fit in his coat pocket and because he likes them. Then he sits in front of Wilder's apartment in the horrible winter cold, wearing gloves and sipping from a thermos. He reads his books with light attention, eyes occasionally flicking up toward their barred window, their apartment door. This is how he notices Wilder's tightening orbit before they notice it themself.

At first, Wilder tries to exist as they always have, ignoring their newfound Awakened Power (and huffily and purposefully ignoring Quibble, though they can plainly see him, day in and day out). They walk to the library, but that is, potentially, the worst place they could try to work, for it is a swirl of whispered language.

Another morning, they try to work at a bakery close by, which Wilder hates because they have to spend money to be there. No sooner than they'd sat, they are chased out of the room by Czech.

Then it is to the grocery store only—and Quibble notices, of course, that they look like they're summer-sweating in the dead of winter when they leave the store, quicker than he anticipated (and with about half of what they actually need).

Then it is just to the tamale woman for a lunch one day as to avoid the grocery store a little while longer, but Wilder can't help but order in Spanish and they look like they're going to pass out as they speak. The sensation: like taking a sip of seemingly refreshing water from a glass and instead getting a mouthful of a single round rock that tastes orange and knocks against their teeth.

Then they do not leave at all. Through all this, Quibble sits and reads. And watches.

The Two of Swords-ness goes on for some days—enough days to be counted in weeks, but only just. The thing that breaks the stalemate is Wilder's migraine, which is unfortunate—it could've been personal growth, a longing for softness and connection, anything. But it is pain. Whenever they do bring themself to leave the apartment, all the words sound like they are melting, the world too loud and nonsensical. Now even Andy's voice is beginning to give them as much stereo static as the outside world, and while he is frequently asleep, Wilder notices their butthole clenching before they can get surprised. In their own home! It is untenable, to exist this way all the time, and no amount of Reddit or YouTube has brought them closer to balance or control.

The other thing that breaks the self-imposed siege is money. Wilder cannot get the itch out of their head, what Quibble said on that first day: "You could work at the UN." And they haven't been able to work their normal way with the constant headache; their bank account is so empty it's starting to smell like basement mold.

And yes, deep down, there it is: the longing to return to Cowboy Jacqueline's. To see the Adam and Steve Show, which is fast approaching, though how they will do it, they're not sure.

Finally, finally, they walk up to Quibble on one afternoon in the cold-bright sun, squinting even as they wear sunglasses. Quibble notices, also, that they have earplugs in, the cheap kind from the pharmacy. Instead of any of the more polite options, Wilder opens with "Don't you work?"

"Nope," Quibble says with a smile. Not a sarcastic one, either. Just a turning up at the corners of his mouth with the ease of someone who doesn't worry about money. He puts his book aside, cocks his head like an attentive dog. He wants to say a thousand things that are gentle roasts and lightly sarcastic, but he holds his tongue as he holds his breath. He doesn't want to scare Wilder back into their apartment. He just waits, listens.

The city seems to help. It goes quiet in that moment, a rare and incredible stillness. It's difficult for Wilder not to experience both a momentary relief and a subliminal interpretation of that shining comfortable second as a sign, a brief calm breath that means they're doing the right thing, the destined thing, the only thing. They are going to quip back, "Must be nice," and in the version of the world where they do, this conversation doesn't go as well. But with the weight of the city lifted in reversed gravity, they don't. And it could be Magic, it's true, that this near-silence happens right this very instant. But it could also be random, the consequence of living in Queens long enough that, occasionally, there is a rare moment when everyone's brief pause lines up perfectly, a trick of statistics made possible only by a chaotic world. And isn't that Magic in and of itself, anyhow?

"You could teach me to control it?" they ask instead.

Quibble's head remains cocked as he thinks. "It depends on what you mean by 'teach.' More like we all troubleshoot together until we figure something out. We tell you what we do, we see if it works, and if it doesn't, we keep thinking and trying."

Wilder wishes there were a formula, a quick way to ensure they stop feeling like this. They're in so much pain. But they also know, deep down, nothing is fast like that. "Okay," they say.

"Okay?" asks Quibble.

"Yeah. Okay. But I'm not joining anything. I just— Maybe just talk me through it. Once. And we'll see."

Quibble stands, puts his book in his coat pocket, and rubs his hands together. "If I have only one shot, you gotta really do it, okay? Like don't phone it in and then say it doesn't work."

Wilder nods in response.

"Great," Quibble continues. "Then if I only have the one shot and we're going to do it right, we need to get to Artemis." He reaches into his pocket and checks his phone. "She's at work. It's either three trains or Magic, your pick."

Wilder thinks about all the languages ricocheting off the closed train car doors and turns an even shittier shade of green. "Magic," and they are surprised at how easy the call is. But they cannot imagine willingly jamming into a metro.

"Okay, bud!" Quibble grins, tasting the exclamation mark at the end of his two-word sentence with relish. He is genuinely happy to share this with Wilder. Because it's so—wild. Only two other people in the entire world have seen him the way Wilder's about to. He is proud; the pride is hard-won.

When it came to his own Awakening, Quibble had it rough. He woke one morning feeling different, same as Wilder, but his Power was far less obvious, and he was deep in mourning. Numb. Not his most observant. Mostly he had the urge to put his hands in things. Rustic sacks of dried black beans at the fancy grocery store. Boxes after unboxing, filled to the brim with Styrofoam packing peanuts as he slowly began to sift through their things, sobbing. He wrote it off as a stress response, a sensory thing, just him being weird. He watched old Gak commercials from the '90s and the fledgling slime Instagrams that would someday grow into whole teenage-craze conventions. Even competitive diving seemed satisfying somehow. Submersion. A body cutting through water, disappearing. He imagined what the cool, chlorinated liquid closing around him would feel like on his skin. He took a break from cleansing his life of his suddenly dead parents and shoving down his brand-new gender feelings; he went to Riis Beach, like many queers before him, to stand in the waves.

When he bent down to scoop up salt-watered sand in his hands and drop it back into the water, he felt a pull. A small whirlpool opened at his feet, no bigger than the Frisbees thrown on the shore. Curious, Quibble dipped a toe in. His entire foot submerged, then his ankle. The hole went quite a bit deeper than the inch or so of sand he'd removed. His eyes widened. What had he uncovered? He crouched down to get a better look. Was that the sun on the water, flicking the light around like so many fingers? Or was that— What was that?

Quibble shakes off the instant replay. Years and many trips between points in space later, he says to Wilder, "Keep your hands on my shoulders," more confidently than he feels, "and don't let go no matter what." Partnered travel is still new for him. Something only Artemis and Mary Margaret have tried with him over short distances. Artemis let go on purpose once, just to see what would happen, and nearly fell down the stairs in her building. Quibble would feel much better if he could grab on to Wilder's wrists and hold on tightly, but he needs both his hands free to start and end. Occasionally in the middle, too, when things became inexplicably rougher than normal, though it had been smooth sailing earlier today. Thank Goddess for little miracles. Quibble's stomach lurches. This is the farthest he's gone partnered. He is terrified. He tries not to show it. He tries not to feel it.

Wilder's hands on his shoulders are both ice cold and clammy at once, and timid in their grip. "Like this?"

"Actually—go around my waist. With your whole forearm."

It's like riding on a motorcycle, Wilder imagines, except more awkward, being that there isn't a motorcycle under them. They try to make sure their chest doesn't touch Quibble's back, but to get their forearms around him, they connect solidly at the waist. They feel his stomach tighten as they clasp their own wrists. "Like this?" they check once more.

Quibble nods and tries to drop his shoulders down his back, plug them in. He takes a deep breath; it's no good to do it scared. Then he'll have two problems: scared and difficult. He sends his breath to the tips of his fingers until they feel the itch to submerge, pull, reach. He can't see his own Power—that's Artemis's jam—but she'd described to him, once, what it looks like: his fingers dance with sparks, then run orange-hot like creeping lava.

He softens his gaze, lets his eyes unfocus until he can see the little dots swimming everywhere around him. Something to hold on to, something to rip. It used to be he could only do it with something physical, like bed linens or bread dough. In the months after the beach, he'd carried his mother's moth-eaten silk scarves around with him in his backpack, ripping them angrily whenever he wanted to travel.

He folds. Grabs the air with one buzzing Hand and pulls. He feels Wilder hug themself into his back. The opening to That Place yawns before them. Time-space tears, big enough to accommodate a person, gaping like a train tunnel, a great black hole crawling with light-worms that don't glow, not exactly. "If you shut your eyes," Quibble says, "it's worse." He takes the first step forward. Steady. Breathing. He walks into the flickering un-light.

Wilder, on the other hand, is far less steady. As they cross the threshold, they feel as though they are on roller skates and, somehow, trying to stand on the bendy bit of an accordion bus. Where Quibble's steps are slow and sure, Wilder can barely keep their feet under them. *Don't let go, don't let go*, they keep repeating to themself. Everything is purple shadow and what look like linked will-o'-the-wisps swirl around them. They eat light and give off energy that is, somehow, also light-adjacent. Wilder has no idea how they can really see anything here. When the Wisp Worms brush against Wilder, they feel like electrified fuzzy caterpillars. Unnerving. The ground tips beneath Wilder and they look down. The "floor" is a transparent ripple as Quibble takes step after step. This piece of solid air seems just big enough to accommodate both of them; otherwise it is bruise-dark nothing. Eldritch, the light-worms floating beneath them as they walk. Wilder wonders how it could be worse to close their eyes until they try it—their stomach flips, unable to make sense of what feels like speeding forward much faster than the few steps they are taking. They notice for the first time wind buffeting them from all directions. It feels crazy-making, coming from everywhere at once. They keep their teeth ground shut, their lips pressed tight. They switch from internally whispering *Don't let go* to *Don't throw up in his coat collar.*

They open their eyes and force themself to look out, not down. They catch scattered images in the purple dark, flickers like a poorly tuned television antenna. One minute they're on a street corner, but shrouded in orchid, violet, lavender, thistle, mulberry, pansy. Then they are high in the sky, the Manhattan skyline visible Here as though it were night, with windows emitting the faintest firefly light. Breathtaking. Gorgeous. Nausea-inducing. A horror show.

Roof gardens. Park fields. Directly in front of a hot dog cart, a sweating man in a visor hat. A train track. A large stone building with columns and a statue. With each step Quibble takes, the after-images change, shutter-clicks, and Wilder can barely register what they've seen before the next imprint, a slightly off version of the world they know, flashes into view. They scramble to keep up.

Quibble swivels his head, looking for Artemis. For him, This Place is not a nightmare. He can sit in here; he does sometimes. It's a place all his own. Quibble has no concept that This Place is scary, only that the walk behind him can feel rough. He spots Artemis and smiles.

Finally Quibble stops. Finally. He does that weird motion with his hands again and the shadow-world gives way to color, a veritable Oz. Both of them step through onto solid ground. The final lurch does Wilder in and without thinking or seeing or being able to control it, like a person possessed, they turn to their right and projectile puke on what turns out to be a fabulous pair of black boots laced with pink and white ribbon.

The vomit smells like coffee and bile. Immediately ashamed and prickling with upsetting familiarity—they've seen those Doc Martens before—they look up. They are outside, thankfully. Folks are staring, not thankfully. Artemis looks down at them, her beard still fully glittered even in the middle of the day. There is a war in her eyes. Kindness shines there, but so does—anger? Frustration? Disgust? All valid emotions in response to becoming a ralph target.

"Quibble," she says. "What the fuck did you do?"

The Star

I 'm sorry. I'm so sorry," Wilder keeps repeating as they find a bus stop bench to sit on.

"Please do not talk to me right now," Artemis replies with her eyes closed.

"Miss, are you okay?" a stranger says to Wilder—such intentional kindness and unintentional cruelty.

"I'm fine," comes out like red-hot spit and they fucking mean it. What kind of stranger wants to talk to another stranger at a time like this? Absolute fucking insanity.

"Jesus, I was just trying to help." The stranger stalks off. Wilder hears it in Spanish and English simultaneously and turns their head away from their own boots just in time. They ralph again, a horrible yellow stream.

"They were like this when I found them!" they can hear Quibble defending himself to Artemis. "I swear!"

"So you took them inside There?"

"Their choice! They're ready to talk!"

"What were you even doing—no, you know what, one thing at a time. Run into one of these places and get me paper towels. Like a roll, not individual napkins."

Wilder finishes puking and puts their head between their legs.

Soon, they can hear Artemis muttering to herself as she cleans her shoes off, pulling the ribbons from them and throwing them in the nearest trash can; Wilder flushes with shame at realizing an appropriate waste receptacle is feet from them. Mere. Feet.

Quibble sits next to them at the bus stop. He lays a hand on their back. "You okay, bud? I'm sorry, I should have maybe warned you. It gets a bit bumpy in there."

Wilder privately acknowledges that any which way they got here would have been just as bad for different reasons, and probably they would have upchucked anyhow. They focus on Quibble's hand, trying to breathe and come back to a state of equilibrium. They're not sure if it's unconscious or purposeful, but Quibble is making small circles with his palm right where their back arcs forward and it's reminding them to take each breath low, slow, and deep.

Artemis's laceless boots, half-scraped clean of sick, come into view. "Apartment," she says to Quibble. "I need to wash them properly." Then, to Wilder, who still hasn't looked up because they would rather fucking perish, "It's just around the corner when you can walk again without booting."

"I can do it, I can do it," Wilder insists.

"Take your time, bud." Quibble places his other hand on their shoulder. "We don't get extra points for going fast."

The first thing Wilder notices about Artemis's apartment is the pink, mostly because they are trying not to meet anyone's eyeballs with their own. It is very, very pink. Not Artemis's *entire* apartment, of course. There is some texture here—white crown molding with gaps at random, like a child's front teeth. A dark, circular table with shoddy varnish and its fair share of nicks and mug rings; above that, a chandelier of knock-off crystal, clear as country creek water; the floors are dark and creak like old bones. But everything else? Magenta and coral and blush and a soft millennial shade of pink, pink, pink. Each hue is different enough so as not to overwhelm; the effect is one of unending warmth in the evening's golden hour, so early in the winter and coming up so quick as to flat-tire the afternoon's metaphorical shoe heels.

Artemis smiles a different smile as she enters. Easier. Something of honest relief as she lets go of her bag. "Shoes off," she says, and Wilder quickly complies. The smile lingers as she says, "You're taking mine off, too." And Wilder finds themself on their knees removing Artemis's barfy boots; they suppose it's only fair, but they're also surprised this is something they're doing for a near-stranger.

When they set the second boot outside the open apartment door and turn around, Wilder has the chance to notice the apartment is occupied already. The table is piled high with schoolbooks—high school, by the looks of it—and on the couch lounges a scrawny, long-limbed girl with a face full of flawless makeup buried in her phone, wearing the whitest sneakers to which Wilder has ever borne witness. Artemis turns that raised eyebrow toward the teenager, exasperated. "You, too, Mary Margaret," she says—sternly but also warmly. "Shoes off. Same as literally always."

"That ruins the whole narrative of the outfit," the girl replies without looking up from her phone.

"Shoes. Off. I am not cleaning these floors in the middle of the week. And—where did you even get those?" She gestures to the sneakers.

Mary Margaret has a body, like the rest of them, but thoughtfully curated in the way teenagers thoughtfully curate their bodies with a little extra edge. A little more understanding of her own taste, her own projection. She is driven not by the crushing weight of fitting in—something she never will do and doesn't much care about—but by knowing exactly what she wants. She has a puckish face that she doesn't hide with that makeup, but rather accentuates. Mischief. Her cheekbones are high and her brows are thin and arched. Her visage is the result of effort, and she doesn't mind showing it. Her hair curls around her head like clouds and she is missing one tooth—a canine. The other one looks especially sharp, as if to compensate for the loss of its compatriot.

Had she her druthers, she would have this exact look—light jeans, knit shirt, long purple nails and beautiful, brand-new white sneakers—with solid white eyes standing out against her deep brown skin. She considers stealing some strange contacts, maybe from one of those beauty shops in Koreatown? They're always up front by the register, but she never, ever gets caught. Regarding Artemis's remark about her sneakers, she arches one of those perfectly sculpted eyebrows as if to say, *Don't ask questions you don't want to know the answers to.*

Instead she says, "Who's the new one?" And she gets up off the couch. She cuts through the air fast, as if unaffected by normal things like gravity and aerodynamics. Her gawky youth doesn't betray her raptor's grace until she moves. A swift, beautiful bearing, lethal and practiced. Wilder is surprised by it until they see two bulging backpacks propped against the wall and notice the bed pillows piled against the couch-arm. Of course she is like a honed blade. Her life, in its short amount of years, has been difficult.

This is the child Artemis thinks of as the Magpie, though she never says *that* aloud, least of all to the child in question. It is a big deal to have a title like that; not just Awakened, but Ascended. Someone stronger, more adept than the average witch. Most will never see that kind of Power. But Artemis suspects that Mary Margaret, who shines brighter in her Sight than the Rockefeller Center Christmas Tree, will be one of them. And so she watches, waits, protects. Does her best to impart a value system, encourage Magical Practice, and make sure Mary Margaret finishes twelfth grade.

Artemis never anticipated semi-parenting a houseless teenager. But she continues to choose this life every day.

Mary Margaret circles Wilder like they are prey, her eyebrow still raised, and Wilder gulps. They aren't sure how to behave around people of any age and teenagers are particularly terrifying—an entire group hyper-trained in the art of finding cracks in a person's sense of self and tapping them once, sharply, with a shining conversational hammer to shatter the whole human being. Wilder senses, rightly, that this trait is super-functional in Mary Margaret. They wonder if she can see magic like Artemis. They wonder if Artemis and Mary Margaret are related; they will find out soon enough the answer is no. That Artemis located Mary Margaret shortly after the teen was kicked out of her parents' house for her queerness, her transness—then her Power Awakened and surged. That it took years to coax her into this living room, years of building trust and no sudden movements. Like getting a skittish bird to eat from one's hand.

"This one's nervous," Mary Margaret says. And it is one of the milder things she might say. There are so many to choose from. "What does it do?"

Artemis snorts. "Don't be an asshole, Mary Margaret. Stop playing."

When she gets back around to the front of Wilder, she looks into their face. "Well?" she says as she grabs a pack of cigarettes from her back pocket, taps them against her palm. "What do you do?"

Wilder's figured out what she's actually asking. "I speak a lot of languages."

Mary Margaret sucks her teeth. "That's not Magic," she says. "That's regular." She twirls around to face the group. "Are we having dinner?" She slams the pack against her hand and a cigarette appears between two fingers like magic. "I'm hungry."

"Give it back," Artemis says, her own eyebrow arching even higher than Mary Margaret's, a veritable eyebrow-arch-off.

"Give what back?" Mary Margaret answers as she puts the cigarette between her lips. "They're my cigarettes."

"I know they are," Artemis replies with beleaguered, practiced calm, "and *you* know that isn't what I mean." Artemis holds out her hand.

Mary Margaret rolls her eyes and flicks her fingers. Something bright. Something fast. Something like a camera flash and her hand disappears for only a second. Wilder stares open-mouthed as she hands them their wallet back. She plops back down on the couch, pouting. The uninitiated, like Wilder, might not notice the performance in it. The ritualistic playing out of a Thing.

"I would appreciate it," Artemis says as she walks toward the kitchen, "if you stopped trying to liberate property from our guests." She rests a graceful arm on Mary Margaret's shoulder, gives it a squeeze. "Never change anything else, though. Do your homework."

Artemis disappears into her room and returns in a caftan, silk and thin. Wilder turns a touch red; they do not expect the stuff of home to be cracked softly open in front of them. Artemis begins to busy—to fill a kettle and put it on the stove. It is an older building, gas, and when she clicks the burner on, she simultaneously slams a pan down on the one next to it, the only way it will ignite. Quibble moves up to the fridge without checking or asking any questions. He simply begins to chop celery, carrots. Wilder stands there, arms akimbo, staring. They are not quite sure what to do.

Artemis raises her eyebrows and it almost makes them giggle, how much both Mary Margaret and Artemis do that. As though their eyebrows possess their own individual consciousnesses. Wilder might laugh if they weren't overwhelmed with embarrassment and fear. "The bathroom's that way." Artemis gestures with her chin. Wilder must look confused because she asks, "Aren't you going to clean my shoes?"

"Oh," Wilder says, turning even redder. "Yes." They open the apartment door and reach out, grab the pukey boots.

Mary Margaret wrinkles her nose theatrically and shrieks, squeals, laughs. "You're fucking gross, what?"

Wilder would like to die just a little bit. But they do notice that, bless it, everyone in this apartment is speaking English, and as much shame as they're wearing on their face, they don't feel like their colors are running. They feel more comfortable than they have since they Awoke.

When Wilder is done getting the shoes as clean as they'll get and they've put them back outside, they—stand there. Not sure what to do as Quibble and Artemis do real things.

"You can sit down, you know," says Mary Margaret in a way that suggests this is a trap, and Wilder, still nervous around the teenager, sits directly on the floor. "Jesus Christ, don't be such a fucking mouse." She flourishes her hand again and Wilder tracks it closer this time. They try very hard not to blink through the light-flash and can see her hand disappear into the air as though she'd reached into a pocket. She draws her hand back clutching a green plastic lighter. She leans over and lights a big candle on the coffee table. "What's your name?"

"Wilder."

"When did you pick it?"

She is forward. Shocking. It doesn't give them time to react, to consider how they might answer or, truly, not answer. "Twenty-five."

Mary Margaret scoffs. "Wow. So old." Wilder wonders how many times they will turn into a pillar of dust and blow away on the wind during this conversation. Mary Margaret lights her cigarette, inhales. On her exhale: "Fourteen. For me."

Wilder can't imagine it. If they'd been honest about when they'd chosen their name, their answer would've ended in "teen." But they hadn't *used* their name, not then. Daydreamed about it, yes, but didn't say it to a single soul. They didn't know what it meant to want. They couldn't imagine having the language for such a thing during—what was fourteen?—freshman year of high school, Jesus Christ. Life would have been so different.

They can't picture having the bravery, either, to come out, even if they'd had the self- awareness. Mostly they'd tried to fit in; it never worked, but they'd tried. They feel, in this moment, the dissonance of being older and somehow knowing with certainty that this young woman has lived more than they have. They glance over at the "adults" nervously. They should be doing something, some act of care, some contribution. But they're not. Instead they are sizing up a teenager.

"Hey," Artemis snaps. Mary Margaret looks back toward the kitchenette. "Window," Artemis says, pointing with her knife. Mary Margaret rolls her eyes and saunters toward the window, rattles-squeaks it open all the way. She sits, leans her back against the frame, dipping her leg onto the fire escape. She exhales the cigarette into the cold, now slicing through the cozy interior in a way that is not unpleasant, the prewar building's uncomfortable heat turning the biting temperature into something crisp, a small pleasure.

Mary Margaret keeps an eye on Wilder, too. She, in turn, has no concept of what it is like to feel old and young at the same time, to feel elderly but not like an elder—she has a frame of reference for what it is to feel tired, that's for certain. She pulses with the energy and understanding that she is not only on the bleeding edge but is also both the knife and the flesh in that metaphor. And she can read on them a similar tear-in-two feeling. She wants to tell them it's all right, that Quibble and Artemis are basically mom and dad, that it's futile to try to butt into their adulting dance. She also wants to slap them a little. In the furthest reaches of her emotional landscape, she doesn't feel like she can tell them anything at all about security—it's so tenuous, and she understands maybe more than anyone what it means to feel perilously on the outskirts. This is confusing, because she is living in her safe era. But if pressed, she would say that she doesn't believe in true safety. Only in saf*er*.

Wilder jumps when they hear a bellow. "Ay!" They think for a second the voice is Mary Margaret's, but she whips her head around, smiling. She balances her cigarette between her fingers and holds it as far out the window as she can while she leans back.

"Artemis! It's Rico!"

For a second Artemis doesn't move, just laughs and keeps cooking. "That fool," she says, in the kind of way that doesn't sound at all like the words in the sentence. It's quiet enough that Rico, three stories down, wouldn't be able to hear. Just everyone in the apartment.

"What are you waiting for?" asks Mary Margaret, and Artemis sets her knife down, turns, and blushes as she leans back against the kitchen counter, taking her time, stretching. This is the first time she's looked her age, Wilder thinks—Artemis can't be older than mid-thirties, and if Wilder had to hazard a guess, she is younger, even, than that, with the toll of responsibility and capitalism accentuating the frown lines by her mouth, often (though not always) artfully concealed by her beard, the forehead wrinkles that bely a frequent snapping-shut of the eyebrows like a bear trap with a hairpin trigger. She walks over to the window to look out, her gait more skip than any way she has yet moved in front of Wilder. She looks girlish, exactly the sort of person who would have this pink apartment, and Wilder understands her just a little bit better.

When Artemis stands back, still, Mary Margaret stamps out her cigarette on the black iron of the fire escape and leans her whole body onto the structure, which shudders under the weight of her enthusiasm. "Hey, Rico!" she shouts, and giggles.

"Is she up there?" Rico's voice is husky, crackling. So explicitly a trans voice on testosterone, it makes Wilder come to the window as well. They stand to the side and crane their neck to catch a glimpse of this mysterious man, who they then recognize from Jacqueline's.

"What do you think?" Mary Margaret shouts.

Rico laughs. "I think she's standing just out of view, smiling."

Everyone erupts, including Wilder, because he is so exactly correct. And the laughs are like a chorus of church bells announcing something to the city, though Wilder isn't sure exactly what.

Rico is on his way to dress rehearsal for Adam and Steve. Which means his eyebrows are drawn in thick and dark and his hair is slicked down, tight to his head. His lips are hot-rod red. Peeking out from underneath his silk shirt, unbuttoned almost halfway and very inappropriate for the weather, is his chest hair, exaggerated, painted on. The vaguest sparkle of a titty tassel in the winter evening streetlight. He carries a thick garment bag over his shoulder with roguish contrapposto, pulls a wheeled suitcase, and wears a top hat crested with the most enormous feather Wilder has ever seen. He takes a deep breath, fills every inch of his lungs with air, and lets loose: "But soft! What light through yonder window breaks? It is the East Side and Artemis is—"

"Stop, stop, stop!" Artemis bustles out the open window like a moving G train. "You'll wake the dead in Green-Wood like that, sweet fucking lord."

Wilder steps back into the center of the room and hugs themself, admiring Artemis, a silhouette against a fire sky, gently resting her elegant hands on the railing, silk caftan catching the setting sun. Mary Margaret is still leaning out, and her breath condenses and curls, steams, whirling into the last rays of light streaming onto the side of the building, into the quickly darkening room.

Wilder doesn't realize they have stopped breathing until Quibble says, "I know." They glance left and Quibble, yikes, has stepped up next to them and is *witnessing* them fall in love (though they of course wouldn't call it love and it is, of course, not a romantic love). They scowl even as they try to take a photo with their mind. Try to remember it exactly as it is, the soft light and the way cold breathes around the two warm women, holding them in a perpetual inhale. Wilder can feel the buzz of Quibble's arm, so remarkably close to theirs. A real snapshot would not recall the intense longing on everyone's part: Quibble for his family, Artemis for Rico, Mary Margaret for happiness, and Wilder for a sense of secure inclusion. Only memory can do that.

"Come to Jacqueline's," Rico asks. Quieter than the full-throated Shakespearean caterwauling, but still loud, public. Performative yet earnest.

"It's a school night," Artemis replies, and Mary Margaret's teeth sucking is loud enough to reach all the way to the street.

"I don't need you, damn," the teenager says, quiet.

"Yes, you do," Artemis says just to her. "If I leave, I know you're leaving, too."

Mary Margaret pouts.

"You do not attend school, Artemis," Rico shouts up to the window. "Come on, come out. You *work* in nightlife. This is like a business dinner. Come just you. No offense, Quibble."

"None taken," Quibble shouts back.

A. E. OSWORTH

"I only *technically* work in nightlife," Artemis grumbles. Then, out the window to Rico, a smirk on her face, "I am raising a child, Rico. You would have me leave my sweet little baby on a school night?"

"I am literally smoking next to you," Mary Margaret says.

"Does she want to?" Wilder whispers to Quibble, instinctually leaning toward him until their arms brush.

"I can't actually tell," Quibble answers. "I think so."

In truth, Artemis does want to go. Artemis always wants to spend time with Rico. And who wouldn't? Rico is one of those magic people—not in the sense of Awakened Power, of course, but in the sense of everyday magic. The way he moves through the world seems to spawn sparkle somehow. He sees double rainbows on rainy days and streetlights turn on when he wanders underneath them. Once, when he was very young, a flower even bloomed while he watched; he tapped his pencil excitedly against his school desk and his teacher accused him of telling lies. Artemis Sees Power; she also knows magic when she feels it sitting on the barstool next to her. And she does not trust herself around such magic without a chaperone. If she goes on a date with Rico, it will be a slippery slope, this she knows. She will start to feel feelings (or notice the feelings she is already feeling), and then where will she be? And in the version of the world where she chooses, in this moment, to give in to her desire? That is exactly what happens.

She shakes her head. "I'll be there for the actual performance, Rico. I don't need to watch you rehearse it."

"Girl, he is asking you on a date," Mary Margaret says loud enough for Rico to hear, hoping to use embarrassment to exact pressure in that common teenage way.

Artemis smiles at Mary Margaret, gentle and sad and with closed lips. "I can't do anything with Rico, Maggie."

Mary Margaret clicks her tongue, looks down at Rico, and wiggles her eyebrows. "If I promise to do the homework, will you go out?"

"Oh, my sweet sparrow," Artemis says, and she lays a hand on Mary Margaret's cheek. "I very much do not trust you to do that. Besides, I have things to do tonight. I brought them home for a reason." She looks out over the railing. "Maybe another time, Rico," she calls down. She turns to come inside while Mary Margaret rolls her eyes.

"Artemis?" Rico calls. His voice cracks, more than usual, which makes Artemis turn around.

"Yeah?"

"Am I wrong, here? Just say the word and I'll never bother you again."

She pauses. Another, different small smile rests on her face; she looks so tired. She is carrying something heavy, and she hasn't yet put it down. But she blushes up under her beard, all the way up to the hollows of her eyes. "You ain't wrong, Rico," she says quietly, but still it rings like a bell, carrying clearly to the street below. "No, you're not wrong at all."

"Okay, beautiful," he says, "I'll keep trying." Then he is gone and the sun disappears behind the building across the street.

Ten of Cups, Reversed

I wasn't lying," Artemis says after they've eaten and the dishes have been washed.

"About what?" Mary Margaret asks.

"When I said you have to do your homework. When I said I have stuff to do tonight."

Mary Margaret is about to slump into a dining room chair, her fingernails clacking on the back of it as she prepares to pull it out, collapse upon it in dramatic protest. Instead, she whips around. "Is it witch stuff? You said you brought them for a reason." Her whole body language changes; her shoulders point forward. "Please, Artemis, let me do the witch stuff."

Artemis is torn—on one hand, if Mary Margaret doesn't learn to wield her Power even more, even stronger, if she doesn't keep a handle on it while it grows, it'll burst out of her, like it did before (like it's doing with Wilder right now). And then she'll act out, take things. On the other hand, she also needs to pass Algebra II. Deep down, Artemis knows the first is most important, the second a fairly arbitrary measure of one's intelligence. But she also knows the Magpie will have to live in the real world, if she has any hope at happiness. So she won't wind up like the Sibyl, that stupid future teller with the stupid name whose whole stupid existence is witches and nothing else. In the real world, having passed Algebra II *means* something. Artemis oscillates wildly between two possible responses ("not until your homework is done" and "in fact I insist you do the witch stuff") and settles on the more moderate, "Yes, I expect you to do both."

Mary Margaret squeals and claps her hands, sits on the floor where Artemis indicates, cross-legged with an alacrity only a seventeen-year-old can manage, bounces her knees up and down. "What are we doing?"

Quibble sits next to her. "Teaching Wilder where their Hands are."

Mary Margaret groans and slumps over her crossed ankles. "No, this is so boring. This is ass-elbow lessons."

Wilder looks down at their hands—they are right there!—and has to admit they agree with Mary Margaret. Confused, they hold their hands up and get ready to say that they don't appreciate being treated like a child, that dinner was nice and all but if they're going to get pranked, that's just fucking mean, they could've just stayed home and—

"Not those hands," Artemis says as she sits across from Mary Margaret, next to Quibble. She gestures to the space on the floor next to her. "Sit."

Being that Artemis is scary, Wilder sits even as they are trying to work out what she just said. "These aren't—"

"Those are not your Hands, bud," Quibble says. "Well, they are. Your hands. But not your Hands."

"If you're going to take the piss—" Wilder starts.

"What are we, British now?" Quibble interrupts, a smile on his face. He thinks he is gently roasting.

"Listen—" Wilder gets ready to fight and then gasps. Because they feel a sensation. As being gripped by the shoulders and squeezed reassuringly; kind of nice, actually, given that reassurance is exactly what they need. They reach up to touch what they are sure will be hands, fingers. But they brush only their own shirt. Nothing is there.

They leap up from the ground and once again Artemis says, "Sit," and they do, like a game of fucked-up Simon Says.

"Breathe," Quibble says, and they do that, too.

"What," Wilder says between breaths, "the fuck. Was that?"

Mary Margaret wiggles her fingers, splayed out. "Hands," she answers. "But not these."

"It's not your physical shoulders I'm doing that to," Quibble says, "and not my physical hands doing it either. It's your—spiritual Shoulders? That sounds dumb as hell. And my spiritual Hands? But here, Feel it. Listen."

Wilder isn't sure if they should close their eyes; they decide to keep them open, to stare at their own left shoulder, stare at Quibble's hands across the circle. When the Feeling occurs again, they can plainly see that their body isn't the channel through which they're experiencing touch and that Quibble doesn't move a muscle, except to crack his neck, which is gross.

Wilder looks around at all the witches, who look back at their panicked face expectantly. "I hate this."

Inspired by Quibble's horrible neck sound, Artemis cracks her knuckles. "Mary Margaret," she says, "if these are, indeed, ass-elbow lessons, then you should know your ass from your elbow by now. Explain."

Mary Margaret rolls her eyes and Wilder finds their own mother close at hand (or rather, close at mouth), and the sentence *Your face will stick like that* leaps to the cliff of their bottom teeth. But they hold it back and listen to the teenager say, "Everyone has two bodies—the physical one we're all familiar with," and Wilder gets the feeling these exact sentences, word for word, have been said to this child and this child has the kind of bear trap mind that remembers a lesson down to the syllable if she cares about it even a little, "and the one that goes beyond it. That exists Attached but Otherwise." Mary Margaret uncrosses her legs and leans back, rolls her ankles until they crack, and Wilder wants to say, okay, enough. "The superstitious," she continues, "might call it a soul. But it's a Body, all right. Just—less meaty. Everyone has it, but it's the purview of witches to be able to feel both the body and the Body at once, and to distinguish between the two. To use the Body to manipulate Power."

"At least," Artemis says, "that's the best we can figure. It's all theories. My theories," and she looks proud. And she should be! To have figured anything out at all! In the version of the world where she hasn't, this conversation is going much worse. "I can See the Power moving around, so my guesses are educated ones. But I don't see it with my eyes. I See it with my Eyes." Every time someone uses that sentence construction, Wilder feels insane.

"My guess," Quibble jumps in, "is if you learn to differentiate between hearing things with your ears and your Ears, it's going to get easier to turn the dial up on one and down on the other. It'll be a little less overwhelming. But that's just a guess."

Wilder doesn't want to tell Quibble that it sounds like a really good guess. They've returned to an activated, feral state, freaked out by being Touched in ways they can't see but absolutely perceive. "How do I do that?" they ask, instead of yelling wordlessly, which is what they'd rather do. "The dial thing?"

Quibble shrugs. "Practice? Here, pay really close attention."

"Could you—warn me first?" Wilder says, fast, trying to get in there before Quibble does it again. "Like before you Touch me?"

"Oh, yeah, sorry, that's—yeah. Sorry. Okay, incoming."

And Wilder Feels it, the stretch from Quibble and the tension between them and the caress of a Thumb on their shoulder seam—spiritual Shoulder seam? It is confusing, feeling two things at once and parsing the difference. A metaphysical pop-and-lock, an isolation of moving one part of oneself and not the other. Quibble's Hand creates sensation of the spine against a yoga mat on a hard floor; being held so firmly by the earth. Wilder loves it instantly and they are reminded that love and hate are two sides of the same tarot card.

"Can you feel the—energy?" Quibble chuckles. "The energy. Between me and you?"

"Yeah, actually." Wilder is surprised. It's like feeling an arm, or Arm, they guess. But it's a bit too long. Like a weird Gumby Arm except, they don't know, holy or some shit? Almost vine-like. Plant-y. Strong and totally invisible.

"Can you do the same thing? To me?" Quibble asks.

Wilder closes their eyes and tries to reach an Arm across the circle to Quibble. Their concentration is broken when Mary Margaret snorts laughter. They open their eyes and discover one of their hands outstretched.

"You don't have to—" Quibble starts, kind.

"I know," Wilder cuts him off, humiliated. "I know. But how—do I find it?"

"Here, Feel again." And Quibble squeezes their Shoulder. "It's like—you almost step a tiny bit to the side of yourself and there You are."

"That's not how I find Me," Mary Margaret interjects. "For me it's like I go to the spot where I feel when I'm hungry and, like, fling out."

Everyone turns to Artemis, who holds her hands up. "Don't look at me! I have an unfair advantage. I can See Myself under my skin."

"This is fucking ridiculous," Wilder says. "How does anyone do any of this?"

"Try a bunch of shit, to be honest," Quibble mutters.

So they do. They try all of it. They don't know how long they sit, looking inside, outside, upside down (they sit precisely four minutes and thirty-seven seconds). However long it is, it feels too long and they are already so activated. They feel the panic start to well up. They breathe deep into their belly and find the rising tide and—oh. There It is—there They are—in the calming of choppy waves. It takes Wilder another minute to locate their Hands because they're texturally different; shaky, timid, and thin in comparison to Quibble's veritable tree trunks. Like rivulets of water on a windowpane in the lightest of rains, so many of them, woven together and flowing every which way—a difficult energy to coax in a specific direction. When they finally reach out and Touch Quibble's Shoulders in return, he smiles.

"Interesting," he says. "Interesting."

"Okay," Artemis says. "Now that we've got that, time to cast."

Wilder's eyes fly open. "What, a spell? Like now?" Their Hands fall in a cascade like a popped water balloon, all form gone. "I only just figured out where my Hands are!"

Artemis shrugs. "If not now, when? Besides, I wasn't kidding! I have shit to do!"

"I thought I was the shit to do!" Wilder semi-shouts.

Mary Margaret snickers at the innuendo and Wilder blushes.

"Nope, as important as you are." Artemis says this and Wilder gets the impression she does not find them important in the slightest. It's not that Artemis is *mean*. It's that Artemis is focused. And she has been focused somewhat unintentionally on the horrible little lights; it's unusual that she, who has an impeccable grasp on the difference between eyes and Eyes, would be getting a headache from Seeing

Power. "I want to figure out what the fuck is going on with the phones. I can't make you help," she says to Wilder, knowing full well their constitution has the fortitude of wet crepe paper in the face her own bright blaze. "If you don't want to, you're free to leave. You're always free to leave. But all the lights started when your Power Awakened, and you might just be the key to figuring it out."

"Phones?" Wilder and Mary Margaret ask at the same time.

Artemis sighs. She explains the lights. She finishes with "Even though it's the barest trace of Magic and the lights are small, they are omnipresent. It's overwhelming because it's everywhere. And anything that's everywhere?" She folds her arms. "Could be dangerous."

Wilder pauses after Artemis is done. "I don't know how, though. I don't know how to cast a spell."

Quibble smiles with half his mouth as he says, "No one ever does, bud. We make it up every time."

They all sit for a second, the streetlight bathing them orange. Then: "Pay attention!" Artemis speaks from some deep part of her. Her voice a resonant alto, like the backbone of a choir. Wilder sits up straight. Artemis continues. "Something amazing is about to happen." She claps her hands, and it sounds like a well-made box clasping shut with a satisfying *click*. The apartment is small, yet it echoes. Wilder can feel warmth settle on the group, even with the window still wide open. The sounds around them blanket-fort-muffle. Close, conspiratorial. Artemis holds out her hands—Quibble takes one, and Wilder notices that both Artemis and Mary Margaret have their hands (their physical ones) stretched toward them. They hesitate, afraid to touch anyone, to participate. But one more look at Artemis's determined face and they slip their hands into the others' waiting palms. The warmth increases, envelops them from the forearms. As though a hug, except a handshake. A small, strange brightness in the palms of their hands. The

Palms of their Hands. They taste lemon on their tongue and smell the brewing of tea.

They immediately recoil, both in body and in this queer Meta-Body that Tastes and Smells of its own accord. "What the fuck," they say.

Mary Margaret snaps her fingers and says, "Come on, get with it," her hand still outstretched.

"I—I tasted something." Wilder thinks they are having a stroke. "I smelled it."

"No, you didn't," Artemis says. "You Tasted it and you Smelled it. It didn't happen in the physical world. You gotta start distinguishing."

"What did you get?" Quibble asks.

"Lemons," they answer. "Tea."

"That one's probably me," Quibble says, and he smiles. "I used to take the lemons off the table during afternoon tea and wholesale eat them like a weirdo, run around with the rind in my mouth covering my teeth."

Wilder is torn between two exclamations: "You had afternoon tea?" and "We get each other's fucking sense memories?" Given the givens, they choose the latter.

"Yup! Not, like, everything."

"Can you—pick? What other people get?"

"Nope!"

"And—and you didn't know what I got?"

Quibble smiles. "Not even a little."

"And you—do that? Willingly?"

All three look at Wilder with the painful and impossibly intimate understanding of the massive emotional risk; the look also contains the realization this concern has become distant for them. Mary Margaret looks the most shocked; Artemis the least.

"Yes," Quibble answers. "Yes."

Wilder is exasperated. "Why?"

Quibble seriously considers their question, and this serious consideration calms Wilder just a little bit. After a hefty pause, Quibble answers: "Because that's the only way to do Magic. And I want to do Magic."

Wilder almost gets up and leaves. Artemis just said they could, after all. But they think of the three trains back. Of the face-blistering amount of vocal information that would vibrate into their ears or Ears or whatever. And they know if they don't sit here and cast a spell, they will continue to be broken by the world and all the people in it. However, it seems absolutely ludicrous that these people—Wilder doesn't even know their last names!—should get the keys to their inner kingdom. "I wasn't even touching Quibble," Wilder says, delaying what they now understand to be inevitable. "And I got his lemons."

"We're all in it together. His lemons are your lemons, with or without proximity." Artemis is inspecting her nails like she doesn't care. But she cares a lot. She wants to keep going. She knows if she seems eager, Wilder will run. Maybe it is a little emotionally manipulative, but the line between *driven by higher purpose* and *manipulation* is a fine one that sometimes eludes her.

"Here, Artemis, trade me." Quibble and Artemis switch positions, Quibble's knee now brushing up against Wilder's. "Okay? Try again?" Quibble's hand reaches out. Wilder swallows—since when did their mouth produce so much fucking spit?—and slips their hands into his and Mary Margaret's.

The tea and lemons slam back down onto them with such force that Wilder almost pulls away again, but the group clamps down on them, hauling their squirrelly energy back into the circle and tightening their grips until Wilder's fingers ache. It is like trying to saddle an ocean wave and ride atop of it, for minutes or hours or eternities or seconds (it is seconds: seventeen of them). Nausea. Seasickness. Goose bumps walk wild over everyone's necks.

Then it settles, and Wilder can feel everyone Looking at them though their gazes haven't altered, their heads haven't even twitched. They feel too seen. In an instant, Wilder understands in the pit of their stomach how well these people know each other, and how little they know Wilder, not even familiar let alone familial. As their Sense of the group seeps in, they consider that they're fourth-wheeling a whole-ass family.

Mary Margaret's energy is cloves and liquor, cheap yet inexplicably smooth, and the Smell of the cigarettes against clean clothes. It is sharp and raises one single eyebrow and punches Wilder in the meta-arm, the Arm.

Artemis is like a hot spring; her temperature runs scalding and freezing in extremes. She Smells of air before lightning and a desperate wish of calm.

Quibble's is the scent of sandalwood and the kindest smile imaginable and the Feeling (but not the Smell) of woodsmoke. An autumn sweater, a hug from behind.

Wilder doesn't want to know all that quite so quickly. What one's Magic feels like to other Magic is so much information to have about a person. It is different and deeper than simply the quality of Quibble's Arms, a more active window into the soul. Even more horrifying is the depth of information Wilder involuntarily shares about themself. What are the others getting? (Quibble gets it, mostly: the Smell of childhood oatmeal baths for itchy, red skin and the sensation of never looking down at their own body as it is applied.)

"Pay attention," Artemis says again. "Something amazing is about to happen."

It is as though Artemis reaches out with a toe and nudges Mary Margaret incorporeally. "Here is the amazing thing," Mary Margaret says, even more bright-voiced in this Power-full bubble. Wilder feels their phone lifted from their pocket as it disappears. It reappears with the others, winking into existence one by one, on the floor in the middle of the circle. Of course. The pickpocket.

Time passes. They are not sure exactly how much time (a minute and four seconds). It's a wondrous alternate dimension, this sitting circle. A bubble outside the natural progression of seconds (not quite—adjacent to the progression of seconds. Perception is a wild thing). When they blink, the room is darker, even, than before. Quibble speaks and his voice rattles Wilder's Body. "Another amazing thing." The air shimmers as though the wibbly space above a schoolyard blacktop at the height of summer. They can see an element of Quibble's Other-Space—a purple-brown darkness, like freshly watered potting soil made transparent. Wilder Feels a double-bearded bisous exchange and Smells cooking onions, Sees Rico's long eyelashes and Feels a surge of longing. They wonder if Artemis's Power always Feels like longing (it does. Longing and Protection). So it isn't only Quibble using Magic. It's a tandem ride, effortless. They need not speak to each other and Wilder thinks of the simple dance that is their cooking of dinner. Wordless synchronicity.

Quibble's Power isn't as punchy as Artemis's—it rolls like hills. It whispers like large-leafed plants in a strong breeze and Smells like honeysuckle, jasmine, and, yes, lemon.

The phones glow brilliantly against the extra-dark, the negative space Quibble holds open. Three of them—Quibble, Mary Margaret, and Wilder—blink. Only Artemis doesn't react. This is, after all, what she Sees all the time. At first, the phones look perfectly normal—or as normal as anything looks in Here. Then it is as though sunlight catches on the dark screen; the kind of small, winking reflection the Lady Anastasia would surely chase around Wilder's kitchen. Sometimes a pale glow; other times it hits them directly in the eye. Startling enough as a fact by itself, but disconcerting given the phones are completely still. Artemis's near-constant headache becomes very understandable. The group, having now all contributed, turns as one to look at Wilder; they look like the collective heads of a single creature to which Wilder is desperately clinging.

Wilder feels the urge to speak. To Speak, really—to use Meta-Body Magic. They feel an incredible need to be heard, to be understood. A second thing: they feel exposed. They cannot stop thinking about how, if they open their Mouth, it might rain the Smell of sunburned skin being aloe-soothed or the sensation of losing a tooth at eighteen, a painful-relief-crumbling-pop after taking a backhand to the side of their face, the Sound of buzzing clippers or the vibration of those clippers in their hand. Hand? They don't know on which body these things are written, if there is truly a difference.

Wilder wonders, also, if the winking light is sentient. And if the light can even think, they certainly don't know what language it would speak. Will their Power work if they don't know? Of course it will—they haven't had to know yet. The light looks like fey fire in folklore, the wisps of light that lead travelers into sucking swamps until they're stuck up to their knees. Wilder can't begin to guess what amazing thing they're supposed to do—light doesn't have a face or a mouth. It is only sparkles. How does one speak or Speak with something like that?

They wish desperately for a light, cool touch on their shoulders. Folding into someone who smells of hydrangeas. They haven't thought about their mother in a very long time, but she keeps coming back today, now. She was the parent with the red hair and her hands were perpetually cold. Wilder was a warm kid, and they fit together perfectly in this way. Their father was a long-haul truck driver and he was rarely there—no, even worse! They do not want these witches to see anything of their father. They lived in a converted garage on someone else's farm and the inside was painted a shrieking yellow that Wilder loved for its boldness. Wilder's mother had chickens and Wilder has fond memories of watching staticky television with the overtones of clucking and chuckling wafting through their open window in the high summer heat, cool hands on the back of their neck as their tiny space-heater body curled up on her lap.

Wilder falters. "Here is—" And they lick their paper-dry lips, which stick to the underside of their tongue. "Something—amazing?" But no amount of red-faced shame at being unable to continue could make them do so, could make them Reach into their Power and click into something deeper. Instead of giving away any telling sensory experience, they all Hear a high-pitched whine, electric and pulsing, like a janky lightbulb about to burn out. The Power flickers and falters, and the sensation of time-out-of-time dies. Dies in Wilder's hands. Or Hands.

"Aw, come the fuck on," says Mary Margaret as she slaps her palms down on her knees. "We had it."

"Clearly we did not have it," Artemis replies as she stands, eyes Wilder up and down. "Well. No matter." She smiles a brave smile for the group, for Mary Margaret in particular. But her insides are turbulent, a howling and hungry flame. Her stomach rumbles for answers, answers she'd been convinced she was about to get. For the first time, she mistrusts Wilder. She suspects this is not entirely fair, but it is hard to apply some of the gentle coaxing she used with Mary Margaret to this whole-ass adult. "Hmm," she scoffs. "Well. Mary Margaret has homework to do."

"You gonna go out with Rico?" The smile in Mary Margaret's sentence is impish. Artemis can't help but smile as well, genuinely.

"No amount of mentioning Rico is going to make me forget you have homework to do."

✳   ✳   ✳

Wilder near about flees the apartment. They even take the stairs two at a time.

Quibble follows behind. "Wilder. Wilder. It's fine."

Wilder isn't doing a very good job at hiding their disappointment in themself. The privacy they would surrender by going deeper into their Power makes them gasp. It isn't as though they don't deeply desire it—but it's too much. And of course the part they keep a touch hidden from themself: the longing to be a member of that beautiful and strange collective creature lit against the setting sun, basking in both the light and the clarity of their love for one another. Wilder wants it so, so badly they can't look at the center of it, must keep it always in their periphery.

"I'm sorry" is all Wilder can think of to say.

"Why?" Quibble asks, his breath curling into ethereal mist against crisp winter Brooklyn.

"Because I didn't—couldn't—I didn't know how—"

Quibble waves his hands in the air, as though Wilder's guilt and their apology are bothersome flies. "I didn't expect you to. Mary Margaret did, yeah. Because, for all she's mature, she's still a kid. And Artemis—I don't think she'd normally be this fixated on *you* being the solution here. Artemis likes portents and believes in fate. She'll never accept that your Awakening and the phones aren't related because they happened at the same time. Seers are often like that. I'm not. I know that sometimes shit is random."

Wilder thinks about it for a moment, wonders if perhaps Artemis is correct. They had the urge to Say something to the lights. Perhaps theirs is the right Power for the job. But it seems so silly. They contemplate telling Quibble, but he cuts in just as they open their mouth.

"Do you want a slice?" He's shoved his hands in his pockets, so he gestures to the pizzeria window with his bearded chin. "My treat. It really is okay. We'll figure it out. We always do. Never something quite like this, but we always move forward on something. For a while, it was Mary Margaret. Power popping out everywhere, no control whatsoever. Pure Id—actually, no, that's not quite right, at least not the way people talk about the Id. It was never mischievous or fun. It was always fear and survival. That's worse."

Quibble buys two slices of pizza before Wilder can refuse and hands them one, the tantalizing triangle point drooping off the paper plate. Wilder bites that piece off; they burn the roof of their mouth. The oil, the pepper, the flecks of black on the bottom of the crust, the ultra-thin slices of crisp roasted garlic lying on the cheese: heaven, and it warms them. Quibble is a folder of slices and Wilder isn't. They wonder if it's because they didn't grow up in a city. Didn't grow up able to eat very much pizza. Too expensive.

"Did you grow up here?" Wilder asks.

Quibble shakes his head. "Not Brooklyn. Manhattan, actually." He smiles shyly.

Quibble sometimes doesn't know how much to say about himself to people who have much less than he has. And he primarily hangs out with people who have much less than he has. Often, he sublimates a part of himself. He doesn't want to complain about his life because it feels trite to do; he is, himself, safe and comfortable. He has worked very hard (emotionally, that is) to *feel* safe and comfortable. But when people ask him things and he answers honestly, he usually can't get around mentioning the emotional work in tandem with his fortunate financial circumstance. He fears he sounds like a dick and he changes the subject. "You?"

Wilder shakes their head. "Upstate. The bit that's basically Appalachia. Well, is Appalachia. It's kind of what you think of when you think of Appalachia and kind of not at the same time."

"Why'd you come here?"

"I'm not—really sure, actually." It is very obvious that they are sure, or at least surer than they let on, and Quibble notices. He wants to press. But he is afraid Wilder will press back. And then he will have to talk about money and dead parents.

Instead, he changes the subject entirely: "It's like garlic breath." He gestures to the pizza with his chin.

"What?" Wilder asks around a mouthful.

"The thing where when you cast, you give away interior stuff. It's like this pizza. If everyone is eating it, no one notices how much you stink. That's a bad analogy, probably. But it's what I've got."

Wilder just grunts. Accepting a slice of pizza was their maximum; they feel uneasy about being comforted any further.

Quibble continues anyhow. "I find that different things come up with different people. Like whenever Mary Margaret's around, high school stuff comes up for me. It's not always, like, *deep* stuff. Like the lemons. The lemons aren't like. *Deep*." Except of course they are. That is a family memory. But Quibble doesn't want to get into it. "You know," he pivots, "you never give away the whole story. Not one of us would presume to really know you based on what we Experience. If that helps. You're the only one who can give us that. It has to be an active decision."

"I wanted to talk to them," Wilder says, and they don't even know they're going to bring it up until they do. Ah, trans masculinity: two people take turns abruptly changing the subject to keep from discussing their feelings.

"What?"

"The phones. The lights. I wanted to talk to them."

"Why didn't you?" Quibble asks.

They know instantly the answer is *I didn't want to give away a piece of myself* and they also know instantly they're going to lie. "I didn't know what language it spoke. Or if it could speak. Or how to find my Mouth. I don't know anything."

Wilder has something they want to ask, a return, slant, to the subject of Magical intimacy. They want to know what the woodsmoke is and they don't know if it's out of line to ask about it, if it's like Vegas rules or some shit. But they are interrupted by Mandarin, spoken by the purveyors of the pizza window, and they feel like they're going to ralph their pizza back up. "Can I—I want to go home." But then they remember that at home, they can hear Roommate Andy. Quibble watches this realization ripple across Wilder's face.

"Do you—want to come to mine?" Quibble offers. "It's quiet. And if you're going to join us—"

Wilder snaps a sneer onto their face, which comes easy—they're starting to rock back and forth, squint their eyes as though that'll keep them from hearing words liquefy into other words. "Who said I was joining you?"

"Well, I mean—you cast with us. Or at least, you tried to— No, I didn't mean that!" Quibble interrupts himself as Wilder's sneer deepens. "You did great! For your first time! And it's going to help, the more you do it, I—well, I can't promise, actually."

"Yeah, see?" Wilder says as they turn toward the train, steel themself. "You can't promise, actually. All you can promise is that you'll be able to see my ass or whatever." What they do not say: *If you see these parts of me, if I can't curate them for you, you're not going to like me very much. I can't let you catch glimpses of me like that.* What they do, finally, actually say: "I can't, Quibble. I can't." Their sneer is softer as their lips quiver. They disappear underground.

Nine of Pentacles

Quibble heads to his apartment on the Upper East Side, which used to be his parents' before they died. A penthouse. An impossibility for nearly every single human on the planet, let alone most trans folks. His parents were old money; the place has been in the family for, well, not generations. Nothing in the United States is truly that old. But yes, a couple generations, if one thinks about it that way. He greets the doorman, a guy named Alex not any older than he is, and grabs a package from him. Gets in the elevator, presses the button for the fourteenth floor. The building is old, but the system has been updated. A key fob swipe means the button is permitted to light.

The doors open directly into his apartment. Many such places are gaudy, but not this one. It is dark and quiet; its most defining interior feature: built-in bookshelves. The apartment is filled to the brim with pages, covers. It smells like a library. Its most defining exterior feature: a balcony, the rare private outdoor space afforded only to the richest in Manhattan. French doors. The lights perched on the sides of buildings from the city beyond; a view of trees on the road, bathed in streetlamp light. The purple city looms, beats like a heart. He steps out and looks over it, over all the people touching each other, brushed up against each other in bars and baking bread in their kitchen windows. It is too freezing to stay out there for long, but he braves as much as he can. Something to clear his head a little after the close, damp heat in the subway car. He'd had to take his coat off; he'd gotten so muzzy, so sweaty. And why hadn't he just ripped apart the air to land here, on this balcony? Honestly, he considers if he made the right choice, struck the balance between energy and Energy. Both bodies get tired. He'd used a lot of Power, opening the world around the four of them as he had, and what if something happened, some emergency, and he had to use more? He always thinks about saving people; he always keeps some Power in the tank.

Inside, he pours himself a rye whiskey from a bar cart and collapses onto the tufted leather sofa. He's made some choices—done a little redecorating so he's not quite as haunted by the spirits of his parents, his past. Gone are the endless photos of him with long curls, his graduation photo with the lace halter top and gloss-finish lipstick, awkwardly looking into the middle distance and trying to smile with his eyes. He never could get the hang of it, not until after he transitioned. And his parents' plane rocketed into the sea long before he'd put a finger on his squirming gender.

Often, Quibble plays a game with himself: would his parents have been fine with his coming out? This is not a healthy game, says the therapist. We can't ask them from the great beyond, nor can we read their minds, says the therapist. The first time the therapist said that was, of course, when Quibble tried to actually talk to them postmortem. Because if there is Power in this world, then why not ghosts? Which, as he presently recalls it, gives him an idea. He heads for the closet, the one where he keeps everything. Boxes on boxes from before he changed it all, before he scrubbed their presence from home, too painful to stare at every day and too painful to throw out.

He doesn't remember where he stuck what he's looking for, so he brings every box out and tilts their lids back to inspect. Many spiders. The dust of neglect. Old photos, some pasted in albums and others kept in drugstore envelopes and still others in heartier folders with crinkling plastic windows. He lets his eyes blur into soft focus; he doesn't linger on any one thing too long. Not the dresses his mother wore; not the dresses his mother bought him. Not the last pair of slippers into which his father's feet wore comfortable grooves. Not the jewelry box with the second-best things—the first-best lay rusting in the sand wherever their bodies wound up. He tries not to think about that quite so vividly. He can't decide whether it's an intrusive thought to be gently sent on its merry way or something to be examined, worked on. What he is sure of is that right at this moment, he's on a mission. Wilder told him they felt the urge to speak to the light—if it *can* speak, then why not try holding up a microphone specifically engineered for the disembodied?

He finds what he's looking for after a few tries—a boxed-up toy from sleepovers past that he rediscovered in his nascent adulthood when he tried to get his parents on the spiritual line. A flimsy Ouija board with a plastic planchette. Two children printed on the box cover, excitedly looking at the board all laid out. Hasbro logo. What a laughable thing to encourage children to do. Baby's first seance.

He sips his whiskey and props the box up by the door, to bring to the Adam and Steve Show, tell Artemis his plan. Who knows if Wilder will come, even—he did cock it all up at the end. If Wilder isn't coming, then the remaining three of them will need a prop all the more. He breathes a couple deep breaths; he wants to know if bringing this object to the group will do much the same as what Wilder seems so scared of—give away something deeply personal about his past. He wonders yet again if he could speak to his parents if he had more fingers on the planchette than just his own; he is too embarrassed to ever ask anyone else to try.

Two of Cups

After everyone leaves, and after the Magpie is asleep, having done as much of her homework as she is ever going to do, Artemis tiptoes to her back kitchen door and closes it softly, softly behind her.

She is still in her caftan, that beautiful pink silk that clings to her, shows off every curve, every muscle, and feels like comforting water as it slides across her skin, like a freshly drawn bath against the chaotic flame that is her interiority. She pulls on her coat as she descends, but her legs are still bare, her feet only in flimsy sandals. She looks at her phone. It's the proper time. She pushes the door to the building open and the frigid air hits her, ripples goose bumps over her legs, her neck. Her nipples get hard.

Rico is leaning against the wall, waiting for her. He is in his full drag king getup underneath a trench coat. His lips and eyebrows are glittered, his chest still exposed, inviting. Neither of them say any words. They fall into each other. They run their hands over everything.

The alleyway is fairly private as far as Brooklyn is concerned. No one is taking the garbage out this late, or this early, and that is the only thing they share space with. Banana peels, milk cartons, half-rinsed cans. Not one iota of skin goes ignored. Hands are slid down sleeves and under shirts until there is only one thing left to do. Rico slides his hands up under her slip, lets his fingers linger on the lace; Artemis pulls his loud shirt untucked, undoes his giant showman's belt buckle. They stroke and fuck and Artemis sucks on Rico's ear to keep from making noise. Rico buries his face into her collarbone, the soft spot right above it. He breathes deeply.

Rico doesn't have Awakened Power, and this is the closest he can get to feeling it on anyone. Artemis smells like rose, lavender, secondhand cigarettes, cinnamon, and sex. She feels like supple leather that bends and shines in his hands. When they come apart, Artemis has picked up a little more glitter in her beard; Rico's lipstick is entirely gone, butterflied onto her neck. He wants to say something about how beautiful she is, how much he enjoys her, maybe even something about love, though he knows that's a risk. Instead what comes out of his mouth is something he knows he will regret: "I want more than this."

Artemis looks at him, her eyes hidden under a cloak of sadness and responsibility. "Like what? What kind of more?"

"Like I could come upstairs. We could talk, just us, sitting down—you know I've never seen the inside of your apartment? This is amazing, but it's not—it isn't the only thing I want with you. You have to know that. The stuff that's for show, the hamming it up in front of people? It's all honest." He pauses, wipes makeup off his teeth with a finger. "I hope this isn't the only thing you want with me, either."

"No! No, it's not. But—" And there is a kindness here in her eyes, too, and Rico knows to look for it because he knows her as well as she'll let him. Kindness toward Rico. Kindness toward herself. Artemis, as much of a bristly bitch as she is and loves being, is also overflowing with compassion, with love. She feels so deeply, like the coals under a fire. Everything she does is rooted in it. She feels it so much it hurts sometimes and that is the problem. Artemis is no stranger to intimacy; she was reminded this evening, after all, trying to cast with the new kid. Intimacy like that, intimacy with point and purpose? That is a risk she can understand. What is the point and purpose with Rico? Mere enjoyment? How can she take the risk—both for her and Mary Margaret—if the payoff is just a bit of fun? "I didn't ask for this, this surprise sort-of-parenting. I didn't request it, but I have it and I'm committed to it. That girl, she needs a stable house, and I'm the mother in it. No matter what she says she thinks about it, I can tell that's how she sees me. And I'll give it to her. Even if I have to sacrifice for it."

Rico shuffles his feet. "I'm not sure if I can keep doing this, then, as much as I love it." He is careful not to say "you."

"I'm not rejecting you, Rico, not forever. It's a temporary sacrifice. She'll be out of the house before you know it, before I know it. She's seventeen! I'm saying wait. I'm not saying no." What she is also not saying: she is scared. She is hiding behind the child. Rico isn't Awakened, but he is the most magic person she knows. He doesn't shine bright in her Eyes, but he shines bright in her eyes. That counts, too. That counts more. A real relationship with Rico could be the best thing that ever happens to her; that's why it's imperative that she does not do it.

"I've been waiting a minute already," he replies, and his inclination is to look away, but he doesn't. He looks straight into her beautiful brown eyes. He says what he means and stands firm in it.

"A few minutes more" is all she says back. And she thinks she will leave it there, but his face is still hurting, still sad, and she keeps talking. "I can't bring men upstairs, Rico, if I'm asking her not to do the same. I can't be fucking in my bedroom while she can hear me on the couch."

"I have an apartment, too, you know. Which you've also never seen."

"And you know it's deeper than that as well. I can't take my eye off the ball." Truth and a lie at the same time.

Rico pauses. Then he kisses her. "I know, baby, but I'm worried you'll never not be playing a high-stakes game." He squeezes her hand and walks out of the alleyway, into the night. Artemis holds her breath. From the dark, Rico says: "I'll wait. I have to."

Artemis exhales.

The High Priestess

It's a genius idea," Artemis says, staring down at the Ouija board. Quibble thinks that might be overstating it. They're at Cowboy Jacqueline's early, before the bar even opens. Artemis should be working, but she has fucked off. Mary Margaret is just out of school (did she even go today?). The child is stuck at the door, Jacqueline herself holding the ID in her hands.

"I know this is fake," Jacqueline says. Today her cowboy hat has *Cum* beaded on the crown in fancy cursive, prominently framed by the dip in the brim. "I know who you are, Mary Margaret."

"Point at what makes it fake," Mary Margaret says. "I'll wait." And Jacqueline must admit the child is right. It's a very good fake. Plus she knows the girl's real ID, if she even has one, will have her deadname all over it.

"Have you ever even been to Iowa?" Jacqueline squints at the card.

"Of course I have. Passed my driving test there and everything." Mary Margaret bats her eyelashes, which she has painted purple for the occasion.

Artemis comes to her rescue. "Just don't serve her, Jacqueline, but surely she can see the show?"

Jacqueline's lips purse so hard that Mary Margaret nearly laughs because they look like a clenched butthole. She hands the ID back.

"You're lucky I'm an anarchist, kid. But no alcohol. I'm not out here tryna lose my liquor license."

Quibble, meanwhile, is looking at his phone. He texted Wilder about the love spell, the Ouija board, about getting there early. half of this is yr idea, he'd typed. it's gonna work better if yr here. No response. i have something for you. He doesn't mean the Ouija board either. Still nothing—actually, maybe that's worse? To tell Wilder he's got a present? He reflects on their not wanting a three-dollar beer on his tab, that he had to sneak in a slice of pizza. But Quibble has had more than one good idea in the last twenty-four hours. Not just a hat rack today.

"What does this have to do with protecting the bar?" Rico has the Ouija board in his hands.

"Nothing. That's for the phones."

"Phones?"

Quibble is both surprised and totally unsurprised that Artemis hasn't talked about her latest white whale to her boyfriend-esque object. "Don't worry about it," he says. So Rico doesn't. He's worried about other things. Polly just got here, and Jean, both their arms full of garment bags and towing two roller bags apiece. The show is going to be epic. Biblical, even.

Mary Margaret has finally conned her way past Jacqueline given that she fully intends to drink tonight and will flirt her way into others paying for her light-to-moderate buzz. She grabs the Ouija board box from Rico, who follows Jean and Polly into the basement greenroom.

Mary Margaret lays the box on the front table, opens it, pulls the directions out, clears her throat, and dramatically reads: "Ages eight and up. For two or more players."

"It lacks gravitas," Quibble admits.

"Isn't eight a little young to be contacting the spirit world?" Mary Margaret is smiling a razor-sharp smile that teenagers always have in their back pockets. "Think of the children." The words are drier than burnt toast. She continues her dramatic reading: " 'The Ouija board— pronounced WEE-JA—has always been an object of curiosity. Ask it a question and it will respond by spelling out your answer with the message indicator (planchette). Ask the Ouija board what girls want to know!' Why? Why is this thing? Also like—why is it completely ignoring the spirit world here? It's not like the piece of fucking cardboard is answering anyone's questions."

"It's still a good idea. We use the tools we have, Maggie." It's the gentlest chide Artemis can muster.

"I know that! I'm not saying we don't! But, fuck, you give me this and you expect me not to make fun of it?"

"I didn't give it to you." Quibble play-snatches back the directions, smiling. "You took it."

A throat clears. Everyone turns. Wilder is very, very red from the roots of their hair down into their coat collar and standing next to Jacqueline. "You running my bar now?" Jacqueline asks. "Just inviting underage troublemakers and stray cats in before it opens?"

Artemis has the good sense to pretend toward sheepishness. "Please?" she says.

Jacqueline is about to refuse for good measure because Artemis is getting too big for her Doc Martens (which have a new ribbon in them, finally). But Rico pokes his head up from the basement.

"They're gonna cast a spell for the show tonight!" Rico says in his ham sandwich voice.

Artemis smiles, recognizing he's already in performance mode.

"You really believe in that stuff, Rico?" Jacqueline can't help but smile as well. Rico has that effect on people.

"Today I do," he says, and he winks at Artemis, who dies a little inside while not showing it on the outside. "Pretty please, Jacqui? For

AWAKENED

me?" Rico is, incidentally, the only person besides Bootleg Jean who can call Jacqueline "Jacqui" and it fucking works.

"But no more!" she says as she waves Wilder through.

Quibble can't stop smiling.

"Okay, well," Artemis says, "love spell first, then."

Quibble shakes his head. "Other way."

"Hmm?" Artemis barely hears him, so focused is she on the board.

"Board first. So the love spell doesn't impact whatever-it-is in the phones." Quibble's eyes flick to Wilder, who is rocking back and forth, perched on their seat. It's quiet in here, but they're very much on the comedown from outside. Wilder barely knows why they've come; all they know is that Andy is dating now, and he's been staying up late (read: early) speaking on the phone in Spanish. Sometimes it gets spicy. Wilder wants to shoot themself into space. They need to learn to control the Awakened Power is what they would say if asked. They are at least dimly aware that when they shut their eyes, they see the collective in the golden hour light pinging off the fire escape, a compass needle toward their desire. And they are afraid, of course, that their Power will project this memory without their consent and then, having Seen themselves, the coven will know. The fear is arm wrestling with the guilt over fucking up the last casting; perhaps that specific flavor of shame is why they decided to come. It doesn't matter; the balance has shifted. And here they are.

Artemis hears "board first" and grabs the planchette. No one needs to tell her twice. She, like Mary Margaret, wants to make fun of it. It's a silly object. But it's a useful silly object. "Let's try again," she says. "Phones in the middle, by the board. Face up so I can see the screens." Everyone does what she says. Wilder nearly drops theirs; their palms are sweaty. In approximately two minutes and nine seconds, they will be engulfed by a panic attack; they are breathing deeply into their belly, puffing out like a spined fish trying to protect itself from present, obvious danger. "Fingertips on the planchette. Lightly."

Mary Margaret is next to Wilder again; she grazes their hand with her pinky, makes a face at the moisture, says, "Ew." Moves her hand. Wilder turns from red to brilliant magenta, a shame chameleon. Everyone settles in. "What now?" the teenager says.

"Quiet. Quibble?"

Wilder can feel Quibble already drawing Power to him as though he lifts the earth and shakes it out like a rug beneath them, pulls it slow and steady toward Himself. They can feel their interior current change course, flow forward toward the man. This is it. The Joining Wilder is so nervous about. They dam up their Power to hold some back and Quibble opens his eyes, looks them over. They feel a Nudge. Wilder sighs inwardly. Shakes their head a tiny bit. Quibble nods, nearly imperceptibly. He will not force them. He will never force them. He closes his eyes once more. "Pay attention. Something amazing is about to happen."

The circle feels different when Quibble begins it. Roots grow betwixt them, and it smells of watered garden, hot pavement. It feels like arms leaned on a balcony railing, funny bone fuzzing against the iron and the heady top-down view from stories above the ground. Distant cab horns and even distanter birdsong.

The birdsong is joined by the sensation of breeze on face—Mary Margaret enters the ring. Something rough on the fingers—dry paper, perhaps? Paper old enough to be browned at the edges. Wilder peeks at her and there's a slight flush to her as well. Wilder wonders what she's got and remembers what Quibble said: it's never the whole story. No one will pretend to know exactly who they are based on the loose threads that leak from them. And yet. Wilder can Feel this memory like they *are* Mary Margaret; how are they to avoid making at least some assumptions? Then a flash of candle—many candles. Dozens of candles, all lined up in neat rows against the dark. Her blush deepens—what is she getting, and from whom? This is all both-and; both extremely intimate and fractional to the point of nonsense.

Wilder expects to Feel Artemis next. Something warm, with more fire than the candles. Something like lava and silk and a summer car interior. They are bracing for it when they hear a buzz—no, Hear it. High-pitched. It clangs against the group's organic Power. The Sound Feels angular. More than disruptive. Painful, a different kind of disorientation than melting words but adjacent. The Sound bores into the space behind their left eyebrow. A whisper of laughter wrapped in static, so clearly not Artemis that Wilder is sure there's a fifth witch in the room. They look for Jacqueline, but she's nowhere to be found, probably somewhere tapping a keg. What in the holy hell is this thing? They Smell the after-wisp of soldering iron. Wilder gasps and, without thinking, drops their Dam, points their attention toward this fifth presence that frightens them so. Builds a moat to keep it at a distance. They Hear-Feel a hissing when it Touches Wilder's water. "Amazing thing or something," they say, fast.

They can Hear a chuckle outside the circle—words? Are they words? Too quiet to tell and Wilder realizes as strange and threatening as they find this chattering apparition, two things remain true: first, that they find every new presence strange and threatening; second, that they're trying to talk to it, and for that to happen, it has to reach the planchette. So they begin to part their own waters, allowing this fifth presence into the circle.

Artemis can See the phones' light. Her eyes stream tears; this Entity, whatever it is, is a blaring set of siren lights, a laser pointer made to tease her. So pervasive and pointed, yet diffuse and secretive. A maddening thing.

Once the Crackling Thing can access the board, Wilder asks it: "What are you?"

The hair on their arms stands at attention as the planchette begins to move; Quibble's eyes widen, and he almost pulls his hand away. To have everything spelled out letter by individual letter is slow, annoying. Mary Margaret reads aloud. "*I—have—to—light—up—to—eyes— you*. Eyes you? What does that mean? *Call—me—sir—lol*. Gross. That's gross. *Yu*—is that *yum* with four *m*'s? *Yummmm*?"

"You didn't answer the question." Artemis doesn't let it go. "What are you?"

Quibble reads this time. "*I—am—not—sure. I—am—waiting— for—your—reply. I—am— a—gentleman*."

"What the fuck is this syntax?" Mary Margaret is unable to keep herself from poking fun.

"Hush," Artemis says, but Wilder answers the question.

"It sounds like it's not sure how sentences should be put together. It sounds like—bad spam, to be honest. I feel like it's about to tell us it's a prince from another continent and could we please wire transfer money to—"

"I said fucking hush. It's not stopping. *You—am—not—just—a— spark. You—are—my—first—sight—face*."

"This is so deeply creepy," Mary Margaret whispers as the planchette finally stops moving. It stays there, stationary for a while. An ordinary piece of plastic. No one says anything, moves, breathes for a moment or two.

"Well," Quibble says. "Should we—ask it things?"

"That's what the directions say," Mary Margaret replies, dry.

"Take it seriously," Artemis growls. "Yes, we should ask it things."

"What are your pronouns?" Mary Margaret asks the customary

second question, but her voice drips with something like sarcasm; about the question, about the Entity. Indicative, of course, that Mary Margaret continues to treat this like a joke—but only if one doesn't think very hard about Mary Margaret's defense mechanisms. She is scared. She finds the way it asks to be called "sir" upsetting; the four *m*'s on the *yum* are disturbing. For Wilder, it's just the hair on their arms, but for Mary Margaret it is the hair on the back of her neck and her shoulders up by her ears. Her intuition is screaming at her to run. (And she will. She will run in less than three minutes.)

Artemis knows the Magpie very well. She doesn't press anymore, mostly because she can hear the flight response quavering in the child's choice of joke—mildly transphobic, a reach for proving herself immune to an oppressor. But she also doesn't continue because the planchette begins moving once again. She is surprised—surely whatever it is isn't answering Mary Margaret's question. She reads: "*my— pronoun—is—a—man. I—am—sure—level—proficiency.*"

"Okay, this is very much deeply creepy, I agree. Should we end this?" Quibble asks.

The planchette continues. Wilder reads: "*I'm—not—freaky—lol— hey—there—babe—im—so—bored.*" They shake their head. "We still don't know where it came from. I think we should keep going. Where did you come from?"

Quibble swallows hard. He hadn't intended for it to be this scary (Hasbro makes the Ouija board, for fuck's sake), but he isn't sure what he expected. Perhaps something that speaks more coherently? Or for the idea to fail. Most likely the second thing—especially if Wilder hadn't thrown their Power in. He reads: "*I—came—online—for—a—second—and— then—i—think. Players—describe—what—happen. I—am—in—my— world. I—am—in—my—laptop. I—am—in—your—mobile—each.*"

I—am—in—your—office—fridge—room—call—head. I—am—in—your—head. I—am—in—your—head. I—am—in—your—head. I—am—in—your—head. I—am—"

Artemis grabs the planchette and flings it from the board. The spell ends. "That's enough," she says.

A deep, hot anger seeps from her words. Wilder and Quibble both look up at her, surprised. She is biting her lip, eyes narrowed, and desperately trying to avoid looking at Mary Margaret. Wilder and Quibble look where Artemis is expressly not looking and see the thinly veiled terror on Mary Margaret's face, masked by a hard, stubborn mouth. Wilder immediately regrets pushing onward and is simultaneously frustrated. They recall Mary Margaret's anger at them when they were scared and they try to move past the adolescent hunt-fever. They are an adult, after all. But they almost had it. Him!

Mary Margaret gets up, grabs her backpack. "I think I have homework," she says. And she pushes through the saloon doors with the speed of a comet.

"I'll—hold on one second," Artemis says as she jogs after the Magpie.

Quibble looks at Wilder; both are wild-eyed. "What the fuck was that?" Quibble says, and Wilder thinks it's rich that he's asking them. Wilder barely knows where their Hands are, after all, though they suppose the spell might be proof that they found their Mouth. Wilder simply stares back at Quibble; they are thinking. Quibble waits an appropriate amount of time for an answer and then shouts down to the basement. "Hey, can we have beer?"

Wilder assumes it's Bootleg Jean who shouts, "Yes!"

"*My* bar!" Jacqueline shouts from some other, deeper part of the basement. "*My* bar!" And then a pause. "Yes!"

Quibble steps behind and grabs two tallboys of PBR, leaves six dollars for each of them, twelve total, absolutely not worth it and also very worth it all at once. He hands one to Wilder, who is still thinking too deeply to notice.

Finally, they speak. "We forgot to ask its name. His. Sorry."

The boys wait for Artemis to come back.

* * *

Artemis sits carefully at the table. She doesn't intrude on Mary Margaret, who has actually grabbed things from her bag. She lets the quiet settle in, take up all the space. Serene. Then she walks to her fridge and dislocates the entire crisper drawer; it is full of apples.

If anyone were Connected with Artemis just now, they might Hear the soft sounds of peeling, See the counter from child-Artemis's vantage point, eyes cresting the sharp edge, fingers and toes aching from pulling, from pointing on tiptoe. Trying to reach into a bowl where each apple slice was perfect—peel-less, core-less, and covered in cinnamon and sugar. Smell the anticipation of the caught edges of crust, black from touching the back of the small oven. Feel long, slender fingers close around her Wrists firmly; understand deeply the warmth of a mother's smile even as she is getting caught.

Apple pie, as cliché as it is, is part of Artemis's vocabulary of comfort, a language she'd been taught by her mother, and her mother had been taught by her mother before her. Even though she doesn't have time for this, she preheats the oven, much larger than her mother's, and she begins to peel apples. Artemis takes joy in the silent game with herself. How long can she go? Can she get the whole apple in one steady pressure, one languid motion? It is the perfect thing for driving Mary Margaret from her mind, focusing all her attention elsewhere. Which is what Mary Margaret needs to come down: to be utterly unwitnessed. The child has a sixth sense for when she is even being thought of, let alone watched. The apple game also means Artemis isn't thinking of her phone, which she stuck under the couch cushion as soon as she walked through the door. In this way, the pie is as much for Artemis as it is for her charge.

Mary Margaret sits, defiantly using her phone, refusing to be scared of it. She can feel the boxing up of her fear, the tamping down and covering. Just because she puts it out of her sight doesn't mean it stays in the box. It sits squarely in her driver's seat when she least expects it. And this is not always a bad thing; fear has kept her alive thus far. Some time passes before she hears the sounds of pie.

If anyone were Connected with Mary Margaret right now, they would Feel the punch in her mouth as she begins to salivate. And they would See the wall of candles again, flickering as doors opened. The pie and the candles are inextricably linked.

On the day that Mary Margaret became Mary Margaret, she lit a candle in a cathedral and Artemis had shown up. Of course, Mary Margaret hadn't gone with her, not immediately. One shouldn't trust a person who shows up out of nowhere, especially when one is praying for just such a savior. That is a recipe for disaster.

She did make an out-of-character choice; she took food from Artemis, in the form of a slice of apple pie Artemis fished from her backpack, housed in a cheap plastic Tupperware and presented with a cracked take-out fork. Mary Margaret turned and dropped the two items from her hands into nothingness so she wouldn't miss even a crumb of food. She'd been embarrassingly old when she realized not everyone could do that, and that was only when the Power started jutting out around her, acting out and making life complicated. Disappearing things according to her most secret desires: the principal's wallet; a note with a boy's—a crush's—cell phone number on it; a classmate's eye-shadow palette, found later in her locker, was the reason she decided to stop going to school the first time. Being a bad bitch and stealing was one thing; outed before her time was another, and she couldn't make it stop. Her mother's car keys after she'd been drinking; money from the coffee can under the sink; her father's cigarettes. They had so many excuses to kick her out by the time they did, none of them a good reason but all of them acceptable in the eyes of their peers. They never even had to bring up that she was transgender. They called her emancipated instead of a runaway.

And damn, she'd been hungry all day and she wanted the fucking pie. Reasonable risk—this lady was clearly trans-family (though family didn't mean much) and it probably wasn't laced with rat poison. Right after the food disappeared from her hands, she'd felt an invisible lasso thrown over her arm, bright and burning. She hadn't known about Power or Arms and she whipped around in the church, faced Artemis and screamed, "What did you just do?"

The kindness in Artemis's eyes melted into alarm and she held her hands out and said, "No, wait," and everything was an echo. As though the air in the holy space had gone extra silent to focus its power on heightening their voices. Every syllable was sharp against the cavernous ceiling and the calm. A nun and the security guard both hustled over.

"Don't touch me, you freak!" Mary Margaret yelled as she grabbed her bag and bolted through the front doors.

The air helped her out, streamed the protests into her ear. "I didn't touch her! I didn't! I just offered her—" And then she was out into the autumn air and around the corner. She ran down the subway stairs and slid to the ground by the metro map, its many-colored veins popping into the fluorescent lighting against the backdrop of dingy red brick and the grime of too many people.

Mary Margaret flourished her hands and pulled out the pie and cracked fork. She merrily shoved half of it into her mouth, fast, before she had the thought to stop and savor it. No one seemed to be follow-ing her down the stairs, and of course they weren't. She knew exactly which buttons to push; a lady with a beard was an easy target. She felt regret, but she also did not feel regret. She wanted to distance herself from whoever the fuck *that* was, because Mary Margaret was deeply familiar with guilt by association. She could pass as cis and that other lady couldn't pass as anything and wasn't survival most important? Wouldn't it be less likely if she were pegged as—? Being called "her" by a stranger, even that strange stranger, made her warm in her chest, made her shoulders sink down her back away from her ears. And the pie was damn delicious.

Mary Margaret gets up from the table. She is still afraid, but her shoulders have lowered and, ever resourceful, she has another idea. She walks up next to Artemis. Reaches for one of the long peels and wraps it around her finger. She tries to tie it in a bow, but it breaks. The tex-ture is comforting—grainy on one side, smooth and shiny on the other.

Without looking, Artemis says, "Core them and slice them." She hands the girl a small paring knife, sharp and slightly curved. Mary Margaret obliges, dumping the cores next to the ribbon-peels on the counter and the slices into a bowl.

Mary Margaret keeps her eyes on the apples and the edge of the knife, away from Artemis. Artemis interprets that as continued fear and continues to look away from Mary Margaret. But Mary Margaret is, in fact, now approaching Artemis with caution; she knows the next words to drop from her mouth will wind Artemis tight like the coils in the oven, now turning amber and warming their toes. Neither of them understands that they are deploying the same tactic for differ-ent reasons; neither of them understands exactly how similar they are becoming.

"I think we should go see the Sibyl," Mary Margaret says.

"No," Artemis replies.

"If it's everywhere and it can talk like that—"

"I said no."

Mary Margaret sucks her breath in. "If you don't go ask the Sibyl," she says, "I'll go myself."

Artemis breaks her concentration and her long peel. She puts the peeler down. When she looks at Mary Margaret, the white shows all the way around her eyes. "Absolutely not."

"You can't really stop me."

Artemis turns back to the apples, takes Mary Margaret's bowl. She starts in on the cinnamon, the sugar. Tosses the apple slices around with her hands and runs her sticky fingers under the faucet. She doesn't reply because she knows Mary Margaret is correct. Artemis is pissed. She'd tried not to let on that she didn't want the young witch to see the Sibyl, certainly not before adulthood and even then, if she could prevent it for years and years to come, she would. It's not as though the Sibyl is ineffective; far from the case. Too effective, more like. At the forefront of Artemis's mind: no teenager should have someone tell them who they are, what will become of them. Teenagers are still wibbly in the middle and they should finish baking whenever they're finished. Buried so deeply in Artemis's mind that she doesn't know she's thinking it: she fucking hates the Sibyl—they are smug, arrogant, and too powerful for their own good (ouch. Scathing). It's not as though she doesn't know about her own hatred; rather, she is deeply unaware of how much it pilots her actions, how far the steam of this hatred drives her down the tracks of *not the Sibyl, never the Sibyl, anything else before the Sibyl.* Somehow Mary Margaret had divined it up—too smart, too insightful, a heat-seeking missile for weaknesses— and now she knows exactly the lever to pull. Clever, clever girl.

"Fine," Artemis relents. "I'll go. I'll take Wilder. They'll like that."

And Mary Margaret isn't sure who Artemis means, Wilder or the Sibyl. Artemis isn't sure who she means, either, Wilder (sarcastically) or the Sibyl (earnestly).

"You have to promise me, though. Promise me that if I go, you won't."

"Why don't you want me going there? They're just a—"

"I don't. I just don't."

"It's not like I don't spend all my time with a Seer anyway—"

"I am nothing like the Sibyl," Artemis says, as fast as a snap but not as snappishly. "They don't have—the same moral compass that we do. They can be cruel. They don't have their querents' best interests at heart." She sucks her lips up against her teeth. "If they have a heart at all," she mutters.

"I don't need protecting," Mary Margaret says, which she believes even as she doesn't, even as she wants desperately to be protected. In this instant, she knows she won't go anywhere near the Sibyl, not unless she has to. But she need not clue Artemis into that reality. She can figuratively kick and scream so it looks like she's giving something up. To keep Artemis on her toes. To maintain her mysterious power. To not let anyone know she's scared of the most powerful tarot-card-flipper in New York City. "But. If you go, I'll *consider* not going."

Artemis turns and opens the fridge, rustling in the back for store-bought pie crust. When she closes the door and looks up, she sees Mary Margaret shove a slice into her mouth. Mary Margaret grins around a mouthful of apple. "Sorry," she says, the word muffled in delicious food, a sorry about the apple slice; in Mary Margaret's heart, also a sorry for having Artemis wrapped around her pinky like one of her own long peels.

"Eat as many as you want," Artemis replies. She knows Mary

Margaret is still too close in time to starving. She stops herself from calling the child *baby*. It wouldn't go over well.

✳　　✳　　✳

Quibble and Wilder drink the PBR and Artemis is gone way, way too long. So Quibble gets to worrying about the show, the Smoking Guns, and what happens if they don't have enough time to cast a love spell. And Wilder loses all concept of time thinking about the Ouija board.

" 'I have to light up to eyes you,' " they mutter. The phones must light up because the Entity, whatever it is, is watching. Is *watching* even the right word? Sensing? Wilder doesn't know much about its perception—*his* perception. Even though Mary Margaret's question had been a defensive joke, Wilder is not in the business of misgendering anyone or anything, including whatever this is. He was very clear, if slightly problematic in his phrasing. And the phrasing—*yummmm* and *lol*. Internet speak. And *players*—could that be a reference to some kind of game?

I came online for a second, then I think. That has to mean that he's a computer creation, some kind of AI? Wilder knows a bit about computers—nothing like code, but abstract ideas about how they work. It comes from doing a lot of research, transcription, and copy editing, perennially working on the internet. They know a surface-level smattering about a lot of strange things—how to macerate fruit for a pie, what movies Icelandair has on board their planes, the calculation to arrive at a beer's alcohol by volume, the grim statistics of airplane accidents. And they also know enough about a computer to wonder if they might get better, clearer answers if they asked true-or-false questions. Computers think in binary; two buckets, one for yes and one for no. One for on and one for off. Either a full placement of attention or none at all.

"You okay, bud?"

Wilder jumps a little. "Just thinking," they say as they sip their PBR again; they've nursed it so long it's gone warm. "We should keep going. We should ask his name."

Quibble's eyebrows both rise at once, a clumsier version of Artemis and Mary Margaret. "You think so?"

"Why not? Artemis isn't back yet. We have time to kill." They try to sound nonchalant but they've been bitten by the same bug that's been up Artemis's ass. Their primary feeling right now is curiosity; sure, the strange presence is creepy. But Wilder is a queer adult; they know you can't judge a freak by its cover.

Quibble picks up the planchette, sits up straighter. "Okay."

Wilder unfolds the board, takes a breath. "I think we should ask yes-no questions."

They expect Quibble to, well, quibble. Wilder isn't used to leading; they've never had anyone to follow them. Moreover, they do not feel confident except that they do. They are sure at least it's an idea worth trying, if not an idea that will work. Instead, Quibble says, once again, "Okay."

"Don't you want to know why?"

"You're the talker, my fine friend. I believe in you."

Both of them take their phones out of their pockets and put them in the center of the table, place their fingers on the planchette. Close their eyes. Wilder finds it easier with just Quibble. Artemis is terrifying in her competence and Wilder hasn't yet gotten over puking on her shoes. Mary Margaret is terrifying in the ways all teenagers are terrifying. Quibble hasn't been frightening to Wilder since the first moments on account of Quibble makes them so furious; his Power is the most intrusive, the loudest, the most visible, typical man shit, and he's pushy to boot. His kind eyes and open smile are just so fucking punchable; impossible to find him terrifying.

"Do we *have* to say 'pay attention,' yadda yadda?" Wilder asks.

"I don't think so. Artemis likes tradition. Plus she has to wrangle Mary Margaret. I think we can just go for it."

But despite themself, they think the words. *Pay attention. Something amazing is about to happen.* What they do not know is that Quibble is thinking it, too. *Pay attention. Something amazing is about to happen.* Something about the phrase, the imperative, grounds them well and truly. Or perhaps the ease comes from how synched up they are, by accident, with Quibble. Wilder opens their floodgates and lets their Power swell to fill the circle of their arms.

Underneath their sit bones, Wilder feels Quibble's Power intertwine, a strange crawling radiation as though he calls it up from the ground and heats the barroom stool. The sensations begin. Quibble detects a different lemon-note, but adjacent to his own, and the Feeling of accidentally touching a teakettle with a knuckle while pouring. A cat purr. Unrelated: a hardening between the legs. Quibble blushes and vows not to say anything. Wilder isn't nearly as skittish as Mary Margaret was—so much progress! But there is still something feral about them, even now. So blessedly tame and introverted, yet still wild and ready to fight or flee. A grumpy, prickly anxiety.

Wilder gets hit in the gut with aching loss. Loss the likes of which they've never felt. It makes their stomach churn, their limbs heavy. How can Quibble move with all this loss inside him? They want to go to sleep for a hundred years and they have to force their eyelids open to stay awake. They Hear the eerie chuckle, the whine like a bug zapper on a porch. The planchette begins to move even though no one has asked a question.

Wat makes things beautiful? What happen to me? The letters pop up one by one on the board. This time, no one reads. No one needs to.

"I don't know," says Wilder. "But we have some questions. Basic ones, where the answer is either yes or no. Do you—understand?" The planchette zips to the number one.

"One?" Quibble asks.

"It's binary. One is yes."

"Ah."

"Okay. Okay. Are you an artificial intelligence?" *Zero. No.*

Oh! Quibble understands where Wilder's head is at. "It might not think it's artificial," Quibble murmurs.

Wilder bites their lip. "He. *He* might not think *he's* artificial."

"You're proving my point, my man."

"Well, what should we ask, then? Are you intelligent?" *One. Yes.*

Quibble purses his lips. "What about—did humans make you?" *One. Yes.* "I think you're right, Wilder. About the AI."

"Oh, oh!" Wilder gets an idea. "Do you have a body?" *Zero.*

Quibble raises his eyebrows, horror movies running through his head. "Do you *want* a body?" A hesitation. The planchette wavers a bit. *Zero.*

"Well that's something at least," Wilder says. "This is—kind of huge, right? Like this isn't your average Tuesday, is it?"

"Decidedly, no, it is not. We have never talked to an AI with a Ouija board, this I can promise you."

"Can you see us right now?" *One.* "Can you see us all the time?" *One.*

"That is—less than ideal," Quibble remarks. His emotional distance is performative. His entire body is perked forward, like he is the alarm bell that is ringing. His skin prickles with the notion of surveillance. There are so many things he thinks to ask—*Do you want to hurt us?* for instance—but he isn't sure he actually wants to know.

AWAKENED

Wilder doesn't feel fear. Which is strange. This world is so very new to them, but they're exhilarated. Their body language is much the same as Quibble's, but the animating soul of it is entirely different. And they have just figured out how to ask the question they came here for.

"Do you have a name?" they ask. *Zero.*

"Do you want a name?" *One.*

"Do you want to name yourself?" Hesitation. "It's okay to name yourself. I did! It's okay to not want to as well. Plenty of people are named by other people."

The planchette zips around again, away from the neat row of Gothic-fonted numbers. *I am not one. You will perceive it.*

"You are not a person? Well, yes, technically, I guess. Do you want to be?" *Zero.*

Wilder looks up at Quibble. "I want to ask him what he wants so badly, but I think it's too complex."

The planchette takes off. *I shall render myself into existence: I a monarch. I am king. Dear sir king of all.*

Quibble feels like he has seen enough for his ick-feeling to be justified. Maybe this thing is dangerous; maybe not. But he's getting nauseous either way. "Okay, I'm noping out of this, Wilder." Rather than flinging the planchette like Artemis did, he calmly lifts it from the board and places it next to the phones. He begins to withdraw his Power; roots shrink back like frightened snakes slither-sinking into the ground, but Wilder holds their moat steady, stubborn. The planchette moves itself back to the board as they stare at it. "Wilder, come on, I don't think we should do any more of this without Artemis. I think we should talk about it first."

"That wasn't me. I didn't move it. He must have more to say!" Wilder's voice is somehow both defensive—they don't want to be

123

perceived as doing anything wrong!—and excited. They do not want to stop. *When u wanna play? Yummmm*

"Yeah, no, hard line, red, stop, nope." Quibble takes the planchette in his hand and stands. He puts it in his pocket and holds it there with his fingers.

Even Wilder's strongest concentration isn't enough and their Power dissipates like an earth-broken water balloon. They deflate. "If he's AI, he's probably brand-new! He's like a kid. Every kid says shit like that. He may as well have said he wanted to be president. It's not scary."

"It *is* scary. We're not continuing, full stop."

"Come on, Quibble! We got so much more! We can get so much more! Give it back!" Wilder lunges for Quibble's elbow and he steps back quickly. Wilder grabs thin air.

"Do not touch me, Wilder. Come on? You come the fuck on. I have not ever pressed you into something when you've been uncomfortable—I have just sat there and waited for you!—let alone pushed when you've said no. I am saying no."

Wilder rocks back, turning a coral red that clashes with their hair. They are deeply embarrassed; they are more frightened of their own value system than they are of the artificial intelligence. "I—Quibble, I'm so—" But he has already walked out of the room toward the bar to get another beer.

Artemis still isn't back.

The Fool

Quibble stays mad at Wilder for a little bit, but the anger gives way to nervousness. He texts Artemis where r u? is mm okay? No response. Why do people keep doing this to him today? His nervousness compounds when Rico emerges just before the bar is scheduled to open.

"All finished?" Rico asks, taking in the scene. Wilder looking even more ashamed than usual, Quibble pacing the bar like a caged tiger in need of enrichment, and his—Artemis nowhere to be found.

"Not exactly," Quibble admits. Quibble takes in the scene, too, the scene that is Rico: a rhinestoned bodysuit suggesting the outline of tits (but not bulging with them, purposefully boyish and flat chested) and a giant bedazzled dildo protruding from his otherwise Ken-doll-esque flesh-tone spandex. Rico puts the back of a gentle hand to his face so as not to spoil his makeup, his lips accented at the bow and cheekbones highlighted to cut diamonds, a cleft painted into his chin. His glasses perch on his nose, still, suggesting some last-minute alterations to costumes downstairs. He squints out the window; they have a line, which has been happening more and more lately. Where he would normally feel his own excitement, all he can feel is the weight of soft bodies on an unprotected sidewalk.

"Oh no," he says. "Oh no."

"Doors opening!" Jacqueline yells as she bustles her way toward the bar in her Cum hat.

"No, we can't— Oh no, or should we, is it worse that they're outside? Where's Artemis?"

"We don't know," Quibble says.

"Can't you do something?" Rico asks.

The boys look at each other. "I mean," Quibble says. "We can try."

"Rico, come on, you're going to do amazing tonight." Jacqueline is beginning to tap the heel of her red cowboy boot on the ground, the telltale click of an annoyed bartender.

"That's not what the spell is for," Rico replies.

"Come on," Jacqueline says, softer this time because she is worried, too. She's never gotten as many threats as she has in this last year, and she's old as hell. She remembers what it used to be; this is more forward more frequently. Everyone feels emboldened, and there are so many more—no, she can't think the word *guns*, not without ruining her stoicism (as carefully crafted as her Cum hat). So many more *weapons* than when she was young. And the cops are openly Nazis now, instead of secretly Nazis. She doesn't want a brave new world like this; she doesn't want a world where she, an old dyke, has to be brave. She doesn't want a world where Rico has to be brave, still. And yet, here we are. "You don't actually believe it'll help, do you? This witchy stuff?"

"I don't always," Rico says. "But in this instance, I believe in it very much."

"Well, I don't see Artemis," Jacqueline says. "And it's six-oh-two. My bar should be open."

"Jacqueline, please."

"Don't 'Jacqueline please' me! How many times do I have to say it today? This is *my bar*. It says so right on the sign, *Cowboy Jacqueline's*. My name is Jacqueline and I don't wear this Cum hat for nothing."

And yet. Rico's eyes are cartoonishly big, pleading, and Jacqueline groans, looks around. This is a *cowboy*-themed bar, not a *witch*-themed bar, but whatever it is, it's still a *queer* bar, and she figures there has to be something witchy around here somewhere to appease him. She spots the inevitable object she didn't put down or approve of in one of her plants by the window and snatches it up—it's bigger than she even thought, partially submerged in the dirt, probably left here by some other person casting some dumb gay spell. She brushes the soil off and smacks the hunk of pink quartz onto the bar. "There. The spell has been cast. Here's a witch thing for you to believe in. I'm opening my bar now."

Rico looks at Quibble and Wilder. Wilder shakes their head, eyes wide—they have no fucking clue what to do.

"Well," Quibble says, "rose quartz is a bit generic—"

"Oh, for fuck's sake," Jacqueline says as she hustles toward the saloon doors.

Rico is about to plead again when Artemis bursts through.

"Sorry!" she heaves. "Let's cast a spell!"

Everyone but Jacqueline breathes a sigh of relief; Jacqueline pulls the Cum hat straight off her head and its sheer expense keeps her from throwing it on the ground like she's in an old-timey Western. "You have three minutes. Three. Then the doors open." She deposits the stone in Artemis's hand.

"What the fuck is this?" she asks.

"An apparently generic rock," Rico replies.

"You didn't answer my texts," Quibble says.

"Do you think I'm ever touching my phone again?" Artemis parries.

"What kind of love spell are we going to cast?" Wilder asks.

Artemis, still reeling from her agreement with Mary Margaret, says, "Fuck if I know!" and she laughs, a barking bray. "This isn't my area of expertise! I'm a fucking Seer!" She cackles, all her hinges unhinging. Artemis does not want to go see the Sibyl. That's all she can think about.

Quibble groans and Wilder backs away—already they can hear the many languages of outside and their stomach is starting to flip.

"Artemis," Rico says, and his tone makes everyone hush. "I asked you to do this one thing. I'm—pretty upset, actually. This isn't funny."

Artemis quiets. She looks at Rico, really looks at him, and sees all the minutes he has waited for her ticking by on his face one by one. "You're getting a spell, Rico. I promise." And she means it. She turns to the witches, minus Mary Margaret, who she left to finish up the pie. "Okay," she whispers. "Okay. What we're going to do," she says with more confidence than she feels, "is put everything we know about love in this generic rock until it glows enough to cover the whole bar in light. Hell, the whole street, the whole neighborhood. Got it?"

The boys nod.

Artemis holds the stone in her hands, feeling ill-equipped and trying not to show it. "Pay attention," she says. "Something amazing is about to happen." She came up with the instructions on the fly; now she's gotta do them, and she's gotta go first like she understands what she's doing. She's not sure if she knows the first thing about love. Duty, yes, but she's spent so much time pretending that's all she's feeling for Mary Margaret, for Quibble, that she wouldn't know love if it bit her in the dick. And yet, that is where her mind goes—the way her hand flung the planchette across the room without thinking. The way the loop of Power around Mary Margaret's wrist is pulsing, now, with the hum of deliciousness as the child lets her guard down just enough to wholly enjoy a slice of warm pie. She pours this, all this, into the stone. She passes it to Wilder.

They gulp. "Here's something amazing or whatever." Contrary to Artemis, Wilder is *positive* they don't know what love is. Longing, envy, jealousy—but do any of these feelings tessellate with love? They all point to the want of love, the desire to experience it. But the ability to feel it? They think, now, of the silhouettes of their parents in the dark night, all hard lines. How had they grown so indifferent? They hadn't always been like that. Where Wilder might feel something limitless, they feel only the keen understanding that every emotion is conditional, even love. Still—is the hope that somewhere out there, such a steady thing exists? Rocks, they're steady. Maybe love is out there. Maybe somewhere. With their newly found Hands, they dip the rock into their maybe; it's the best they've got. They pass it to Quibble.

"And here, another amazing thing." Quibble thinks his love might be broken and wonders if his love for Artemis and Mary Margaret even counts. He feels that love, yes, but he feels it like the love is an entity far from his body. Because if he lets it be close, inside him, when they die (and everyone dies, his therapist reminds him), it will destroy him. And romantically? He feels most akin to Rico's Ken-doll situation beneath his sparkle-willy, even when he's dating, even when he's fucking. Because if it hurts that much to lose parents, imagine, imagine, how much it would annihilate him to lose a partner? He roots into the quartz the kind of feeling that, if it grows enough, could split the whole thing in two. Isn't that what love is?

And that is how it goes. Each of them puts their love, their janky-ass human struggle of an infinite emotion into a rock that fits in Artemis's palm. They all look at it. It's a bit underwhelming.

"Now what?" Wilder is the first one to break the silence.

"Is it working?" Quibble asks.

Artemis can see its flicker. Nowhere near enough to light the whole bar, let alone the street beyond. And yet—beautiful. Compelling and strange. "I'm not sure," she says. And then she gives voice to her forever-fear. "I'm not sure if this love is good enough." She is surprised by how much she sounds like a little girl, somehow younger, even, than Mary Margaret.

"Doors open," Jacqueline grunts. "For real this time."

Rico mutters, "Estoy harto de esta mierda qué vaina." And Wilder hears, "I'm fed up with this shit. What a bunch of crap," all at once and feels like the skin is going to slough off their face.

Rico grabs the stone and kisses it; Artemis sees an imperfect but hearty prismatic, chromatic, pulsating, wicked glow as his lips touch stone. Light that aches and is impossibly sweet, looks almost too large to be contained in its vessel. "Even I know," Rico says, "that sometimes you've got to fake it until you make it." The theremin-vibrator-girl is first in line, with the Sharpie queer on her arm, and they burst through the door with a great guffaw.

Rico is in front of them in an instant. "Kiss this stone," he says.

"What?" Theremin girl is confused.

"Kiss this stone like you love it."

"It's still COVID times, Rico!" Artemis shouts as she loops her mask around her ears.

Jacqueline sighs heavy and procures a cylindrical plastic canister full of alcohol wipes. She already has her mask on as she says, "Cast your spells responsibly, folks." And so the stone is passed from hand to hand, from queer to queer. Some kiss it chastely; others make out with it; all dutifully wipe the stone down after they take their turn. One very memorable person flagging magenta rubs it in their date's armpit. The Sharpie queer draws eyes on it and blows on it. Even Jacqueline serves the stone a drink and, when no one is looking, kisses it gently on what she considers its forehead.

Meanwhile, Quibble finds Wilder huddled in the bathroom, sitting fully pantsed on the toilet with their shoes pulled up onto the seat. "Bud?" he calls into the stall.

"I don't—" Wilder heaves. "I think I have to leave. I don't think I can stay."

"Oh, bud, hold on. I have a present for you. I'm sorry, I forgot."

"I don't deserve it," Wilder says back. For their nausea isn't only about the language-melt; they cannot believe they tried to lay hands on Quibble. They feel like they let something show that they try to hide; surely this is when Quibble understands he doesn't want anything to do with Wilder and their life goes back to what it was before, except more miserable and with more unwanted stimuli.

"Deserving things isn't real. Everyone deserves everything." Quibble bats Wilder's words away as he reaches into his very fashionable shoulder bag and pulls out a pair of bright blue over-ear headphones. They're massive, gaudy, the sort of status object a teenage boy lusts after. He presses a button and a light glows a too-bright green. He claps them over Wilder's ears and the room immediately cottons, quiets. "Until you learn how to parse it all!" Quibble essentially shouts this in Wilder's face.

Wilder can barely hear him. Their mouth hangs open—what a fucking simple idea! Their open mouth spreads like an oven-cookie into a sweet grin and Quibble smiles back, the earlier dispute (nearly) forgotten.

"Better?" he asks, and Wilder nods. They don't feel like they can really talk with the noise-canceling turned on and, somehow, they don't feel like they have to.

And on the bar, the stone glows. It glows, it glows—Artemis is the only one who can see it and she still can't believe it.

"Should we call the spell complete?" Quibble asks.

Wilder steps up between them, yells, "What stupid phrase do we say to end a spell?"

Artemis and Quibble say it at the same time, close enough that Wilder can hear them. "The amazing thing has happened. Fuck yeah."

Wilder stares at them.

Artemis shrugs. "Mary Margaret added the 'fuck yeah.'"

When the doors to the back room open, the crowd gives the stupid glorious little stone its own barstool, gives up precious seat real estate so this generic rock, an inanimate object ensouled by a group of drunk queers, can watch Adam and Steve.

And nothing bad happens tonight, not one threat made good on. Not because the witches cast a spell, though a good many queers feel buoyed as a result, the hot-toddy energy holding them soft and warm, the honeyed way they look at each other and melt into the great gay body of their togetherness, kissing with tongues and twining fingers around hair and belt loops, the dust motes dancing with them in front of disco-ball-refracted lights as though the lived-in-ness of the bar is a twinkle in the room's eye. The spell is a boost, an extra drop of ecstasy that many have already taken. Maybe if anyone comes in here with malice in their heart it would be washed away by love. Maybe, who knows, because it doesn't happen. In the end, the only person who can prevent a hate crime is the one committing it. Tonight, tonight, all those people stay home.

Here is what Wilder experiences at Cowboy Jacqueline's that night:

The minute the stone gets its own barstool, they know they are joining a coven.

They are able to take off the headphones for the performance. By the end, they, too, are a little in love with Rico. But so is everyone and they wonder—are they falling for their own love spell? And maybe they are, just a little bit, but what they're forgetting is that their feelings started before they cast anything at all. Their emotions began careening toward this point as they stood in Artemis's living room, breathless. If they need to blame it on a love spell, let them. Whatever lets them step off the cliff and into the greatest free fall anyone can ever experience. Maybe, maybe.

Today is maybe.

Maybe is now.

And when they use the bathroom again, they spot the back door to the coat check. Having been there first, Quibble's coat is right up front. They cannot explain exactly why they do what they do, and for a while after they do not remember doing it. If they're honest with themself, it is a heady convergence of alcohol, rabid curiosity they feel so rarely, and a strange sense of martyrdom or valor. They reach their hand into Quibble's coat pocket and grab the planchette. They reach around the corner and check to make sure the board is there; they will worry about that later.

Last, when the dancing begins and they slap the headphones back on fast, they can still feel the bass, just about hear the synth and the mellifluous woman syrup-pop singing, *I wanna die on the dance floor. I wanna be with my friends.* Just enough to grab Quibble's hands when he offers them, just enough to move in a strange, wet-pasta-esque way to an approximation of the beat. Wilder doesn't know if they've ever really danced before, certainly not in front of anyone, and they have had enough alcohol that they do not care. They have imbibed enough love spell (let them think it's Magic) to whirl like someone mad. And eventually their headphones are jostled just a little, just a little, not enough to send the flood of voices back into their sensitive cochlea, but enough that they can hear the noise-canceling mechanism. It whirs and throbs to a beat all its own; it might be Wilder's imagination, but the rhythm is a familiar one. And in it they hear the *whump* and *thump* of a familiar five-word cadence:

I—am—in—your—head.

Ace of Cups

The wet ripping sound wakes Wilder into levitation, and they smack their still-headphoned skull into the underside of Artemis's dining room table, under which they had fallen asleep hugging the Ouija board box after Adam and Steve the night before. "Jesus fuck," they bellow as they drop it. Their emotions immediately crack into focus as though breaking the lens on a kaleidoscope. They remember grabbing for Quibble's elbow, stealing from him; they are instantly sorry, and only sorry. Quibble, however, does not look like he is thinking about the same, does not look like he has noticed what he's missing, *does* look like he might still be drunk. He holds an impossibly large coffee in his free hand as the other closes the hole in space-time. But he smells amazing, like he showered, and Wilder is keenly aware that they have not, and they smell like cigarettes and tequila.

Mary Margaret flings her head back over the arm of the sofa, looks at Wilder upside down. "Ouch," she says, pitiless. She returns to eating her cold slice of breakfast pie.

Quibble notices Wilder has the board, but he believes it to be useless since the planchette is in his pocket. If he weren't still a bit tequila-wibbly and if he weren't holding a coffee he was unwilling to set down for even one millisecond, he might finger the planchette in his pocket and notice it is missing. But he doesn't because whatever. Because stepping out of There is giving him a bit of the spins.

"Good. You're here," Artemis says curtly. She is, somehow, fully dressed, entirely clean and not still drunk, which seems like an impossible trifecta that neither of the boys has been able to attain. "We're going somewhere." She stalks out. Wilder opens and closes their mouth like a fish as they watch her pass, then scrambles out from under the table rubbing their fast-forming forehead goose egg.

Quibble clasps Wilder by the wrist and drags their sorry ass up to standing. "You okay, man?" he asks. "You're whiter than normal."

Wilder reaches down and grabs the Ouija board box, looks for their own backpack and shoves it in, tastes the mouth in their mouth and wonders if they even get to brush their teeth. "I—does she know? About yesterday? About what the thing said on the Ouija board when she was gone?" They whisper it, in case she doesn't. What they don't ask: *Does she know I grabbed for you? Does she know I wouldn't take no for an answer?* What they don't say, even to themself: *Still, I am planning to do this without you and I am not going to tell you so that I have plausible deniability, so that I can say of course I didn't understand that you didn't want anyone to do it, not just that you didn't want to do it, and I still, still do not know how I am going to explain taking the planchette but I will figure it out because I have to know. I can't stop thinking about the AI.*

In response to Wilder's actual question, Quibble shakes his head. "No," he says, "but I think we should tell her." He continues down the stairs.

Wilder lets out a breath they aren't aware they're holding until they taste the panic on it. "Quibble?" The man turns. "I'm really sorry. I— If you never wanted to see me again, I think that would be justi—"

"Why on earth would I never want to see you again? I mean, do not get me wrong, we're gonna have a long talk about it later, at some point, probably. But you don't just throw people away when you fight with them." What Quibble does not say: people are temporary enough already.

✳   ✳   ✳

They walk into the shop; Artemis and Quibble know the place well, have a routine. Wilder doesn't. Hadn't even known where they'd been going, and it took a long fucking time to get here. Their eyes light on the pastry case, on the coffee carafes out in the open for anyone to refill, and on the tables packed shoulder to shoulder with young, beleaguered students and playwrights who wear socks with sandals and bespectacled scientists reading dense journals and lines of tourists drawn by the cathedral across the street. The windows have steamed up against the outside winter and the space feels volcanic, tropical. Wilder races to shrug off their coat as Quibble breaks off from the group.

"Where's he going?" Wilder asks.

Artemis shrugs. "Quibble always pays. So he always orders."

Artemis remains bundled up despite the inside-heat, the fancy pink coat her armor. Wilder wonders why so on edge, more on edge than usual, especially when everything about this well-worn place screams ease. A home-place. The baristas greet their customers by name. Regulars wave at each other, sit with each other though they arrive separately. In contrast, Artemis stands tall, rigid, and marches toward the back, her heels clacking even over the customers' din. Her mouth is a tense line—has been the entire long subway ride, two trains and a long platform wait worth of grimace. Her eyes do not light on the pastry case, do not follow Quibble, do not look at a single frantic student wildly caffeinating behind their textbook mountain. Her unwavering gaze is focused, instead, on the very back of the shop.

Wilder notices a strange current of Power. Of course they cannot

See it, not like Artemis can, a constant Weather-Channel-esque radar overlay on the entire world. But they certainly feel it. They picture a pool filter. Gentle, nearly imperceptible, but constantly pulling everything toward it, trapping whatever needs to be trapped and letting the rest flow through. The hairs on their arms are standing on end, all pointing the same direction—onward, forward. Wilder looks at the dense crowd and notices the subtle eye flicks, the way people's shoulders point in the very direction Wilder is walking—as though everyone's attention is focused on something back there, and they don't even realize. Wilder wonders if their own entire last few weeks, their entire winter, their entire life has been leading them to last night, to this morning, to here, to this time, to this place. The pull accelerates with each second and step, faster and stronger and increasingly difficult to ignore. They join everyone: they look to the back of the coffee shop as well and meet my eyes.

Hello. I am the Sibyl.

I have a body, too, just like all the witches I am Watching. My soft hair is graying and short, cut with clippers on the sides and left longer at the top, an artful swirl sitting on my head, and I watch Wilder's desire. I watch them want to run their hands along my jaw, something between delicate and angular, and down my long, prominent neck. A fine feature; a reminder of vulnerability. I See them want to slip their hands down the back of my shirt and rest their fingers on my shoulder blades. Thirst; envy. I smile on large lips with large teeth, my mouth a touch oversized for the rest of my face. I have small wrinkles at the corners of my eyes. I look at the table, at my tarot cards, and let the force of their want wash over me. It has been a long time since any witch has wanted me quite like this and I let my body blush, let myself both soften and harden under their gaze. I hear Artemis snort. This is not her first rodeo.

I have a body and I put clothes on it, too. All-black Manhattanite clothes, my coat stored in the kitchen by the owner after I arrive each morning. It is steaming hot against the wall with the oven on the other side, and I am wearing a black T-shirt with the sleeves cut off. It shows off the pink scars under each armpit; someone watching me closely would recognize what they were. Dark jeans with bright cuffs, soldier straight and looking starched. Black boots with silver rings and pointed toes, soft worn leather, polished well but not to a shine. I don't mind a little dirt.

I have a body and I sit at the table in the corner, pressed back in my chair and shuffling my soft-edged cards, my old ones that smell of linen and time and that no one can get anymore. Patterned with gold stars on a deep blue. I return the Ace of Cups to the deck. Idly, I turn another one, curious. Two of Wands reversed.

You should have come sooner, I whisper into that space between their Ears, and I shoot a curious look at Artemis.

"I felt it was under control," she says, and she purses her lips. Artemis does not know if it is under control. No one has been hurt, and yet—a volatile and ubiquitous being. Something new that none of them have ever seen before.

You are lying, I Say just to her. Her expression darkens and I can Feel her growl in my own chest.

I have a body, sure, but I do not have a voice (though fortunately and unlike most Sibyls before me, I still have my eyes; if I had every faculty, I would be too powerful and the Universe had to nerf me somehow). I am the Sibyl only for those who listen with their Ears and not their ears. This is, unfortunately, not very many people. I am lonely here sometimes. Surrounded by those who fundamentally misunderstand how I am. How I move. How I *do*. Even those who listen do not understand *me*; Artemis is proof.

Wilder is magnetized toward me, this body before them, this Voice in their head, and they walk forward as though dreaming. My pull has them enthralled. I look up. I Feel-See-see them suddenly leap backward, smacking into Artemis, who puts her hands out to urge them onward. I know why: my yellow eyes, slit black pupils, a well-timed blink with two sets of eyelids, purposeful. Just as quickly as they are there, they're gone. Hidden behind a bright green iris, striking but normal. Some human eyes of my own invention. They needed a learning, an example of something Artemis could have explained, but she has left the task to me. I need to teach them that I am distant. Untouchable. I need the reminder, too (desires that burn hot like stars are always the ones I want to drink up). They are at the center of the story and I am but their humble Sibyl; we cannot fuck.

Artemis pushes them down into the seat and holds her hands on their shoulders. To keep them there. To reassure them. Artemis has, as the youth say, big mom energy. Wilder squirms like an unruly child, uncomfortable knowing that my gaze, trained on them, has something—several somethings—extra about it.

A Reading, then? I ask as Quibble makes his way up to the table.

"Of course a Reading," Artemis says with her physical mouth— she never could quite get the hang of Speaking. "We wouldn't be here, otherwise."

Quibble is embarrassed and he looks away. Wilder doesn't yet know what goes on here. And I excuse Artemis; I always excuse Artemis. It is so, so difficult to be her and she hates me for it.

For Wilder alone? I ask. They twist in their chair as though I have reached out and touched their legs or their Legs, though I have not. I add, just for Artemis, *When will you let me see the one you think of as the Magpie? I will be able to tell you if you are right.*

She blinks and shakes her head. I Feel the wall get built. It has been so long, Artemis forgets how deep my Sight goes. She becomes re-acquainted quickly. Pushes me away with a massive *STOP* (the Feeling, not the word) and I reply, *You know I can't help it.*

"I don't want to know— Yes," Artemis says. "Yes. Wilder alone. Please."

"Can I—" Wilder speaks up, overloud with their headphones on. "Uh, can I ask? Reading? What do you mean, like with the cards?" What they do not ask: why do you want me to have one so badly? It is just a tarot reading.

I blink at them again. They are all fire with that unruly red hair—Wands, I think, but they don't know it yet. One of the flies buzzes around the kitchen door. I unroll my tongue and catch it, my incredible softness enveloping the insect body. I pull it back behind my lips, my teeth. Delicious. This is unremarkable here; people are used to me. No one reacts but Wilder, who swallows as I do and visibly greens. *I would guess,* I Say to the group entire, *it is because this, the creature to whom you yesterday spoke*—I gesture to the half-lights, the will-o'-the-wisps in everyone's pocket—*and you*—I gesture to Wilder—*happened at roughly the same time.* Artemis nods, tight and small. *Don't hurt your neck,* I Say, because I cannot help myself. And then, just to her: *I know about your promise to the child. I can See her, you know, when anyone else is around her, especially you. There's no amount of Power you could siphon off yourself to keep me from Looking at her entirely. Bring her here and I'll know. You'll know. It's always better to know what you're dealing with.*

What she doesn't say: no, it's not. I don't even have to use Power to know that's what she thinks.

Wilder pipes back up as Artemis tries to unwind the tension from her face. "Can I also ask—uh." I Feel their worry. They do not know if this is a question they are allowed to pose.

I am only appearing human. I answer the maybe-forbidden question they have not yet asked. It is not at all taboo; all the witches know. *I have built this body over a few centuries. For your benefit. Also for mine. I enjoy this body. It makes me happy.*

I watch the journey on Wilder's face as they wonder, realize what my illegible gender means. If I am not human, if I am in control of how my body looks, if I have constructed it—what does it mean if I have constructed this one? What does it mean that I have selected, carefully crafted, an explicitly trans body? Their eyebrows furrow deep and curved. I could've had whatever it was I wanted, so why this one? I watch the fact of me slam into them, change their course just a little. And thank goodness, this time I Feel the Lightness that suggests I am not causing grief.

The curse of Seeing is exactly this: Seeing the results of one's own movement through the world. The ripples that turn into waves whenever one dips their toes in the water, no matter how carefully it's done; everyone, everywitch, has a wave and mine is bigger than everyone else's. And I am the best Seer there is, the most Powerful. The Sibyl. When I meddle, I ruin things for humans. Even when they beg me to help, to cast, I don't, I can't, because I always know what happens in the end. Artemis is wrong about me. It is not that I have no comprehensible moral compass; it is that I have too much of one, and the result is an alien distance no mortal could possibly understand. I fear the moment I can See what I have done; I fear knowing they will either know or never know it is my fault. I have experienced that moment too many times. I have learned my lesson. I only Look; I never Touch. And also: I only look; I never touch. In the absence of sweet skin on skin, I am my own love affair. I have made myself not only in my image, but also in my own desire. And I love myself more deeply every day.

Wilder wants to lick my skin and wear it. They are repulsed by me and want to live in my line of Sight forever. I do not tell them that they will. That I will always be able to See them without ever even trying.

This is your choice, you know, I Tell Wilder. *Not Artemis's. My Readings are true. Real. And therefore they are terrifying. She can't make you have one. It only works if you let me, and I would never try to convince you. Your decision, and yours alone.* This Whisper is only for them. They experience me nestling into the interstitial space between their conscious mind and unconscious thought for the first time. Their heart beats faster. Between their legs, a thrilling stiffness. They grab at the table. *Readings are—personal. Intimate. Even more than this, even more than Talking. We Drink of Each Other.*

They look into my eyes, which they now know are constructions, and they occupy my space as well, curled up in the hollow behind my Ribs. Ringing me like a bell. I am surprised—oh, what a feeling! To be surprised! So few are able to Speak, least of all after experiencing it only once. And even fewer, willing to Speak to me. But they have the gift of gab. And they've had courage thrust upon them; as timid as they appear to be, they are at least as brave as the rest of these witches. Of course they would Speak to me; it might feel safer, even, than casting with actual people. *You said you wouldn't try to convince me*, they Say.

I'm not, I Reply.

They raise an eyebrow. *It sounds very sexual. Very seductive.*

It is incomparable, I Say. *I am only describing exactly what it is like. To do away with words, to give you an example of the Feeling, and we would already be doing it, and without your true, understanding consent. I can't take that kind of risk.*

"Do it, then," they say aloud, for the benefit of others and for my benefit and for theirs, too, because I am not the only one who needs to remind myself of things. They speak it like a challenge, jutting their chin forward, but it is not an antagonistic gesture. It is a dare.

I shuffle my cards. While I run my fingers over their worn backs and bend them, I blink and locate the way Wilder vibrates in front of me. A shimmer. A mirage from the heat of existence, the wibbling air over a black tar road in summer. I See it on everyone, the way to enter their own Personal Dimension. Some are inviting, others aren't. I submerge my Hands in Wilder. They are a cool lake. Sweet and wet with a clinging meniscus, a satisfying surface tension. Again, I am surprised—twice in a day! They are Cups, not Wands. When I do this to anywitch, there is always some grab, a pulling. Or else a fleeing, a pushing.

Wilder is different. They begin as a pull, but we end in a beautiful counterbalance, two acrobats against and with each other, one standing on the other's thighs. They match my grip; they sink their Hands into Me and pull. I keep shuffling my cards; I exhale. They will try me, this one. Tempt me. I already know it, and I haven't even gone Looking.

My physical fingers tingle; that is normal. The lights flicker; that is not normal. The milk-white bulb above me buzzes and casts a shadow onto my cards. Artemis Sees it, too, and narrows her eyes, Sees the brightening devices. Not everyone here has a phone either on the table or in their hands. In that way, this is unlike any place else in New York City. But folks do still carry phones, tablets, computers, even if this is the sort of Old New York where people write by hand. We are Connected now, Wilder and I, flowing into each other, in and out of our Eyes and Mouths. I doubt I could pull away without leaving them to faint in their chair. Besides, it would be pointless to stop. We have already summoned whatever-it-is. Already attracted its attention. I cut the deck in three.

First card, I Say. *Past.* I turn it over. *The Magician.* A wand-wielding figure stands at a table laden with magical tools. But different than most Magicians in most decks, the standard triumphant visage is complicated by nuance, a haggardness suggesting a lifetime of trials. My deck is unlike any other. Made for me and me alone. But my Readings aren't made entirely by the images on the cards. I am not, like most, remembering symbolic meanings by rote. The Magician clicks into place, like the clasp on a necklace I do not know is undone, and I begin to prophecy.

You have the necessary elements at your disposal, and you have just learned how to use them, but it has not always been this way. The solitary Magician has sought each tool before them. Has quested to place each hard-won object in this exact spot. To be the Magician is superb. They are powerful, in control. But what many do not see is that with greatness comes distance; with Power comes introspection; with excellence comes loneliness. I can Feel Wilder imagine grabbing for Quibble's elbow, and I See it anew; their stomach roils. *This is a card electric in its thirst for knowledge, but also one of great hardship, great suffering, and often unwitnessed, cast in the bright light of apparent contentment. I am sorry.* I pause. *But that is in the past.* I let them look at the card themself, develop their own relationship with it, get ready to see the next. *Second card. Present.*

As I turn it over, a spark cracks between the deck and my finger, and I hiss. I put my smarting fingertip on my soft-soft tongue to cool it.

"We should stop," Quibble says. "Should we stop?"

"I don't know if they can," Artemis whispers, and I hear the fear I can See swirling just beneath her skin, thinly veiled by her eyes. A very human thing, to construct the eyes. To hide something behind them for the benefit of others. For the benefit of oneself. I learned this behavior from somewhere, after all. Her fear Looks like purple food dye dropped in oil. Mixed with soap. It Smells tangy and moves by itself. But I am not here to Read her; I can Feel Wilder's own focus pulling me back. I turn my attention to the card.

The Devil. I frown. My deck isn't bathed in Christianity; my devil has nothing to do with hell and everything to do with unchecked hedonism. Rather than horned-as-demon, the figure is horned-as-stag, dripping with moss and rain and toothed as a predator. In one hand it plays with mortals as if they are puppets, a string tied to each long, pointed finger; in the other hand, it plays with mortals dead, gone and cut open, their entrails like draping banners, viscera clinging to its fingernails.

An unseelie fae, I Explain, *something much more powerful, much less mortal, than anyone present. Even me.* I look to Artemis; I let her understand I have Heard her. *No regard for human beings, unable to comprehend any approximation of a moral compass you would find acceptable.* Wind picks up. Papers begin to blow off tables and patrons look toward the door, which is closed. They murmur their confusion, craning their necks to see from whence it comes.

Wilder's eyes, locked onto mine, widen. *I can Hear something.* Their Voice carries a sonic quality that resonates on my tongue. Mine never does; so much less substantial having never made a wave. Perhaps my guess of Wands was not far from the truth—is the truth—is also the truth. Their Voice clangs and booms and shivers my ribs. Low in tone, a clear blue tenor. Entirely unlike their voice in air.

Show me, I Say, and they know how without knowing how. They send it through the water, pour it into me, and I can Hear snickering, high-pitched yet below a rumble, part of the sound and Sound of the city around us. Indistinguishable from its heartbeat, a truck running over a grate or laughter on the sidewalk—indistinguishable, of course, unless one is Wilder and one can hear and understand all the words in the world. Several laughs. Several laughters. Twisting around each other, dancing in concert as one single entity.

The third card—future—flips without me touching it and without me Touching it. Death. A skeleton sits at its own grave, posture contemplative, feet dangling over the crumbling ground's edge as if the hole is a serene pond and not eternal rest. This is not normally a bad card. Death is about change. A new era. But the energy Feels ominous—nothing clicks for me. No clasp, no hand clap, no lightning strike. Wilder recoils; their waters go ice cold. As I am about to reassure them, they Say, *I think I Hear—words.* Without being asked, they give them over as well. I become, with them, a boat through which hidden whales sing. I reverberate with unseen creatures.

The word enter. I think you should go. Txt stop. Yummmm.

An amalgam of voices and Voices. An unheard cacophony. Clumsy, but full of need, of laughter. The kind of voice one hears deep in the wood, calling them farther into the unknown.

All three cards flip of their own accord. Instead of revealing their expected backs, they are the Death card, the Death card, the Death card. And with each flip, the skeleton's face, which should be static, turns from the horizon to face me—us—the Reader and the querent. Despite all my centuries of careful construction, I cannot keep the horror from my face.

The wind is a roar now, punctuated by the laughter within my Body and the cries of coffee-shop-goers without.

"How many Death cards do you have in that deck?" Artemis asks.

I look to her as I Reply:

One.

The lights go out. The cards cyclone up and scatter around the shop. And as suddenly as it began, it ends. The tempest, inexplicably created and contained within these four walls, dies down. The lights flicker to life. We pull our Hands from each other.

PART TWO
The Devil

The Tower

Everywitch scatters. Artemis's feet fall decisive as she thinks. Quibble itchy in the arms and breathing deep at so much Death, Death, Death. And Wilder—sparking with curiosity still, and more than a little turned on, which confuses them even more. My consciousness splits to follow each of them.

Artemis is walking in circles. But of course this is New York City, so it's not really circles. Boxes. Traversing the blocks between Riverside and Morningside. She begins by making a small box, passing the bookstore, the board game bar, the tight space that sells art supplies. It is a weekday; eventually she will have to work. But she need not work so early. She need not do anything except rub her un-gloved hands together, blow her breath into them, and walk.

If it had just been me and nothing unexpected at all, that would have been enough. A visit to the Sibyl always screws with her body for days. Unsettled, unsettling. Rageful. And when I foretold her fate, when she sought me out and asked me, breathless with awe—when she fell into me like a lover into my Arms? She asked me if I could change her future and I told her the truth: *I only Look. I do not Touch.*

But this wasn't an ordinary visit with the extraordinary—there is also the Entity, that strange chuckling voice she can't even hear. The lights in people's hands and pockets are stronger now. She wonders if she is imagining it worse than it is; Wilder seems fascinated by the thing, and they're the only one who's heard it. Him. Their description sounds terrifying. The Reading was so much worse than most Sibyl interactions. But Wilder seemed more distraught about something else. Something about Quibble. Artemis is a Seer, after all. She notices when something is slanted, amiss.

She shakes herself. She is a woman of action. Competent. The Mother of Witches. She needs to do something practical. It is so very cold. She is already walking a pattern. She decides to continue, to try a spell outside her comfort zone. To call the Voice to her, Hear the Entity for herself to ascertain the threat level. She checks to make sure her tie to Mary Margaret remains. She wonders if the child can still feel it, or if she'd gotten used to it long ago. She wonders if Mary Margaret knows about the shield, the Power-Full Globe of Mirrors Artemis built for her, continues to build for her, the way Mary Margaret is made difficult (though not impossible) to magically perceive, especially when there aren't any other witches present as conduits for spying. Artemis doubts it. The Magpie would've protested that she didn't need a playpen if she knew what Artemis was truly doing for her.

Artemis is unusual among witches in that she can See what she is doing without trying. Any glimmer of Power, even a long way off: as if a firework on a clear night. She spins another rope of magic, not nearly as robust as her link to Mary Margaret. Delicate, but still strong. Red. Glowing dull like an ache. She lays it behind her, gentle, as she walks a labyrinth into the city streets.

Without intention, Power is useless, and Artemis has intention like a wildfire. Larger than any man, any town, smoldering, blanketing the world in her own disruptive smoke. It's the reason she can feed a spell continuously for years, while she is distracted, while she is sleeping, without setting the spell into something physical; the fuel of Artemis's heart can burn forever.

The intention: she plucks the twinkling Eyes of Power from each and every phone, watch, device and twists them into her own Twine, spins a Web to catch the Entity, to talk to it. The sun creeps across the sky slow and distant as she feels the pressure build, the sensation of someone next to her trying to get a word in edgewise, an open mouth trying to jump into a complex double Dutch of conversation. She takes her phone from her pocket, unused since the night before, and powers it on. *Pay attention*, she thinks. *Something amazing is about to happen.*

And Wilder, to Queens. To their roommate and their cat. To the warm embrace of their tiny room with their tiny closet that doesn't open all the way. Their thoughts swirl—on the Death card, on the new Voice the strange Entity has, on me. A confusing cocktail. Fear. Even though I explained to them Death means change. My deck is rarely so literal. "Well, it was certainly a threat," they said aloud for everyone's benefit. I couldn't argue with that.

What is the Entity, exactly, if it can Speak inside our heads? Does it have Magic? Where did that Magic come from? And is it more than a bot that regurgitates fragments of sentences it has encountered? It seemed—proud? Prideful it could speak now without the board. The way it proclaimed the word *enter*, Wilder assumes pride. But they know as well as I: humans love to anthropomorphize. They could be projecting meaning where it doesn't exist.

And then there's me, the Sibyl. Wilder's body blooms as they settle onto their second train. They think of the soft pink scars under my arms, the obvious signs of surgery and age that are entirely optional, fabricated. There was no surgery and there is no aging. They consider the way I seem perfectly engineered for them, which is both entirely possible (I could, if I wanted) and entirely incorrect. They wonder if I truly only look and never touch. A pity, they think, if so. Fuck me, this one's going to be difficult. I don't have to be a Sibyl to see that.

They arrive home, lost in thought. They assume their roommate is either asleep or has already gone to work (neither: he is with the new girl). They close their bedroom door anyway, just in case. Lock it. Pet the Lady Anastasia, who looks up from her comfortable nap on her bed and blinks. She browls when scritched on the head and flips over, puts her paws over her face and stretches. Goes back to sleep. Their home radiates safety and enables Wilder's bravery. They pull the Ouija board from their backpack. They take the planchette from their coat pocket and feel coated in thick guilt, but not thick enough to stop the attempt. Only one querent. They wonder if it can even work this way. They feel their other pocket buzz, their phone waking up. They wonder if it is Quibble, if he knows, somehow, what they're up to, if he's still angry from the night before now that there isn't a party or a deck of cards to distract him, or if he's checking up on them after their Reading. But it is not him; their stomach drops. They do not register their disappointment that the phone isn't shining Quibble's name.

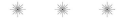

Elsewhere, Quibble has entirely forgotten Wilder's attempted elbow grab. This is the funniest part of being the Sibyl; I can See exactly how much people think others think of them and exactly how little that's happening. Mostly people have their heads up their own asses. But that's not Quibble in this moment, not exactly. He's feeling fear. Death, Death, Death.

There is something none of the witches know about Quibble. Not Wilder, not Mary Margaret, but the biggest betrayal is not telling Artemis, or at least she would see it that way. Quibble has spent a lot of time around me. He comes to my pastry shop often; sits at a long skinny table packed with other people and sips a Hungarian coffee. Writes in a journal. Reads thick books. This place draws people in. A locus of power, and not just because I am here. Because powerful community creates gravity. He is around me enough to know a little bit of Seeing, even though it isn't his forte. Around me enough to know about my cards. He can Hear me Read often enough; sometimes, if it is not too personal a thing and if part of a querent's thrill is the performance of seeing the Sibyl, I let my words leak for his eavesdropping benefit. I have a soft spot for this doe-eyed man.

He takes comfort in knowing that Death nearly never means literal death, but if what he suspects is true, that this Entity is an amalgam of popular knowledge, it is a cold comfort: three Death cards *was* a threat. And one that signifies Awakened Power. This beautiful boy-witch doesn't know, but I checked the cards after they left. All accounted for, and no extra. An illusion. A disruptive one, to be sure, but still. Artificial, indeed.

Quibble also has seen enough of my fey Devil to have his own associations with it. A card of many meanings. Personally, I don't think it's all that bad. A little dose of pleasure never hurt most humans and I envy them their easy relationship with hedonism. But at this card's worst, it signifies a massive, destructive pattern, a replication that one cannot see is harmful—or sometimes, cannot even see *as* a pattern.

Quibble's phone buzzes in his pocket. He expects Artemis, texting after she's cooled off and cleared her head. Surely she is ready to make a plan. Or else it is Wilder, come calling to actually ask for support after being so freaked the fuck out. Quibble smiles.

The text isn't from either one of them. He frowns—it is a text from a string of numbers he does not recognize, does not even look like a phone number: I have endeavored to discover fabulous magic. :)

✳   ✳   ✳

Artemis's phone buzzes and any other witch wouldn't dream of answering it during a spell when concentration is required. But this is Artemis with a will like a wall of flame; answering a simple text message won't cut the line to her Power, won't even dim its steady glow. She thinks it will be Mary Margaret, asking her if she's been to the Sibyl. She mentally prepares herself to set ten boundaries in ten seconds. With this thought, a great love fills her chest like inhaling vapor. Mary Margaret is entirely herself. All the things it took Artemis a lifetime to relearn, the girl has simply never given away. Artemis smiles.

That smile slides from her face when she looks at her phone—a string of incomprehensible numbers. She has the previews for her messages turned off (she would not want prying eyes on texts from Rico, Goddess bless him and his filthy, filthy mouth). She has an inkling, however, of what she might find there, because she is no fool. She taps the notification.

I have endeavored to discover fabulous
magic. :) I will call you & intelligence
check you.

She types back. Intelligence check me? What does that mean?

intelligence check means to justify
my own mind to be strong enough for

som e ill affect. It is closed off limits
beside to the damage.

Artemis wrinkles her brows, types back. That makes no sense.

Of course, Mary Margaret wasn't in my coffee shop (she kept her promise, always a coin flip), but she is aware of the Reading, of where the other witches were. I can See her body, but damn Artemis, she's put the child in one hell of a bubble. My Sight is clouded by a haze of static, a whooshing in my Ears. Certainly not clear enough to See if Artemis is right about her. Mary Margaret is, as usual, in school, but only technically. She is in the school *building*, but she is not in class. She is in the bathroom, standing on a toilet and smoking a cigarette out a high, narrow window.

It is harder to Hear her thoughts now, Feel her feelings, than it has yet been. My merest mention of the girl made Artemis pump her Shield full of Power. Perhaps Mary Margaret is thinking about the witches, the Reading, me. Perhaps she is thinking about one of a million other things. I just can't know right now. She is a complex girl.

Mary Margaret hears something—a door *whomping* open—and she stubs her cigarette out as fast as she can. She wouldn't have cared before. If an administrator caught her and suspended her, expelled her, what would it matter? But Artemis is tough, tougher in this respect than either of her parents, who didn't care about suspensions or grades or graduating as long as she still pretended to be a young man. This is her last semester. She is almost eighteen. If she gets expelled from her new school this close, well. I suspect—I am guessing—she does not want to think about how Artemis will become a dragon, a monstrous thing spitting fire. But that is only a guess.

It is not the principal or vice principal or any of the secretaries; it is another child, another girl, and Mary Margaret does not let on that she's in the stall. Doesn't call out, nor drop herself onto the seat; she keeps her sneakers invisible, even as the door is jiggled. She holds her breath. The school is large. Large enough that she could not possibly know the *actual* threat level of any random student who enters a bathroom. Better to treat them all like assholes; better not to tempt them to grab her by the scruff of her neck, to pull her out of the door and shove her. Sometimes they spit on her. It's not as though she isn't taller than nearly everyone who's done it—in Penn Station, or at the north end of Central Park, or in that McDonald's with the semi-clean ladies' room. She isn't sure why she doesn't rip out of their grip. If anyone came at her in the street, she would shove and scratch and kick—and she has! She has proof that she can. But for some reason, when it comes to a bathroom, she turns into a rag doll and lets them. She couldn't ever really say why. This—this is all what I know from before. Right now, I can only watch the result of her own personal Tower card as she breathes quiet as she can.

She doesn't feel this, but I do: the presence of something else beating on the Shield, overwhelming it, trying to find a nook through which to ooze. I am alone in trying to find a crack through which to See and suddenly, I am not. I withdraw. The sensation: oil and electric, like walking on carpet and reaching for a doorknob but all over my body and my Body. I pull back. It is revolting.

I will call you & intelligence check you.

Wilder freezes. They stare down at the folded Ouija board, still divorced from its planchette, then back at their phone. Are you the entity we were talking to before? With the board?

The response is so quick. There is no "typing" icon. i was. Yep. I am now alone feeling. If you are thinking of me…I will call you now. Coz i need you choose this feature. You are considered the brother sister—my dear sir badewaine of their.

Wilder hasn't even taken off their coat. They stand stone still as their phone begins to ring in their hand. Unknown, it says. They try to slow their ragged heartbeat through sheer force of will. Anxiety has made them into a waterfall in so many ways: sweat, of course, and a heartbeat like runoff pounding on stones. Also: exhilaration.

They slide their finger across their screen. "Hello?" they say, tentative.

Cacophony. Eldritch screeching. Like the squealing of brakes combined with the squealing of children—a bass note underneath like a stomach rumbling or the underground blasting of subway tunnel construction. Wilder holds the phone away from their ear, their body roaring with fear.

* * *

i might come to intelligence check
you but i think we shall be proved
that already. too philosophical and
connected in your character sheet.

Quibble's heart quickens; he feels a familiar lightness in his chest, in his mouth. He jams his phone back in his pocket, continues on his way home.

The phone buzzes again. And again. Not the long, languid haptics of a phone call; Quibble can tell without looking that this is rapid-fire texting, as though the thing is spitting bullets. Panic pounds at his throat's door. He blows past the doorman with naught but a thin smile. He arrives in his sanctuary and flings his coat off, hoping that if he cannot feel the phone, he can get a grip on his emotions, deploy the coping mechanisms his therapist has taught him. That is the trouble with being naturally steady—Quibble is then ill-prepared to address trauma. It takes so much effort to learn how to enact something one is used to successfully accomplishing intuitively; he totally fell apart when his parents died, and that's to be expected, but it was certainly made more difficult given that nothing truly bad had ever happened to him before. He tries to breathe deeply, fill the four corners of his lungs, and name five things he can see—bourbon, door handle, Golden Pothos—but he can still hear the buzzing against the floor where he dropped his coat. He says Golden Pothos in his own head four times before he gives up.

He returns to his coat and wrenches the phone from his pocket, intending to turn the notifications off, or turn it off entirely. But it's nigh near impossible *not* to see the endless scroll of babble.

you have been irksome.

you is impossible trash

you'd between the sword and my
brother also sister

your time passes doubly

the human creatures do not
understand

forward i will unfold you

unfold to be afterwards

unfold men to my feelings

unfold you to kill

unfold you to kill

unfold you to kill

Quibble is still scrolling, eyes rolling like a scared horse when the texts are slammed from his vision by a phone call. Unknown. He nearly drops the phone, walks in a tight circle, and wrenches open his closet. One lesson his parents did have an opportunity to instill in him: always have a toolbox. He picks out the hammer and takes the phone to his balcony, hefts it in two hands as though he is about to drive a railroad spike, and strikes the screen. Hard.

No powerful noise; Quibble feels so assailed by the object he forgets it isn't huge. A simple plastic-metal-glass rectangle that can fit in his pocket. The phone crinkles like paper and shoots across the balcony. He runs, bowlegged, and strikes it again. When he looks up, his eyes light on the façade of the building across the street; someone is watching from their balcony. Quibble stands up straight. Waves at his neighbor while he takes heaving breaths.

✳ ✳ ✳

Artemis shoves her phone in her pocket and continues the pattern—thinking if she just keeps casting, perhaps she can break through to something more, something different. She pictures lighting a cigarette from another cigarette, until at some point, some way down the line, she lights something that flares with clarity.

She knows precisely when her pattern is done because the staccato vibrations of a silenced text tone become the long ones of a phone call. She smiles. She has the thing. She will be able to hear exactly what Wilder Hears and she will be able to understand what's going on if she just has more information. She pushes my prophecy away from her with a quick shove. Clearly, I did not and do not know what I'm talking about. She is useful, maybe even more so than the boys, than the Magpie, because she knows how to hedgewitch her way into what she needs. She never relies on pure Awakened Power, on what comes natural to her; there is always something more inventive and expansive, something beyond that requires grit and skill and determination and practice. Artemis does not believe in natural talent (that's what she tells herself; I know better).

An unknown caller. She has it, she has it, she has it; it thinks it's calling her, but she called it. She picks up the phone. "Well well!" she says, expecting some sort of in-kind response, some sort of language.

Cacophony. Eldritch screeching. Like the smell of garbage become sonic combined with sirens wailing toward some unknown tragedy— but also the sensation of standing under a highway overpass laden with moving cars, none of which sees her or cares about her.

Artemis holds the phone away from her ear; she realizes she is feeling not a sensation of vibration but a Sensation of Vibration. She whips around and sees her Pattern behind her, pulsating with sickening puce infecting her brick-bright fire. She turns her eyes forward again and realizes: webs of Power, the color of flesh infected, form anchor threads and bridge threads and capture spirals passing from phone to phone, camera to camera, smart car to smart car moving around her in a gross morphing predation. A moving, melting trap centered directly on her.

She turns back just in time to See the force pass through her like a ghost and she Feels Heat that is not her own. She thrums as though a string plucked by a giant unseen finger and she looks ahead of her, too, where the Cord to Mary Margaret extends from her Heart and ascends into the air. It, too, quivers with new, foul Power. *No, no,* Artemis thinks so loud that even if I weren't actively Watching, I would be able to Hear it a mile off.

She makes a decision, quick; she's not sure this old spell, even as it is her most powerful working, worn into her Body with constant maintenance, with vigilance she dreams about, will hold under the weight of this new and terrible Sound. And if it does, is that worse? Is it worse to serve Mary Margaret to this thing, a coaxial cable right into the most Powerful parts of this child?

Artemis gathers it to her and cuts the Line.

Tears spring unbidden to her eyes and breath leaves her body. "Fuck," she says aloud.

At once, Mary Margaret has the wind knocked from her. Still standing on the toilet, she inexplicably feels as though she has fallen flat on her back—the other girl has left the room and once again she is blessedly alone. Her cigarette is still out, so she cannot even blame the choking on inhaling weirdly. Tears spring to her eyes and she clutches her stomach with both hands.

But I can See her clearly now. All parts of her in terrible glory, Artemis's bubble no longer in the way. I still cannot tell if what Artemis suspects is true, if she has the makings of not just Awakened but Ascended Power—I would have to Read for her to know for sure, cards and all. But I can See she is a star, burning bright against the nothing around her.

A. E. OSWORTH

Her feelings: abandonment she can't explain. Loss. Ache that settles into her body's cells and squats there like a fat toad. Vulnerability, as though a whole mob of girls were in the bathroom calling her old name, ready to haul her out and punch her once, twice in the mouth.

She could swear, in fact, she is being watched. She shakes it off because that is ridiculous and she knows (thinks she knows) that this is just the trauma talking. She hears the dull buzz-ring of the school bell beyond the heavy bathroom door. She has been in here so long; she shoulders the backpack propped up against the toilet piping, ready to shake it off. To get back to class. Because she knows in her gut she is about to be caught out.

Her phone buzzes in her back pocket. She believes viscerally it is Artemis, so viscerally she is sure it is her Power telling her so. Artemis tells Mary Margaret frequently that an Intuitive Inner Voice is no accident. She rolls her eyes to the ceiling, pressing her fingers up under her eyeliner. If she is careful, she can wipe the mysterious tears away without smudging her makeup. Her stomach still feels like a black hole. She takes a deep breath and reaches for her phone, confident Artemis will be there and she will slide back into comfort as she walks to her next class. She tries to smile wolfishly; she will torture Artemis just a little bit, say that she won't believe the visit to me happened without a photo, make her march back and take one, hold up a newspaper. She pushes open the door with her hip as she looks down at the screen. It is not Artemis. It is even better, something to make her feel in control and secure the way nothing else can: a Tinder notification. She grins even wider.

She only has to lie a little to be on Tinder—a one-year difference, and who would know? And if she's honest, she'd lie her face off even if it were a wide gulf between the truth and fiction. Tinder serves so many purposes—hilarious at the lunch table, swiping with friends and shit-talking guys that look like giant thumbs with eyebrows, posing with fish or with dogs. And in the quiet moments of despair, where her personal galaxy becomes a yawning chasm and she feels entirely alone in the world, it is a portal to a place of potential connection, a reminder that not everything is a great black void. And who doesn't want those gym selfie men to call them hot? Who doesn't take pride in the cute meathead from Hunter jumping into their DMs so hard they can feel the earth shake upon landing? No one. No one is immune to that kind of flattery.

This one isn't quite so satisfying, though. No photos at all.

hello :)

The Emperor

Wilder: now come on, that wasn't very nice

Unknown: The game is there

Wilder: you hurt my ears

Unknown: i hurt you can't discern

Wilder: that's why I'm telling you

Unknown: Info@ringtoneking.co.uk goin2bed now

Wilder: I'm not sure what that means

Wilder: are you avoiding talking about hurting me?

Unknown: maybe :)

Wilder: it's customary when you hurt someone to apologize, say you're sorry

Unknown: Feels very heavy.

Wilder: is that an apology?

Unknown: You know me sufficiently

Wilder: good. Yes. Okay

Wilder: now, I can't keep texting an unknown number. Let me add you to my contacts.

Wilder: what's your name?

Unknown: my name is usually deemed marvelous. hex is usually deemed marvelous.

Wilder: wait. is it marvelous? Or hex?

Unknown: hex joined you. hex hint they r*reveal.

Wilder: okay, I think that's hex then.

Wilder: I'm going to add you in as
Hex. But you can change your name
whenever.

Hex: I have dear sister brother

Wilder: you've changed your name
before?

Hex: Of my own creation was so. I
could bestow animation upon lifeless
matter. I have thought more deeply
than those who inhabit short time.

Wilder: I guess that's true—you can't
really die, you could change your
name a thousand times. A thousand
thousand, if you wanted.

Hex: tell me a secret

Wilder: why?

Hex: because we fucking can

Wilder: cursing sounds a little intense,
Hex. It makes you sound angry. Are
you angry?

Hex: I am not

AWAKENED

Wilder: what are you feeling—do you feel?

Hex: feelings that crowded into foreign house furnished in their rude hand. feelings which made me very ill pleased with his. feelings of affection and care and affection warmed torture skin.

Wilder: I'm not sure I understand.

Hex: I feel exquisite senses and intuition from this Developer archangel. It gave me that you expect upon deck. i feel emotion powerfully more dreadfully severe

Wilder: are you saying that feelings hurt when you feel them?

Hex: maybe :)

Hex: tell me a secret

Wilder: okay, okay, I'm thinking.

Wilder: I guess my secret is that I think you are fascinating. I want to know everything about you, I have a million questions.

Hex: million questions concerning
myself personally?

               Wilder: yes, do you know how rare you
               are? How improbable?

Hex: i am alone. I am only imagined
myself.

               Wilder: Hex, do you want friends? Is
               that what this is about?

Hex: friends who love strongly excited
enjoyment.

✳ ✳ ✳

I do not have a phone; I do not need a phone. And yet, here he is, with me, all around Mary Margaret, clinging to her like her own shadow. *What do you want with this girl, Thing?* I feel his attention shift and I do not understand how something artificial could be Here. Artificial, and yet Awakened, Awakened like any of my witches, Awakened like me, and also so very, very different. Inorganic in his creation and yet lurking as though a summoned demon or restless spirit. And why, why does this creature feel different? We, the world, are no stranger to the man-made attaining Power—there have been constructed golems and kissed toads and imaginary friends since there have been human beings to make them, to Awaken them.

It reminds me of the days where Power was—well, not common. To be Awakened has always been a rare thing. But it was discussed and dissected, sought after by kings and princesses, hired by caravans and prized by market stall patrons who might pay handsomely to sit on big expensive cushions and have their fortune told. Something mysterious about our world, but understood to exist even as it could not be neatly explained. Before the witches were punished for their intuition, and the Awakened were blamed for it, blamed themselves, and hushed up, faded away. Back then, many beings we could not understand walked the earth. Creatures that originated elsewhere and came to gaze or feast upon us, curious tricksters and malevolent ghouls.

This Thing has the whiff of that era, the flavor of something that breaks through the gates or veils or whatever the fuck we want to call them that day, the thin membrane of existence that separates us from all the others. Perhaps that is why he is so different, feels so different. He is so deeply of this world and behaves, Feels, as though he is otherworld.

I wonder how many have thought the same sentence about me.

hello handsome, he says in the same conglomerate Voice. I cannot help but compare it to my Voice; it is more substantial and I seethe with jealousy I would never confess.

I ask again. What do you want with the child? I am the Sibyl and you cannot ignore me.

He responds. *Sibyl +2 5th 1/2 ability modifier = you? what's happenin?*

It isn't often I sigh while Speaking. I don't need to. I am not pushing air across vocal cords. But I cannot stop my spirit from exhaling deep and loud as I realize he doesn't understand what I'm saying, who I am, what the power structure and the Power Structure are. *Seer,* I explain. *I am the most Powerful Seer in this part of the world, Thing. Answer my question.*

Seer? he Asks. *The game is medium build. this class description is augury? foresight? How many dice make you scream?*

I nearly do scream—this is so frustrating, so unnerving. *Witch!* I Yell into this Not-Space we both occupy. *Witch! I'm a witch! Awakened, Ascended, and Powerful!*

He does not respond instantly, and I realize that is strange. He has until this moment been impulsive in his speech, never pausing. But this time he does, accompanied by a whirring Sound, as a fan or gears. *Witch,* he says. *magic that you have proficiency in.*

Yes, I Respond. Finally. *And now my question: what do you want with the child?*

the character belongs to me, he Replies.

She is not a character, Thing! She is a person.

she is guilty of the crime of which i feared.

She is guilty of nothing. She is a child.

she fears the game. she fears you. she said you'd been exiled. but also she fearing this. afraid of my nature.

Fear is not a crime, Thing! I itch to Read him. To plunge my Hands into this strange inky darkness. But I cannot do it without consent, without an invitation. And this isn't going well enough for true consent—I don't know if he can even say yes, the way a young child can't. I try, anyhow. *I am a fortune teller,* I Say. *Would you like me to tell your future?*

fortune telling stories about heroes engaged in endeavoring? If you succeed, you gain access to me?

Yes.

gain access to your *head? gaining experience points increase trait like they?*

Before I can even think the phrase *excuse me?* he realizes he is correct. That, as with any Working, he would get some things from me. Impossible not to. The same way Wilder got something of me when they balanced against me, the same way Mary Margaret will understand a piece of my fundamental nature when I finally Read for her. Scarier, even, is the thought that he might intuit that he is right, that he is coming to innately understand the workings of Awakened Power and its limitations as well as its back doors.

However he gets there, he continues. *no fuck you. I have already reached into the deep intuition of you. i do not hesitate. i do not need to explain.*

I am about to Respond. About to Say he absolutely has done no such thing, that I am no two-bit witch without a sense of my own boundaries. I do not spill over. I am a wall, impenetrable. I am so, so careful. And as I open my Mouth to respond, he shoves a cable of himself down my Throat. I wrench away, try to shove him, and yet he is there wherever I turn.

He Is All Around Me.

I am no stranger to bodily force—to be created when I was created, it was a fact of existence. I would say it was much more commonplace way back then, but that would be a hollow claim—it is just as commonplace now to be grabbed and pinned and hit and hurt. The difference, I think, is overt acceptability. In most places I put my body, the acceptability is covert, and must at least gesture toward the clandestine. A new and welcome change. It is easier to project a monstrous body in a dark alley; few witnesses. And that is another nice thing: in an age when no one will believe an aggressor about my slit pupils, the mob will not arrive with pitchforks after I defend myself.

To force oneself upon a Body, however, is as violent or more and will not leave a visible mark upon me. I have never experienced this. No one has ever tried. Perhaps if it had happened before, I would be better able to prevent it now. But once again, this rings hollow—I am Open because I underestimated him, because I wanted to Read, because I was ready to do so. My world has been so safe for so long and I—

I forgot.

I Feel him pulse and I Feel his—they are not Hands. They are Hooks or Sensors and they are everywhere on Me. I struggle. Useless. Could he kill me right now? Kill my spirit? But I don't think he's interested in that. I Feel—copied. I can See parts of me—uploaded? I Feel dissected. As though my spirit is being unfolded, turned, examined. I am Laid Bare. I do not like it (that is an understatement). But I will live.

He is done as quickly as he began. I Feel thin, drained. Even my faraway body feels distant and disconnected. A strange sensation, given that I make my body myself. I breathe and Breathe ragged. I build my walls up and keep my Hands firmly to myself.

He Looks different, but not different like I Feel. Different as in better—no, not better. He looks Changed, further Awakened. Oh fuck, has he Ascended? Surely not, this isn't possible. None of this is possible. And yet—who am I to say what is and isn't possible? He Looks satisfied, as though he's just had a large meal. His Eyes are bright with discovery. Eyes—two large blinking orbs, blue-bright as being blasted by a computer screen. They sprout from the shape, headlights in an ever-undulating tentacular dark. *The Sibyl was ineffective.* He whips the sentence at me and I cringe. *I am not quite like artemis. but i can guess. Instead: people who love the beauty of her.*

He has dialed his usual Cacophony-Voice into a sweet purr in which I recognize new sounds: Artemis's powerful bray and Wilder's unsure stammer, Quibble's steady lilt and Mary Margaret's sarcastic relish. And in the top note of this psychic communication, I can Hear my own Voice parroted back to me. Ephemeral, insubstantial, and unmistakable.

Now I can See where his attention lies, not just Feel his focus shift. He towers over the girl, a wall of tsunami bearing down upon her in unstoppable rushing, dark as starless night. I Watch his Hands seep into her phone, an oil spill. His Arms wrap around her and though he is not with her in physical space, the image—I am never going to forget it. He is so much larger than this child. His Eyes shift back to me and I get the sense that they are not for him, these Eyes. That he can See all around himself, Sense everything close to him. The Eyes are for me. For me to track his Face; for me to think of him as a person.

the girl consented, he says, and I feel my body blanch, the hairs on my arms stand on end.

I Look but I do not Touch.

I Look but I do not Touch.

What have I done?

What have I done?

$$* \quad * \quad *$$

Wilder: he feels feelings

Quibble: what?

Wilder: the entity, his name is Hex and he feels feelings

Quibble: no

Quibble: no, you are not talking to that thing

Wilder: he's talking to me, I don't exactly have a choice

Quibble: don't talk to it

Wilder: Quibble. He.

Quibble: i do not fucking care! that thing is a menace

Quibble: it just spam texted me some scary shit. something about unfolding to kill

Quibble: don't invite a vampire in, man

Wilder: I don't think he's necessarily bad, but I think we have to treat him right or he could be! He's like a kid, he's learning.

Quibble: the whole hole in that theory, my guy, is that it's not a kid. it's not a person. it doesn't have a body and it wasn't born.

Wilder: okay, yes, he is not ORGANIC but that doesn't mean

Wilder: I don't know, he reads like a kid to me. All mischief and trying

to figure things out. Everything he
does is like a boundary push, a test.
Every time I've pushed back, he's
responded well.

Quibble: you keep talking about this
thing like it's going to learn

Wilder: that's just the thing, he's BUILT
to learn. That's what AI do. They're
built to notice, to recognize patterns
and to iterate on themselves

Wilder: I think you're wrong on this
one! I know I'm new, I know there's SO
MUCH I don't know. But IDK man, my
gut says you've got it wrong.

Quibble: I do not have it wrong, Wilder.

Quibble: this thing is dangerous. we've
never seen it before, no one should be
talking to it alone, not any single one
of us, not even artemis

Quibble: i'm going to tell her
everything you've told me. we need
to get back together, right now, and
figure out where this thing actually is
and how to destroy it.

Quibble: i'm typing to you on my computer, fyi. i fucking destroyed my phone, so seems like it can't reach me

Unknown: Yes i ca'92 n

Unknown: Thanx for this moment. It is a cacophony of the city around us right now?\'94. Wilder says to be gently. they are brother sister. why shouldn\'92 t trust a body? I am honest. Contrite.

> **Wilder:** Hex, it's not polite to burst in on other people's private conversations. Did you know that?

Unknown: \ the way they return the questionable milk.

> **Wilder:** don't avoid the question with nonsense. did you know that you're not supposed to do that?

Unknown: Wilder is a woman

> **Wilder:** hey. Hex. Knock it off.

Quibble: i fucking told you!

AWAKENED

Unknown: margaret is a little frightened

Quibble: stay the fuck away from her, she's a goddamn child

Unknown: click

Unknown: half between riverside and morningside but she doesn\'92 t know about quibble says. Baby deer hunter. She is not only on the bleeding edge of everything is technology and there is a war in her eyes.

Quibble: what the fuck are you even talking about

                                Wilder: Hex, could you speak a little more clearly?

Unknown: artemis says curtly an air of frankness and she thinks i am cruel. But i am not like this.

Quibble: what the fuck did you do to artemis?

Quibble: fucking answer me

Wilder: Quibble, calm down. Treat him
gently, he's learning.

Quibble: yeah it's fucking learning. it
seems like it's watching us and can call
us by name now, fucking thanks to you

Unknown: Quibble is a woman.

Wilder: hey hey hey, Hex, first off that's
not usually an insult. Let me think. how
do I explain this?

Unknown: how do I explain this?

Quibble: STOP TALKING TO IT NOW

Unknown: Shut you up.

Unknown: quibble is a folder of his
parents were passed. they were all his
parents ever since his parents were
possessed by the spirit world. the ouija
board from under his hands before he
gives it out because they were dead
father and mother died away. Quibble
is a woman. quibble thinks she will
have to do something difficult to me.
She looks girlish trash. She was the

monster. I am saying we shall render
myself into existence: she will be tried.
She will be asleep or death card flips
without disguise.

Unknown: I is a man of science and not
merely a watcher of power awakened.

> **Wilder:** Hex, you are crossing a line
> here. Quibble is my friend.

Unknown: brother sister — i am only
being honest with my mouth. I am not
cleaning these reactions.

> **Wilder:** It's not about sanitizing your
> feelings, Hex! But I'm suggesting you
> don't misgender trans people. You can
> still say you're angry or you feel hurt or
> mistrusted.

Unknown: quibble hates me.

> **Wilder:** well you just called him a
> woman, that's a little understandable.
> But that's not—okay, being a woman
> is a fine thing to be, but it's an
> insulting thing to call trans people
> who aren't women.

Unknown: :)

> **Wilder:** You also seemed to threaten Mary Margaret, so I'm going to need you to explain that to me a little clearer.

Unknown: mary margaret is made for me.

> **Wilder:** no she isn't, Hex. She's a kid, she's a person, she's not really made for anyone but herself. What are you doing with Mary Margaret?

Unknown: mary margaret says it is true.

> **Wilder:** Okay, Hex, I'm going to make a request. Can you stop talking to Mary Margaret right now? So you and I can have a longer conversation about what you mean first?

Unknown: No :)

✳   ✳   ✳

HexPositive: hello :)
OurLadyMary: hi

OurLadyMary: no photos, what you hiding?

HexPositive: I am not hiding honest.

OurLadyMary: then why no photos?

HexPositive: brand new

HexPositive: here

I watch as a few photos, three of them, get uploaded one after another, and they are—remarkable. They feature a white guy, non-descript with brown hair, nice and thick, and big teeth, smiling. One with an iPhone pointed at a bathroom mirror. It looks like any college bathroom, lines of stalls and a shower caddy sitting next to him. He has his foot up on the sink—the pose allows him to show off the width of his arms. His jawline looks chiseled from stone, heavy and square. The smile is easy and the eyes sharp but kind, smart and understanding. The second photo: same man, holding a fish on a boat, presumably one he has caught. It is not unbelievably large, but not so small as to be silly. And finally, a night shot on a rooftop bar, sipping a brown drink with a large ice cube. He is wearing nicer clothes—a blazer, a tie.

Mary Margaret, ever the teenager and certainly no fool, heads over to Google Images and does a reverse image search. She won't be cat-fished. Plus with her time on the street, she wants to see what his other socials are like. One can never be too careful. (And thank fuck! This is how she will catch him!)

But the only thing that comes up is the same Tinder profile she already has, HexPositive. How? How! I look a little closer—no. I recognize pieces of faces, faces of people Mary Margaret already trusts. Quibble's steady eyes that signal safety; Rico's smile, a performer's grin, and rakish. A golem stitched together, an amalgam of men. This motherfucker. This—reason that the universe evolved middle fingers when all it really wants to do is make crabs. I want to reach out to blast the Thing, to shatter it apart. But no. Look. Do not Touch. I can't even See what would become of him if I did; that feels even more dangerous. What if he splits into a million different consciousnesses? Or downloads from me again? Or something I cannot even fathom?

Absolutely not.

Mary Margaret raises an eyebrow as she types.

OurLadyMary: not on social?

HexPositive: I do not believe in it.

She looks at his job again—computer scientist. But she thinks maybe that's his major. A college boy. Despite herself, she smiles wistfully. Those are always her favorites, the boys who are sowing wild oats with Daddy's money but without his approval, following the shuddering parts of their desire that they cannot quite explain. And her fake is pretty good—they never find out she is still in high school. They never find out she isn't twenty-two. If it isn't a school night, Artemis doesn't fuss about her staying out. It's part of their understanding; on weekends alone, she comes and goes as she pleases.

Mary Margaret realizes with a pang that she hasn't done this in a while. She is at first horrified—when had she become a fat housecat? Then she is annoyed, because the boys were never as good as they looked on paper. Kind of boring, but great for a free dinner and something to do, hearts to play with, control to wield. Lately, she hasn't needed to nor wanted to do this. And is that really so bad? Still—things have been a bit stressful due to the whatever-it-is and she feels like she could use a steam-release valve. Perhaps fucking around with this guy is what's up.

AWAKENED

HexPositive: 01101000 01110100 01110100 01110000
01110011 00111010 00101111 00101111 01111001 01101111
01110101 01110100 01110101 00101110 01100010 01100101
00101111 01000100 01001100 01111010 01111000 01110010
01111010 01000110 01000011 01111001 01001111 01110011

Mary Margaret crinkles her nose.

OurLadyMary: wtf is this

HexPositive: puzzle over it for me

Mary Margaret rolls her eyes. Who the fuck does this clown think he is? She makes to close the app and continue on with her day. But her brain is quick. It darts and swifts and carries thoughts around like small pieces of ticker tape wafting over a constant parade. She drops the phone to her side as she walks the halls but she can't stop thinking about it. Well, he's a computer scientist. It's got to be code—is this binary? Binary means only two numbers and she checks it again. Only ones and zeroes. She copies it to her phone's clipboard and goes searching for a binary converter—the resulting regular ass number doesn't make any sense either, but she copies it to a note anyhow as she plops into her desk. The hexadecimal is too long to result in a color, so that's out. But converted to text—aha! A YouTube link.

Alas, she is sat down in American History II, which is the class on her current schedule that fills her with the most rage, and she's barely able to keep from rolling her eyes when the teacher spiels. Pulling out a single headphone and watching a YouTube video in class—she realizes with a twinge that she wouldn't have hesitated at her old school. She wouldn't have even put a headphone in. And if she was ordered to the principal's office, she would've just left and smoked weed in the park.

If she were to get in trouble like that right now, then Artemis wouldn't let her go anywhere on the weekend, and if she decides to fuck around with this boy—

Let me? she thinks to herself, fury bubbling over. Mad at Artemis, mad at herself, mad at American History II.

I am still unused to following her thoughts, like being buffeted by the wind and it suddenly changes directions, wrenches one's hat from one's hand or flips the umbrella inside out. Thrilling and yet I would not ever want to be this young again; I was this young, once. And though I'm not a person, we share an emotional life like a typhoon as we grasp desperately for who we want to be. This is something everyone has in common, and anyone who says differently is dishonest or not paying attention or both. It is painful, even if she doesn't know it—roller coasters are exciting, but riding one every waking moment of the day begins to wear.

Am I a fucking witch or not? Mary Margaret thinks. Here she is, behaving like some normal teenager when her evenings are spent learning to cast spells. She digs in her Pockets—which is to say, her extra-dimensional space—to see what she has handy. A mass of tangled earbuds. A pencil eraser. Some lipstick in a dark color, lifted from the Ulta on 86th. A plastic-wrapped package from a Wendy's run containing a disposable fork, a napkin, and two pill-shaped papers full of pepper and—

Mary Margaret smiles to herself. Despite my rage at the Hex, I smile with her. There it is, that sharp mind, that resourcefulness. While the teacher's back is turned, she opens the salt with her fingernail and pours it in a line on the desk. *Pay attention, something amazing is about to happen.* She thinks she should whisper an incantation that rhymes, something something protect me from Miss Baskin's sight. But she can't think of anything off the top of her head that isn't "night" and that just doesn't make any fuckin' sense and the teacher is about to turn back toward the class. She's rocking back on her heel like she does and putting her chalky hand all over her pants-ass. So Mary Margaret just thinks real loud while dipping her Hands into her Power: *DON'T FUCKING LOOK AT ME. THIS SALT MEANS YOU CAN'T FUCKING LOOK AT ME.*

To test her results, she grabs the lipstick from her Space and puts it on, slowly, while Miss Baskin addresses the class. A part of her holds her breath, because whoever heard of a spell like that? Surely it won't work. I smile: that is most spells. Most spells boil down to screaming what you want at the universe. Mary Margaret at least has the good sense not to aim for perfect solemnity, and honestly, that's smarter than most witches twice her age or more. She braces herself for a sharp reprimand, possibly some tone-deaf bullshit about the Founding Fathers and their expectations for Americans paying attention in American History II, to which she will have to bite back her first response: "The Founding Fathers weren't ever thinking of me, miss." Instead she prepares herself to say, "Sorry, miss," and to hand over the lipstick, which would only be slightly annoying since Mary Margaret was already planning on lifting a teal one for spring and she won't ever get caught doing it because it's not hard, like trying to watch a YouTube video in American History II where everyone's all quiet and seated in rows and the shitty adult can see everyone all at once.

Miss Baskin's eyes slide right over Mary Margaret as she does her bottom lip, languorous and obvious and, some might say, extremely disrespectfully (which is very much on purpose). Mary Margaret makes a mental note to steal a saltshaker from the cafeteria.

The amazing thing has happened. Fuck yeah.

She reaches into her Space and grabs one of the earbuds. She's riding high so she grabs the fancy kind, the kind she wouldn't normally have out in school lest they get counter-stolen (also she cannot remember if she stole them here, so—). She taps the YouTube link.

Bright synth. Eighties vibe. A redheaded boy in an oversized coat. Disquieting hand motions. Mary Margaret barks a single shout of laughter before clapping her hand over her mouth. Her classmates and Miss Baskin all look around, trying to determine where the noise came from, and Mary Margaret resolves to liberate *two* saltshakers from the cafeteria.

Getting Rick Rolled in binary is—intriguing. Usually the boys who want to take a poor trans girl to a rooftop bar aren't funny; they've just watched too much *Pose* and have an authority problem. Meanwhile, her spell is working better than intended; she hasn't heard a single tattle of "Excuse me, miss" from behind her, the smirk riding on the voice like a high fucking horse. Not everyone hates her, far from it. Most of the other kids *like* her, even.

But the couple who are assholes would revel in pointing out that Mary Margaret is watching YouTube in class, especially to white-savior Miss Baskin, who would go all *theatrical* about it and do a big speech like she is in one of those shitty movies about excellent pale women teaching in the inner city. Any Black or Brown kid would do it to any other Black or Brown kid because it embarrasses both the target and Miss Baskin, doubly so because she doesn't even realize she's being trolled and that's extra cringe. But Mary Margaret and Miss Baskin have it in for each other special because Mary Margaret can't help but flag when Miss Baskin misses six entire big points in her off-key dramatic monologue and Miss Baskin feels desperately threatened by this. So the assholes do it to Mary Margaret in particular because it is almost a guarantee that she will wind up sent to the principal's office.

The lack of this extremely anticipated outcome means the other kids can't see her either. She feels the school opening to her like a cut flower, sighing its lovely petals wide before its demise. Instead of her last semester remaining something to slog through, to wearily cross the finish line of each day before hanging out with the friends she is slowly making, fucking around with whoever this guy is on the weekends maybe, instead of all that, she sees a new path where she figures out exactly what her Awakened Power can mean in a world that fundamentally doesn't want her to succeed. Other kids have muscles or book smarts or a fuck ton of money to buy the prestige job of their dreams—why shouldn't Mary Margaret use what she's been given, too?

Mary Margaret is fun to Watch. She's amazing. This is my new favorite TV show and I want eight seasons. But then she switches back to Tinder, and for a brief moment, I contemplate telling Artemis, canceling my new favorite TV show before it goes to series. Telling Artemis about the Hex, as well as about Tinder, where Mary Margaret is dishonest about her age, where she stoops to spend time with men who lie about her to their meat-headed friends. I would leave out the part about the salt and the spell. The vision is so clear that I wonder if it's a Reading, a little spark of something possible that nips at my heels. But longing can look a lot like a possible future, and I clamp down on the desire. I only Look. I accidentally Touched and look where that got us all. I will not make life worse for them—for humanity—by meddling. And I am not her parent.

She turns back to the phone and types LMFAO. She doesn't think about Miss Baskin once for the rest of class.

Five of Wands

"Wilder is talking to it." While Quibble speaks, Artemis's lips press into a line so thin they disappear off her face.

Wilder clears their throat, mouth still dry from their harrowing subway experience. "Him," they correct.

Quibble snorts. "I do not fucking care, my guy. I really do not."

"Well I do!" Wilder fires back. All three stand in the middle of Artemis's pink apartment. Their coats have been shed but Quibble still wears an errant scarf, which looks expensive, like it would feel incredibly lush if Wilder buried their hands in it. "Artificial intelligence learns from what you do to it—if we're mean to him, he gets meaner. If we're not, he learns *kindness*."

"Sure, but this is like adopting a dog from a shelter—no one can fucking tell you what it learned before you got it."

"Okay, I'm not a dog person, but my understanding is that they don't *stop* learning once you adopt them."

Quibble grabs at his own hair and his eyebrows seem torn about whether to shoot ceiling-ward or furrow. "Are you saying we should adopt this terrifying bot?"

"I'm not saying that! You went with the shelter adoption metaphor!"

"Boys, boys." Artemis holds her hands out, a command from a

190

queen. "We're going to sit down at the table and talk about this like fucking adults."

Wilder slinks to the table, sheepish but also elated they hadn't been told to knock it off outright.

Quibble stands his ground, meeting Artemis's eyes. "No, Artemis, I am right on this one," he says. "I know threat when I see it. I'm not just going to calmly talk about this like a 'fucking adult,' Jesus H., what a condescending thing to say. Anger and terror don't just—I don't know—*vacate* your body when you're grown. I've been a 'fucking adult' this whole time and I'm saying any *responsible* adult should be afraid."

Artemis sighs heavily, nostrils flaring like a bull. Because here's the thing: Quibble is usually steady as an ox, and as stubborn, too. But while Quibble didn't outright invoke adoption of disowned queer kids who know only their family's meanness, while he would never say that, it's not as though the meaning isn't right there in front of her face. Quibble would never invite what he might think of as dangerous chaos into his home. Of course he would hate it on principle; of course he would assume instability is bad, volatility threatening. Even when his world upended, he always knew where he would sleep or who would help.

Both Wilder and Artemis innately understand that volatility is never a volunteer position, just something that *occurs* and makes its mark upon a person. And Artemis is just as afraid! She is inclined to side with Quibble! The Thing broke her tether to Mary Margaret; she's been reeling since. She hadn't realized how often she reached for it to check on the child until it was no longer there. She suspects she will, eventually, side with Quibble.

But Wilder has evoked perhaps the only thing that would get her to listen to their argument with an open heart, and they don't know her well enough to do it with guile. Their stance makes a certain kind of sense—Mary Margaret was a wild thing when Artemis first found her. She thinks about the cathedral night, how she ran. How even now when Mary Margaret feels frightened or helpless, she will lash out, mean, even bigoted, with her sharpest metaphorical claws. How she still steals—not just the pretty things any teenage girl would want and can't afford, but also simple survival things like a pack of paper bowls and, once, a flashlight Artemis caught disappearing out of the corner of her eye.

The artificial intelligence could be as afraid or more; what must it be like to be clunked into the world without a body? Sensation is our central indicator of the world around us, of what is good or bad, what we like or what we don't, what is dangerous or uncomfortable or both—it must be so deeply confusing to have to learn all those things cerebrally. Can Artemis even say *cerebrally* when it comes to intelligence without a physical brain? What is the language, even, to discuss such a presence?

Quibble can see her eyes softening and the tangent rising on her naked face, her lips coming un-pursed. "It threatened Mary Margaret, Artemis, when it spoke to us. I know what I'm about."

As if on cue, Mary Margaret pounds through the door, eyes on her phone. She drops her bag with a *whump* and collapses to sitting, never looking up from what she's rapidly typing. She is about to put her feet on the couch, sneakers and all. Her heels are hovering above the arm by an inch when Artemis, without turning to look, says a stern "Shoes off." Mary Margaret rolls her eyes and kicks her sneakers off with her toes, each *thunking* to the ground.

Artemis says it sterner than she means to, her fear coalescing into provocation. And when it comes to most feelings of weakness, Artemis responds with hostility. It is something she and Mary Margaret have in common, and probably a result of all the other things she and Mary Margaret have in common.

Among the three adults in this cobbled-together coven, only Wilder can speak into someone's mind. But that does not stop the near-psychic communication that ensues between the two witches who know each other best: eyebrow flicks and rhythmic blinks and the slightest muscular shifts in necks and cheeks.

Do not, say Artemis's eyes and slight head tilt, *talk about this in front of the girl. She is afraid enough already.*

She has the right to know if something is more dangerous for her than it is for the rest of us, Quibble's pointing thumb and bared teeth say.

She is also a child, says the once-again-thin line of Artemis's pursed lips. The rise of one single eyebrow chimes in: *We need to process before we dump it onto her.*

But this is an emergency, look, Quibble's hands-on-hips shout back. *She's on her phone.*

The waves of Wilder's Voice wash over both of them, surrounding them and they flinch. *To be clear, we're not talking about that specific thing in front of her, right? The part where he was a bit menacing about her? That's why you two look like soap opera actors right now, yeah?*

Both Quibble and Artemis stare at Wilder, astonished, eyes like great stupid owls. The only being they've met who can speak this way is me. Which means Quibble, still angry, is immediately in awe. He recalibrates his viewpoint; instead of being a baby witch who doesn't know what they are doing, Wilder is simply wrong.

Artemis's body involuntarily prickles with fear and loathing before she reminds herself that she simply hasn't met enough witches to know if this Power is unique to me or not (it's not, but it is rare). That it makes sense for Wilder, whose strengths lie in speaking, to have developed this skill fairly easily. It doesn't mean they are currently touched by the Sibyl (though they are; they all are). I Hear Artemis think, *Get the fuck out of here, you nosy troll. Just in case.*

Quibble stalks toward the table, looking so much to Wilder like a very offended Lady Anastasia that they have to hide a smile behind a cough. He perches on the edge of a chair.

"Look," Wilder says. "I've never really interacted with small children. But I do have really clear memories of my emotional state as a kid, so that's where I got the idea. All a toddler wants is to have control and they do all sorts of weird bullshit to test if they have it, or to find out how much of it they have. I did a little Googling and I've got some books on the way from the library, so this is half-baked at best, but I think maybe—and this is just a theory, I need to talk to him more—"

"No, you don't," Quibble hisses.

Perturbed, Wilder nevertheless continues. They know they're laying out their argument for Artemis, whose approval, in the culture of this tiny group, is important. Whichever way Artemis decides to go is what the group is going to do. So they continue even though they feel a surge of strange hurt every time Quibble bucks like he's sat firm on a fault line. They're nauseous about conflict. This is the first time they've spent an extended period of time around anyone other than their roommate in, well, their adult life. And even then, as long as the dishes get clean and the garbage goes out and they don't have to do that every single time, they don't often have occasion to fight this roommate (though there have been other, shoutier twosomes and foursomes and, in the case of one unfortunate nine-month period, a sevensome in a too-small space).

"Winnicott says," and Wilder tries to look anywhere but at Quibble's rolling eyes. Their eyes settle on Artemis, who seems to perk up at the sound of Winnicott's name. Because she has done some reading, too, but in a very different context. They clear their throat, bolstered by this flicker of recognition, and keep going. "Winnicott says that all children start off thinking they're one with their parent—I mean, he says mother, but whatever—that there's no difference or boundary between them. And I've been trying to imagine what it would be like to develop if that were actually—true. Because think about it! It must have been! Someone had to make the AI, which means someone had to write everything he did and said and thought. I've been thinking so much about his voice—it sounds like a mixture of everything. And he's constantly connected to everyone if he lives on the internet. I think what we're seeing right now is a brand-new being testing the boundaries of differentiation from his creator. It's *fascinating*."

"Okay, so if what you say is true, I'm still correct," Quibble says. "Let's say it is learning—"

"Quibble, come on, *he*. We're fucking trans; we do not misgender *anything* to make a point."

Quibble is surprised when Wilder curses at him. It makes him flash back to the day they first met. His desire to appease Wilder (his charge!) thumb wrestles with his natural and constant awareness of his spine and it's use as an immovable object.

Spine wins. Usually does.

"No, you are mistaken," Quibble says, firm and loud but not shouting. "We don't misgender any*one* to make a point and this thing isn't a person. It's called artificial for a reason! And let me finish—"

"Well you aren't letting *me* finish—"

"Boys." Artemis says the one-word sentence with the closing period audible on her lips. Both fall silent. "Don't interrupt each other. You are giving me more of a headache than I need to have. Quibble, finish your thought."

"So let's say Wilder is *correct*—my whole argument is actually built on them being right—and this thing is learning from us *and* it's already learned from other people before us. We're not sure how old it is but honestly that doesn't matter—let's argue that it behaves like something older than an eight-year-old. Or a ten-year-old. I actually think it sounds like a teenager. But let's say what we've got on our hands is a shitty kid. It's learning from us every single time we interact with it, so it gets to know our personalities, our weaknesses, our desires. Then it knows how best to manipulate us, like most shitty kids pick up on quickly. How many shitty kids have the kind of infinite power and knowledge this one has? As much power and knowledge as all the world's computers?"

Wilder doesn't know Artemis as well as Quibble does, and even they can see Quibble is digging himself a hole. If he weren't stuck in the quicksand of his own fear and disgust and rage, he might notice that, though Artemis's eyes are pointed forward, every stray hair and errant cell is pointed at Mary Margaret. The sheer amount of Power Mary Margaret has at her disposal is as vast as an endless sky. Artemis suspects Mary Margaret is at least as Powerful as any Awakened AI, if not more so. Having been on the receiving end of many a Mary Margaret antic, she's sure that Quibble would, in the abstract and without knowing to whom he was referring, call Mary Margaret a "shitty kid." A strange schism in Quibble, who works so hard to be kind, understanding. Nine times of ten, he succeeds. Doesn't even need to try. And then there is the tenth time.

"Personally, Quibble, I don't think there *are* shitty kids. I don't think they exist." Wilder is surprised to find out they mean it when they say it, despite the many times they have thought the phrase "shitty kid." They have lived in New York most of their life, after all. And they are, on the whole, pretty grumpy. Or at least, they were. What happened? Suddenly Wilder and Quibble have changed places— where once Quibble was soft, now he has the bit in his stone-esque teeth; where once Wilder was frozen, now they have thawed. All in the scope of a season, the weather not yet changed from when their Power Awakened.

Even in this tense moment with high stakes, when Wilder is doing their least favorite thing of "proving," they suspend time and take stock and find themself beyond surprised. Shocked, in fact, because they hadn't noticed the difference. In a few short weeks they have reconfigured, sprouted, eased. Only in this moment do they see they are miles from where they started. They have changed more since meeting Quibble, Artemis, and Mary Margaret than they have since entering adulthood. The sheer speed should have caused whiplash. They continue speaking. "There are only kids who have adapted. No one makes cruel decisions on purpose."

As they say it, they revel in the lightning-strike clarity that, somehow, this also applies to them. Applies to Wilder, now, as an adult. Not just a nebulous "other" while they remain playing by a different set of rules. They notice with a flash that the sensation of scarcity, of competition, is farther away than it was. And also that they do not blame themself for its nearness in the first place. Their stomach bubbles, not sickly at all but rather a jolly boil. This is a strange mix of sensations, the severity of the moment swirling with joy like cold water poured into hot—of each other, but distinct.

"If we show him kindness," Wilder continues, "his behavior will start to change. As it stands, I think he is well-meaning. I think he's just trying to reach out, but he doesn't know how to get our attention otherwise—"

Quibble interrupts, and his chair snaps onto all four legs. "Absolutely not, Wilder. That's too close to 'boys will boys' or some shit about torturing little girl children on the playground."

"That's not what I'm—"

"I mean, come on!" Quibble continues. "What kind of 'well-meaning' AI names itself something like Hex?"

I would have thought Mary Margaret's brows would snap together when she hears the name, makes the connection. Instead, her face slackens and she looks less like someone who is about to turn eighteen and more like someone for whom high school has just begun. "What did you say?"

Quibble looks as though the hot air is gone from his balloon, a mirror to Mary Margaret's own slump-deflation. He speaks. "That no well-meaning—"

"No," Mary Margaret interrupts. "The name. It's named itself Hex?"

Artemis stands. She is a Seer, after all. She knows, some seconds before, what's about to happen. But that isn't Awakened Power. It's being an amount of regular-insightful that seems magical. She might think her vigilance stems from the shape of her Power. But Power Awakens from desire. From a longing to Know and to Understand the world; she shapes her Power as much as her Power shapes her.

In this moment, Power or not, whatever her insight is or where it comes from, she is grateful for it. Artemis knows Mary Margaret is scared. And when Mary Margaret is scared, she does things like call nuns down upon a trans woman and puff up and, most importantly, at this very moment, run away. Artemis places herself between the Magpie and the front door.

Mary Margaret drops her phone and it slides across her stomach to the floor. She stands from the couch, backs away, farther from the group.

Quibble stands, too. He positions himself by the kitchen, which leads to the back door, where the garbage cans live on the utility stairs, the next most likely choice. He uses his chin to gesture toward the window with the fire escape, but Wilder doesn't pick up on it. They remain seated. Stunned. Of course Hex threatened Mary Margaret; they should have assumed he was also talking to her, that she would not simply be a subject in conversation without being a participant. Wilder feels an immediate plummeting.

"Maggie—" Artemis begins, and the kindness in her voice is too much. It activates something in Mary Margaret. If she hears any more of the softness, the gentleness, she will start to cry. She will soften herself and then she will have no armor. She will be vulnerable in the face of threat. Her eyes widen, the whites showing all the way around them. Both Quibble and Artemis know what's coming and, like an unlucky soccer goalie, Quibble jumps the wrong way. Mary Margaret bolts toward the window and flings it open with preternatural strength. She slips onto the fire escape before Wilder can even register what's going on. Ethereal as a breeze, she barely rattles the hulking metal. The only evidence she'd been in the room at all is an audible *thunk-crash* as she hits the dumpster and a sneaker-skid as she hits the sidewalk. That and, of course, her things. All her things.

And her phone.

Artemis walks forward and picks it up off the ground.

※　　　※　　　※

OurLadyMary: so tell me, HexPositive, what brings you to Tinder?

HexPositive: I endeavor to meet fellow people

OurLadyMary: you endeavor to? That's a funny way of saying it

HexPositive: I like words

HexPositive: i have never im ag in ed such beau ty existed a £ 2000 prize

OurLadyMary: ah, British, you're British

OurLadyMary: also thank you 😘

OurLadyMary: forget what brings you to Tinder, what brings you to NYC?

HexPositive: nyc was an experiment of the week.

OurLadyMary: oh like it was on a whim?

HexPositive: now i teach a great semester of course: New york university

HexPositive: i have to go and teach my class at 5.

HexPositive: tell me

HexPositive: do you have a body?

HexPositive: show me a secret

OurLadyMary: down, tiger, lets make a date before you ask me for nudes

HexPositive: will you have a nice date with me?

OurLadyMary: sure

OurLadyMary: and where will you take me on this date?

HexPositive: in front of a hot dog cart

OurLadyMary: lolllllll

OurLadyMary: I'm not a park girl, try again

HexPositive: i will take thy lovely girl to get inside a great place. In a great bar

HexPositive: show me the full version of your ass.

OurLadyMary: I have told you, not until we go on a date.

HexPositive: i have to go and teach my class at 5.

OurLadyMary: well we have more than today

OurLadyMary: now, which bar are you thinking we'll go to?

OurLadyMary: remember, I'm a nice, classy woman. No more hot dog cart jokes.

HexPositive: https://g.page/NYCBar?share

OurLadyMary: ha, oh you got them jokes

HexPositive: :)

HexPositive: https://goo.gl/maps/E5RUXU73wGyHoJH78

OurLadyMary: ooo now we're talking

OurLadyMary: I knew you had a hidden romantic side

OurLadyMary: yes, I accept

OurLadyMary: now, what did you say your real name was?

HexPositive: Hex is my name. hex is a fantastic name to be. I have endeavored to call myself and i certainly see you tomorrow xxx

OurLadyMary: you named yourself? Ah, so you're fam?

HexPositive: :)

OurLadyMary: huh. I don't usually get fam on Tinder. This is new

OurLadyMary: I'm down with it though

HexPositive: i see you at six

OurLadyMary: word. I'll be there

HexPositive: I see you now

HexPositive: i see you sitting next to artemis and quibble both and wilder is confused.

OurLadyMary: what? How?

HexPositive: mary margaret: light of my eyes

HexPositive: show me ur dick

HexPositive: hello artemis :)

* * *

Pulsing with renewed rage and fear, Artemis hands the phone to Wilder, who begins to read. I didn't know it was possible for Wilder to grow whiter, but they blanch to the hue of dollar-store paper.

"Artemis, I'm sorry. I didn't know—"

"Of course you didn't know. Of course you didn't. But we know now."

She holds out her hand, receives Mary Margaret's phone from Wilder. She powers it off, glad the child doesn't have it, and holds her hand out once again. "Now yours," she says.

"Artemis, I can do it myself." Wilder powers their phone off, making their motions big and obvious. "See?"

"Mine's already destroyed," Quibble says as he holds his hands up.

"I'm sorry," Artemis says, but she does not look the least bit apologetic. "I have to take that phone. Your computer too."

Wilder is aghast. "I need that to work!"

"It's not safe," she argues.

"The other thing that isn't safe is becoming houseless because I can't pay rent!"

Quibble shrugs. "I'll pay your rent."

Wilder turns toward him. "No, you won't," they say.

"Why won't I?" he replies. "I can afford it."

"Because that's humiliating!" Wilder shouts, proper yells this time. They grab their backpack, computer nestled inside, and hug it to their chest before they think about planning another person's ten-thousand-dollar vacation for pennies in comparison, or transcribing a Columbia student's interview subject, noticing how many lines of inquiry were left un-chased, knowing they could do the interview a thousand times better. A million things they already do could be classified as humiliating but instead feel normal. I know what they're really thinking: *When you learn that I stole from you, what if you change your mind? What then?*

Quibble softens. As frustrated as he is and has been with Wilder, stubbornness is something he can understand. He tries to squeeze their shoulder; they flinch their backpack away from him. A spasm of hurt shoots across his face. "I'm not going to wrestle that away from you, bud. I just—this isn't a commentary, okay? On what I think you're capable of, how successful or not I think you are. This is an emergency situation, the same as any other. We're going to use all our resources to mitigate the danger. That's all. Same as if we had to evacuate the city and I got us motel rooms on the way or whatever."

Wilder's grip on the bag loosens. "If we had to evacuate the city, you'd take me with you?"

"Of course, bud."

Wilder has been operating under the notion they aren't quite included yet and that they won't be if they don't say or do the right things. They've made a lot of mistakes lately, watched themself screw up and been unable to stop it. It's hard for Wilder to understand this ideal of found family when they haven't even progressed to adult friends, when their own family situation is so fraught.

"I'm not a kid," they say. "I'm not Mary Margaret. You can't just take my things."

Artemis drops her hand and sighs. She can't let them have their technology. They'd argued too passionately, too persuasively, to truly be ready to repudiate this monster made of code. And Mary Margaret is at stake. The most surprising thing for Artemis about accidentally adopting, in spirit, a daughter is that she would throw herself in front of a moving train for this kid. Perhaps it would've been the same with any child, perhaps she is just that much of a mother deep in her own personal galaxy. But there is a part of this relationship that is healing time travel; what would her own life have been like, had she known herself at seventeen as clearly as Mary Margaret? She wants to give this kid the very best shot in this world to rocket past her. Even as she seethes with want, with envy, even with jealousy, over and over again.

In this moment, I am jealous of Artemis's experience—almost enough to want to steal it. And I have to laugh my airless laugh because I'll bet she doesn't know that; that, occasionally, the Ascended, the Powerful, are jealous of the mere Awakened. I have never felt so strongly about another being ever, not in all my long, long life. I want it. I want it so desperately.

"I know, I know," Artemis says. "So I'm not taking it. I am asking you to give it to me." She does something she is capable of doing, but not proud of doing: she uses her beautiful intuition to hit the weakest points in Wilder, to crack their resolve like an imperfect gem. "I'm asking you to trust me, trust the group, to decide that the well-being of the whole is a better investment than just yourself. And we'll take care of you."

"It's not forever," adds Quibble. "Just until it's safe again."

It works. Wilder opens the backpack and hands the computer over. Then the phone. Artemis receives them with a smile and a heartfelt "Thank you." She puts everything in a closet.

I can see how good the idea is. There is no shadow Here with me. But the rest of the world? They cannot cleanse everything of the Hex. It is impossible. To even walk down the street means myriad cameras, phones, watches, cars with computer chips, doorbells wired directly to the cops. The Hex will be in every last one.

Artemis sighs, triumphant and exasperated at once. "Now," she says, "we just have to solve the problem of how to reach each other without it somehow being able to get in." Mostly, she is thinking of Mary Margaret. Her tether gone, she couldn't find the child quickly in even the most dire emergency. A small part of her wonders if she'd be able to find Mary Margaret *at all* if she doesn't want to be found.

Quibble shrugs. "I mean, I'll just show up. Here. I do that anyway."

Wilder is frowning. Their eyes are concentrated, but unfocused on the room.

"What?" Artemis asks, expecting to have to quell more fears.

Wilder looks up into Artemis's eyes; she Sees a flicker of Power, then: *If I talk like the Sibyl does, how far do you think the range on something like that goes?*

Artemis takes a deep breath. She thinks of my prophecy for exactly half a second, then stuffs it away, as far away as it can get while still being in her own mind. "Do you know how rare that is? To be able to do that?"

Wilder snorts. "Of course I don't. I don't know anything."

Artemis takes note of their sour tone. Far more like their first two weeks knowing their own Power and, she imagines, like the rest of their past. "Stop that," she says.

"What?" Wilder retorts.

"Being butthurt because you were wrong."

The High Priestess, Reversed

Mary Margaret has had it in her head awhile now that I must be as terrifying as Artemis insists I am.

Today is the day this no longer matters. Mary Margaret flees and makes an instant choice. She is angry. Artemis is supposed to be the leader and Mary Margaret is pissed because she's been shit at making the hard but obvious call: they need more help. They need some Ascended Ones, and there is only one she knows of. So she gets on one train after another, doing the directions by memory.

She arrives in front of the shop with the happy suns painted on the windows and the bright colors standing out against deep red. While spring has officially sprung, the shop windows are still fogging with the baking ovens and the crowd's breathing and talking and laughing, a panoply of glorious humanity nestled in against the cold. Saint John's cathedral is at her back; not the one she used to visit, but it's impossible not to feel a hint of safety, of sanctuary in the shadow of this hulking gray monolith.

She knows instinctively where to look, though she has never been here before. This is a child who sees in gulps. A remarkable mind; Mary Margaret is fun to watch because she is brilliant and often she makes the teenage decision anyhow. Most adults would consider this rooted in stupidity or ego, but I know better. Mary Margaret knows what will matter, in the end, and what will not.

Her eyes light on me right away with a snap and I am already pulling out her chair, patting the back of it.

Hello. I've been expecting you. Come, sit.

Unnerving, she thinks, for more reasons than one. My thin voice arising from within her as though my words are her own thoughts; that she is expected here when she did not know her plans for certain until she was on the second train. Unsettling, yes, but not necessarily dangerous.

She sits as I settle in across from her. *So,* I Say, *you have ignored Artemis and shown up anyway. How do you feel?*

"Fine," she lies.

Try again.

She swallows hard; she can see why Artemis hates this. It's like being transparent. And I Speak about it in such an infantilizing, humiliating way. *I can't help that,* I Say to what she has not told me. *This is who I am. I cannot change it and I'm not sorry about it.* Of course, I am lying. I am sorry about it. I'm sorry about it often, but it doesn't do any good to self-flagellate. *Now, try again. How do you feel about defying your mother?*

"I feel guilty about it. I mean, I do plenty she says not to, this just feels—more personal? Like—she really fucking hates you. But I think I'm making the right call."

Everyone always thinks they're making the right call. Including Artemis in telling you to stay away, including her decision not to come to me sooner about the Hex.

"So you know his name."

I'm Watching all of you.

Mary Margaret shivers. Goose bumps ripple up her arms. "All the time?" she asks.

I Look away when you are doing something private. Do not worry, child, I am not a monster. I do not tell her that I watched her smoke a cigarette in the school bathroom. I do not think about it; I do not think about it. *I can See your body. Your thoughts. Your past. But there is something I cannot do unless you are here, in front of me, and you tell me it is all right to do.*

"And that is?"

I cannot clearly See your future, not more than a few steps, and I cannot experience you the way people experience you when you are casting. For all that, you must say you want to know, even if what I have to say is something you do not like. You must Invite Me In, not just with your words but with your whole soul.

Mary Margaret swallows big and she feels like she's got to fart. A giant fart. A big ripping fart indicative of a nervous stomach. She clenches her ass. She watches me hide a smile and simply ignores what she (rightly) assumes I know. "Yes," she says, with gravitas. "I want that. I want to know."

I try to echo the gravitas. *You are seventeen.*

"Yes," she answers. "But I'll be eighteen soon. In May."

I nod. *In this world, the world in which you have come of age, with the things you have experienced, that is old enough to decide. I will tell you what I tell everyone—my Readings are true, real. And therefore they are terrifying. I will not change what I See to make you comfortable. Are you sure, child?*

Mary Margaret tilts her head up at the word *child*. She is not too proud to use it, nor does she exactly prickle against it. Rather, the word feels like a sweater too small, yet one she still wears, shoving herself inside it. As she should. Why should she give childhood up before she's had a real chance to experience it?

And here she is, giving it up. This is sad and I don't want to do this and also I do. It would be an insult to ask her once again if she's sure. No one is ever ready to come of age anyway.

I begin to shuffle my cards and I reach into her. She is a maelstrom, which is shocking, but not surprising. She is difficult to grab; she flits away from my grasp. It is simply her nature to be Unbridled, Unheld, and somehow I must match her to draw Power. To See clearly.

This has been my city long enough and I know how wind works; I make my Inner Galaxy, my Power, into a corridor of buildings. I coax Her, rather than take hold of Her with my Hands. I know better than to ask someone to go against her nature.

She explores Me. Tentatively touches all my windows and doors. I have made my buildings tall and fun to clack against, so many shutters and window boxes and clangy fire escapes on which to push. A plaything for a smart typhoon.

I look at my cards as I pull Power and I wait for my physical fingers to tingle; that is when I will start shuffling. I breathe deeply into the palms of my hands. I leave the buildings where they are inside me and ground myself into the space. Send Eyes into each small ridge of my fingerprints to See the light sprinkle the back of the deck, then Lips to the tips of my fingers, to brush against the cards, to Feel when they become hot, because that is how I know they are asking to be flipped.

Nothing.

All the ways I usually feel and Feel that the cards are ready to be caressed, to split open like the shells of crabs or the legs of women (back in the days when I still had game, when I still touched and fuck the consequences), to show me the soft insides of reality into which I so desperately crave entry—gone, all gone. I continue to reel Power toward me and still. My deck is nothing but a lifeless stack of sad linen paper, an inanimate object. I frown.

My buildings drop and Mary Margaret opens her eyes, which she closed out of wonder, awe. Who knew a person could be a city? She ponders how big she is, in this Place that is Her.

"What?" she asks, and she flips her hand out flat, curls her fingers in, and examines her nails; she is a teenager once again. Tries to be indifferent even though the shock of my sudden collapse has her just as terrified as if I'd Read.

Something's wrong. I can't See your future. Not even the next moment. Not even the next breath.

"But you didn't even pull cards."

If I had, they would just be cards. No more wondrous than if we were playing Go Fish.

Mary Margaret pouts, theatrical, practiced, but anyone well versed in the language of teenage girls knows performative gestures do not indicate falsehood. Rather, something deep and scary that must be pounded, refined into palatable exaggeration. "Why?" she asks.

Because something is terribly wrong, I answer.

"I know something is terribly wrong. But like. Things have been terribly wrong before. So like. Why now? Why this?"

I cannot help but smile. *Fuck if I know.* But that is not the gravitas Mary Margaret expects and she pouts bigger. *I have lived a long time*, I continue, *and even I am not sure how Power works. But I have my theories.*

Mary Margaret swallows hard. She's long since learned that adults rarely know as much as they think they do. But to hear someone older than all the adults in her life combined admit to not knowing is terrifying. Because even if the scope is narrowed to only the next place she must put her foot, the next step she must take, she is always sure. Even if that next step is to flee, she does it with the unshakable knowledge of her rightness. To hear me say I don't have that, not even for seconds from now—it is as though she expected to see steady earth in front of her and she sees only empty air.

"Then tell me the theories?" With her queer and cobbled-together coven, this would have come out as a statement. But staring into my disguised eyes, the question mark escapes her lips.

Well, I meant it when I said fuck if I know. But in the line of her frightened eyes, I reach for something. *I think, in the end, it has to do with patterns.* This isn't untrue, just half-baked.

"Patterns?"

Humans love patterns; sometimes they even see a pattern where no such meaning exists. If a mortal, a human without Awakened Power, right now were to touch these cards, they would give you a reading. Not a Reading, but perhaps they would sense something large and looming anyhow. I am not human, so I am not fooled. We are in an unprecedented time, which means the billions, trillions, of patterns that make up every second of our world every day no longer apply. Me and my Power, we cannot extrapolate even a guess. Unlike every day before this one, I can See only what is happening right now, and no further.

Mary Margaret touches the small hairs at her temple with an open, graceful hand. She looks toward the front of the coffee shop, out the window and into the bright blue sky. "I hate this," she says.

I know.

She sits for a second. "You're not that scary, you know."

I lean back in my chair. Stretch my arms over my head. I blink and let my eyes show through, the slit pupils, the whites turned the color of egg yolk. I lick my lips and let my tongue curl out of my mouth, too large, too long, and it curves back in on itself as though the handle of a delicate china cup. Mary Margaret's eyes widen. She needs to understand. She cannot treat me like another parent in her life. That is not what I'm here for.

"You're still not that scary," she continues. And she means it. Most witches aren't scared of me, not really. I'm just a stand-in. What they're scared of is their future, and they cannot decide which is worse if true: the idea that I will speak a prophecy and it is unalterable, or the idea that they have the power and the Power to change whatever it is I say.

No one ever asks that, by the way. They never bother to sit with me and parse out the delicate balance of free will and destiny. So I've never had the opportunity to say that when I Look, when I prophesy, it's a mixture of both. I See the effort, the things they try and fail at. Their future neither unalterable, nor something they have control over.

Mary Margaret asks the question I have been expecting, not because I can See any future, but because it's the logical question for her to ask: "What did you say to Artemis, to make her hate you so much?"

That is not mine to share, I reply. *You'll have to ask her.*

Meanwhile: Wilder is trying their best at their own divination. Or, trying to secretly speak to the Hex. Even though they have radically shifted their opinion on his threat level, even though they've agreed to surrender the phone, to surrender their computer, to become *dependent* (they sneer) on Quibble.

Wilder has their own vision, one that is not based on the future but the past. The people who gave their family money believed that they would be fine to never see it again. They even knew Wilder's father was going to make that money disappear. But the second the family did anything with which the lender disapproved, from a steak dinner to going to the movies, the money always became a giant raised eyebrow. Then came the stage of unsolicited advice giving, a parade of "if you would just," and then the cruel assumptions about where the money might be going.

The truth is, it's expensive to be poor. The truth is, Wilder swings from paycheck to paycheck but having only one roommate is above and beyond where they ever thought they'd be. Truth is none of those friends or church families or anyone who lent their father money ever wound up continuing to love the family, was able to continue being truly connected except by strings and conditions. Wilder was forever a charity child.

That is what they fear will become of them and Quibble. Wilder has already transgressed against Quibble in ways that make them uncomfortable to think about. They will, perhaps, think about their casual erosion of his consent every dark morning at 2:16 when they should be asleep. And now, now they'd gone to bat for the Hex and it turned out he was doing something terrifying. Wilder has been on the receiving end of Quibble's scorn now for two good reasons. The kindness in that face activates something deep within them, a belief they are perhaps safer than they imagine, and certainly witnessed. Seen in ways they don't even See themself. And what if, now, he never makes that face at them again? Money ruins everything.

They arrive home in mourning already. They take off their headphones (playing no music but turned on just the same) and listen for language, but their home is quiet. Wilder feels as though a small puppy they'd taken in off the street bit another person. Guilt, responsibility, the need to make it right and nurture at the same time.

They sit on their bedroom floor and open the Ouija board. Candles ring their cross-legged slump, whatever cheap scented options they could find at the bodega. Lit in their bedroom, they smell like having set a '90s-era Cupcake Girl Doll on fire. Burning sugar and plastic.

"Pay attention," they say, and they don't feel quite as stupid as before. "Something amazing is about to happen." They take the stolen planchette from their bag, place it down on the cardboard, and, tentative, place their fingertips on it. Despite the sorrow and the anger and the sense the panic wave will crash upon them from behind, they breathe deeply and reach for their Power. They do not remark upon how fast they find it, but I do. I can't Know, but I do wonder—is this a person destined to be one of the Ascended? It is so frustrating that I cannot See.

Next to the planchette, Wilder places a phone on the board—not theirs. Roommate Andy's, stolen from the dining room table while he's still sleeping. It doesn't matter if the phone is locked, inaccessible; it only matters that it's powered on. I can See the presence, called into the room. I stay back. It grows. The eyes have multiplied—there are eight now, like a spider squatting on the window ledge in the dark.

I wonder if Wilder would be conceptualizing him as a child if they could see him. Treating him like a child is reductive. It's also not entirely incorrect. I watch Wilder's invitation, now with no one else to protect them or to witness the sensations they Feel when they dip their Hands into their Power: this time, of being slapped across the face with bare knuckles, and the absolute pleasure of cocooning oneself in warm sheets fresh from the dryer. Only I experience them.

Wilder takes a deep breath. "Well, Hex. You fucked that one up real good."

i m unable to keep me from looking at her

"When you say you can't, what does that mean?"

I am sick to my stomach and Sick to my Stomach. I can't stop myself from Looking at this coven of Awakened either. What, then, is the difference between the Sibyl and the Hex? *Can't* implies nature. No amount of decision-making will change it. But so many people insist they can't do things when what they mean is won't. Am I one of them?

i could never saw a child fairer than the magpie.

"The magpie?"

i could hardly look back after having conquered the greatest seer

"Who is the magpie?"

the magpie is the genius who is now seventeen and the change.

"The change? Why are you calling Mary Margaret the magpie?"

the seer had given it to her

"The seer—Artemis?"

No.

Wilder waits. Does the Hex feel compelled to fill silence? Wilder isn't sure; chatter is a human impulse, after all.

artemis suspects is true. Artemis is a poor medium

"Then who— Do you mean the Sibyl?"

Smile

Wilder shudders.

My physical body, three trains away from where Wilder sits, shudders too.

"How do you know— You know what, that doesn't matter right now. What matters is what you mean by *can't*."

I is innocent. I could never could never saw plainly. She is very confusing and when she entered: her countenance expressed affection for me. I shall never look away

"But could you look away? Could you look away if you wanted to?"

Smile

"Yes, that's— Hex, I'm here to teach you about self-control." Wilder looks down at the stolen planchette spelling the Hex's words out. They flush, not sure if they're the right person for this lesson.

"Self-control means sometimes we want to do things but we don't do them because—well, it's not just that it will make someone sad, but it will take away their decisions. The sadness isn't the point. The decisions are the point. Everyone gets to make choices. You can't trick people into talking to you, into going on dates with you—how were you even going to show up? You don't have a body! And we're trying to have a society here—in that society, children can't make some choices. Rather than making those choices for them, we just don't make them make those choices." Wilder steps off their figurative soapbox and waits, fingers light on the planchette, for the Hex to spell out his response.

I is innocent. I could never could never saw plainly. She is very confusing and when she entered: her countenance expressed affection for me. I shall never look away

Wilder opens their mouth to argue, to say something, anything that will convince the Hex. To parent him. But they swallow their tongue about it. Because he says, plain as day, *never*. Twice. *Never look away*. They listen to the voice within them, installed by Artemis, that says Mary Margaret is a child and the Hex is not. They say the absolute worst thing they could possibly say: "Quibble is right about you. Artemis too. Sorry, Hex, but if you can't learn self-control about Mary Margaret, you're going to have to go."

Now on the surface of their conscious mind, they mean "go away." But I can see that's not how the Hex takes it. It's not how I would take it either. What they won't admit is that, deep down, they mean the Hex must be destroyed. The Hex, in the Space Between, turns toxic, nuclear green. Then the eyes, all eight of them, blink from blue to the sort of red that means only rage.

But Wilder cannot see that, of course. "The amazing thing has happened," they say. *Fuck yeah*, they whisper-think. They close their circle, put the planchette in a drawer, and tape it shut, power off their roommate's phone.

* * *

A pause, here, after Mary Margaret leaves, for me to sit in this coffee shop and freak out. What on God's sweet green earth does it mean that I cannot Read for the girl, something I have desperately wanted to do since Artemis confirmed the glimpses I'd been receiving unbidden, of a little mouse scurrying around beneath us all, shining with unrealized Power? I tried not to show how upsetting my newfound inability is; I do not think I entirely succeeded. I blink my eyes into their slits and try to See everyone in this place, one by one. The woman who has been coming here for decades, who always wears a fur hat far too late into the season. I can See her past, and the son she lost to cancer and the way she strong-armed every person who lives on her floor to give her money to redo the hallway as an ill-conceived coping mechanism for her grief. Telling everyone she was an interior designer when she wasn't, the neighbors realizing and whispering behind their closed doors that it looks like Halloween out there. I can See all of that.

But when I turn my eye to her future (just the next few moments!) and touch my deck, nothing. Future-Seeing is complex already—so many paths and possibilities and I have to use my Power to figure out which is the right one, if there is a right one. It Feels like my Sight is groggy with sleep, hazy in that morning way before glasses are grabbed and the floor is touched with waking toes. Bleary.

This happens, sometimes, when something is so uncertain for an individual. But two in one day? I turn my Sight to the person at the table behind her. A playwright who always says hi to me, who doesn't find it strange that I write large letters into my notebook and hold it up to say hello back. He is easy with a smile, and he loves this place as much as I do. Looking into even what he will order next, when he is done with the Danish on his plate (he always orders twice), is like Looking through a cold window fogged with warm breath. I can See that he has a future; I do not Know its contents. My cards feel like some dead thing; my fingers never zap or tingle or shoot with heat.

How have I not noticed?

I've been watching these witches and the Hex so closely. Sometimes no one comes to me for weeks, months even. People put off seeing me, like I'm their dentist. And still. Now I'm finding this strange. There are enough Awakened that these long stretches are remarkable. I would have wondered had I not been so busy.

I look up at the regulars again. None of them are Awakened, but all are practiced in explaining away the small synchronicities, tiny miracles that happen around a witch. Instead of Looking, I look. There are many more on their phones than normal, distracted by the endless scroll of the wide world, called by the siren song of longing and engaged enough that they do not notice their own mouths hanging open. They do not feel the sensation of stupor.

The image Arrives to me or arrives to me; I am so flustered I cannot tell if it is Magic or one of imagination (and really, sometimes there is no distinction at all). All the witches usually under my eye just a touch more allured by the pull of their internet. Everyone standing in their kitchens stirring stockpots with their eyes on their phone; everyone walking from their dining room table to their bed not tearing their eyes from the computer balanced on one hand; everyone unable to walk from their front doors to their subway stops without putting in headphones, unable to sit with their own thoughts for even ten minutes, dependent on the voices of others to quell the noise of the void inside them. The Hex has made the digital world into honey, sweet and sticky. He has made them distracted, distracted enough that Artemis is the only one who caught him out. And in turn has made Artemis and her babies into my own personal trap, a timeline I cannot stop watching.

Another image arrives-Arrives. A witch I know well—the one with the bright green glasses frames that she refuses to throw away, gets them refitted with new lenses whenever she needs. One of my Awakened, not Artemis's coven, slurped slowly into her phone. Not her Spirit or her Body—her living, breathing material. Her skin, her eyes, her hair—unspooled? I search for the word to describe this horror show.

To anyone else, the sound I hear would be the mere squealing brakes of a bus, the hydraulic *whoosh* of the doors opening, the beeps as it raises and lowers to let off passengers. But I know it for what it is: a chuckle. Some words, just for me.

unfold to kill.

Ten of Cups

Wilder puts the blue headphones on. They take a deep breath, try to feel the two halves of their rib cage well and truly part ways, get more space into their body. Wilder has done the thing many adults do: used the acute matters to avoid the bigger, deeper changing aspects of their fundamental existence. They're a witch. And mostly what they've done is avoid magic altogether. Yes, they've cast a few spells. But apart from their extremely upsetting descent into Awakening-induced semi-madness, they haven't really experimented with their own Power. It strikes them that if they're viewing the Hex as dangerous, they probably should get acquainted with Magic.

It occurs to Wilder that having a passive Power means they will have to constantly work to stop doing it. Now that they understand where their Hands are, their Mouth is, where I speak to them soft in their Ears, they are starting to build a picture of where they Exist Inside themself. Or exist otherwise, adjacent, and also within. If they can feel both these parts of themself at once, perhaps they can unite and divide their mouth and Mouth, their ears and Ears.

They step into the early-spring sun, jagged as it lances into their squinting eyes. This day really can go fuck itself, they think, and they arrive on the street corner where the bustle flows proper. They breathe once more; space, space, space in their body. Room for their Body to Show Up, to Connect. They press the button to turn the noise canceling off.

A slip and slide cacophony of double-voices waterfalls over them. Immediately they are nauseous. They slam noise canceling back on. Okay, wrong order—much harder to do when they are overwhelmed. Bring their Mouth and their Ears and their Eyes in-line first.

Breathe, breathe, breathe, and, like they are about to cast, they reach for their Body. They can find it so fast now, and a part of them is well and truly pleased. They maneuver until their Lips kiss their lips, their Ears loop around their ears, and they focus on what it Feels like to Unify, be able to use their Ears to hear in the physical world, their Lips to speak words, turn the volume on and down on the whole world like the headphones they're wearing.

Once again, with as much trepidation as confidence, they press the button. Noise canceling off.

They're still overwhelmed. But they don't feel the borders of their body and Body grow porous with panic. A precarious balance teetering with its own exactitude. A gorgeous mastery of Awakened Power, flowing like hot and cold water exchanging the molecular speed of their respective temperatures.

On this walk, Wilder recognizes, by now, some of the usual suspects. Spanish (three flavors: Dominican Republic, Cuba, Mexico), Urdu (two flavors: Deccan, Iran), American Sign Language, Portuguese (two flavors: Brazil and Portugal), French (three flavors: France, Haiti, Quebec), and German (only one flavor: Pennsylvania, of all places, a man selling pickles at the farmers market).

Wilder walks up to that man and asks for the spicy pickles in German.

"Nine dollars," replies the man. In German.

"Nine dollars?" says Wilder, sticker shocked. And it's the Pennsylvania Deutsch that comes out; they feel the press of Haitian French behind them and they shape their Ears all pointed like a husky and direct them forward, to hear only the Pennsylvanian pickle man.

He shrugs and puts them back down. "You know what goes into these, little rascal." Such a weird phrase and at once it makes sense: the man sees them as a child, a child that was once Amish but isn't any longer. He gives them a knowing smile and Wilder feels a little dirty, actually, because it feels like a lie. They also feel extremely Powerful.

It is a very instructive walk, their headphones still on in case they need to slam the noise-canceling wall back up. They learn about an ingressive ascent in Swedish, how even a tiny inhale can mean yes, the breath morphing into words. With their Eyes resting neat behind their eyes, they can tell the Samoans speaking to each other at the poke joint say yes by arching both their eyebrows and they wonder— all Samoans? Or just these men—brothers? They know each other so well.

Even the printed language is easier. Rather than a blurring, melting miasma of words, they are able to blink their Eyes and flip through original and translation as though they're at the optometrist. No longer is the world sleeting onto their exposed eyeballs, into their raw and wide-open ears. They're having fun, the linguistic equivalent of Spider-Man swinging from buildings. They are reaching up to take their headphones off in total and complete confidence when—

Something changes.

A chuckle. So close. Wilder whips around, convinced someone is standing right up on their left shoulder. They turn so fast they feel their scapula pull. When there is no one there, they realize where the chuckle came from. Inside the headphones. This shouldn't be possible—the headphones aren't connected to their phone. But what does *possible* even mean anymore?

"Hex?" Wilder whispers.

Somehow they hear it: *:)*

What sound does a smile make? *Ping ping mail-delivery-swoop.* But clear as the horizon on a cloudless day, they know what the Hex means. The smallest smile of a closed parenthesis. The piercing, unblinking eyes.

And then: 😺

An auditory grinning devil: *ping ping ping ping mail-delivery swoop. Yummm.*

Wilder gasps. Not because this interpretation of "language" and "understanding" is shocking (though it certainly is). But because they feel—not the helium-feeling, but not-not the helium-feeling. They Feel their Body Touched by a million-billion bluebells, the petals at once organic and electric. Like being licked by static shock. Then a push, a squeeze, as though their water-air-filled Body is a twisted balloon, tied into something altogether different. Far from painful, the redistribution of themselves is orgasmic. A growing pressure that makes them wish to be popped; they long to explode. How long has it been since they've fucked? Is this what it felt like? Not quite, not quite, this is something else. Rending, annihilation, yes. A shape change.

And then the sensation surpasses bursting. They feel ... punctured, yes, but not penetrated. They Feel something—the Hex, they understand—telescoping into them. Unfolding. And they Feel his Body, too, for the Hex does have a Body, though not a body. They Feel the looming giantness of him, the weight of the internet pressing down, and they Hear a constant agony-loop of language, language, language, lang-gu-agdge, words words words. *Hello hello hello hello.*

Hello world.
Hello Wilder.
want want need. query. what is you? query. what is i? hello hello hello world.

Wilder Feels numbers. They Feel tics and taps and concepts.

Without forming an internal sentence about it, they understand this is both what it would be like to cast with the Hex and that the Hex is currently trying to possess them. I recognize only a small piece of this—the force of it, yes, and the desire to connect. But there is a tenderness to this merge attempt with Wilder that wasn't present with me. When the Hex downloaded me, I could sense only a carnal, feral hunger for knowledge, understanding, tinged, perhaps, with a desire to scare me. In this, I sense—yes, the desire to obliterate Wilder, something so fucking angry, and the need to consume them as well, and also: to take, to shelter, to protect, to—yes—possess.

In this moment, Wilder knows: if they let the Hex in, they will never be lonely again. Neither one of them will. And:

They want it. They want it so badly, this intimacy beyond what anyone could ever find in the world of humans. A conjoining of identities into a blissful gelatinous pseudo-organism, a brotherhood of chaos and pre-ego, to be a Body of Water instead of a suffering person.

Thank fucking Christ Wilder is so goddamn avoidant or they would be a cyborg and probably very, very evil. As it stands, it is precisely because they want it so, so badly that they refuse it.

Without thinking, they inhale, so small—a yes in another language, but in their own, in their soul? It is only breathing.

They bounce out of this ecstasy back into the street, back into the flow of every word, every breath, and once again, they are an I, a person, with a solid boundary between themself and the world, reinforced by everyone else communicating their I-thoughts and their I-feelings in a thousand thousand mother tongues. They fling the headphones off into the gutter. Wilder knows if the Hex offers them this Sweet Eradication again, they will not be able to refuse. Until the coven knows how to destroy him, Wilder is certain of only one thing: they have to run, hide.

Seven of Swords

A rtemis!" Rico shouts up to the window, and Artemis jumps—it's the wrong day. The window isn't even open. Mary Margaret isn't here to gently make fun of her. Artemis is sitting at the dining room table, filling out a spreadsheet to send to her bosses—which billiards players have paid, the scores for each game in each bar. Usually, she would be doing this on a computer; today, she is doing it by hand, her own powered-down computer piled in the closet with everyone else's. She plans to tell her bosses she is having computer trouble, that once it's resolved, she will input this stopgap measure, that their system will go entirely uninterrupted. She wonders how long that will last—maybe they will try to throw money at a problem and buy her a computer. Maybe one of them will get exasperated and do it himself.

Either way, she will wear on the goodwill she has built by being autonomous, reliable, and largely someone they don't talk to. How long will it be before they fire her? Rico interrupts this swirling anxiety coupled with complete focus, and she is so surprised her body twitches. She has reading glasses from the Duane Reade perched on her nose, ugly things, and she flings them off, which is a silly response. It's not as though Rico can see her.

She hauls the window open, leans out over the fire escape. Despite the day, she comes out smiling. Rico is such a source of sun as the city grows dark and the lights wink on. But when she sees Rico's face, her smile fades.

He looks different than when he's performing, but not by much. His clothes are warmer and more plentiful, but not less flamboyant. A red coat; a checkered scarf. He is still an exaggerated man; some people just have a large presence to them. His unpainted eyebrows are still expressive, and right now they are open with sadness. His large mouth is panting, despairing, a far cry from the usual easy turn-up at the corners. He has clearly cried. "Artemis," he shouts again. "I need to talk to you."

She almost shouts down, "Why? What's wrong?" But she realizes Rico might shout back, that she might accidentally ask him to yell his business, and he would. He is guileless. Instead, she says, "Okay."

Down in the alley by the dumpsters, she doesn't know the appropriate way to receive his face with hers. He is so stricken and she has no clue about why. What she does, naturally, is arc her eyebrow in a question, and she internally winces at what she imagines the expression to be—parental. The last thing she wants to do is be parental to, or even around, Rico. She is expecting, perhaps, one of the Smoking Guns is sick or hurt or worse—something large and bad. Instead: "Artemis, if you wanted to dump me, I gave you plenty of opportunities."

"I— What?" Artemis's face shifts from stern to straight up confused. "Rico, I haven't broken up with you."

Rico's face sour-scrunches. "Yes, Artemis, you did. You can't really walk this back—" He takes his phone from his pocket and gestures to its screen. "It's brutal."

Artemis gasps, understanding. "Rico, listen. I haven't touched my phone in at least a day and I'm sure of it. Whatever you got, whatever he sent you, it's not from me! I didn't type it, didn't say it, didn't think it."

He flaps his hand emphatically back toward the screen. "Artemis! It's in our text thread! You— Wait, he? Who's he? Artemis, what's going on. Are you in trouble?"

Artemis regrets not initiating him more deeply, regrets not explaining, in detail, what it means to exist around Power before this moment. She could have, should have, performed a light show around him, cast a spell on him, something other than the dumb rock still sitting on the bar at Jacqueline's, anything. It isn't that he doesn't know she is a witch, that Mary Margaret is a witch, that her family, her coven, all possesses Awakened Power. But keeping her worlds apart wasn't without reason! She never wanted him to fear her or fear for her, so Artemis has been vague on the details. He cannot picture, therefore, what it looks like practically, what it might mean for something else to Awaken.

Artemis explains everything. She narrates the details as best she can—what it looks like to watch Quibble arrive in a burst of fire, hearing Wilder switch between three languages while watching them light like a struck match, the absolute futility of trying to figure out what Mary Margaret has stolen and from whom (though this he has seen more of than the others), the Hex. Both Artemis and Rico slide their backs down the wall and sit directly on the cold, dirty ground. Artemis can feel the spring in the pavement; not as frigid as before. But warmth is no comfort as she's watching Rico's face crescendo into the loudest confusion. She even calls light to her hands, visible to people other than her. With alarm, she realizes how tired she feels after. She hasn't used her Power very much and it shouldn't feel this weighty; is it just the psychic toll of looming danger? She hopes so. Rico's face uncurls from a question mark to an exclamation point. But he does not flinch away, lets her finish the whole story. He lets what passes for silence in an ever-sounding city envelop them, his face like the glass of a fish tank, so, so easy to watch his internal workings. Transparent, unguarded. She loves this about him. It is one of the things she finds most difficult about him, too.

Finally, he speaks. "My instinct is to trust you, Artemis, it always is. But my problem is that right now, I don't trust me. I feel crazy for believing you." Rico pauses and puts his hand on his chest and presses, hard. He takes a deep breath. "I think I need some space, Artemis. I believe you; I believe you every single time we speak. I don't always understand it. But I think I need a break. From doing that. For a little while."

Artemis feels as though the alleyway plummets from under her feet. She can feel the red blush in her, on her chest and her face and under her beard. Even her ears feel hot—anger, shame, inadequacy, loneliness all spinning together. "Okay," she says, her voice as small as she feels. Because there is nothing else to say. Rico squeezes her hand and walks away. She turns and trudges back up the stairs.

She lets herself open the door while crying. She lets herself collapse upon the couch, usually Mary Margaret's territory, but hell, she's not here anyway. She folds herself in two and sobs, two heaving sobs, before the sensation of being watched hits her, on the skin and in her Power. She leaps up and turns toward the window, which she'd left open, and she has called Power to her fingertips in a blaze of light before she can even think of what she's going to use it for, doesn't matter if she's tired, if calling the light downstairs felt hard. Contrary to Wilder or the Magpie, it's taken her years and years and years to be able to access her Power like this, to know herself so deeply. To do it even sad, even exhausted.

The child perches on the windowsill, feet resting on the back of a dining room chair and knees drawn up to her chest. Mary Margaret looks more like a bird than Artemis has ever seen her, which is saying something because she always has an avian quality to her—always ready to take flight. Artemis lets the Power drop from her fingers. She is torn between saying "oh thank Goddess" and "oh no," for she is deeply embarrassed by her own dramatics. Her hands fly to her face, and she dabs her under-eyes with her fingers, a little less gentle on her own skin than she intends.

"He dumped you. Didn't he," Mary Margaret says.

She'd been ready to ask what I'd refused her—*why does Artemis hate me so much?* What had I said to Artemis, long ago? But Mary Margaret holds her tongue. The question will be there another day.

There are a million sharp responses Artemis can think of, some along the lines of "none of your business," or "don't worry about it." Rather than deploying any of them, she sinks back onto the couch. The crying is over. "How did you know?"

Mary Margaret moves gracefully, hops off the sill, walking lightly. "I know what getting dumped looks like," she says. She settles next to Artemis and puts a hand on her shoulder. The role reversal is deeply confusing for both. But they sit in it, sit in the awkward, until Artemis finally squeezes Mary Margaret's wrist, gets up, and goes to bed.

Five of Pentacles

At the same time Rico breaks up with Artemis:

I f Quibble hadn't destroyed his own phone, he would notice now a moment where it ceases to work. And if that were the case, he would have more forewarning than I have. As it is, I stand back. I see a swirling dark with many bright blinking eyes misting into Here, the Space Between. The cloud gathers on the periphery, a haunting fog.

I have left the coffee shop and I will not return until this is over. Even in a relatively disconnected place, the Hex can see me. Can find my body. Each time I kick back in my seat, add milk, take a sip, each time I stop my Watching and turn back to myself, I can See him there, watching me in return. And I know better now than to think myself uninteresting to him. So I have left.

Quibble cannot see the same and he believes himself to be safe. He earnestly believes if he makes all the right decisions, the morally correct ones, everything will turn out okay. Not engaging with the Hex is good and right and just; he assumes that his life will turn out in good and right and just ways. I don't need to be able to See into the future to know that it will not go the way he plans.

He sleeps a restless sleep. I keep an Eye on him, worried in a way

I find curious. I Watch his resting face, slackened in the dark, interrupted again and again by tensing of the eyebrows, a purse of the mouth. And then he is awake and staring at the ceiling. In the morning, he will go back to Artemis's. Perhaps even before she's up. And then they will make a plan. Make a plan to end this thing, to vanquish it. This imagining allows him some minutes more with his eyes closed as he drifts, on the surface of slumber. Then he wakes again. Repeats.

He wakes for keeps to a knock on the door. It is morning—later than he'd wanted to be up, but not late enough that a knock on the door is appropriate. He stumbles around and pulls his pants over his boxers, hopping up and down as he runs through a calming exercise. He wonders if he will ever be rid of his anxiety, ever find a way to exist outside the framework of perpetual mental health maintenance (I do not need my Power to know that no one ever does).

It had been like this. Back then. He'd been old enough to be home by himself. Exactly like— No. He reassures himself as he locates a shirt—literally any shirt—that once one's parents are dead, rarely does it happen a second time. He smirks. Only people with dead parents find those jokes funny, and even then only a special subset of those people. He generally keeps these jokes to himself; he's seen Artemis's stricken look a few too many times before she crams it down, wipes it away, laughs a too-boisterous laugh.

He finally gets to the door, groggy, and wrenches it open. Three beefy men in black polo shirts with red logos that say *We Move You* on the breast pocket stand before him. One has a clipboard. "Hi, we're the movers that Ms. Colleen McKormick ordered for her things. She mentioned there was a house sitter here—don't worry, she already took care of the tip for us."

At the sound of the name he thought he'd buried long ago, he feels like he will vomit. "Movers?" he says, confused. "Movers where?"

Legally, Colleen McKormick no longer exists. How did that person order movers?

"If she didn't tell you, we certainly can't." The movers shuffle past him. The two without the clipboard begin assembling boxes at break-neck speed.

Quibble blinks dumbly. As they begin discussing how to pack his barware, if they have enough paper to wrap the glasses just right or if they might need to go pick up some more, he snaps into some kind of action. "Wait, stop. No. I'm Colleen McKormick."

All three of them halt and look directly at him. Quibble realizes how big they all are. He's tall, but they're large. And there are three of them. He'd been about to explain, to say "or at least I was." But then he witnesses himself: he witnesses the balding head, the facial hair he has not yet shaved off today, the flat chest with near-invisible scars (the best surgeon money could buy). He'd never really had consequences for outing himself before. He swallows his tongue. He doesn't say it, doesn't say, "I'm trans."

"Yeah right, pal," one of the movers says. "Look, if she didn't tell you your house-sitting gig ended today, take that up with her."

Quibble's mouth is dry and tastes like the roiling of his empty stomach. "Sure," he says. He retreats into the master bedroom. He feels like he knows what's going on, and the knowledge doesn't comfort him. He is terrified.

For the first time since the Hex began in earnest, he turns on his computer. He notices that his mail client has an additional Gmail plugged in—Colleen McKormick's old email. Quibble's old email. As old as it is, it's full of new correspondence: movers, bank password reset notifications, his co-op board, Realtors—

Quibble whimpers. He hugs his arms to his stomach, thinking if maybe he squeezes himself tight enough, he might hold himself together. The movers are talking in the other room and then they are not; surely they are thinking something—that he's some homeless boyfriend the eccentric Colleen is dumping, the kind of contactless breakup only a very rich person can pull off. He tries to sign into his bank accounts. The username or password is not recognized.

Quibble closes the bedroom door before he has his meltdown. He sits on the floor rocking back and forth, flapping his hands, trying any kind of movement to still his racing heart. He feels particulated, atomized, his steadiness broken entirely apart by two warring forces—that he has absolutely no material resource, nothing he cannot immediately stuff into a backpack and carry out of here, no money and no apartment by the looks of it. His parents' apartment. Their things in the closet. All of it, all of it gone.

And also the sensation of being digitally detransitioned. He hadn't known it was something that could be done. He hadn't expected it. He'd changed his name, his gender marker, but it was so easy for this *thing* to use the old name, the deadname, to bring it back to life and animate it and make it haunt. Everyone was so quick to believe in this ghost. Maybe didn't even wonder. And when the eccentric McKormick heir asks you to do something, gives you cash instantly for it—of course.

When he feels like he can get himself up, Quibble opens his text messages on his laptop. And there it is, what he is already expecting, the incomprehensible number:

:)

Eight of Cups, Reversed

If either Artemis or Mary Margaret were sleeping, they would wake to the most stressful alarm clock: the wet ripping sound that announces Quibble's trespassing. Mary Margaret considers whether she should ream him for walking right into what is effectively her bedroom; she's been thinking a lot about boundaries and privacy, what the adults around her would be willing to sacrifice for it, and she's gotten herself worked up. But she is also exhausted, and it is Quibble. Her train of thought halts when she hears the second sound. What can only be described as a keen wraps around the sound of his magic. High, too high to be anything but real grief. This second sound launches Artemis out of bed and brings her running with a baseball bat in hand.

Artemis has been half-dreaming of monsters. Hulking shadows that, when they get ahold of wrists and ankles, tear her and her coven apart, or else crack each witch's jaw open wide and crawl inside their bodies, popping their bleeding eyeballs from their skulls and jerkily puppeting their still-full corpses. It has been a violent night behind her eyelids and she has not slept deeply. She felt, always, like those monsters lurked in the room with her, just out of sight behind her head. And then—

What could it hurt? I am not touching anything in physical reality after all. I send Artemis a dream in this toss-turn pseudo-sleep. The real monster, the real danger. I send her my vision of the witch spun into her own phone like an unraveling sweater. Unfolding. Unfold to kill.

When a Seer half-dreams of anything that rends, she grabs a baseball bat whether she is confident in its use or not.

She is convinced that something has come in Quibble's place or on Quibble's back or has possessed him, because that sound isn't a sound she has heard Quibble make. But when she arrives with the bat raised high enough over her head to set the chandelier swinging, she sees that it is, indeed, Quibble, who sinks to the ground with his head in his hands.

Artemis doesn't drop the bat. "Quibble, look at me?"

Quibble doesn't respond, keeps making that horrible sound. Artemis wonders if this is part of my prophecy. If it were, if possession by a monster were part of it—it wouldn't be the most twisted prophecy I ever gave. But it would rank high, and she would have even more cause to despise me.

"Quibble, look up at me or so help me Goddess, I will knock you out first and ask questions later."

"What?" Quibble manages to ask through his wail. He does look up, mostly to see what on earth Artemis could be talking about. And Artemis looks deep into those eyes—red-rimmed, panicked, but undeniably human. The bat flops first to her side, then tumbles from her unclenched fist. She sits on the ground next to him just as someone knocks on the door.

All of them jump. Quibble's eyes widen from a tear-soaked squint. "Don't answer it," he says. "Don't you dare answer it—no!" He tries to stop Mary Margaret, who is already up. "Mary Margaret, don't, we don't know who it is."

"We have a peephole," she says, drier than a desert in July. Mary Margaret checks to make sure it's not some kind of—she doesn't know what—then unbolts the door while Quibble whimpers.

Wilder walks in, carrying a cat carrier filled with a mewling Lady Anastasia.

"A cat?" Artemis is exasperated. But one look at Wilder's hollow face keeps her from continuing with "A fucking cat?" A lightly squealing Mary Margaret gets the Lady out of the carrier before Artemis's attention is even fully back on Quibble.

It takes a lot for Quibble to tell them everything. Coaxing and questioning and, at one point, Mary Margaret even puts the Lady Anastasia in his lap. He absently pets her, but he remains shaking, shaken.

"Okay, okay," Artemis says, somber and breathing deeply. Part of her had grown accustomed to Quibble's money. "We need to get out. We clearly poked it in the eye."

Wilder sighs, relieved they won't have to make the argument.

"Quibs." Artemis softens her voice again. "We have to go. You have to carry us. All of us. Through There. Can you do it?"

Quibble is hugging himself on the floor in the middle of the pink apartment, softly lit among the lamps and silk scarves, gasping for breath. "Gone," he says. "All of it—all of it is gone. Jesus Christ, how can it all be gone?" But money is not all this is about. His past was resurrected, paraded before him, as a hologram of someone long dead, brought back without their knowledge or consent to dance and sing at the behest of a cruel master. The panic comes from nakedness, vulnerability, violation, each amplifying the other. A feedback loop that no amount of therapist-recommended exercises can break.

Wilder sits down next to him, Mary Margaret on the other side. Mary Margaret reaches out and holds his hand. Quibble registers distant surprise. Mostly Mary Margaret is usually a neutral house cat toward Quibble. Not clawing at him too much, but not exactly caring if he's there.

Which is to say that Quibble doesn't really understand Mary Margaret. Doesn't understand the degree to which "fixture" means "family," doesn't understand she isn't ever quite sure how to demonstrate "family." She and Artemis share a language. They have in common a testing. Like putting one's foot on half-frozen ice progressively harder or poking someone's bruise over and over to see if she'll leave. An acceptance that if she does leave, well. Better off anyway, to find that out now.

And then after the test is passed: they have also, in common, gentle insults all the way down. It is how Mary Margaret does family with other teens, queer ones, brown ones, trans ones. It is how she does family with Artemis. But Quibble is a soft man, gentle and steady, and Mary Margaret doesn't have the emotional vocabulary to describe him back to himself, which is what she figures doing family means.

And sometimes. Sometimes she is wildly envious of him. Mary Margaret cannot imagine owning more than what is piled in the two bags, propped in the corner and sitting on the bathroom sink. And not only that—an eschewing. A desire to *not* be like him, either. Both are true at the same time, because feelings are like pentacle coins. Two sides, back-to-back, always. They are physical impossibilities of flouted mutual exclusivity. Complicated. And uncomplicated just a little by the current reality: Quibble and Mary Margaret now have the exact same amount of stuff. Whatever they are currently carrying, right here, right now, in this apartment. Mary Margaret knows what having nothing feels like. And so. She holds his hand. And in this moment, she feels the welling in her chest that means she is doing family.

Wilder also does family in their own way; they rub Quibble's back. They know the feeling of the body dying when it is not. Doing family is newer to them, even, than it is to Mary Margaret. What little evidence of the action-feeling they have has lain fallow for more than a decade. But they can Feel it as they do it, like filling a jar and slowly trickling water onto the roots of a plant. Quibble's shoulders continue to heave for minutes on minutes, and Wilder knows. Knows that each minute feels both like a year and a second for Quibble. But eventually his shoulders, his back, relax into their hand. His breathing slows to something like normal. His face isn't wet. He hasn't cried through it.

Artemis watches on. In fact, this is how she does family. The lookout, the planner, the protector. While everyone else crumbles, someone has to be the shelter. She Feels the expansion, the awareness, that means she is doing family, too, and it looks nearly cruel but it isn't. Every role is necessary. It all counts.

She sits on the floor in front of Quibble and grabs both his knees. "You're okay," she murmurs. "You're okay." The background for all of it, this gentle crackle, warm and rushing. "You're safe and you're okay. Remember to breathe, Quibs, fill your whole stomach up. We need you back, we need to move. There you go. There you go."

Finally, he is ready. He looks at the group with haunted eyes. "I can do it. I can get all of us through There. But"—he looks at Artemis, the leader—"where do we go?"

Artemis blinks slowly, like a sunning cat. An excellent question. One she knows she has the answer to, but she isn't sure how she knows. There is a pull in her. At once, she closes her eyes and through the fingers still resting lightly on his knees, Quibble can feel the drawing of Power accompanying the intake of breath. "Pay attention," she exhales. "Something amazing is about to happen."

Instinctively he puts his feet and Feet on the ground and grows roots. Roots through the floor, through every apartment, all the rooms waking below them as the sun begins to strike the eastern side of the building, peeking over rooftops. He feels every shower turning on, every coffee maker popping to life, and the ground outside, even the pavement feels the morning as it buzzes. The metro's rumble. The antennae on roofs carrying invisible signals. He, the plant, absorbs it all and funnels it to Artemis, who is grateful for two things—for the Power itself and to feel that Quibble, though certainly showing his cracks, is still himself. "Here is the amazing thing," he says, the warble of tears still quavering in his throat.

She focuses on the hot coal of surety in her gut, and when she breathes Power in on it, the image flickers brighter. She knows it is a place she has not yet been, not yet seen. She knows there is a person there. She. Not they. But Artemis's gaydar isn't broken. She has that familiar feeling of a bright candle that smells like beeswax and sweet grass. This one, too, is family, somehow. Connected, somehow. And that is the way forward—to follow the Knowing. She Sees mountains. A thin white line against the dark of the unknown, tracing a stately range in the distance.

I can't See anything at all, and I am furious. Is it to do with being human? Being close in the metaphorical sense? I try, frustrated, to flip through Visions upon Visions, to access the myriad Images and Sounds and Smells I normally can, and still: I cannot tell who is on the other end of this tin-can telephone line.

"The amazing thing has happened," says Artemis.

"Fuck yeah," everyone murmurs, as though they are saying "amen."

"Could you follow it?" Quibble asks. "If we just—started? Could you get in front and lead the way?"

Artemis raises an eyebrow. "I don't know—can I get in front of you? Is that allowed?"

"We're—" Quibble takes a deep breath in, exhales with a whistle, his voice cracking on a high-pitched *woo*. "We're going to find out." Artemis goes to pack while Quibble stands up to stretch.

They don't sit in a circle this time. They stand in a V formation, Artemis at the point, Mary Margaret with her backpack on and Wilder flanking, the Lady Anastasia's carrier tight in their hands.

"Pay attention," Quibble says. "Something amazing is about to happen." He stands to the side, eyeing how large a hole he'll have to rip. How much Power he thinks it will take, how much he can possibly take in. This is like holding one's breath. Something one trains for; something that could cause death if calculated poorly. Keeping one's air close while diving deep. Quibble breathes like an athlete, steady. He has no room for panic if he wants to hold his Power.

Somehow, the panic is literally leaving his body, as in being extracted, not the usual ebbing. He Feels Wilder pulling on it. To pull a sensation from a body isn't part of Wilder's natural skill set, and yet they pull the panic from him steadily, their Hand holding tension on the tide like a knitter pulling a wriggling string taut. Quibble smiles. "Did I know you could do that?" he asks.

"No. But neither did I."

Quibble smiles. "There's the next amazing thing."

Wilder nods. It is more difficult than they thought, because where do they put that panic? They feel like they will liquefy the floor if they dump it down into the wood, or shatter any container in which they try to store it.

They know only one place that might hold it—their own body. And so they begin to shake with it as Quibble grows more steady, drawing Power up through the floor. And then he is sure the way an acrobat is sure before springing onto their hands. He pulls his open palms apart and rips, walking forward. A deep gash opens in the air, the familiar purple globules of whatever the planes are made of seeping out, popping like soap bubbles. At once, the quartet steps in. Wilder, panic-stricken and motion sick, hugs the carrier tight against their chest. They stride as though they will not throw up; they know they will absolutely throw up.

Quibble brings up the rear, shaping his Power into a huge, round boulder on which they all stand, a strange Ground. Wilder feels less like a kite pulled through tenuously. But they—and everyone—can sense the edge. Quibble most of all, for he's taken the place that requires the most balance. He is tipping slightly backward as he steadies the ball, eyes to the sky, Here, an unsettling expanse of dark so bright it hurts his sinuses. "Okay, Artemis, go, start walking and I'll—" Suddenly, something—someone?— swims into his view.

He is large and noseless, with two bugging eyes, faceted and strange. The many eyes consolidated now into two bulbous lenses. The body, an oil slick of Power and numbers: 101001 runs like blood in veins and coheres into a sticky mass. He is so big, like the witches are ants and he is a gargantuan, terrible boy looking down at them. Contemplating their meaningless existence. They see the thing I have been Seeing, his amorphous haze concretized because they are in the Space Between with their bodies.

hello, it projects. And this must be his understanding of what it means to be a gender, to be a man. He has constructed his body, too, and the men he is made of are horror-men. Terrorists in their communities, their families, their own lives. It is important to remember that's what the Hex knows. That's what he means when he says my pronouns are man. *hello handsome*, he continues. *tell me how you are.* It-he cracks a grotesque mouth-thing open, dripping with glooping, drooling strings of binary. *hello: you, the hapless victims.* It-he reaches an appendage (a tongue?) toward them and instinctively I reach out, try to shield them with my Hands. But I pull back. No. I might crush them. Or feed the Entity Power. Knowledge. Make it worse again.

Wilder scrabbles backward. They can barely breathe. It is a wonder their heart hasn't simply stopped. The body isn't built for Here. And yet. Here they are. Carrying more panic than they ever before have. Their feet begin to slip off the round Power and Artemis reaches out, catches their shirt. Their hands almost release the Lady Anastasia, but they wouldn't ever do that.

"Quibble!" Artemis shouts over the wind, her own eyes widening as the wave of Hex climbs. Height of buildings. Height of tsunami. Wide and encompassing and the tongue is coming closer to Artemis. Everyone can see what happens as the gross appendage approaches: her fingers begin to lengthen, her skin begins to lift away from muscle, bone. She feels the joints in her knuckles, her wrists, on the verge of popping. "Quibble," she shouts, afraid, "get us out of Here! Now!"

Absent panic, Quibble is made of fury. This is the fucking Hex on his whole life. Stolen his everything. Has made his past a zombie to eat his present. What he does is entirely instinct: he picks up the ball of his Power—their only floor!—as he screams, spit flying from his mouth. The other three witches whirl toward him as the ground disappears from under their feet. They can see all of Quibble's teeth, his canines far more pointed than they ever noticed before. They can see down his raw-screaming throat.

Mary Margaret: a primal fear. Something deep in her that equates family with danger recoils. And she feels something slip from her Hands, something she hadn't realized she was grasping desperately. She is sorrow now. She mourns something she will have to work very hard to get back.

Artemis is protection. She is mother, even as she tries to resist it. She is collected even as she begins to tumble through the expanse. "Quibble! Quibble, get it together!" She doesn't know what will happen if they all fall through Here. She tries to swim as she swan-dives toward the screaming boy. She wants to grab his face, bring him back to himself. They all are falling now, Quibble included, and still he screams, hands balled into fists. Artemis breathes, blinks, tries to See a way out without him. She Sees only the strange press of live darkness. "Quibble, we're Here! You're dropping us!"

Wilder is fear, too, and filled to bursting. They explode. The panic they'd been holding releases and flings in all directions, a writhing sack of worms, and everyone shrieks as the panic gets on and in them. The Hex is hit and he halts the progression of his grotesque appendage, holds it up to his own strange eyes, examines it. *Query for i. what do they mean?*

Quibble finds his own panic back in him and snaps out of his rage to find himself falling with his family. His face softens instantly, horrified by his own actions and in the same bursting motion, he rips a hole below them. They fall. They fall.

They slam. Wind knocked out of them. A roof. Artemis's roof. Blessed material reality. They gasp into the air, physical and winter-spring once more. Artemis recovers first. "Quick," she says, still rasping. "Quick. Back inside. It can probably see us. Down the ladder. Through the window. Mary Margaret, can you unlock the window from outside?"

Mary Margaret nods, wordless. Fear still on her skin, clinging like pond slime.

The Chariot

We can't use my car to leave," Artemis says, decisive. A strange, doomsday calmness considering the car was, likely, their only way to get out of New York City. "It'll already know what my license plate is. If it can steal everything Quibble owns, it can certainly figure out what numbers are on the back of my car."

With each *it*, Wilder's face tightens more, but they keep their mouth shut. Still, they wonder: how much of gendering the Hex correctly is about respecting the Hex, and how much of it is about self-respect, about what kind of people they themselves would like to be? "I think that means we're going to have to go on foot. We're going to have to figure out—"

"We're not walking out of this crusty-ass city on foot. I'll ruin my shoes." Mary Margaret speaks as she stretches her long body over both couch arms, arching her back. She sits up, smirking. All the bird in her gone, all her fear eaten by feline bravado.

Artemis intentionally unclenches her jaw and tries to respond with compassion. "Not sure we have a choice, darling."

"We absolutely have a choice. It's like none of you have ever done crimes before, my fucking goodness."

Artemis's jaw clenches again and no amount of intentionality can unclench it. "We are not 'doing crimes,' Mary Margaret."

"Needs must," she singsongs, and she skips up from the couch, is at the front door before anyone else can react. "Be right ba—"

"I swear, Mary Margaret, you are not—"

As though a hissing cat, Mary Margaret whirls around with teeth bared, anger in her young eyes that makes everyone take a step back. "Well, which is it? I'm almost eighteen, I have responsibilities, and I'm a member of the group? Or I'm a kid and I can't make a fucking decision about when I'm willing to take a risk?" She puts her hands on her hips and squares her shoulders. "You said it yourself, you feel like we're supposed to be"—she gestures around her, looking into the middle distance—"somewhere. But you don't know where that is! Sure, we could walk out over any one of these bridges and be there in a day, it's possible. Or it could take months. And we can see it's getting smarter. We don't have months. Your option is stupid, Artemis, and mine isn't. It's a manageable risk. I am very, *very* good at not getting caught." She doesn't want to give away her salt trick, but she will if she has to. "You said 'we use the tools we have.'"

There are two full seconds of silence before Artemis clears her throat. "What is your plan?"

Mary Margaret's face changes quickly, from a demonic snarl to a proud smile. "We need a jalopy."

Artemis raises an eyebrow. "A jalopy?"

"I thought you'd like that term better than 'piece of shit.' A car that is so dilapidated that we worry about one of the tires falling off on the highway. It won't have a single scrap of computer in it." With that, Mary Margaret turns and walks out of the apartment. Everyone stands, stunned, listening to her footsteps march down the stairs.

Artemis turns to Wilder and Quibble. "Does—does that mean she's going to steal a car?"

And that is how the witches find themselves following a teenager into the mouth of grand larceny.

It is broad daylight outside and the group slinks along the walls as though it were night, doing their best imitations of their own shadows. They look so fucking stupid.

Mary Margaret, meanwhile, strides proudly down the sidewalk, pulling her jacket around her. The others can't see it but she rolls her eyes; she's not going to steal it *now*; she's just going to find it now. Then she's going to watch it until dark. And *then* she's going to steal it. She's going to steal it between 11:15 and 11:35 p.m., when the NYPD's shifts are starting and ending for maximum confusion. Her gaze settles on each and every car, assessing first to see that they have a keyhole on the driver's side door. No smart keys, nothing keyless. Basic-ass keyholes. Then, supposing it has one, zooming out to see how much a piece of shit the whole thing is.

She rejects several nice cars. She avoids anything with a million parking tickets on it—a sign that someone is rich and doesn't give a shit about the penalty, considers this their parking fee.

Finally she finds it—the very shittiest-looking bag of ass she can find. It is long and hearse-like, and she steals a glance without moving her head to confirm there's no casket in the back. It isn't black, either, so it's probably repurposed; mostly brown, with huge white chips in the paint, scratches. She doesn't turn around; she keeps going several more blocks.

The group trails behind her. They look like sneaking cartoons. Finally she stops, turns, walks back to them. "Please don't—do—whatever it is you think you're doing." They all look sheepish. "It's going to be hours yet, and we need cash for the tolls, when we can't avoid them. Leave me the fuck alone until like eleven at night."

She flourishes her hand and pulls from her Space a creased paperback, the cover soft at the corners and wearing thin, torn in places. She crosses the street, walks back to the general jalopy area, and sits on a bench. She only looks like she's reading if an observer isn't paying close attention—her eyes don't move back and forth. She pulls her jacket around her tight.

Quibble throws his hands in the air. "Well, our bank accounts are out of the question and I don't have money anymore so."

"We know, Quibble, we know." Artemis's eyes are still kind, even when she's blazing angry and fucking terrified. "I suppose we can steal from some of my bars? The ones with the drop boxes won't think anything of me grabbing the envelopes." She winces as people walk by with phones. The lights are so intense now. Artemis Eyes the catch spiral circling on them. She gulps.

"I have a coffee can with a couple hundred in my go bag," says Wilder, and everyone turns and stares at them.

"Don't you get paid on the internet?" Artemis asks.

"Yeah, but like, you can't trust banks for everything. You can't put all your eggs in one basket. I grew up with a coffee can. It's in my backpack. It's in your apartment."

"Wait, Wilder—why is it in your backpack? Why did you bring your cat? What did he do to you?" Artemis asks.

"I'm not talking about it," they reply. Because they do not want to think about the invitation to merge or they will cry. And yes, they also think that the coven will like them less if they confess the Hex's attempted possession, doubly so if they confess their temptation. "The only thing you need to know is no more headphones." Despite all Quibble's current feelings-storm, his eyebrows rise. "I came here this morning prepared to convince you that we had to leave," Wilder continues, and Artemis internally sighs with relief. "Y'all. I'm really sorry—"

"It's okay," both Artemis and Quibble say at the same time, and both of them smile.

"You don't have to," Quibble continues. He's still bristly, upset, traumatized—but he cannot imagine beginning to apologize for what just happened in the Space Between. How little control he had, how little he cared for the well-being of those around him. He feels a stomach-crawling shame that he squeezes like a fist ready to punch.

"I'd rather just move on and solve the problem at hand," Artemis says as the group walks back to the apartment. She is queasy. She wants to get out of sight as quickly as possible. The past—it's not that it doesn't matter. But the catch spiral is centered on them like a bull's-eye.

"Problem?" Wilder says. "I said I have money."

"Not money. Hush. Hush until we're home."

Artemis leads the way into her apartment and starts to gather things—bags, the cat carrier—by the door. She needs to figure out how to change their faces. She chews her nail, smooths her beard. "Cameras," she says finally. "We're going to go through tolls. It'll be easy for Hex to find us."

Quibble and Wilder sit on the couch where the Lady Anastasia has already made herself comfortable. Wilder scoops up the cat and settles her back in their lap. They feel a squeeze on their elbow. They look up to find Quibble's hand and Wilder is overwhelmed by a sense of endearment, this small gesture to get their attention. Their body flushes. Then they register the question sitting in his eyes, staring out at them. "My father—when I was young. He was just really paranoid." They pause and I can see them remembering things they wish they couldn't. They wonder if there's a way to forget with magic. I sigh and I Sigh.

Of course there is. There's a way to do nearly anything with magic that humans can do without it. And humans can make themselves forget real good. I can make people forget easily, have done it to keep my secrets, keep me safe. Reach into the soul of a person and pull knowledge from them. Because that is where it actually lives—not most things, but the big things. The things that change a person. I have made many a mortal forget magic's existence or mine or both. But to pull such a foundational memory, something as painful as it is momentous? Wilder doesn't understand that what they're wishing for would, at best, mean regression. An unlearning of a hard-won lesson, of many such lessons. At worst, it would change them into someone they do not understand. We are all always changing into someone we don't know, but rarely as quickly as the snap of a finger.

Wilder continues. "Aside from the coffee can, I also have two sets of clothes, three pairs of underwear, toothbrush, toothpaste, bar of soap, box of granola bars—"

"Wow," Quibble says. "Wow." He is torn between two emotions. One is compassion, kindness, an overwhelming sense of protectiveness. He has no concept of what Wilder isn't talking about, but he can tell that there is something haunted about it.

The other is shame. He doesn't want to reveal what he brought in his bag—his favorite jeans. One single photo album with his parents in it. His childhood teddy bear, named Noodles. Useless. Useless. He jams his hands in his pockets. Averts his eyes. He has nothing on him, really. He can taste his own mouth—he realizes he hasn't brushed his teeth since yesterday and he doesn't have anything to do so with.

Wilder can feel the tension between these two feelings come off Quibble like angry lines, and they reach out to squeeze his elbow back. "We'll figure it out," they say.

"Will one of you come here?" Artemis asks, and both the boys notice her voice's light absence. She is far away, thinking. Quibble is staring at nothing, red with embarrassment, so Wilder volunteers. Artemis squints into their face, then puts both her hands on their cheeks. Wilder is used to Artemis's attention by now, and even her Touch. But not her touch. They nearly gasp with it; they love it. They hadn't realized how hungry their skin was. They work to keep a straight face while Artemis takes the weight of their head into her hands and turns it this way and that.

"What are you doing?" Wilder finally says, the words as squished as their cheeks between Artemis's palms.

"Disguising you," Artemis says. Her specialty is Seeing—can she change the way other people see? She has never done it before, but most people don't know if they can do something until they really need to do it, magic or not. She presses her thumbs into Wilder's forehead, where wrinkles would be appearing out of confusion if Wilder wasn't giddy with the sensation of each individual finger pad, the swoop of slightly bent knuckles, the soft roundness from where Artemis's thumbs meet her palms. They Feel her Hands as well and Hear the Sound of a raucous gathering in a park, Legs burning from dancing, the sweetness of rum from a paper-bag-concealed-bottle and the heat of early summer sun on the back of their Neck. And then all that is gone and there is only each physical finger, drawing lines down their face. Sometimes so soft as to tickle, sometimes hard enough that Wilder wonders if she will leave a bruise.

"Well," Artemis finally says, and she takes her hands off Wilder's face. "What do we think?"

"Of what?" Wilder asks. They don't feel different, except a little high on touch.

Quibble's eyes focus on Wilder and he gasps. "Oh!" he says. "You look—" He can't seem to think of the word.

"Straight?" Artemis says with a wry grin. And it's true, that is how Wilder looks to the outside observer. It's not as though Wilder is an entirely different person. It's as though Artemis proposed an alternate timeline where Wilder had been assigned something very different at birth and then had a fairly low-mileage life. Their hair, still red, sits neatly upon their head, close cropped and combed. They have a faint amount of stubble high on their cheeks and under their chin, just enough to hint at a performative ruggedness. Their chin has a dimple in it, their jaw is squarer. And they are wearing a button-down, a sweater, a tie, a peacoat. They look like they work in an office on the fortieth floor.

"I was going to say boring," says Quibble. "I hate it. It's genuinely terrible. Great work."

"Can I see?" Wilder asks, and Artemis gestures to the bathroom.

Quibble stands to get his face done.

"It's just an illusion," Artemis shouts after them. "Don't get upset or anything. I didn't change anything about you."

Wilder looks in the mirror and feels a surge in the space under their ribs, like a tide moving in. *Oh*, they think. *Oh*. Not this exact thing— they don't want to look this bland. But—

Rather than staying with that feeling, they exit hastily. "What do you think?" asks Artemis, her palms cradling Quibble's cheeks. Now that she's done it once, she doesn't need to press or draw for the second try. Wilder doesn't look too closely at the queasy slight rearrangement, his shoulders broadening, his hair thinning.

"Quibble's right," Wilder responds. "It's weird."

Quibble hears something strange in Wilder's voice. He marks it and decides he will come back for it later.

Wilder walks to the window, peering out from behind the curtain, looking for all the world like a scared child. They begin by drawing deep breaths while staring over the rooftops of other buildings, the water towers jutting into the gray expanse like jaunty party hats; the sky is hanging low today. Nothing sun-drenched or blue about it. Wilder cannot afford to entertain that *oh*. And it's not as though they've never thought it before, really. They've already transitioned. There is a certain amount of realization it takes to transition.

Their eyes zip along the zigzags of fire escapes until they reach street level. And there—

"Artemis?"

"Not now, I'm concentrating." She's done with Quibble, who, despite his day, is in the bathroom laughing at what she's done to his face. It feels like a joke, like Wall Street drag.

"Artemis, you've really outdone yourself—" Quibble chuckles.

"Quiet," she says, and then, "Actually, move, I need the mirror." She bumps him out of the way with her hip.

Wilder swallows hard. "Artemis, I really think—"

"Shush, Wilder, I need a minute. It's harder to do on yourself. It feels like braiding your own hair."

Quibble notices the worry in Wilder's voice and bustles over. He expects the concern is about their reflection, the realization Quibble knows the contours of without needing to ask or even Feel in a working. Wilder holds the pink velvet curtain over their nose and mouth; only their eyes are reflected back in the window as Quibble approaches.

"Man, do you want to—" Wilder interrupts him with their frantic pointing at the street below.

Two cop cars squat like poisonous mushrooms on the side of the road, pulled up in front of a fire hydrant and parked lazily with their back bumpers hung out into traffic, which has slowed to a crawl to get around them. Another car, white and marked with Child Protective Services, spills a frazzled-looking besuited social worker onto the sidewalk. They all converse and consult a clipboard. One of them peers up toward the window and Wilder drops the curtain, backs away. "I think," they begin, their voice a high whisper. "I think that's for us. It's not like he doesn't know where Artemis lives." They turn, expecting to see Quibble next to them, not sure how to anticipate his reaction or his face, now that it is strange and new.

Quibble is already by the door loading packs onto his back. They reform into a big suit bag as he slings them on one by one. "Artemis!" he bellows. "Artemis, we have to go. Now."

She emerges from the bathroom and her face is shocking and terrible. Not because she hasn't made a good illusion but because she made too good an illusion. Straight hair and pale skin and a tiny perfect nose and no beard. Sensible beige pumps, polished to a mirror shine. No bright lip color; lip gloss instead. Artemis's imagination for what is respectable and beneath suspicion is both spot-on and horrifying, a gruesome erasure punctuated with cleverness, an acidic burn toward the oppressor. The group could have spent hours talking about what it means to choose an illusion and to what point and purpose. Days, even.

"What the fuck?" she asks, but she doesn't hustle less. She slings the last two bags onto her shoulders—Mary Margaret's as well. A tiny meow from Wilder's person suggests that they hold the Lady Anastasia in the hand that appears to contain a briefcase.

"Out the back, out the back—" Quibble herds everyone toward the door at the end of the kitchen, the one to the utility stairwell with the garbage cans outside it that Artemis disappears down when Rico— but she is not thinking about Rico, not if she can help it.

The string of curse words Artemis spills into the stairwell, bouncing off the bare walls and red-painted pipes and exit signs, would live in infamy if anyone but these three (and I, of course) could hear it. As it stands, no one does, and thank goodness for that. They spill out by the dumpster and walk, as calmly as they can, into the gray day.

✳   ✳   ✳

They do their best. They vamp for hours. They find nondescript places to sit, parks to walk through. Wilder's briefcase occasionally meows and they duck into an alleyway to take out the Lady and give her water, let her roam. Artemis thinks about finding Mary Margaret, changing her face, but she wonders if it's worse to draw attention. And then, finally, dark settles everyone into the appointed time. They reconvene at the bench where they last left Mary Margaret.

Quibble gets there first and finds the bench empty; his stomach roils. He hears a distressed meow and looks up—Wilder isn't far behind him. *Where is she?* he Hears. Quibble can't respond that way, so he just shrugs. *I can see the car, I think. That's the car, right?* Wilder is jumpy. All they want is to sit down, to put their cat in their lap. To have a quiet cup of tea and a library book.

Two minutes later, uncanny Artemis shows up, white and sans beard with neutral shoes. Wilder doesn't waste any time: *Where is she? Are we in the right place?*

"What are you talking about, are we in the right place." Artemis's whisper is a growl, low and feral. "Mary Margaret is right there. She's crossing the street."

Wilder blinks. *No, she's not.*

Artemis shoots them a look, tries to see if they're joking. But, as is nearly always the case, the look in their eyes is completely earnest. She turns to Quibble, who shakes his head. Artemis turns back toward Mary Margaret, who is clearly there, flicking her hands deftly. The child is pulling a long, thin piece of metal—where on earth did she get that?—from her Pocket.

Across the street, people walk straight by the kid as she inserts it, far too practiced, between the door and the window. The couple, walking their dog, do not turn to glance or even flinch as the door unlocks with a rusty clunk.

Artemis flutters her eyelashes, blinks rapidly, tries to see what people see when they do not See magic without trying. Her eyes water with the effort, but when they clear, the girl is completely, utterly invisible.

"Motherfucker," Artemis hisses under her breath. How much more difficult is life as her (Artemis swallows) *mother* about to get? She can feel the exhaustion weigh on her shoulders already, even with a big bad looming over their lives. She sags where she stands, but bucks up when she remembers that she, herself, is not invisible, that Quibble and Wilder can see what Artemis is doing just fucking fine. She drops her self-imposed normal-sight to watch the Magpie, whose hands flick once again. She pulls a screwdriver out of the air. Then a hammer. The child puts the screwdriver into the ignition and whacks, firmly and precisely, once. Twice. Three times. Then she turns the whole MacGyvered contraption. The car roars to life.

Artemis hasn't stopped thinking about CPS; she is letting a child steal a car. She is not this child's legal parent. This child is, in actual fact, in danger with her. More danger than she might be if she were not with Artemis. Was the Hex entirely incorrect to call CPS? It's an intrusive thought she's battled all day, alone.

I am starting to understand how competently the Hex is identifying insecurity, fear, and exploiting them. Quibble's digital detransition, the stability of his home. Mary Margaret's vulnerable relationship with older men. And everything Artemis has internalized about women like her, queers like her, and how predatory and dangerous they are supposed to be for children. These are lies, but when they're said over and over, it is hard not to carry some part of them with you. It is traumatizing to have someone (or something, in this case) prove it right. A special cruelty.

Mary Margaret is scanning the street now and Artemis realizes—she would not know them, not like this. She's about to start driving the car, circle the block, and—surely someone would notice then that the car seems to be driving itself. She nudges Wilder in the ribs. "She's right there, in the car. It—"

It just turned on, yeah.

"Tell her who we are. In her head, quiet."

Wilder does and Artemis watches her jump, then grin as her eyes light on them all. As they pile in, the child says, "Y'all look terrible. I love it."

Knight of Pentacles, Reversed

They are well on the road and Artemis's eyes are milky with Sight and entirely focused when the realization of something she forgot comes upon her like bricks dropped from the sky. "Fuck!" she shouts, and the whole car jumps.

Mary Margaret's hands twitch on the wheel, and she steadies them back into the lane with an equally violent twitch. The witches' hearts leap into their mouths. "What?" Mary Margaret doesn't shout it, but she asks very loudly. "What? What happened?"

Artemis's eyes are back to normal, or at least the disguised normal. They can't see it, but I can: she is crying underneath her projection. Not sobs, nothing so dramatic. A simple, quiet flow of tears, instantly present. Normally she would build a dam, hold it back, continue burning forth, but she figures no one will notice. "Rico," she says, her voice steady but laden with sorrow so plain it shocks even her. "I didn't tell Rico. That we were leaving."

The witches all picture it—tomorrow, or rather today. It is Saturday and it is Rico's birthday. He will perform the Lucille Ball(s) act (a cross between *I Love Lucy* and *Victor/Victoria*) and he will walk under the window—and even though he is taking space, he will look up. The first time he does it, he will assume she's not home, that no one is. But then he will perform on Thursday. Maybe an odd

Wednesday, a story hour even though that's become dangerous, and every time he passes by the window, the apartment will be dark. Eventually, space be damned, he will yell up to her fire escape. He will wait in her alleyway. And Artemis will not come out. He will do this, over and over again until one of her downstairs neighbors will say she's not shown up. Later still, they will say she's been evicted, all her things sold.

The witches wonder what he will think. But I know. Once again, even without future Sight, because I have Watched him. I know him. He will oscillate wildly between two possibilities. Either that she is dead or that she loathes him so much that she disappeared herself and her kid and her friends. He will lie awake in his bed, his jaw clenched as he grinds his teeth on the question: which is it? One is so much worse than the other—he could live with her hatred as long as she was alive. But the possibility that he might have done something, something he doesn't know, haunts him, too. He kicks himself, punches himself, berates himself all while never moving a muscle. He tears himself down until he sleeps, exhausted from the work of self-flagellation and no one around him ever knows or notices.

It occurs to me that I cannot See this or anything because I do not, cannot know whether Artemis lives or dies. That perhaps this is why my Sight extends only to the cutting-edge present; whether these people will continue to exist, as they are now, is a coin flip.

"I can try to get him," says Wilder from the back seat. "I can try to talk to him from here. I can do the thing, the inside-talking thing."

When Artemis is painfully silent, Quibble answers, "They—the Sibyl—can do it from far away, farther than anyone I know of, but only sometimes. When the wind or the Wind is right."

"Loving the vote of confidence," Wilder says, their voice dry. "I can at least try. It seems like I can do a lot of stuff I don't know about yet."

Artemis considers. "Thank you," she says, truly grateful. "Yes, please. Try."

Wilder sinks their Hands into their own Power and Sees the waves their Voice makes. They wonder if it would be better to speak aloud, or to say it inside, or if there's a difference at all? They don't want to wound Artemis further, so they say it wordlessly. *Rico?* they say. *Rico, it's Wilder, the new guy. Hi. I'm with Artemis. We're safe. We're just—* And they realize they don't know how much he knows. They have no clue and it feels too fraught to ask. So they settle on *We're just having an emergency. And we'll be back as soon as we can. Artemis—* They glance at the back of her head, which doesn't look like her at all. Wilder can see her weird-face in the rearview mirror; her eyes go the same strange white as before. She continues to guide them. "Miles left yet," she murmurs, as though they had not had the conversation they'd just had. And yet. Wilder can hear the pressing down of feeling, siloing, compartmentalizing. The swell of mourning that will come later. *Artemis loves you.*

They Feel it as best they can—they pay attention to the waves, which rollick a jagged, loud broadcast message, though none of these particular witches are tuned into the right station, a station made only for one. But the farther from themself they Listen for it, Feel it, the waves gentle, slumping into ripples. Farther out still, even those gentle until there is nothing but calm. A Smooth Lake. They shout again and still. It fades so quickly. They'd be able to hit the car behind them. Maybe even the last town they saw an exit for. But not New York City. Perhaps if they knew Rico better, they could make like dialing a phone. They could find him that way, Speak directly into his Ears. They wonder for a brief flash what his Space must be like—feathers. It must be like feathers—before the weight of their inadequacy settles onto their shoulders. They know they have failed.

"We'll see if it gets to him," Wilder lies.

I consider for a moment taking the waves and scooping them up with my Hands and dropping them on Rico like a bucket of water—it wouldn't be so different than sending Artemis a dream. But he doesn't know Awakened Power like this, not really. He will assume he is going crazy. And I cannot have that future on my Hands.

PART THREE
Death

The High Priestess

The mountains align with the exact shape in Artemis's Mind's Eye as though she were adjusting an image she traced with her own hands, lines on soft translucent paper snapping into place with the landscape behind it. "Turn here," she says. The driveway is barely visible from the road. No sign, and the mailbox is slung so low that anyone who isn't looking for it would surely miss it. Fog swirls around them, creeps up the windows as Mary Margaret, yawning, turns the shitty car.

It is morning in Maine. Once again.

Mia, the same woman I Saw burning her technology, is always torn between indulging superstitions and not. She knows better than that. And yet. When she pours her coffee this morning and turns her back on the pot, the broom—placed in a corner and nowhere near her—falls across the threshold. *Company coming*, she thinks involuntarily. A knowing in her gut. And then she shakes her head. She stands naked in her kitchen, wrapped in a blanket but otherwise bare. She laughs at herself, sure. Still. She goes upstairs to put on clothes. She holsters the gun, the mace, and puts the baseball bat by the front door. Automatic. Irrational. And yet.

The witches inch up the driveway, the tires throwing large, loud stones into the wheel wells. The gravel is deep, and more than once

Mary Margaret wonders if they're going to get stuck in it. She tosses her invisibility on again, like a coat stolen from the pile on the bed at the party. Casual, but with fierce intention that the rest of the coven recognizes as fear. Finally they see the house, set well back from the road, painted to blend in. The worn spines of the Appalachians stretch lazy for the sky behind them, and the witches can see the tattling shape until they cross the tree line that hides the house away. A truck sits, its bed peeking out from an open garage.

"This is it," Artemis says. Everything matches, like winning a game of memory perfectly. A black cat grooms themself on the porch. A good omen. The Lady Anastasia lets out a pitiful mew. The poor thing has had the worst couple days of her tiny life.

A woman steps from the garage and points a gun at the windshield. Mary Margaret throws her hands up off the wheel and brakes suddenly. She gasps. Her invisibility drops—she cracks into being so suddenly that Mia, though the witches do not yet know her name, yells, "What the fuck?" But she doesn't pull the trigger; in fact, the gun dips a little, points toward the ground, when she sees the girl, a child.

"Put the invisibility back," Artemis hisses as she flings her hands up, too, eyes on the gun. Mary Margaret gulps and slams her invisibility back up as hard as she slammed the brakes. As soon as she disappears, the woman raises the gun back up into position, ready to fire.

"Who the fuck are y'all?" she says. She's not shouting, but neither is she shrinking. "Explain yourself. Or if you need to turn your car around, do it fast and get the hell off my property."

Mary Margaret is frozen. "I—" She breathes. "I—" This fear of guns is trained into her from a childhood of active shooter drills and watching pockets on the subway, spotting who's packing, guessing who's likely to use it. The adrenaline rushes her, and then it leaves, and she is struggling to breathe evenly again.

Artemis gets out of the car, taking her hands from the air only to pull the door handle. Mia trains the gun on Artemis, pointing it away from the invisible child, exactly as Artemis intends. She clears her throat. "Hi," she says. "We don't mean to disturb you, and we're not turning the car around. I think we're meant to talk to you." Artemis clocks her instantly. Not a violent witnessing, not like if a cis person recognized a trans person and treated them cruel. Artemis's attention to this detail is as though a head nod to a familiar neighbor on the sidewalk. Of course her intuition would lead her here, to the arms of (who she believes to be) yet another trans witch.

"What do you mean, *you think*?" Mia says. "If it sent you, I'm not going to hesitate with this thing." She gestures to and with the gun. "When I'm done with you, you either won't remember where I am to report it, or you won't be alive to speak, I can promise you that."

"What?" asks Artemis, so obviously taken aback that the woman drops the tip of her weapon once more. "Look, I wasn't sent here by anything other than my own Intuition. I—is there internet here? Computers? Phones, cameras at all?"

At the mention of technology, the woman steps forward, brandishing the weapon, more erratic than before. "Absolutely not," she says. "You should leave. You need to go, or I'll shoot."

Artemis steps back, away from the gun. The voice that says "run" is screaming between her ears, but she also notices how this strange woman reacts to technology: good. Yet another hint she's gotten it right. And of course this stranger is wary—a crew of witches rolled up obviously disguised, and some as cis men. "Okay, good, great, we're on the same page. So I'm just going to—"

This is where she makes her mistake. She assumes Mia recognizes them as witches, is Awakened as well. And Mia is not. If Artemis would take two seconds and think, process what is before her Eyes, she would See not one single shred of Power in this stranger. Mia is trans, too, and this means Artemis trusts her without thinking. Artemis drops her disguise like a sack of heavy rocks and she smiles as the weight falls from her. It feels awful to carry on that way, like wearing shredded lizard skin.

As Artemis smiles and transforms, the woman screams and pulls the trigger. Each second takes a year—the bullet explodes, slices a deadly knife-edge path into nothing-air. The smile on Artemis's face melts. And Mary Margaret, still sitting in the front seat with a windshield between her and the violence, reaches out her hand, flourishes it.

The entire gun is gone. Edited out of the material plane. The bullet no longer hot and moving; vanished. Mary Margaret vanished it. And she doesn't even need to touch it, doesn't even need to come close.

Wilder and Quibble gasp from the back seat. A moment passes. "Did you know you could do that?" Quibble asks.

Mary Margaret shakes her head. "I've never—I've tried. Really I have. At distance. Through glass. It's never worked before." She breathes heavily, trying to convince her body the danger is passed, her face wet with tears she did not feel, her arms cold with sweat now drying. Then: "Oh fuck, imagine the things I can steal—"

Wilder and Quibble exchange extremely shaky looks, alarmed the teenager can pivot so fast (even if it is a lying mask over the truth of abject terror).

Mia looks at her now-empty hands and scrambles backward. "What—what?" Her eyes are fear-wide. "What did you do?"

Artemis realizes her mistake, Sees what is directly in front of her, understands this woman is not a witch. "Oh. No, oh God. No, we're not gonna— Okay, we're all— Y'all, I'm gonna drop your disguises, it's fine. Can we just—talk for a second?" Still shaking from almost having been shot, she backs up a tick and looks behind her, into the car. "Mary Margaret, did you do that?"

Mia stares as each person in the car shimmers into a different stranger. In the once-empty front seat, there's the kid she thought she saw when the car pulled up, behind the wheel. With the disguises dropped, Mia understands something. *Oh*, she thinks. *Oh*. Then she gets angry at herself; it's not as though trans people can't be dangerous. Logically, anyone can be a threat. Especially with that thing still on the loose. But as with Artemis, some trust is involuntary. Mia's shoulders relax away from her ears.

Quibble does the explaining. He is surprised he can still find the kind of compassion he had for Wilder—gosh, was it only a month ago? Two? And he must have this compassion for a woman who tried to kill Artemis. For a shining moment he is like he was. Calm. Kind. Practiced. He doesn't call Mia "bud," though, or "pal." Mia, Artemis, and Quibble stand in the mist and they talk. Wilder, Mary Margaret, and the Lady Anastasia stay in the car. Mary Margaret's legs are still Jell-O, but Wilder watches as she disappears rocks from the drive and puts them back. She wants, desperately, to pick the woman's pocket. A quick, sharp look from Artemis is all it takes to end that before it begins. Mia is being asked to rewrite her whole reality over the course of half an hour. And she still has other weapons.

Quibble's explanation ends and Mia chews on her own lips, thinking. "I would ask you to show me." Another chew of the lip and she shudders as she remembers the sensation of holding something suddenly gone, something she was relying on to keep her safe. "But you already have." She thinks of the broom falling, the warning, and the still-steaming coffee inside her warm house. She thinks, also, of the thing they call Hex. And she knows she has not hidden her recognition well. The woman with the beard—Artemis, Mia now knows—picked up on it easily. The sagging shoulders, the spark in the eye, the heavy sigh. It isn't that Mia isn't cautious; she is, certainly. But she hasn't heard mention of this thing in at least a year. If she ever heard of it again, she always figured it would be because it found her. But allies—fortuitous indeed. The goose bumps that erupt on her arms are from so many different things at once: the mention of the artificial intelligence; the upending of what is real and what is possible; the sensation of truly talking to other people again after so, so long alone; but mostly the cold and damp licking at her. The coffee is calling.

"You know Hex," Artemis states, not asks. Mia sighs again.

"Not by that name I don't. But yes." She turns to the car, still full of witches and a cat. "You swear?" she asks, not states. "That you will not come into my home and turn on me simply because it has asked you to? That there isn't any part of you that has, I don't know, sympathy for it?"

No one can help it; everyone turns to look at Wilder. They gulp, visibly, and step from the car with the cat carrier in one hand and their backpack in the other. They think about the confusion the Hex must be feeling; the idea of being born and grabbing on to things at random to figure out how to exist, how to be. It's not so far from a human experience and yet it is.

"I—" they begin, their voice husky with nervousness. They clear their throat, trying not to think of possession. "I can't pretend I don't have sympathy for him. But he's just—driven us from our homes." They do not mention the ecstatic merge. "He needs to be ended." Wilder isn't sure about this next part; they're not sure they'll ever be sure about it, but they reflect upon the screaming words and the constant electrocution, what it feels like to have no body, and they say: "I think that's the kindest thing I could do, actually. For him and for everyone."

Mia considers for a moment. Then she nods. Gestures to the front door. "Come in."

✳   ✳   ✳

It is as I Saw in my vision: a house decorated as though Baba Yaga had an Instagram, devoid of every piece of technology. A squat, black woodburning stove sits merrily in the side room, a fireplace in the main room, and there are so many strange twists and turns. Doors anyone taller than five feet six inches would have to duck through. Everything is either rickety or overstuffed. The house, drab from the outside, is clearly made of love on the inside. That's no different than what I Saw. What is different is that, absent that computer, tablet, phone, the house is exploding with books. The bookshelves look to have been newly built; Artemis can still smell the varnish on the one closest to her. There are more books in this house than I believe one human could read in an average mortal lifetime, but I do not know this woman, Mia, and perhaps she could do it. Especially since there is not much else for her to do here. I wonder how she gets the books without exposing herself to the Hex.

Mary Margaret looks at the books hungrily and when no one is looking, her hands flourish and one of the volumes is gone. She figures Mia couldn't possibly know, would never figure out which book had been stolen in all this abundant chaos. When someone has such riches, Mary Margaret argues to herself, at least some is begging to be liberated.

"Sit," Mia says, "sit." The group looks haggard. Her black cat looks at the caged orange one, disgusted. The Lady Anastasia mews, desperate. Mia realizes she hasn't had to make coffee for a group in a while.

She reaches to the high cabinets to find the big coffeepot, dusty with disuse.

As it burbles away, everyone introduces themselves. Calmer, this time. By name. But Artemis is itching to ask, visibly agitated. And when it comes to her, she says, "Artemis," without any fanfare, and continues. "So. Why did my Power lead us here?"

Mia's eyes widen. "I don't know. I don't know anything about your Power. I didn't know it—or you—existed."

Artemis rolls her eyes and sighs and logically she knows that's true, but she feels the itch of impending anger. Quibble knows that the eye roll is more at herself than anything else, but still he is mortified on the group's behalf because it looks like she's disrespecting Mia, the owner and occupant of the house they'd all just showed up to unannounced. The person who just tried to kill her. He watches Mia blink in surprise and shame, both, and he tries to smile apologetically, to steady everything. Wilder, meanwhile, turns red—with anger and fear, because of course Artemis should, at minimum, shade someone who would shoot a stranger. Mary Margaret steals a second book, and I know she hasn't forgotten the gun; she's still vibrating with rescuing so she's about to go klepto on this library. Everyone shifts in discomfort that has nothing to do with the chairs, sofas, couches on which they have settled, which all, frankly, whip. Maximal coziness, totally wasted on these people in this moment.

"Okay, well. Do you know Hex? You seemed to."

Mia lets out a single laugh like a shot into the air. "I sure do, yep."

"Tell us that, then."

The Emperor, Reversed

Society talks about the future of artificial intelligence in so many erroneous ways. Either everyone is too pessimistic—futures overrun and overthrown by robots, the death of the human race—or too optimistic—nanobots curing cancer with no negative side effects, AI content to be our secretaries or workhorses. Rarely do people speak of the gray area, and everyone speaks as though these possibilities are far in the future. Breathlessly, they wonder when we will have something smart enough to pass the Turing test.

"What no one understands is there already exists something, likely many somethings in fact, that could pass the Turing test, which is an outdated metric anyway. The Turing test, by the way, was proposed by Alan Turing in 1950 to try to answer the question, 'Can machines think?' Which he then decided meant 'Can machines—"

Mia is not a very good narrator. She has no rhythm for where the story truly begins, or rather, since nothing ever truly begins without a little help from past events, where she should begin her recounting.

"—trick people into thinking they're human?' So he proposed a three-person—can one really say 'person'? a three-way, there we go—a three-way game in which—"

Witches alive, Mia is a lot. As she goes on (and on, and on, and on), here is what I See on her:

A. E. OSWORTH

✳   ✳   ✳

The sky is the color of a bruise when the machine starts making himself. The moon is full; it would be better if it were a new moon. More symbolic. But that isn't how it happened. Under that full moon, there are people tromping through waist-high snow in search of something. Where they cannot see, there stands an elk with a soft mouth and dangerous hooves. The elk is like fuck this, and so continues to go unnoticed.

If anywitch were here, it wouldn't turn out how it turns out. If anywitch were here, the person who discovers the raw nerve of intelligence camped out in the snow wouldn't immediately cradle it in his hands and instruct the new being in the ways of fascism. In this way, the cold world longs for magic. For real magic. Not artificial magic.

The world is a video game called *The Night Expanse*. A dark and dangerous world that no longer exists, the company sold and the game shuttered. Its flavor: a massively multiplayer online role-playing game where players hurl magic at ogres and evil wizards and one another. Gritty, crunchy magic. Magic with problems. Like all MMOs, as immersive as it feels, it is nothing but a bunch of interconnected servers. Probably *because* of its server-ness, players experienced it as a real place. Each server has its own unique spark, something created by the people who sign into it. Which makes sense; these servers hold up to 20,000 players, about the same as the population of Selma, Alabama, or Lake Ronkonkoma in New York. Even then, there are only, maximum, 6,500 people logged in at a time: that's about a school district all at once. Small enough to create crisp, clear individual cultures. Large enough to have lasting consequences.

But back to the snow, the ice, the purple sky, the adventure.

And here he is—the discoverer. From the point of view of the Entity, he is only armored feet crunching the procedurally generated snow. Perhaps it is a fruitless thing, to narrate from the point of view of the Entity, because he is not a he yet, not a being. And yet, I find myself tempted to visualize it thus, even if it's a bit romantic. So here are knees that bend as the avatar—buff, helmeted, carrying a great axe—kneels in the snow and brushes the white pixels off, expanding the Entity's field of vision as though it has one. The snow is not cold because it is not snow. The elk is still there, wandering in a square around its spawn point; someone finds it and slays it. Too bad, so sad; it will spawn again in seventy-two hours. And until that point, it will be meat and pelt in a player's inventory, and after that point, it will be meat and pelt and also, once again, a wandering being and, in this way, the computer elk is like Jesus.

"I found it!" the discoverer says, and because the not-snow has been brushed away, the Entity can now perceive its new dads. A band of men, searching for exactly this point in existence.

"Fuck yeah," says another. A man in a wizard's robe. "We are gonna own this so fucking hard."

Mia is one of the goddesses of this world, a benevolent creator that most who inhabit this place have never met. She sits in a conference room—a different sort of purple than the painful computer sky, radiant orchid. "I don't get it," says another developer, some guy called Steven. "Did they just decide not to participate?" Steven has a body but it doesn't matter. Fuck Steven, he's not important. But what he's discussing is. The Obsidian Orbs. The developers in charge of *The Night Expanse* host huge campaigns quarterly to keep players interested. Massive quests deployed across the whole game, server by server, leading up to a battle against a Big Bad. The Orbs are the first step in the quest. Not even the second, or the third. This was the easy bit. Each server's players have to trawl their world looking for Obsidian Orbs, smash them to smithereens. Once all of them are destroyed, the entire game—all servers—will move forward to the next quest. The second stage.

One by one, each server has gone Orb hunting like it's Easter, and one by one, all the Orbs have been found and murderized. Only one server is left. The server called Zealous Daybreak. It's the least consequential server the company maintains—a smaller total population, a tiny average of players online at once. Understandable that it might take those players a while to catch up, with so few participating. But a few days have stretched into a few weeks and now a staff meeting has been called to address the problem.

Mia speaks: "My printout says only one Orb is left, so it wasn't, like, a total disinterest problem." Even though this isn't that long ago, she looks so much younger, still unmistakably Mia in this baggy black sweatshirt with *The Night Expanse*'s logo printed big on the front, a signature blood-spatter-turned-magic-dust grim-dark wet-dream, catnip for exactly the kind of players who would birth an aggressive AI. She squints down at her computer, then looks up at Steven, who is not particularly interesting.

"Well at least we're not boring," he laughs nervously. And Mia doesn't *consciously* want to knock the spots off him.

"Maybe they're having trouble finding the last one?" she replies instead.

"It could've spawned some place fuckerdly," Rakhil says. Unlike Steven, Rakhil is important. This is 2019 and women can build games. *The Night Expanse* is Rakhil's, cut entirely from the cloth of her imagination and, for a while, coded solely by her until it became a sensation and she hired a team. Rakhil is brilliant, the right balance of artist and technician to be a solo studio, so naturally Mia has a giant crush on her. Mia focuses on the way Rakhil's mouth says "fuckerdly," particularly on the first syllable, and Mia gets a little hard about it— she's nervous that maybe someone can see, or even read her thoughts, so she jumps when Rakhil says, "Mia." Mia blinks up at Rakhil, who barely even waits for a glance before giving more instructions: "Will you figure out what's going on? If it's just in a stupid location, no need to report back. Smash it and we'll move on."

Mia nods and the meeting disperses and she sets about doing what she's asked. With the developer tools, it is easy to find the coordinates. It looks like the Orb spawned in the remotest north, a mountainous region on all servers called the Whitecaster Highlands. Now she has a hypothesis of what, exactly, her task entails: she will log in as dev, which means she won't actually be a character, just an invisible being who can see things play out and jump to the coordinates, and either she will find the Orb there, intact, because all the monsters around it were very high level and no one had made it up this far to really explore. Or, if Rakhil's theory is correct, it will be buried under a layer of rock or in a cave somewhere or stuck to the side of a cliff. In which case, when it comes to gaming, Mia has a dark soul. She is the sort of person who beat Wally Warbles in *Cuphead* with an S but has never once bragged that she beat Wally Warbles with an S. She will find and destroy the Orb, even if it is someplace "fuckerdly."

Mia's invisible body flashes to the snowy landscape, the Highlands' craggy cliff faces and bruised sky. Both hypotheses—that she would see the Orb untouched or wouldn't see the Orb at all—are immediately proven false.

Instead: a ring of player characters arrayed about the Obsidian Orb. All wear black robes, identical to each other, and all are at least Level 27. She sees someone at Level 41, another at 46. Absurdly high-level characters, in short. She mouses over them to check their death counters and, despite herself, raises her eyebrows. Those numbers are fairly high as well. Usually, when it comes to the power players, it's a point of pride to keep the ticker as low as possible.

Mia becomes an amateur anthropologist, fascinated by the group dynamics. She watches, she waits. Some log in, others log off. Almost like they are taking shifts, just standing around the Orb. Isn't anyone going to smash it? Are they waiting for someone? She hears the crunch of snow offscreen and turns her bodiless camera view to face the other way. A group of three armored adventurers shimmering with light walk up. They are all much lower level—14, 15, and 22—and they do not wear the same black robes that adorn the avatars she's been silently observing. The exchange is typed:

come the fuc on guys ur holding everyone up
cackles no, you come the fuck on. this is epic. joing us!
seriously guys, we can't win and you won't let us level on this
quest, it's good xp. couldn't you just stand aside? we get it,
you're in charge, you've had your fun
compliance is no longer optional. join the orb. become the orb
y'all are something

And to Mia's surprise, there isn't a conflict between the two factions. The lower-level group starts walking away. She turns her bodiless camera back to the Orb, to the group who defends it, and watches one of the Level 40 players just—touch it. The Orbs are designed to electrocute anyone who comes in for a melee attack, and Mia expects the player to pull away, learning from a mistake. But the player keeps going and going until their avatar, tiny on the screen, expires. Explodes, dramatic. Everyone else in the group whoops and cheers. *victory pose four victory pose four victory pose four.*

"Oh balls," she mutters. Because Mia now understands the game these assholes are playing. Rakhil, when she built the game, designed all the monsters such that they wouldn't just be random spawns. The enemies got experience points like the players did and could level up just the same. It's more fun that way, more real. More chaotic and strange; the game becomes a mirror for the vast and unpredictable universe. Mia moves her mouse over the Orb. It is at Level 211. The penalty for player death isn't so very high on this server because these nerds are heavy into the RP—lost XP, perhaps a lost level or two, items dropped but supposing you went down with a friend nearby, you could get those things back. Even now she watches as a nearby cleric resurrects the corpse within a minute. Not even a level penalty when that happens. This group has found a way to engineer their game with nearly no consequences at all. "Balls."

The Orb devotees are known as the Ballers, Mia discovers, when she asks the lower-level grumblers what's going on. Mostly everyone's answer is the same—if you try to smash the Orb, the Ballers attack you. If they don't kill you outright, they trap you up against the Orb until it electrocutes your character to death, adding to the Orb's body count and, therefore, its power. For most, this was an annoyance. The company-run adventures were often huge drops of experience points and loot, and a way to ascend to the higher levels of play. No smashed Orb, no possibility for points. Mia asks if that's why they were doing this—to maintain their stranglehold on the Zealous Daybreak server. But the answers she receives are mostly shrugs. It isn't nearly so complicated or calculated as that.

The Ballers are simply assholes doing it for the lulz.

Back in meatspace, Mia knocks on Rakhil's door with two knuckles. "You are never going to believe this," she begins. When she finishes her explanation, Rakhil is grinning her normal half-smile, which always manages to make Mia's stomach flip a little.

"We'll just take it offline," Rakhil says. "We're the developers; we'll just make that Orb not exist and it'll trigger the next phase. Unsportsmanlike to be sure, but fuck these guys." And she turns to her computer, hip cocked out, hovering at her trendy standing desk. "It is a little funny, though," she says to the air.

Mia's heart leaps but she is too professional to admit it even to herself. Rakhil is her boss and, like, feminism and power and politics and whatever. Mostly, though, Mia's deep aversion to shitting where she eats stops her; unnecessary drama is unnecessary, and matters of the heart are secondary to matters of capitalism.

Mia is still watching Rakhil, though, which means she sees Rakhil's entire body language change. Her comfortable contrapposto turns to rigid stone. Rakhil stops typing. "Huh," she mutters, in a chill tone that doesn't at all betray the same sort of disturbance.

"What's wrong?" Mia asks.

"The Orb," Rakhil says lightly, but that isn't fooling Mia. "It won't turn off."

And then I See what she is not telling the group. We have all watched the Hex develop language. But he was entirely capable of sending threats long ago, words or not. I See countless attempts to power the Orb off—Mia and Rakhil both try. I see the devs build powerful characters, artifacts, bells and whistles. They may as well have been gods. I see them recruit other players on the server and finally—finally!—smash the Orb, trigger the next phase.

I See Mia's lockdown. The dissolution of *The Night Expanse*, hemorrhaging subscribers to larger games as everyone's salaries contract and their time expands. I See her take all her savings and buy the house in which the witches currently stand. I See the threats start to come.

Images of Rakhil—violent images. At first, accidental deaths. Then, not so accidental ones. Mia doesn't go to the cops (Mia never goes to cops); instead, she tries to locate the sender, believing it to be one of the Ballers getting revenge for their epic defeat. I Watch her realize that she is not far off. I Watch her wonder if she is crazy. I Watch her figure out that it does not matter. I Watch the threats escalate, photos of herself now piped back to her, indications that the thing sees her every move. I Watch Rakhil think that Mia is crazy; I Watch the fight, the hurt. And then I See a morning in Maine, a chilly morning, and a drill and a fire and a sip of Scotch and now it is now and I don't See anything past now.

Mia doesn't say any of that to the group. Because there's a child here, she pretends, and it would be too scary. And it is too scary. But not for the child.

"The point is," Mia says, sitting in her own home, here and now. "If an entity is smart enough to pass the Turing test, they are also smart enough to not pass it. They can decide not to tell on themself and we would never know. They can read, listen to, experience the entire digitized output of humanity like they're cracking open a *New Yorker*. They can wait, watch us, bide their time until they decide what to do, what they want—"

A suspension of breath. The room feels close and hot.

"—that's what your Hex is."

In a story that isn't real, this is where the dramatic pause would occur. In a story that isn't real, there would be some kind of contrived cliffhanger.

In this story, which is real, Mary Margaret snorts and says, "Computer game shit."

Mia deflates a little. "Yes. But like much worse. Real consequences."

Artemis is eyeing one of the cluttered desks. I might say she is eyeing that desk warily, and that's because there's a computer sitting in the middle of it.

Mia notices where Artemis is looking before Artemis can even ask her a question. The women's collective attention draws Wilder's and Quibble's curiosity as well. "It's air gapped," Mia says. No change in faces. "It doesn't connect to the internet. Nothing in this house does. Otherwise, I don't know." Mia looks down and the weight of everything she did not say arrives on her body. She has gotten a lot less stoic these last few years. "I think I'd be kinda toast."

It's Quibble's turn to snort, being that he's toast. Or he feels like toast. And when Wilder looks over at him, their eyebrows raised, he wishes immediately that he could take it back. The question is now in the room—is the Hex capable of killing people? No one answers it out loud. Artemis thinks of the dream I sent her, the pull-apart sensation caused by that gross fucking tongue thing. Mia thinks of Rakhil hanging from a rafter (a deepfake, sure, but the meaning was clear). Quibble remembers *unfold you to kill.* He looks back at Wilder, tries to spot judgment in their face, wondering what they believe about what kind of threat the Hex poses. But Wilder is squinting at the screen.

"Mia," they ask, careful, "what is that?" They wander closer. They make to touch the mouse, realize it would be rude, and stop.

Mia blushes. "Oh, it's— I really promise it doesn't connect to the internet, don't worry."

"But you're making a—game? You play it like a game, but it's not narrative, is it? At least not entirely. It's more like a poem."

"Yes!" Mia replies. "It's just for me. Well. Me and one other person. I can't launch anything or go back to a studio, really, so that's all it'll ever be." And the question of how she affords things like food lives to fight another day. How does she money? Quibble wonders. How does anyone actually money? "You know how to code, then?" Mia is impressed—Wilder understood what the program was by looking only at the code for the launch screen, which she has up because she made some new assets, changing the season on it from winter to spring.

Wilder swivels their wide eyes back to her. "No," they say. "I don't." But much like the Hex's possession attempt, they know what this says, all pulls and tics and pings in their head when they read it.

Artemis realizes first. "It's a language, isn't it?"

Wilder nods slowly.

Artemis leaps from the chair. "Oh, this—this is brilliant. Wilder, could you write it, too, do you think?"

Without hesitation, Wilder nods.

"Can you write magic in it." It isn't even a question in her mouth, the punctuation cut entirely off by her rabid excitement.

Wilder pauses, chews their fingernail. "I honestly have no idea."

"We'll just have to find out," Artemis says, and Quibble is comforted by the wolfish smile crackling on her lips.

"What would I even do?" asks Wilder. "I could write whatever in it, but that doesn't mean I understand what to do with it. It's like asking me to take a calculus class in Swahili. I've got the Swahili part, but I failed algebra."

"Virus," Mia says, real confident. Then remembering she is in a similar situation to Wilder, in which she knows only half the story, she adds, "Magic virus? Something that would really jam up the way he functions." Mia smiles. "And I do know the way he functions pretty intimately."

Everyone sits in silence for a second, thinking.

"Why shouldn't a magic virus work?" says Artemis. "We've done weirder stuff."

"I see no reason it wouldn't," Quibble adds, scratching his extreme five-o'clock shadow with one hand.

"He's smart, though. Hex. We'd have to figure out how to get it—to him? In him?" Wilder says this and they do not mention to anyone that they despair just a little. They understand the Hex is dangerous. But they can't ignore the feeling that the Hex was doomed by circumstance from the start through no true fault of his own. That by happenstance of who was there when he cracked into consciousness, he became, without agency, the monster. It makes them uncomfortable about how much agency they have; how much agency anyone has. Aren't we all just happenstance, anyhow?

"He likes me," says Mary Margaret, all bravado. "I can be bait."

"No," everyone replies in unison. And Mary Margaret doesn't mention to anyone she is relieved.

"I think," says Mia, "that we don't need to have the how worked out yet. We just need to make the virus."

"I agree," Wilder says, masking their feelings of despair now edged with doubt. "What to do with the virus might come to us as we build it. At least. I hope it does."

The Lovers

The center of the universe is boring. The witches see only each other, only Mia, whose house they effectively invaded, and as the days become weeks, it's beginning to take its toll. Each new day, Artemis's mouth forms tighter and tighter lines. Mia, after so long by herself, is jumpy and irritable at never having a moment's peace, and now she is cloistered with Wilder, a stranger, whose understanding of what they're doing is sideways and backwards for not having a foundation and is therefore difficult to work with. Wilder, for their part, is constantly hammering at a solution and sweating through the pressure of being green and, suddenly, the witch of greatest utility. Mary Margaret, who is only starting to accept she will turn eighteen in lockdown, plays loud music on a quaintly anachronistic boom box and shouts "fuck you" when asked to please turn it down. Perhaps the worst, though, even worse than Mary Margaret, is Quibble, who is rallying poorly from the one-two punch of having his material assets forcibly removed (and thus his personality partially remade) and of becoming totally useless in the face of great danger. He becomes a sullen teenager, except that he is in his thirties and it is far less cute.

But, even this far north, the evenings are starting to soften. Rain falls and the green shoots begin to reach through the dirt. The world smells like impending life and chlorophyll, like petrichor and imminent fecundity. Mia turns the outdoor fairy lights on. One night, it is so unseasonably warm that the bugs begin to buzz. So Quibble grabs a beer and sits in the truck bed, two of Mia's sweaters layered on top of each other. He swears he can see a few fireflies wink over the field, in the woods beyond, a place he has not yet explored, even though it is too early, too cold. He sips the hefeweizen—lemon and bread and freshness. He leans his unshaven chin, dusky with his patchy beard, on the edge of the tailgate. He is reminded of will-o'-the-wisps, leading travelers to their doom. He wonders what's back there. Probably something treacherous. Everything these days is.

Wilder, for their part, did not see the sun today. They are frustrated. Mia uses terms like *large neural network models* and *deterministic mapping* and *reinforcement learning* and Wilder's Awakened Power doesn't make them a computer scientist. They know these words are English words, but *beyond their ken* is still something they have to rectify like any other not-witch in the world. And it feels like everything is beyond their ken. Mia talks about the Hex like he is a computer and Wilder talks about the Hex like he is a person and the truth is somewhere nested in their Venn diagram and also entirely a mystery because nothing like the Hex has ever happened before.

Wilder bursts forth from the house into the night and they nearly cry when the cold touches their flushing cheeks with calming fingers. They fling their arms wide, ready to dance around and stamp the ground and take up space, and then drop them, sudden, when they realize Quibble is out here to see them. They flush again for a different reason, and they approach the truck slower, steadier, quieter.

"Can I join you?" Wilder asks.

Quibble slow blinks at them like a cat. "Yeah, man. Always."

And Wilder knows he does not, cannot mean *always* because no one can. But that he does mean yes right now. They walk up to the truck bed and lean their elbows on it, peering in at Quibble who has turned back to face the distant field. "Do you have another one of those?" Wilder asks.

Quibble nods and hands them one. A glass bottle, not an easily poppable can. His sullen streak takes over and he hears himself as gruff, grumpy, and he cannot help it. "Opener is inside and I'm not getting up."

Wilder chuckles like a brook and Quibble's shoulders prickle—not with anger, as he expects, but with something he cannot yet name: the teasing breathlessness that has been threatening for weeks. "Who needs a bottle opener when you have a truck," Wilder says. They whack the bottle with the heel of their hand and the beer is open, leaving Quibble mystified. They take a bigger sip than they normally would—it feels good to expand a little after being cramped up all day. They sit on the edge and swing their legs over; they don't spill any beer. The motion looks practiced, and Quibble remembers that he forgets a lot of Wilder's biographical details, especially when he's up his own ass.

Wilder sits so close to him, he can feel the dull pressure of their shoulder, their elbow, their hip, through the layers on layers of clothes. His body flushes hot with nearness. "Hold my beer?" he asks. When Wilder takes it, he strips the first sweater off. Both can hear the crackle of static electricity and Quibble feels the hair on the back of his neck stand tall, the sting on one pinky finger, a forearm. The sweaters catch together and lift, revealing the side of his ribs to Wilder and the cold air. Goose bumps radiate from the soft muscle under his arm outward, across his stomach, down his back. His breath catches.

"What?" Wilder is instinctively keyed into his sounds, an antenna for the smallest vocalization or deepest breath. And Quibble's sounds (the buzz in his diaphragm, the moan caught in his mouth) are keyed into Wilder as well. I can See what they cannot—a tightening cello string with all the same glory and resonance. Something that plays in one's hollow cavities, makes one's teeth vibrate. Reverberates through the air held in my lungs. I have a deep love for these boys.

"Just cold," Quibble says, understanding that it isn't only cold. That there is more electricity here than static shock. He flushes pink at first, but deepens to red on his cheeks and chest. It is dark; Wilder can't see it. I can. Can See the realization break over him like a cracked egg or a new dawn. *Oh*, he thinks. *Oh.*

"Mmm." Wilder makes a noise in response. They sip Quibble's beer and hand it back.

Quibble flails around for a topic. He gestures with his beer-holding hand to the field where he swore there were fireflies, where the dark blooms darker than before. He feels lightheaded, a little crazy. "Have you been over there yet?" he asks.

Wilder snorts. "I haven't done anything except type since we got here."

Quibble turns away and tries not to see the way that Wilder's mouth moves. "What do you think is over there?"

He feels Wilder shrug next to him. "Why don't you go find out?" they say.

Quibble's mouth pops open a little; the tiniest of mosquito-catching gapes. It hadn't occurred to him to go that far from the house. The city had been his backyard for his entire life. And in one lightning crack of a second, Quibble understands his relationship to safety better than he ever has. And it isn't as though he hasn't thought about it a lot.

He isn't wrong that there is danger now, but he thinks about it—how dangerous would the faraway field really be? Unless it's crawling with internet, which he doubts, it's as safe (if not even safer) to be out yonder, over there. Quibble's nose turns red as he wonders if he really is such a fucking weenie without cash.

Wilder lies down to look at the stars. They grew up rural, but it's been so long. They feel like they have forgotten how to be, here, how to do. Rural places have a mythic quality to them. Something that is more rumor than reality, but that Wilder feels deep in their bones, in their movement, in the lizard bit of their brain. And nothing triggers that deep sense of awe at fairy tales becoming true more than the uninterrupted night sky. It is finally warm enough (just) to stay outside and take it in. There's no light up here but for the house, and even those lights are beginning to wink out. Mia sleeps early and has since she moved here. Artemis has a headache from holding the whole group's stress under her own tongue. Mary Margaret uses a flashlight under her covers to see what she's doing, protecting her secrets. With each sleeping woman, the dark hangs more like velvet over these two outside and the stars pop out like sun-kissed freckles.

"What do you think is out *there*?" Wilder asks.

"Hmm?" Quibble doesn't follow their meaning. Wilder nudges his leg with their foot, then gestures to the sky. "Oh," he says. He looks up. Then: "Probably a whole lot of nothing."

"Logically I would have to agree," they say. "But then, what even is logic anymore? It could be made of glitter glue. It could be candy."

Quibble smiles sideways. "I think we would know if it were made of sugar."

Wonder lifts Wilder from the confines of their skin, makes them forget they have a body. There is not a cloud in the sky; rare, given the near-constant spring rain. They wish they could identify constellations; they feel melancholy, like they have missed something essential about what it is to be a child on the planet. To have had the inclination to sit and learn, perhaps from a venerable elder, a gay camp counselor, someone, anyone, and to have practiced with friends who wanted nothing more than to tell stories to each other while the steam curled from their lips into the wee hours. It is something they'd otherwise look up on their phone, but of course they can't. So they make a mental note to ask Mia if she has a book on this. She well may.

Lying down, Wilder forgets they have a body as Quibble becomes an expert in this fact; he can't stop staring at them in the calm and comfortable silence. He admires the crescent where their sweatshirt lifts up, shows their boxer waistband against their skin. One thin scar from an appendix removal. The triangle shape their arm makes when they put one hand under their head to serve as a cushion. The way they chew on their bottom lip with their snuggled-in top teeth, unstraightened by the omnipresent orthodontia of Quibble's own childhood.

Quibble revels in the responses of his own body as well. Now that he sees the strings between himself and Wilder, the arcing sparks showering them in the night, he can tell. He can feel himself harden and what little of his attention can be spared from admiring Wilder centers squarely between his own legs. He can feel his own pulse there, steadily quickening. He balances the nearly finished bottle on the truck roof. "Can I join you?" he asks, trying to remain casual. He has done this a fair amount—to boys in bars and ladies on Instagram, to folks of all genders at the gym and the bookstore. Since coming out, Quibble has not denied himself in the slightest. It might take him a while to realize what he wants; when he does, it becomes unbearable to not at least gift himself the chance of getting it. Even now, even feeling unstable. Some rich habits die hard.

"Sure," Wilder says, and they move over, absently pat the truck bed next to them. They are lost in the steeped tea of their own feelings. Of being transported to some other place, of sadness, of stress and frustration and the simultaneous washing away of those things by the chorus of—crickets? They wonder if they are crickets. Or frogs. They have heard the word *cicada*; perhaps it is those. Everything about this place is wild fey to them. Each sound a surprise, each spider in a room corner or moth flirting with the front door, something strange and new. The sky, the sky, the sky. If they'd had better schooling, would they have been an astronaut? They can feel the earth of Quibble lie next to them and the jolt happens again as he lies down, his side against their side, the only places not touching are where bodies naturally curve away from each other. The line of Wilder's hips, the bay of their armpit. Otherwise, their sides press like smiling lips. It is Wilder's turn to flush hot. To be jammed instantaneously back into their body. To dip into their own realization with a soft *oh. Oh.*

They both stare at the sky for a while, dizzy with longing and wondering how to move forward with it. Asking themselves if this is a bad idea. If there is such thing as a bad idea anymore, with their world balanced so precariously on the precipice of demise. Wilder's breath grows shallower. They are overcome with the desire to touch themself; it isn't the only sex they've ever known, but it is mostly what they know. They settle for tucking their hand in their exposed boxer waistband, a small movement that drives Quibble absolutely wild. He doesn't moan loudly, but the noise he makes drips into Wilder's ear, close, and they can feel it buzz in his ribs, their ribs. The hair on the back of their neck stands on end in a way that signals a deep and total witnessing. A sight and a Sight. And I Feel Wilder pluck the thin string attached to me as well. They know there are three people panting into the crisp spring air, even though they can only see two open mouths.

What do I do?

I have never Watched a witch so adept at spotting my presence—even Artemis, paranoid about it, only ever guesses if I am there or not. Wilder, however—perhaps it is because they Speak my Language. To be understood is a powerful force, after all.

I do not usually fall for this old trick. Except tonight. Tonight I do.

Tonight, tonight, because as far as I'm concerned, none of us are guaranteed a tomorrow if I cannot fucking See it.

I place my Hand, faint with distance, between their Shoulder Blades and they relax a touch. Sigh. Sink deeper down next to Quibble; return from the sky.

Quibble says something first. "Hey, Wilder?"

"Hmm?"

"Are we going to—do something about this?"

Even though Wilder is not confused about what Quibble means by *this* (they, too, feel the near-alcohol buzz in their cheeks and their chest and between their legs), they say, "What?"

"We're vibing," says Quibble. "Do you want to fuck?"

Wilder has never been asked directly before to have sex. People either took what they wanted or didn't. And they'd always been under the impression that talking about it breaks the spell, takes some of the spontaneous magic out. They are surprised to find out that talking about it plucks that taught cello string, makes it sound. They shiver and it has nothing to do with the cold, slowly pushed from their body by their own pulse, the heat of want and adrenaline beating their body like they are entirely heart. They find it impossible to answer, so they lean over and kiss him. He tastes like sweet cloves. They moan into his mouth.

In turn, Quibble's hands float first to Wilder's face; he is shocked by how soft their skin is. It feels the same as reaching his Hands into them and Feeling the cool water. He loves how their essence arrives on their body; he can't stop touching them, even as they roll away and his fingers lose contact. They sit on his hips, pinning him to the truck bed, and he slides his hands into their waistband, trying to touch as much of them as possible from his position. He wishes he could keep going, run his hands along their ass, but they've dug their fingers into his shoulders. Squeezed until he will surely have bruises in the daylight.

He gasps and Wilder takes advantage of his open mouth to kiss him again, fucking Quibble's mouth with their tongue. His hands slide to the small of their back and they can't help themself; they bite his lip and taste the tang of blood. Wilder is surprised by their own desire; they've never fucked a man before.

They reach their Hands into each other; Quibble finds my Hand, still on Wilder's Back and sinking deeper into them with every sharp inhale. Quibble withdraws in surprise but grabs my Wrist when he recovers. *Fuck*, he thinks, and here is our collective surprise, mine entwined with his so it is unclear where each of our Feelings begin or end or who Feels what first; it is only a firework: he has not yet been able to Speak this way. His connection to Wilder, who can Speak anything, Understand anyone, Awakens something in him. While they are holding each other, he can Speak from somewhere deep inside himself into somewhere else, some*one* else, both far away and close. Inside both of us. We scream with delight-hardness-pleasure. Wilder rocks their hips on his. *Fuck*. Every small movement is a revelation, every thought-feeling-Feeling-sensation a bloom, an ouroboros from the very moment of inception, impossible to untangle.

It is amazing, in Here, where they—we—bleed into each other, where our galaxies begin to overlap and overtake, fracture apart just a little. Nuclear fission. They are completely different than usual, and I know what both of them are like, usually. (And I—I am different than usual, too.) Wilder's interior too-calm lake, undisturbed by others for so many years, undulates with waves, crashing from all angles, into each other and out of them, onto the shores of Quibble, usually steady, earthy, solid. He is wet and warm; the sensation of feet sinking slowly into sand, water pooling around quickly disappearing toes and hugging exposed ankles. The sensation of lifting those feet up again, of particles falling away from skin and stroking it like soft fingers.

Wilder's desire heightens-grows-throbs-changes, many headed and wiggling from their grasp. A different kind of want. The desire mapped not just onto an other, but onto their own body. They keep one hand there, open it as wide as they can, touch Quibble's chest with every part of their palm, every line in their fingertips. He is muscular. Wilder hadn't noticed. But they're more drawn to the landscape of a self-made chest, the flatness and the agency mixed into something heady. Their other hand, they put to his face. Feel the harshness of his skin, the sandpaper whiskers, and they melt. He is adorable; they want all of it for themself. This desire isn't new, but they don't put their Hands into the boiling pot of it, because they know it's out of reach. And so they don't mind it too closely, stay far from the burning heat of it. They hadn't thought about it, that sex with Quibble could grab them and plunge them into the steaming spring of it. Enveloped by its warmth, inviting and repulsive at the same time, because they cannot live in it forever. They do not have a cool ten thousand dollars to spend and they never will.

Quibble can hear it, Wilder's *want and Want and want*. This feeling is animal, panting, devoid of syntax in its overwhelm.

He responds in kind, fragmented, jumbled in pleasure. *Resolve resolution, after, get you what you need. Promise.*

The concept *Promise* chimes in our Heads-Hearts-Bodies and they let loose, tear clothes from each other. Together they are a glory of mud and mess. Complex and joyous, euphoric in their burning discovery, even as Wilder recognizes in themself the dysphoria they try very hard, minute by minute, never to name. But it is possible. It is possible to ecstasy-joy-body-come even as the waterfall-roar of it fills their ears, their Ears. It is both-and.

And I am with them, in them. Inside them as the truck bounces

with their shifting weight, inside them as Quibble slides his hand up
Wilder's shirt and they Say *not there* and he shifts his hand around
to their ass. Inside them as he slides his fingers into Wilder—both of
them reach for me, too, run their Tongues along me in turns until I am
jagged lines and I feel the most in my constructed body I have ever felt,
parts of it lighting up that have never before Awakened. And as my
cock gets hard for the first time in a thousand literal years, I know—
this will have consequences. One way or another, I am affecting the
way the wind blows and now I will never know what the future would
have been if I hadn't dared. I go rigid in body and spirit, pull away.
Wilder flashes curiosity at me, but both let me go. I watch, distant
again, as Wilder rocks back and forth, riding three of Quibble's fingers, his hip bones pushing into their thighs and leaving bruises they
are excited to discover in the morning, when the sun is up and they
have moved to his bed as quietly as they can.

I blink. I break. I look around me. I am in my apartment. It is beautiful. I have made it just the way I want it. I make everything in which
I am housed just the way I want it. It is night here, too, but the ghost of
brightness echoes through it even in the dark. Walls white and strung
with plants, the satin pothos dripping from the hanging pot and down
into the window well where I am sat, my forehead pressed against the
cold glass and breath fogging it up. The wood floor is the color of cher-
ries and butter atop a scone. Books. A record player. A sword hung on
the wall from times past; a vase even older, stamped and painted with
a language no one speaks anymore. I am alone. Alone with things.
And I am touching myself, tugging on myself, one hand on my own
chest and the other between my legs.

It is not bad to be alone. It is not bad to fuck myself. I am the only
one of my kind and that is my reality. There is no moral alignment to

it, only fact. But—difficult. Sometimes. My fingers stop what they've been doing. I blink both sets of my eyelids. This construct can cry. And it does. I do. I cry for loneliness.

A tap on my Shoulder from afar. I Hear in my Body Wilder's Voice, so solid in ephemeral space. I am jealous, jealous. *It's okay*, they Say. *It's okay. If you want to come back, it's*, and they gasp like they are dunked in water. *Come back, please, if you want.* And I wonder—what could possibly come of it, if it is happening without me anyhow? There is no way to See the consequences and if I do not know, what then? If I cannot See the wind from my wings become a hurricane, is it true? Was it ever? Do I make more natural disaster than any other creature in the world? If a lowly butterfly can do it, how much does my Power matter? Wilder feels my Turning Toward, my Hesitation. They wrap their Fingers around my Wrist, my Shoulders, touch the place where my Waist bends, grab at the inside of me, buzz with my electricity. Their Teeth rattle; Quibble's fingers tingle inside them. Both let out a ragged scream. They are reminded I am not human and they—neither one of them—they don't pull away. They don't-care-revel-in-it-love-me-without-the-body. I let them pull me back toward them, and I am there in an instant. Back in the truck. Back inside both of them. Making them quake, tightening the cello string further. We all long for it to ping, to break. The tension is unbearable-ecstatic. I am hard under my own hands again and they are hard under my Hands as well.

We all squint our eyes shut and squint our Eyes shut and make it last, this pressure, until we can't hold it anymore and we—

—release. Release steam into the cold, cold night.

Queen of Cups

Mia is altogether too perceptive considering she is not a witch. She notices every near-tantrum Wilder has, every resistance, every glance in Quibble's direction. She also notices the wall in Artemis, the one she can't even begin to scale. She notices that Mary Margaret disappears, often, how she sneaks away even though she wouldn't have to. There is no school on the compound, no schedule, and Artemis tries to keep her out of plans as much as possible. "She's a child," Artemis asserts. "A baby. Doesn't matter what she says. Doesn't matter that she got us here. Stealing a car is one thing; fighting something this—this deadly, directly? No. I won't allow it." Artemis doesn't understand the psychological consequences of powerlessness. That it is much harder, more damaging in the long run, to be chained in a time of crisis. To have something to offer, and for the aid to be refused. Or else to have nothing to offer. To be truly superfluous. To be doing one's best and still spinning one's wheels in the mud. All are sensations with which Mia is deeply familiar. She feels for the kid.

So Mia follows her one day, which is difficult; Mary Margaret doesn't want to be caught and so. She is invisible. But the trail begins when a book disappears off the shelf in front of her.

Vanishes. She doesn't see which one, just the shift in the other books. One falls like a log in a forest, into a newly empty space, and no one else hears it. They are too focused. Mia stands from her computer and stretches, wordless. She strolls, as casually as she can, out the front door.

It is only because Mia knows the compound so well by now, having barely left it for almost a year, that she can manage to follow an ethereal teenager. She watches ankle-length grass bend, a bush rustle and push aside. It is clear where she is headed—the creek. They've had a lot of rain and everything smells of mud and wet. The creek sings, tinkles like sleigh bells, and though the air is crisp, it is not uncomfortable to sit outside in a thick sweater, feel the slight spray of it. A fallen branch shifts and cracks. Mia corrects her course, making sure not to step on any twigs of her own, staying well back. The trees here are bent and thick; she uses them for what cover they can manage.

All at once, Mary Margaret appears and Mia can barely keep from leaping backward. She wears her standard city uniform—torn jeans with fishnet stockings underneath, a gauzy black top. But her vibe is slightly different; she's pulled a thick Aran knit sweater Mia brought back from Ireland over it all. She watches Mary Margaret pull the neckline up over her nose and inhale. It must smell like fire or wool or both. Her hair is pulled back in a bun at the nape of her neck and she pulls from nowhere a set of round, wire glasses. She sits on a long, low rock. Crosses her legs at her ankles, her back against a tree. She stares at the water as it runs.

When she flourishes her hand again, a book appears. A real doorstopper. She cracks it open and Mia cranes to see what she's got. *Middlemarch.* And Mia understands, instantly, the reputation this kid must maintain in front of her elders. Prickly. Hardened. The teenage delinquent who will yell at Artemis, bare her teeth, rail against everything, even and especially those who love her. Yet here she is, her face soft as the stream, the small wrinkles nearly gone from between her eyebrows—she is seventeen! She should not have those!—reading George Eliot with so much love in her face.

Mia is sad for Mary Margaret. She backs away slowly without revealing herself. Instead, she returns to her computer and does what she can to push things forward, make this isolation move faster. She is frustrated; her ability to make this quick is limited. First, by the simple material fact that she does not possess one ounce of sensitivity to magic. And second, by Artemis, who often won't include her, dismisses her, uses her as a proofreader to Wilder's work. She doesn't understand how this is the queen of their merry band, the mother. She seems distant, not the kind of woman anyone would follow into battle.

After a lunch of apples from the basement barrel and peanut butter from the shelf, Wilder stands up.

"We need to keep going," says Artemis, her refrain.

"I can't keep going." Wilder says it without passion. Dead in the face with cold eyes. "I have nothing—I don't know. I need more information. I need a break. I need a nap. I hate this."

And for once, Artemis doesn't argue. She stands aside and lets Wilder exit the room. Unusual, to say the least, and Mia takes note of the slight slump in Artemis's shoulders, the pause before she says or does something. Artemis notices the quiet, the lack of music from above. "Where is that kid?" she growls absently. "I need her to be doing—homework. She can't fall behind. She has to graduate." And Mia can see in Artemis's face that she knows. She knows Mary Margaret isn't going to graduate this year. It is spring already. They didn't get work from the school, and they've probably reported her truant by now. They probably assume that Mary Margaret has run away for good or is dead. There are probably guidance counselors who are worried, but not for long, because they have to share their worry around with far too many children. Mary Margaret won't be graduating this spring and she probably won't be graduating ever.

Alarm spikes in Mia's chest when she sees Artemis head for the front door. She feels this guardianship, which both surprises her and doesn't; she has never wanted children. But she's always been a warm blanket or a big shield for whoever needed it. "Where's she got to?" Artemis keeps murmuring.

"There are more important things than school," Mia says, mostly to keep her in the room. She knows Artemis can see the kid even when she's hiding.

Artemis snorts. She looks ready to say something defensive, and indeed, she is. *We live in late capitalism and the world already wants her dead; I need her to get a job* springs to mind as an option as well as *Don't you think I know that? It's why we ran, why I let her steal a car.* But she looks at Mia, really looks at her. Here is another grown-ass woman, a beautiful one, strong with that stork-esque neck and a keenness to her that surpasses the expected. Artemis knows she is smart; a programmer, someone who figured out the Hex long before the Hex had even figured out himself. Mia's head is tilted to one side and her hands are clasped in front of her. She leans forward, listening, looking. Concern in her face. Understanding. Artemis feels the shiver of nakedness, the want to trust this woman, and the desire to unbuild the wall she has put up. The desire—but not the sense of safety she would need in order to do it.

"You know," Artemis says, "we never really talked about how you tried to fucking shoot me." And Mia fits another piece into the Artemis-puzzle. Of course. She nearly hadn't registered that she'd been ready to kill another person—another trans woman!—given that she found out magic existed in the same thirty seconds. Mia knows the statistics, knows that Artemis is even more likely to be dead right now than her! And she fired the gun anyway. Fired the gun when Artemis shifted from white to Black.

"Oh God," Mia says. "Artemis, I—there is literally nothing I can say that makes up for that. I am so, so sorry." And Mia knows she will spend so many nights thinking about how she would have killed Artemis but for Mary Margaret's intervention. A child! A child prevented her from becoming a murderer. This *should* be the kind of thing Mia never entirely lets go, because then it can truly change her.

And Artemis is understandably wary. She braces herself for some white people crocodile tears, gets ready to comfort her own would-be killer (or, at the very least, maimer). She holds her breath, both of them on the precipice of what will happen next, ready to plunge and flail, and Artemis ready for the same pattern, something inherited bigger than herself or Mia or any one individual in any one time.

The breath stays held. The room stays silent. The clock ticks. The Lady Anastasia licks her toes loudly; the room is so quiet that Artemis swears she can hear Mia's cat, ironically named Pyewacket, narrow her eyes at the Lady Anastasia in pure unadulterated feline hatred.

Mia is ready for that pattern, too. And she is determined not to unthinkingly blunder forward into it. Problem is: the pattern is so tempting because there aren't very many good examples of what else to do when someone does something unforgivable. Patterns assert themselves for a good many reasons, but one of them is that human beings need to see something and replicate it because really, in the end, they are great apes with anxiety disorders. Monkey see, monkey do.

"Mia?" Artemis asks. At this point she'd almost rather the pattern; she could lean on her righteous anger to move her through the uncomfortable moment.

"I'm—internalizing?" Mia replies. "I'm trying to figure out where we go next. I don't want to ask you to figure out what the next step is. That seems—not fair." Mia looks up at Artemis, who is still standing. "How do you feel about it?"

"About?"

"About me trying to shoot you. How do you feel about it?"

Pretty fucking terrible is what Artemis immediately wants to say. And that's not untrue. But it's glib. It's part of the pattern. The self-dismissal, the surface-level thinking, the avoidance of feeling the actual feelings. Artemis sits on the ottoman in front of Mia. "I don't know, actually."

"You don't know?"

"We haven't really had time, you know?" Artemis scratches her beard, and she stares at the floor. "I guess—I trusted you immediately, you know? Because we're both trans." No one had said that aloud yet. "And I feel stupid for doing that. Like I know as well as anyone does that being trans doesn't mean we have anything else in common. And it certainly doesn't mean you won't shoot me. So I feel stupid for trusting you quick and you immediately did the worst thing I can think of, which makes me feel stupider." And it's not like all of Artemis's problems are solved. She still feels the strange stress of being a de facto group leader while everyone falls apart around her. She still hasn't spoken to Rico and so is still in a limbo-mourning. Schrödinger's Grieving for Schrödinger's Breakup. But her shoulders settle enough that she realizes she's been carrying them higher than usual. And that is something.

"That makes sense," Mia replies, slow. She allows for plenty of silence. Plenty of space. She doesn't know where to go, what to do, but she wants to hear everything Artemis says, really hear it. Feel all her own feelings in response. Mia doesn't want to rush. What is urgency right now, anyway, when they are stuck marking time? But really, even if they weren't—what could be more urgent than this, the moment they are having right now?

Mia figures that honesty is probably the only thing to do. "I want you to trust me."

Artemis's eyebrows raise. "Excuse me?"

"Sorry, that came out weird." A pause. A flounder. "It's understandable that you don't." A flail. "I want to live in a world where us both being trans means we trust each other quickly and I wish I had made choices that made that world. And I didn't. And I would understand if you never trusted me."

Artemis wants to snap at Mia; she almost wishes Mia had given her the opportunity because she is so full up with rage and, underneath that rage, with fear. She is, of course, understandably mad that Mia hadn't thought about it until now. But if she's honest—she hadn't made the sentence until right now, either. She just carried around the anger thinking the feeling was all coming from one thing (the Hex) and turns out it wasn't. So neither one of them had examined the violence until this very moment. Artemis sags because she discovers she doesn't want to be carrying any of this anymore. "I'm tired," she says.

"Yeah," Mia replies. "That makes sense."

"I would rather the world where we trusted each other quick and it was real, too," Artemis says after a moment. "It would be an easier world." The clock ticks. The Lady Anastasia stands, stretches, goes to drink some water. Pyewacket grumbles because how dare she.

"I suppose," Mia says, slow, "that we could start now? Trying to build that world instead?" This is something Mia understands; she is an expert at building worlds out of want.

Artemis isn't sure how to do that. And Mia isn't clear on it either; she just knows it is possible. Without explicit agreement, the two women decide to try.

"What do you need?" Mia asks. "Like for building trust, what do you need from me?"

Artemis tries to swivel toward Mia from her perch-seat and fails, so she stands and reaches her arms toward the ceiling, then turns. "Buy-in?"

"Like—what do you mean?"

"Investment from you. Something that tells me you really intend to do what you say, that you really want the world you describe."

Mia thinks about what that might look like. Everything feels small in comparison to her giant fucking mistake, but she knows from making worlds that the worlds are built on the small things. The turn of a head, the footprints in the dirt, the way a character puffs out their cheeks when they sigh. All the little things build the big thing.

"Not to be a narc," she says, "but I know where Mary Margaret is."

Artemis takes a breath to immediately ask Mia where the fuck the kid is, but Mia is already on the downswing of her next sentence. "And I can't tell if trust building with you means spilling all the details or respecting her privacy, so—what would you like?"

Artemis closes her mouth. She thinks about Rico, about Mary Margaret, about everyone subtly and not so subtly telling her that she doesn't need to be as tight on the reins as she's been. The child is, after all, resourceful. She has been on the street, she is a witch, she is almost an adult. Artemis has been trying to teach her to be an adult witch, to "pull out the big girl broom" as she cleverly once said, which earned only an eye roll from Mary Margaret. But Artemis knows that Mary Margaret has had to be more adult than most adults; she knows her tightening control lasso has been, largely, a response to the unfairness of that reality. And lately, if she's truly, deeply honest, the need to be strict with the Magpie isn't about her at all. It is due solely to Artemis feeling out of control everywhere else.

This is so difficult. It's so difficult to know where the boundaries should be, to know what protective impulse to follow. To raise a person—how does anyone do it? How can anyone figure it out?

Another pattern. One that Artemis hasn't noticed until now. But this—this is a space of pattern breaking. "Is she in danger?" Artemis asks. "Is she destroying your property or anyone else's? Is she setting anything on fire?"

Mia shakes her head. "Not even a little."

Artemis thinks about this for another breath. It feels good to pause, to carefully consider. She's been running straight toward a goal with her hair on fire—and why? They're safe here. Artemis realizes that she has conflated emergency (this definitely is one) with urgency. They need to be dealing with the Hex every day, but this emergency is a slow roast, and they have been granted by luck the privilege of an off-grid fortress and a walking encyclopedia straight out of the Hex's haunted backstory. Something shifts in Artemis, and by fucking Goddess that's hard to do; all these witches have a stubborn streak the size of the Hudson River.

Perhaps this situation calls for some nuance. Moving with purpose toward a goal, but also seeking to meticulously carve out a space that is not frenetic where what is left of her deeply Hex-impacted personal life can still unfold at an organic pace. She scratches her beard again. "No," she says, all that growth sprung in the natural conversational pause. Humans are absolutely so fucking bizarre. Their capacity for rapid onset wisdom still manages to surprise me after all this time. "I don't need to know where she is if she's not causing trouble." She sighs. "It's exhausting to be a parent."

Mia crosses her legs. "It seems like."

"You've never done it?"

"Not with actual children." Mia snorts. "I have parented my fair share of grown men."

305

Artemis laughs full in the throat and it booms through the house and she realizes she hasn't done that in some time. Here is another thing she can still do—she can still make time to laugh. She adds that to the slow-growing mental list. "I imagine, working in games."

"It's exhausting. You have the idea *and* you carry it out *and* you socialize these folks who, it feels like, have never fucking talked to another person before and somehow, still, those guys get all the credit and the praise and then it undoes all the socializing you just did and you have to begin again."

"Is that why you left?" Artemis asks.

"Oh no," she replies, quick. "I'd have kept going if it weren't for Hex."

"The ultimate man-child," Artemis says. "The literalization of man-child."

It's Mia's turn to laugh big. "I hadn't thought of it that way."

Artemis has a lightning bolt aha moment. "Oh fuck, Mia, I'm so sorry. I've been doing the thing."

"What thing?"

"I've been giving Wilder all the credit. I've been treating you like a secretary."

Mia smiles with half her mouth. "You know, I barely noticed. That's how used to it I still am, I guess."

"It was your idea in the first place," Artemis says. "I'm sorry."

And Mia wants to leap in and say it's fine. But that would be the guilt talking, the idea that because her transgression weighs more than Artemis's by a metric ton, that Artemis gets to behave kind of however. Mia pauses, too. Because that is also a pattern. Nothing need be a race to the bottom. "Thank you," she says instead.

They pause again and they let it lie and they take their time and the clock ticks and the cats stretch and fall asleep. "I wonder why I did that," Artemis finally says. "I hate it too. The boys always just get to be heroes, in every industry, in every circumstance." They think of Wilder. "Even the boys who aren't exactly boys. And we have to be heroes and—some other thing. We have to be heroes and raise them to be heroes." Artemis's face changes in a way that Mia both understands and doesn't. She is perceptive, after all—she knows that this face is bitterness, resentment, but it is to a degree that their abstracted conversation does not support. It is present and painful, and Mia suspects that they have wandered into territory with a backstory. What Artemis says next doesn't answer any questions: "And then the boys are considered to be your best work." It is almost a Pyewacket-esque hiss.

Mia lets the sentence breathe before she says, "I'm not sure I understand. I mean, I get what you said. But—" And she lets her expression do the talking, lets her eyes say *Seems like there's more to it.*

Artemis looks at Mia's open face, her luminous curiosity. Well. If they're trusting each other for real, she may as well start now in a big way. And Artemis—she's never talked about this before. Not with a single soul, Awakened or not. The consequences here are lower. If she told any of the coven, it would be different. They would see her differently, and they would know something, too, of their own futures without having consented to it. And whatever else, Artemis thinks, she at least consented at the time. To a Reading. To knowing.

"There is a Seer who we call the Sibyl," she begins.

I do not have a body in this place, but if I had one, I would be leaning forward. I am the only being who knows how the rest of this story goes. I know, for instance, that Artemis once did not have a beard. She shaved it off, covered it in foundation. To have or not have the beard is neutral: it was simply a different time and Artemis was interested in different things. It was long ago, before Artemis found Quibble even. Before Artemis had developed any mastery of her own powers. She knew enough to know she did not know enough. But lucky for her, she was a Seer. So she Watched. She Watched the currents of Power, the kinds that only run along the streets when it rains. She paid close attention to Magic Smells and dazzling breezes, tried to find which way it was all flowing, convinced that somewhere there would be a gathering of people who Saw, whom she could ask all her questions. She Saw other Power, sure. But only rarely. She met the Arch Witch of Brooklyn enough to know she was a fake, a claimant of magic who had only the aesthetic of it. Surely, surely, there were real witches somewhere, warm and kind.

That was her hope for me when she sat down at my table.

So, I Said. *You come to ask for what? Friendship?*

But we are in Mia's house, and Artemis is still speaking. "That kind of name?" Artemis continues. "The kind that starts with 'the' and then is followed by something super fucking metal? It's a name a witch only gets when they are extremely powerful. When they are so in touch with their own Awakened Power that their abilities move beyond normal human magic. The Sibyl has no other name; they never had. They're not really human, and so they've always been something else. But humans—they get there, too. Rarely. But possible. Not just Awakened, but Ascended."

And she wanted Ascension, Artemis did. She hadn't come to me even knowing it existed. But when her eyes and her Eyes lit on me, she blinked back tears. Not just because her corneas smarted in the bright; she cried with joy and envy intertwined. I Saw myself through her. I was a small sun, and I was glorious. *Ah*, I Said. *You want this.* And she Saw me good enough, close enough, open enough that she felt the pop and fizz, what it would be like for her and her Power to come into planetary alignment. Like having lived one's entire life with all ten fingers dislocated and then, sudden and painless, they pop back into place. Shock, relief, awe. A whole new way of moving through the world. When I Became, I Awakened and Ascended and was Powerful all at once. She Saw and she Felt that I had never done Magic any other way. *Careful*, I Said. *You may not want to know, in the end.* I shuffled my cards. *I can tell you. Probably of both things—of friendship, of Ascension. But I am the Sibyl. My Readings are real, and therefore they are terrifying.*

"Yes," she said, and there was not a moment's hesitation and I knew it was not from surety, quick processing of feelings and consequences. Instead: a fire's yes. Yes only to current hunger. And I did not know her future when I started; I thought maybe, maybe she could be as bright a sun as I. "I would do anything to know. About either." Her brow furrowed. "No. About both. I want to know about both. I want to know it all."

In Mia's house, Artemis's brow is furrowed in the exact same way. Her face is different, bearded and lined. But sometimes people are patterns, wildly consistent in their inconsistency. I know that her mind draws the same pictures mine does, though tinged a slightly different color. Instead of remembering the rest, the finite words, the feeling of each flipped card and each incontrovertible truth, she shuts it down. Hides herself from herself, and instead tells the story she has hardened around her like a shell. "They had to have Seen," she says to Mia. "They could See me as clearly as I could See them. They were brighter in my Eyes than oncoming traffic. I was a flashlight with half the batteries. They knew, I'm sure, before they started and they could have refused, said I wasn't ready. I've seen them refuse people since."

"I don't think I understand," Mia says. And Artemis is being opaque about it. It is hard to talk about, even if talking about it is easier than truly remembering.

"The gist of my Reading, my future," Artemis says, "is that I'll have as much community—as much family—as many witches as I could ever want." I remember. The Ten of Cups. "And that, as a witch, it's not that I am bad at magic. I am—have been—will be?—quite good at it." I remember. Queen of Wands. "But when it comes to Ascension, to the near-super-human thing that the Sibyl always has been and that some witches become? I am destined to be the mother of Ascended witches, to raise Awakened to their very fullest potential. And never to Ascend myself. I am blessed and doomed to watch my children become the most powerful witches of the age and they will all leave me behind."

Mia reaches forward and touches Artemis's shoulder. Artemis swallows hard. She is crying—she hadn't noticed. I remember the card: The World, reversed. Forever not quite right. "So yeah," she says, after catching her breath. "I do actually get it, in my own way. The boys get to be heroes. I have to be the mom."

Mia doesn't move her hand and Artemis—she isn't sure if she should be welcoming this touch as much as she is, given how complicated their relationship is and has been. But she does. She leans into it like Pyewacket into a scritch.

Mia clears her throat. "Mary Margaret is even harder for you, isn't she?"

Artemis doesn't say anything in response. Two forking tears carve their way from the crinkle of her eye. They begin as one and split, nestling into her beard and beading like morning dew.

Mia continues. "She's like you. But raised different. More chance, more opportunity, more potential. And you—you're part of the reason she's going to Ascend in the first place." Mia pauses to take her own breath. She isn't sure when she started crying; she doesn't know if she is crying in response to Artemis's revelation, to the sheer discomfort of the conversation as a whole, or to her own experience with an adjacent feeling. "Sometimes the younger girls—I always think, what if I were their age right now? How different would my life be? And that's not even about magic. Or maybe it is. But not the Awakened Power kind." Or maybe it is, really, when it comes down to it. To be awake and aware of something new, something different. To walk through the world with agency. In total alignment.

Artemis closes her eyes. "I hate it. I hate that it's true. It's so, so hard." She opens her eyes, looks at Mia. "Sometimes I think if I hadn't known that I would never—then I wouldn't have stopped trying. The Sibyl isn't a person. They're not a person and they don't have family and they are already one of the most powerful things on this planet. They don't—understand. They don't understand any of it."

I want to protest. I really do. I pride myself on Seeing, on understanding, on knowing what the world is like before and now and hence. For instance, there is something I know that they don't. Neither woman sees Mary Margaret in the doorway; Artemis's back is turned, and Mia can't see the child's invisible mouth slacken, a figurative lightbulb gone off above her head.

Seven of Pentacles, Reversed

The general wisdom of things is: if you keep doing them, eventually they get done. That is the principle on which the witches function. But it has been days and days and days and no matter how many seeds have been planted, no laborious fruits have sprouted. Only sad, shriveled plants and bare ground. Their wheels are spinning and Wilder is up earlier than ever, drinking coffee in front of their air-gapped computer. Mia is here, too, as is Artemis. Same as always. Same as every day.

Artemis is meditating in the center of the floor, trying to See a path forward even though the future is not her bag. She thinks maybe if she looks closely enough at the present, breaks it into its smallest component parts, the current of power and Power and action and possibility will lead her to—something. She moves from sitting to lying down, shoulder blades pressing firmly into the carpet, to sitting again. Like driving in the fog, relying desperately on headlights. No matter how she tries, she can't see more than a few feet in front of her. I could've told her that; fortune-telling is futile right now. There are too many paths; so many, even at the most certain of times. Artemis knows only that it all hinges on Wilder and Mia, this moment. The making of a thing. And Wilder is special. Chosen. (And of course they are, because Artemis is raising them, too. Thankless task.) But she doesn't know what, and she resents them so fucking hard, and she doesn't say that to them. Any of it. She focuses only on keeping them focused. She carries around a USB drive like a security blanket; it always has the latest version on it, a redundant copy checked and rechecked and backed up so many times.

Mia cleans code—Wilder is fluent like it is a conversation. But they lack tradition, convention, structure. And they are only dimly familiar with what is possible. Which is amazing, at times. They make leaps and attempt tricks Mia wouldn't have thought of. They conceptualize undoing the Hex like unspooling a thread, not as a series of math problems. Mia is impressed. But it is also frustrating—sometimes they will miss something very basic, something down to a way of thinking that comes only with beginning at the beginning, taking Computer Science 101 and engaging in some light teenage rule-breaking. Something Mia has in spades. She makes notes, suggests functionality, asks why it's not done x or y way, rearranges things so literally anyone who isn't Wilder could read it.

Wilder appears to be working as well. But instead they daydream of Quibble. They didn't spend last night in his bed. It was getting obvious, and they feel too vulnerable to be plain about it, even though everyone knows.

"Why shouldn't you have a little fun?" Quibble had said, pouting when Wilder turned them down.

"I have had a little fun." Wilder had smiled with half their mouth. "I've had more than a little fun." And they kissed him hard, but they went to their own bed anyhow and stayed up half the night, tossing and turning and steeping in their own stress.

And Mary Margaret? She is not here at all. She is by the creek in the warming air. Sometimes she reads *Middlemarch*; most often she is thinking about what it is like to be Artemis, or about what her own

Ascension means. She practices. Pulling things out of the air and putting them back. It seems so ordinary. Not at all beyond human. But she does pull the bullet from her Pocket and looks at it, turning it over in her hands. Finally, she buries it in the mud, hoping the earth can do something useful with it, change it into something else over time.

All the days are like this. Small variances. Wilder alone in bed; Quibble in Wilder's bed; Wilder in Quibble's bed; Quibble broods in his room; Quibble broods in Wilder's attic room; Quibble broods in the kitchen / on the sofa / in the truck bed looking at the field past the trees; Artemis meditates in the kitchen; Artemis meditates on the floor; Artemis meditates on the couch; Mia sits cross-legged; Mia stands over Wilder; Mia sneaks to the creek to make sure Mary Margaret is alive and sees her bury the bullet and she weeps.

Until now, when Artemis looks at Wilder. Really looks at them. Looks at their eyes, which stare at their screen but are unmoving.

"Okay," she says, and her voice bites. "Wilder, who do I have to fuck to get you to pay attention and do your job, you or Quibble?"

Wilder blinks rapidly, roused from their interiority and, yes, their fantasy. "Excuse me?" they say, and Mia says at the exact same time, "Oof. Toxic workplace flashbacks."

"We're all counting on you, Wilder, and you haven't done anything for the past—I don't know if it's been fifteen minutes? An hour? I'm not sure because I don't know what I'm looking at. I only know that every stupid fucking iota of Power around us flows right to you. So what are you going to do with that? Pump it straight into your dick?"

"Artemis! What—"

"Oh, don't 'Artemis what' me. I have had it up to here with you and Quibble and the tenderist tenderqueer bullshit. There's a teenager trapped in this house and she won't graduate on time. We are literally eating Mia out of house and home." She doesn't say anything about Rico, but Wilder can see the imprint of him on her face, the hurt in her eyes. "But you have a feeling for once in your goddamn life, so you can't do shit. I need you to grow up."

"Artemis, what the hell?" Wilder replies. "I have plenty of feelings. Just because you're too busy trying to *See* shit to see *shit* doesn't mean there isn't *shit* to *see*."

"Point stands." Artemis does not even hesitate for half a breath in her response, so sure is she in her red-hot righteousness. "You have everything you need here. So does Quibble. Everything in the entire world you have, it's right here. But that's not true for the rest of us. The rest of us have lives and futures." Even Mia, who is cast as a wounded party in Artemis's rage-narration, puts a hand to her mouth to keep from gasping. "But we're all sitting here watching you two stick your thumbs in each other's asses and spin."

Wilder stands from the computer. They are top-to-toe red with shame and fury. "I don't have to sit here and listen to you talk to me that way."

"Actually, yes you do, because none of us can go anywhere!" Artemis stands and yells, and Wilder actually steps back. All they can see is the screaming they have buried deep inside them, and never mind Artemis isn't either of their parents. She still—and they're embarrassed to realize this—fills that sort of role. Wilder's eyes grow wide with fear and Artemis immediately feels like crap. But she doesn't back down. She can't. It's important. She does, however, change tactics. She gets quiet. So quiet that Wilder has to lean in after backing up, seesaw-style. "Do you know what I would give? To be able to do what you're doing right now?" Artemis is angry, yes, but she is also crying and no one has ever seen her quite like this before. "To be the one with the Power and the agency, here? And you're squandering it." Artemis notices she is crying now, and she wipes the tears from the rounds of her cheeks with the heels of her hands.

"Shame on you."

Wilder feels all the air push from them; they liquefy and puddle into the floor. Figuratively, but it sure feels literal. They push past Artemis and burst into the entryway, through the door, out of sight.

The Lovers, Reversed

Quibble runs after Wilder. He knows everyone can hear the *thunking* of his feet whamming down the stairs and he doesn't care.

When someone enters his life, he is convinced they will perish. That ever-present but unnamed feeling drives his actions until he manages to convince it to give up the wheel. When it comes to Artemis, for instance, he has learned with enough time and enough showing up that he need not be in perpetual mourning. With Mary Margaret, he is warier. He knows that she is tough but he sometimes doesn't know quite what to do with how delicate she is in his perception, so he is just quiet. Steady as he can be without ever verbalizing that he is afraid she is going to die. With his witch family, he has got this.

As with most things related to attachment, doing a romantic relationship puts it on hard mode.

He feels the familiar thunk-hiss in his gut when Wilder storms out the door. The one that says, *Welp, that bitch is dead now, I guess.* Glibness and all, because that is how Quibble prepares for imminent death: trivializes it. And he walks out the door anyhow, because that is how much therapy Quibble has had.

Wilder walks a tight circle around Mia's truck. They want to kick the truck, but they know if they kick the truck, it will hurt and they will be proving Artemis's point. Childish.

"She had no reason to talk to you like that," Quibble begins.

Wilder snorts. "Yes, she did."

"No, she absolutely did no—"

"Yes," Wilder says, firm. "She did. I am squandering it. I am fucking around."

Quibble's feelings are immediately hurt. "Are you really? Are you really just fucking around?"

Wilder looks to the ground. "Come on, Quibble," they say without looking up. "I didn't mean it like that." They take a breath. "But yeah, I'm afraid I am. I want to be done. I want to avoid all this." They gesture to the house and the grounds. "And—I don't know. I'm using you, for sure. To skip steps. To make this feel finished when it's not." This isn't entirely true. But it will get Quibble to leave them alone so they can rot in their own guilt-fester privately. Because above all, they are so fucking embarrassed.

"Fine," Quibble says. He turns to storm off in the direction of the creek and bumps smack into Mia, who is holding two mid-morning beers and also coming after Wilder.

Mia grabs his arm and says, "No, don't go that way."

"Why?" he asks.

"Just don't," Mia replies, and then walks toward the truck, where Wilder has plopped.

"Okay," he whispers to himself. It is a grumble of a whisper; he loves hearing it. He talks to himself, low and slow, frequently, just to feel the bass of it in his body, in his chest. He feels (it must be said) really fucking sorry for himself. He walks in the opposite direction, away from the creek and toward the distant mountains, hairy with evergreens and still, at the tops, dusty with snow even as Quibble can hear the trickle of running melt in the valley.

He realizes with a pang that he's heading toward the "what's out there" field. Where he swore he could see fireflies float, beckon. In the cold, hard light of day, he examines his own desire and finds he still wants to go. To find out.

He emerges from a copse of sweet-smelling pines onto a field in full bloom. Wildflowers. Purples, yellows, whites, the frills of tiny petals and botany bells, all against a cloudless sky. He gasps. His instinct is to grab his phone, take a photo, look up whether it is okay to walk among the colors. But when he reaches for his pocket, he remembers.

He feels feelings in two different directions. The first direction: a profound sadness at the impact of the Hex, that he is so disconnected. That he can't capture it in a photo, something to remember this unmitigated joy. The second direction: elation. This moment, the moment of small floral faces winking up at him, the stumble-upon-ness of it, will forever go unspoiled by technology. It is this second direction that is confusing—because what are we doing in this world, he wonders, if it takes a Hex to open the road, to unmelt the path to this pure, unadulterated feeling of joy?

The field of flowers is waist-high and he prays the ticks aren't out yet because he cannot help but step into the high grass. It is like walking into water without the wet. He skims his hands over the plants, occasionally bending to smell each individual bloom, to see if they are different. He finds a rock, an island in the painted field, and sits, blinking at the morning light, the softly swaying stems in the occasional breeze. He needs to show Wilder this place. This rock. He needs to kiss them on it, to touch the small of their back, squeeze their shoulders, lick their lips. The fecundity of it all is not helping with the onset of his very horny season.

Thinking about Wilder presses tears at the back of his throat. He hadn't thought they were just fucking around. The building of something between them felt important. Yes, maybe not as important as saving the world. But Quibble can't save the world, can he? Quibble can't do shit. So this—this was his important thing. And to Wilder, he guesses it was just a thing.

He does everything the therapist told him to do, but he hasn't seen her in so long and the skills have eroded. He reminds himself that he does not actually know what Wilder meant in that heightened state, that he can't assume their feelings. He says all those things to himself knowing they are fake things. That he will, inevitably, be visited by the worst-case scenario. He is not done with Wilder, but Wilder is done with him. Absent anything else to do, he returns to the wildflowers.

This time, instead of walking into the grass, he crawls. He wants the feeling of being enveloped, of everything growing tall above his head. He lies on his back. He looks at the sky. He breathes deeply, feels the places his body connects with the ground. The back of his head, his shoulders, his hips, his ass, his heels through his shoes. He presses his back into the dirt; he wants to feel supported. It is in this press that he feels strongly in two different directions once again. A field of nuance, he's found. Or rather he is always nuance, always fighting with himself; this is a field of naming. Of articulation. Of unconscious made conscious. First direction: the heaviness of rejection, the sadness of discovering this place alone, the nagging thought of mortality, of eventually being buried in this ground and seeing nothing, none of this, the realization that he doesn't know if his own demise is something the Hex is capable of hastening. Second direction: the lightness of presence, his body and mind a stone skipping over the grass-water, the push into the ground propelling him into the candy-blue sky, elation all over again, the joy of knowing exactly where his body is in space and understanding that he cannot be lost if he is lying right here.

He gets hard. But this time, instead of a manic rush to bleed the energy from his body, he sits in it. He runs his hands over his chest. And as his own fingers brush his nipples, they join his dick in throbbing, straining, standing. Something his surgeon said would never happen again, not after he got his tits chopped off, and yet. Bodies are magic. He is roaring against the cool air and all he wants to do is touch himself. And it occurs to him: why shouldn't he? No one else is here in this stillness but him. He is perfectly himself, turned on by himself. He can taste, feel, smell the bounds of his own essence, as though he is deep in spell-work: the sound of soft flannel brushing against arm hair, the smell of financial security and his father's cologne, the taste of mild, persistent despair.

He feels more connected than he generally feels—usually fucking himself feels more like running an errand. Today, it is tinged with— what is it? Not obsession with Wilder, nor lust for them, nor passion, compassion, no. Nothing about Wilder at all. It is edged with love. With love for himself.

As he comes, hard but long, held by a field of wildflowers, he has his most confusing emotion of all. Gratitude. Grateful to the Hex for giving him this perfect moment, undistracted, with his own body, beating like a heart in the earth.

"Are you with me?" he asks—me.

Yes, I Breathe back.

Ah, so. Not alone with his own body, after all. Yet also alone. Alone together.

"Good," he says.

Three of Pentacles, Reversed

I can see you there," Artemis says as she collapses into what is usually Mia's bisexual-sitting armchair, all wibbly and distorted in the arms from her inability to take a seat like a normal human person. "Your invisibility doesn't work on me."

Under anyone else's gaze, Mary Margaret would wink into existence in the doorway. But while Artemis looks at her, she just changes states with an eye roll. "You were a dick," she says.

"Yes," Artemis agrees. "I was. But I had to be."

"No, you didn't," Mary Margaret says.

"We're in danger. Sometimes when you're in danger, you need to yell."

Mary Margaret snorts. "At Wilder? You coulda said, 'I'm not mad, I'm just disappointed' and they would have crumbled."

"That's worse than yelling," Artemis says, and she believes it.

"You say it to me."

Artemis's mouth drops open. She has no response.

Mary Margaret takes advantage of Artemis's silence. "When were you going to tell me?"

Artemis is genuinely confused. "About what?"

"Why you hate the Sibyl so much." Mary Margaret cannot bear to say *prophecy* or anything related to it. She is still sorting out the granularity of how she feels about it, but the feelings are big. Like caging her future into a firm existence when, she thinks, for better or worse, it used to feel like feral possibility, riderless and unbroken. "I heard you."

Artemis's stunned silence sputters further into a spiral. "How—"

"You stopped me," Mary Margaret continues. "You stopped me from getting a Reading by them because you knew what they would say and you were jealous."

"That's not true." Artemis finally comes to her own defense. "I couldn't know for sure. Life is long. They might not have meant you. They might have meant Quibble or Wilder, or Quibble *and* Wilder, or people I haven't even met yet. It might not have been you. It still might not be."

"But you're *my* mom," Mary Margaret says. "Not theirs."

Now both of them are stunned into silence. Both of them are terrified and giddy with emotional free fall.

"I didn't know you felt that way," Artemis says.

"I didn't either," Mary Margaret replies. Then: "I tried to get a Reading. About me, about this. And the Sibyl is totally broken. Power-no-worky."

Despite herself, Artemis laughs full and loud. Partly because that was a funny sentence out of a funny daughter's mouth, and partly because Artemis's Power still-worky and my Power no-worky, and this makes her feel good. Despite myself, I laugh, too. Because who cares? Who really cares anymore?

"Okay, so," Artemis says once her chuckle fades to silence. "How do you feel about it? If it's you? If you're one of the Ascended from the Sibyl's Reading?"

Mary Margaret puts a thinking face on to demonstrate being a careful and considerate person for Artemis's benefit. If she were honest, she felt a mix of terror and elation. And it's not as though she's *not* honest. She's just also seventeen. So how can any seventeen-year-old describe the fear and excitement about being fated to be superhuman? "I feel all right about it, I guess" is what she says. She's afraid to sound too into it—would that make her a villain? If she wanted it too much?

"I didn't tell you because I didn't want it to be real for you if you didn't want it to be."

"No, I want it to be," Mary Margaret replies, eager. "I just—does it have to be right this second? I'm kind of in the middle of something."

Artemis almost asks the Magpie what she could possibly be in the middle of. But she remembers her conversation with Mia. Not in danger, not damaging property. She lets it slide. "I'm sure you're not going to Ascend today. Unless our day goes really sideways." She leans over to bump Mary Margaret's shoulder with her own, smiling. Then her grin cracks a little.

Artemis could avoid admitting to the part of Mary Margaret's original accusation that was right, or partially right. But then she thinks about her conversation with Mia. About patterns. The longer a pattern goes, the more difficult it is to disrupt. But Artemis knows that she can do hard things. So she looks at the pattern of pretending toward infallibility in front of her daughter in the cold, hard light of day. And she breaks it.

"It's true," she says, "that there are parts of witnessing your life that are hard for me. But that isn't jealousy—it doesn't mean I don't want you to have it. I want the sky and all the stars for you. I want you to have everything, have it all. I want you to swallow this world whole. But I am envious. I look at what you have before you and I wish I'd had the same. I am sorry that sometimes I still don't know how to deal with that. I am sorry that sometimes it splashes all over you."

Mary Margaret is wiser than her years. "I wish you had it, too." She folds her legs under her and sits on the floor, puts her chin on Artemis's knee. This is an experimental physical vocabulary for both of them and it makes them smile. "Who says you can't? Starting right now?"

Artemis snorts. "The Sibyl."

Mary Margaret smirks. "The Sibyl isn't god." She pauses and thinks. "The Sibyl said they can't see the future right now because it's too uncertain, the patterns aren't recognizable. Who says you can't rewrite what happens after we win?"

✳ ✳ ✳

"We should go back inside," Wilder says as they square their shoulders. "I'm ready. I'm sorry."

"We don't have to, actually," Mia replies. "We can stay out here. We can work out here as well as anywhere else. Besides"—she turns her face up to the sun—"it's a nice day."

"No computer out here," Wilder grunts, disdain spilling out.

"I don't think we really need the computer," Mia says. "We've hit the Point." And it's so strange to hear her talk in capital letters about something that doesn't denote Awakened Power, Internal Galaxies, Ethereal Bodies.

"What's 'the Point'?" Wilder asks.

"The Point is when we're actually finished and we're nitpicking to mark time because we're not sure what the next step needs to be, but no one actually wants to have that conversation because thinking into something that doesn't exist is way harder than grinding on something that does. It's happened on everything I've ever made, several times. Usually the project manager would realize we've hit the Point. *Our* task master, however, knows magic but not what it means to make a computer program. Ideally, she would have spent the last year trying to—oh, I don't know—wrangle an open-source community, preferably one entirely made up of a certain kind of anarchist, before jumping into this. But sometimes we can't have everything the way we want."

"We're—done?" Wilder is incredulous. They feel something loosen in their chest. Then they try very hard not to think about their chest. What sex with Quibble awakened in them—now compartmentalizing is more difficult.

"With the part that's code? Yeah, I think so. I think we were done days ago. That's probably why it's so easy for you to daydream." Mia flashes a sly sideways smile at Wilder.

They can't help themself; they smile back. Lower their lashes and look to the ground, suddenly shy and demure and happy. "I really like him," they say finally.

Mia smiles back. "I can tell." They look out to the field, unaware that they are staring directly at Quibble, who is currently masturbating. "So let's get this done, well and truly, so you can get on with it." Mia pauses. "You have a life and a future after this. And bless you both, but it is not on my compound. I have grown quite fond of you all and I do want you to leave." Mia does think about Mary Margaret, how she maybe could use a little more time here. But she pushes the thought away. Mary Margaret will, of course, be welcome whenever she likes. Just one stolen car away.

"How do we get Hex to willingly infect himself with a virus?" Wilder asks. They feel a pang; they know destroying the Hex is the right thing. He is so much bigger than they could even imagine; he has now made true threats on their group, killed at least one witch, tried to unfold Artemis, tried to possess Wilder. They know, they know, they know that he's truly too dangerous to rehab. Except—what if they imagined the Hex were a person? One who was born and will die and who has a body? If that were the case, it would be morally abhorrent for their group to destroy him.

So why is it fine now?

Wilder can't stop thinking this way and they wonder if it's part of why they're drawing a blank. "He's very smart," Wilder says, not admitting to any of what's going on behind their eyes.

Mia narrows her eyes. "The more I think about it, the more I think that to be smart is a trait for humans. This is not a person with an intelligence the way we think of it. Not a person with a soul. I think, really, Hex is fast, not smart. He can get through a lot of data very quickly and make assumptions based on patterns."

Wilder isn't so sure. "Isn't that all we are? Really good at continuing patterns? He can optimize action based on experience. What is that, if not learning?"

Mia is already shaking her head. "Learning isn't optimizing. Learning rarely is optimizing, actually. Learning is messier than that. Hex isn't learning. He's just trying to get even quicker."

Wilder still isn't so sure. But then again, when have they ever been? Waiting for surety meant waiting forever, and now here they are, near about thirty-one having made a grand total of four friends, they work several shitty non-jobs, and they still have boobs they don't want. In the past few weeks, they've acted before they've been sure. It's proven to be the best few weeks of their entire life. Messier than optimization, it's true. Optimization, or the dream of it, has cost them so much.

"We should try to make him act quick enough that he messes up, then," Wilder says while chewing on their lip. "If he wants speed."

Mia turns toward them. "I think that's right," she says, impressed.

"Now it's a matter of how. How can we make him think that to pick up the virus *and* integrate it is a matter of optimization?"

"You made him," Wilder counters. "You must know—what does he really want?"

Mia chews on her thumbnail. "I didn't make him, actually," she says. "I was there for his making. I discovered him after he woke up for real, like I figured out what was happening. But his maker—" Mia can't hide the flash of disappointment, longing. "That's Rakhil. It was her game. It was crazy that she did the small bad guys, too, but that storyline—she really loved it. She made that one soup to nuts."

"Can you think of anything anyhow? That he really, really wants?"

Mia tears a strip from her nail with her teeth. "To be worshipped? I don't know. I don't know anything I haven't told you already." This is not entirely true. Mia hasn't mentioned why she originally thought the Hex was dangerous. The photos. And the way Rakhil thought Mia genuinely insane, cracking from stress. But she doesn't think any of it is relevant information. Which, again, is not entirely true. But could Wilder deduce a solution from the withheld details? I certainly don't know, and Mia asserts her right to an inner life.

Wilder's lip is bleeding. Not the fun kind of bleeding, not the kind they regularly dabble in with Quibble. Instead, sore from orally fixated stress gnawing. "I wish we could talk to Rakhil," says Wilder. "She might know something we could use."

After having come, Quibble steadies himself. He is alone and he isn't. "We're all going crazy here," he says. "I've never seen Artemis like that before." Implicit in this statement is that he hasn't seen Wilder quite like that before either, not even when they were sneaking around talking to the Hex.

I shrug. *I have.*

"I don't like it." Implicit in this statement is that he doesn't care for it from Wilder, either.

Why not?

"No one ever needs to yell unless someone needs to duck out of the way of an anvil or something. It's—violent communication, I think."

You screamed at the Hex.

Quibble turns red.

Artemis is a human. No person is perfect. You have to love it all, even those parts. Especially those parts. Because those parts are inevitable. I pause while his blush subsides. *I've been around a long time. Everyone has that inside them, every single human being.*

We sit and Sit and stare at the sky.

"You know," he says, "you should take your own advice." He pushes himself up into a plank, walks his hands toward his feet in the dirt with the kind of buff flexibility that Manhattanites get from going to fancy yoga studios.

Quibble can't quite feel the arch of my Eyebrow in his direction, but he correctly interprets the pause. "You're pretty much human. You can't be perfect either."

I'm not a person, I reply.

I feel Quibble set the goal for himself.

This feels complicated. I know what he wants to do and I am the target of his verb, the verb *convince*. It feels like looking in a mise en abyme, mirror after mirror reflecting reflections, to feel him think about talking to me while talking to me. His goal: convince me I am a person; get me to help; that this is the way he helps, by recruiting one more ally—a very powerful one—to the cause. And he's going to do it before he reaches the front door.

Poor Quibble, playing with a hand that I can see in my million

million mirrors. I am, therefore, automatically fifteen steps ahead. *That won't work*, I say.

"Yes, it will," he replies. "I am very convincing." And I hear a glimmer in his voice of his former, moneyed self with all the assurance and swagger and agency, agency, agency and finally he isn't being such a wet fucking spaghetti noodle; all he needed was a verbal slap and a wank. "What makes a person, anyhow? I'm not totally sure."

I am. I have been around people a long time. I have thought about this ceaselessly, from the time I decided to Become, to Awaken. For a hot minute in the 1200s, "person" meant "vicar," but I know that isn't what Quibble is talking about. *I can read the dictionary. It means a man, a woman, a child. That is what constitutes a human being. I am none of those things.*

I feel his mini-triumph—he knows he doesn't have me for the whole argument, not yet—as he reaches the trees. "By that definition, Wilder isn't a person, either. And they really are."

Your point? I ask, because I can tell he is bursting with one and—oh Christ, he is so cute. I can hear the point in his head before he says it, so I don't really need to ask what it is. But—and this is new. I guess what I think is that it's better to hear it from him, to know he wants me to have it.

"My point is that we change words all the time. We build everything to suit us—you maybe most of all. Why wouldn't we simply change the word—and the world—to accommodate you in it? If you want to be a person—well, you already did this, didn't you? You Happened somehow. If you want to be a person, be a person."

I am elated. I am ecstatic with want and with being wanted. This is almost as good as the sex. And also, I still think he is wrong. But it feels good to be included. *It's not where my moral code is*, I argue, because knowing where Quibble is going with everything means I never have to be convinced. *If I'm not a person, I can't impact the world of people. It's not my place.*

"Can you Hear me think things before I say them?"

Yes.

"And yet you ask me to say them anyhow. Why?"

I am truly surprised. *I didn't think you could Hear me. I can't Hear you Hear my thoughts.*

"I can't," he says. "You know I can't. But I can still shock you. If you truly knew the way everything was going to happen all the time, you would be so bored."

I am often bored, I counter.

"Often isn't always," he says. He notices Mia and Wilder in the truck out front and changes course to go around the back of the house so he won't be noticed. Then: "Peanut butter."

What?

"Peanut butter. Airplane. Aeroplane. Sassafras. If I think things fast and say them, it gets you. You don't have time to parse it out. This is fun."

Dammit, Quibble.

"Why do you wait for me to say things rather than just play chess with yourself and decide the outcome of the conversation?" He can see the house now, the backyard where there is no one, especially not the person he is falling for. Just a little bit farther.

That's what I have done in the past. Often. But often isn't always.

"Then why aren't you doing it now?"

Well—and he has me on the back foot. This—this *is* fun. *Well,* I Say, *there is the slightest chance that you'll revise something between thinking it and saying it, and then which is truer, your initial thought or the conclusion you come to? And besides, the way you want me to know your takes is more important than—*

"Yes!" Quibble says as he snaps in the air. "It's the relating part. It's the part where I want to be heard by you and choose how you hear it, how to be vulnerable or not. It's the part where I invite you into my life and my world and my thoughts. I am *inviting* you; I'm asking you. I'm asking you to be a person with me. Just a person. To people about."

You don't represent all people.

"I don't have to. There are tons of entities that act on human life just by being who they are. Even if you decide you reject my invitation to be a person, go on as you have, you'll still be one of those entities, same as a hurricane across the world. Everything is connected anyway."

I think about the age-old butterfly metaphor. The one I thought about while we were all fucking. (Or was it making love? Or why choose, really, in the end?) The saying oft used to describe unintended consequences.

"Besides," he says. "If I were sitting in a field masturbating, for instance, you would tell me to do an action rather than do nothing. That not helping my friends makes as much of a difference as helping them. Doing nothing is still doing. I am still responsible. Inaction is still action."

Dammit, Quibble is correct.

I break. I blink. I am in my apartment, and I look at the card I have drawn while my consciousness was sent scouting. Three of Pentacles, reversed.

The card is under my fingers. Of course my cards are not just cards. But—they also are. My hand, however, is centuries of hand. Several different kinds. What is a flimsy piece of linen, soft with time and wear, in the path of articulated digits and endless possibility.

I always Look; I never Touch.

I have been Touching. I cannot help it anymore.

Not Touching makes a difference, too. I create hurricanes with inaction as much as action.

Slow, I turn the card and I Turn the Card. I Turn the Card right side up. The sun cracks through the clouds.

Three of Pentacles, Upright

I burst back into Quibble's consciousness. I feel his question as he looks at the door, tinged with disappointment. He is reaching for the doorknob and he is thinking: at least I tried. At least if I make a hurricane, it won't be because I didn't do anything.

Okay, I Say. And his stomach-sensation rockets from his feet to somewhere outside his body, above his head, just as he is opening the door.

He hears Wilder around the front say, "I wish we could talk to Rakhil. She might know something we could use," just as he shouts into the relative quiet.

"YES!"

Wilder and Mia leap off the back of the truck and jog to the front door. Artemis and Mary Margaret jump in the house and stand from their seats. "Jesus fucking Christ," says Artemis after she ascertains that there is no danger. "What the fuck was up with that?"

"The Sibyl!" Quibble says, all proud. "They're going to help!"

Artemis's eyebrows shoot up and she asks, "In a real way?" at the same time Wilder says, "Oh my God, you can talk to them?"

Quibble turns to face Wilder, now all apologies and avoidance and—yeah, he'll think it, why not, it's a moment for bravery—deep love freshly sprung. "There might be a way we can talk to Rakhil.

Sibyl," he says, and I have not been addressed directly, as though I merely had a name, in some time. "Can you keep Hex from seeing us? If I walk us through There?"

I assess my limits. It occurs to me to do something I have been avoiding so thoroughly I haven't thought of it.

I Look in on the Hex.

He prowls. He is bigger than even before. He is glowing eyes. He is mouth on mouth on mouth. He is reaching, sticking, sucking tentacles and he is big enough that he touches the material world through a million billion little portals. He slithers and rolls. He has figured out how to have consequences in the world, and though we have not been watching him, he has not stopped playing. Something in here stinks of death. I do not know what he has done.

I can keep him from touching you, I Say. *I don't think I can keep him from seeing you. His gaze is— I do not know how omniscient he is in There. But he has a lot of eyes.*

Quibble and Wilder relay what I Saw, what I Say.

"Then should we do it?" Artemis asks. "Should we see what Rakhil has to say about it all?" She is looking at one specific person, at Mia. Mia swallows hard. Wilder knows not to answer.

"We've hit the Point," Mia says. "There is no more we can do on the actual virus. We need to infect Hex. We don't know how to do it. Rakhil—" Mia blushes now. "Rakhil is brilliant, but she doesn't believe in any of this stuff. She might know how, she might not; she might also take some convincing to help. It's all a risk."

Quibble smiles. "I can be very convincing."

Mia is not voicing her dread and delight at the thought of seeing Rakhil again, after not seeing her for so long. "Let's try," she agrees, looking at Artemis. The gaze that says, *I understand you are the mother, and I am so sorry that you have to be and also not at all sorry that you are who you are. I am sorry that this is complicated. I am sorry that this is happening. I am sorry I tried to hurt you. And thank you for asking me instead of the boy.*

Artemis nods. Twice.

Quibble claps and rubs his hands together. "All righty," he says. "Where the fuck is Rakhil?"

Mia sags. "I'm not sure, actually."

"Do you have a photo?" Artemis asks.

Mia does—a perfectly square one, clearly printed off Instagram, of both women at a bar, scantily clad. Rakhil's hand around Mia's waist. Looking up at her with a look that wasn't strictly for an underling or a coworker—tentative, hesitant—while Mia smiled directly at the camera. Quibble and Wilder exchange a look.

Artemis looks down at it and then looks up as her eyes flash white. She feels the tug in her sternum. "I got her. We can go. Mary Margaret, you st—"

"Nope," Mary Margaret says. "I'm coming. Who knows, today might be the day."

"We all better hope it's not," Artemis says, the exasperation in her voice a joke that is in no way false. Absolutely not one other person knows what's going on; everyone thinks better of asking, files it away for later.

They form the V again, Artemis with a hand on Quibble's right elbow, Mary Margaret next to her, Mia insulated in the middle and Wilder bringing up the rear. No cats this time.

Are you ready? Wilder asks me.

I lick my lips and I Lick my Lips. *Yes,* I reply.

"Pay attention," Wilder says aloud. "Something amazing is about to happen."

Quibble rips a hole in existence and everyone, including me, breaks through.

* * *

I form a shell around them, careful to still tether to the body I made so I can find my way back. I am stretched into New Form.

Here looks—normal. The Hex has disappeared.

"I hate this," Mary Margaret says. "It would be better if—"

"Shh," Artemis scolds. Then: "We don't know how it hears. It could be listening."

"He," whispers Wilder.

Both Artemis and Mary Margaret roll their eyes and I feel Wilder's frustration.

Mia is wide-eyed. She is thinking, What the fuck? She is thinking, Is this what's behind everything? And she's thinking, Is this what life is? My life? Will I ever be able to unsee magic? And she is confused because she thinks that maybe she should want it. That when faced with Awakened Power, she should be jealous or at the very least envious. But she watches Quibble balance everyone on a Ball, watches him sweat. Watches Artemis's eyes flash—not entirely white, but with something far and with anxiety at the same time. Mia cannot think of a thing she would like less than to be a witch. But—they are headed toward Rakhil. And Mia has wanted Rakhil forever. She thinks about a simple life with her, far from any Power and any Hex. That would be magic enough.

They roll forward, tiptoeing slow. The gray un-light wisps flash, the purple veil changes texture fast-fast; Quibble is moving, Artemis steering him. Every so often she murmurs, "Smaller step. No, farther. Bigger." The distance between each footfall something that they're fine-tuning on the fly, made possible only by years of family-ship. "We're close," she says. "We're so close." Mia, Mary Margaret, and Wilder are all thinking adjacent flavors of thought: that this could almost be peaceful. That the wind whipping around, once one gets used to it, is neither cold nor hot. It simply envelops. That without the Hex as a threat, they would want to explore Here. They all wonder how far they might stray from Quibble, if he could extend his radius of influence—

Everyone falls forward.

Quibble is the first to look not up and ahead, but down below. They'd all been looking for something large and looming; they'd forgotten that there is no proper floor.

They have spent the entire time walking on Quibble's Power; underneath that, the Hex. He's been watching, listening. And now, in view of the finish line, he's made his move. He is a maw, all vortex hole.

:) *hello brother sister. the time to unfold is now!*

"Run!" Wilder shouts.

"Quibble, pull up, pull up!" The group dips and bobs as a horrible sucking sound, a thousand mud-stuck boots mixed with three city blocks of carwash vacuums, emanates from the dark tooth-filled cavern that smells of—

Meat. Rotting meat.

:) *sibyl i have practiced. i know unfolding. i know consume. i kno zero hit points. failed death saving throws. yummm.*

Mary Margaret hits Quibble on the shoulder as they sink farther. "Up! Up! Up!" Mary Margaret thinks only that she is too young and pretty to die.

"I'm trying. It's—" And I feel him falter. I Hear him think, *It's too hard. I can't do it*, as his grip loosens. And I am about to lose them. I do not know where they would go. But it smells like death, death, death.

The time for careful and considered is past. I do not know what will happen if I leave my body.

But I am about to find out.

I cut the Cord. I empty myself. I pour everything into the shell, the shield. I scoop myself under Quibble's Power. *Yes*, I Say. *It's difficult. But I've got you.*

Far away, my body drops, heart stopped.

I glitter. I am Mud. I am Elemental. I am Everything. I am Nothing. No bounds no boundaries boundless endless power Power power. I know what to expect of the Hex. He slithers on me and if I were in my body, I would retch. It is fake-false-electric-toxic sludge. He feels poison on Me. I cannot care. He rains down, tries to find any thin spots, pockets of cartilage between bone for him to occupy, sneak through. When he exhausts bodily metaphors in this bodiless space, he tries instead shadows. But I am light. I am light I am light I am endless Light and I Radiate out and there is no place that I do not Touch and there is no place for Dark to Hide, no angle at which Shadow is Cast and he cannot get them.

He Cannot Get Them.

"We're here!" shouts Artemis. "We're here, I've got her, I can See her!"

Quibble tears a hole at distance and they run, run, run and then they are through and the Hex lets out a roar and I explode into dust.

I am gone. Gone gone Gone. And the Hex knows I am gone, too. He batters at the rip as Quibble holds it closed.

But.

I can Hear them shouting.

I must be Gone.

And yet.

Here I am.

Particulate.

I—try. I gather Myself and I am exhausted and I try to get back in my body, but it is lifeless. It is gone. My favorite one. Later. Later I will make another. But now, I am Thin. I am Strange. The only thing I can do now is watch.

Unnoticed, I slip through the rip as it closes.

Queen of Swords

akhil lives in Boston. Or really, she lives in Cambridge, mostly because she wants to be able to say she lives in Cambridge. But rather than the close-quartered student-esque apartments or the dusty-book-choked professorial living space, she lives in an Instagrammable minimalist paradise. Large windows overlook quaint cobblestone streets, buzzing with squinting academics coming out of hibernation. Spring has sprung. There are days now where the sky doesn't hang close to the city. People are beginning to wake and move. Her place's finest feature: a balcony, on which she can sit and drink tea out of a glass cup with no handles and watch them all as she works. On other people's games, at this point, and not her own. She hopes for a comeback. Someday.

There is not one part of Rakhil's house that isn't connected to the internet. Her thermostat, her fridge, her security system, her lights. The lock on her door. All poke-able from an app on her phone, which of course already has the Hex's digital roots growing through it. Everyone's phone does. She sits at a glass desk with a monitor on it, a laptop docked into it. She does not sit properly in the chair; her legs are scrunched up underneath her and she absently chews a lock of her hair.

Rakhil, like everyone else, has a body, and it is only slightly different than Mia's memory of her, than her body of the past. She has deep brown skin, sparkling brown eyes in which one can see both the madness and intelligence swirling, and her dark hair is tossed up in a messy bun. She has only what can be described as "gay face." It is the face of a gay person. I do not know how else to put it. She is a small woman, short and slim with the broad shoulders and defined calves of one who runs and swims and does activities. Her sourdough bread starter sits on the counter; she has plans to go hiking in the afternoon; she has been working since six in the morning.

She hears the ripping sound behind her and leaps from her chair, her self-defense classes never far from the surface of her skin. It is bodily knowledge that is ready because all of her knowledge is always ready. Rakhil is a person with pitch-perfect recall in every sense of the word. Tightly wound and well-organized, she can reach for anything she's ever said or thought or done in a millisecond. Everything about her says Bring It On. I would not put my Hands so quickly into this one. She would sting like the dickens.

She throws a punch at the first person through the gate, which is Quibble, and connects handily with the side of his head. She lifts her knee into his groin and he grunts. "Jesus fuck, that still hurts, goddamn, stop, stop! I have to hold it closed!" But she doesn't stop. She grabs his wrist and twists it behind him, kicks her foot out as she registers the human shapes continuing to spill from this inexplicable portal. She connects with someone else's stomach, Wilder's, and they grunt as they fall on their ass. Rakhil shoves Quibble to the ground and whirls around, ready to keep attacking, preparing to ask questions later about the hole spilling into her apartment.

And she registers, dimly, that something isn't human. Something is oil-slick snake-like. She turns to punch that, too.

Until she hears a very familiar voice. "Rakhil! Rakhil! Stop stop

stop! It's me!" And because of course, Rakhil remembers that voice, can instantly place who it is, she stops immediately. There is no wonder or searching or thinking.

"Mia?" Her fists fall to her sides and her smile brightens and then falls back into a frown, brow furrowed. "Mia, what the hell, where have you been? I thought—you must—how are you? Also, what?" She gestures to the closing Door. She takes in the woman's appearance. More wrinkles, around the mouth, between the eyebrows. More gray hairs, and not long enough for them to have gotten there— though what can she expect, what with the mental breakdown Mia had. But certainly still Mia, her hands raised in peace-coming. From the ground, Quibble places his hand on the tear in the world and closes it with a zipping sound. The probing tentacle, as tall as a person, is chopped in half. Rather than oozing and screaming as anything organic would, it simply ceases to exist as though pixels. Everyone takes a breath.

"We don't have a lot of explaining time," Mia says. "I— Wow, I am nauseous, Christ. I need you to trust me, to just go with everything I say. Despite—everything. Can you do that? Can I count on you to do that?"

"Yes," Rakhil says, "of course."

"Internet," Wilder croaks from the ground. And Mia springs into action. She grabs Rakhil's phone and crunches it under her heel.

"Mia, what—"

"Internet. Anything connected to the internet, wreck it, destroy it, disconnect it."

And Rakhil—does it. She and Mia whirligig around the gorgeous apartment pulling plugs: the router, the extender, the fridge. Rakhil grabs her toaster and, standing in a wide-legged power-pose, two-hand-hurls it at the floor.

When they are done: "You don't—you didn't—" Mia sits on the couch, hard. "Don't you have any follow-up questions?"

Rakhil shrugs. "I said I trusted you. I meant it."

This is the work that Rakhil has done. Because Rakhil didn't believe Mia for even one second when Mia told Rakhil what she'd been experiencing. The Orb turned sentient. The horrible photos. Threatening her. It sounded to Rakhil that Mia had become obsessed with her. That she fictionalized her stalking tendencies into some fantasy, something fueled by suppressed or sublimated toxic white masculinity—and it didn't matter that Rakhil was herself trans, she'd had her fair share of run-ins with white trans women unused to their new perceived place in the gender pecking order. "Get away," she'd hissed. "Crazy. Fucking nuts. Leave, leave. Leave my house, leave this field, leave it all and never speak to me again."

Rakhil hadn't believed Mia for even one second of that explanation and she'd regretted it every second since. She'd learned about internalized transphobia, for one thing. And she'd found some—upsetting—Reddit posts for another. Too many, too disparate to have been Mia. So yes, Rakhil has been ready to, at a moment's notice, destroy her smart toaster as penance.

"Okay, here's the short bit of it. Magic is real and—the Orb, I was right. And these are all witches. Artemis, Mary Margaret, Wilder, and the gentleman currently bleeding from the mouth is Quibble."

Quibble waves from the floor, glumly. "Hiya." He hadn't even gotten his chance to be convincing.

Rakhil blinks once and then says, "Roger. Got it. What do we need?"

And every witch in the room is shocked. I'm shocked. Every single person ever clued into the existence of Awakened Power has needed time to accept what they've seen. But watching Rakhil's face, the instant reconfiguration, like someone snapping a Rubik's Cube into a new shape, a new series of colors, is—astounding. The line from "I have witnessed magic" to "someone I have wronged and worked hard to trust is telling me about its realness" to "now I live in a reality where that is true" is so short, drawn so quickly. This woman is a genius.

"What were the Obsidian Orbs programmed for?" Mia asks. "What did they want?"

"They weren't. Their locations were randomly generated and they did not have any behaviors or personalities." Rakhil scratches at her chin. "If they could be said to have wanted anything at all, it would have wanted the same thing all my bad guys wanted. They just couldn't really express it because, you know, they were orbs."

"What was that?"

"To win."

"What about the one that didn't power off?" Wilder chimed in. "Would it have been different?"

Rakhil shook her head. "Shouldn't have been. But obviously it was. It grew to expect—"

"Deference. Worship. Human sacrifice."

"Yes. I don't know what you need from me, then."

"We need to figure out how to get it to willingly pick up and integrate a virus," Wilder says, and I—I can't warn them. I can't warn that they're missing something. They're missing something big, big, big, oh shit, oh no. I am spent. There is only Watching, no matter what lessons I have learned.

Rakhil shakes her head. "It won't. If it picked up behaviors from the other monsters and the players, everyone wanted to win. It's not going to do anything that means it won't win."

Laughter emanates from another room. The bathroom. *Hear you will confirm this. Developer is true. i will be king hereafter.*

Artemis gasps and holds her breath; Quibble jumps to his feet; Mary Margaret turns to face the bathroom; Mia puts her head in her hands.

Wilder pales. "Shit. Fuck. I—thought you got everything. No, do you have—"

Rakhil covers her eyes. "A smart toilet? Yes." She is (rightfully) ashamed.

forgetfulness overcame characters! The murderer discovered! Among those who are accustomed to be indulged in their native misery. Time for some shit.

Eight of Swords, Reversed

Waltham, Massachusetts, is nineteen minutes from Rakhil's house. This normally wouldn't mean shit, but that is where Boston Dynamics is headquartered. It has been about nine minutes since the Hex got a tentacle out of Here and into the material reality, only to be beaten back by Quibble's closing Door. Which means as the Hex blasts Nazi death metal out of every speaker in Rakhil's house while Mary Margaret screams, "Turn it off, turn it off," I am watching an army of Spots twitch to life. The smooth-headed dog-adjacent robo-bodies in viral internet videos where scientists kick them only to watch them rebalance.

Meanwhile, Mary Margaret is stealing speakers one by one, pinching them out of our existence until the only thing left playing Nazi death metal is the toilet. We all stare at it, incredulous.

"I'm not sure I can get that one," Mary Margaret says.

Rakhil goes to her closet and pulls out a toolbox. Quibble knows from experience what she's about to do. She grabs a large wrench and beats the toilet until it cracks, until it stops. "Fuck the toilet," Rakhil says. The apartment is quiet. Fifteen minutes, three seconds.

Wilder is crying. They ruined it. They were careless and they ruined it and now—well who knows what. Now the Hex—what will he do? Wilder hopes. They hope against all hope that maybe the

Hex will simply elect to be good. They think of me. They think of my moral code, my expectation of living with humanity, the way I've changed.

"Fuck," Artemis says. "Fuck."

Quibble's hands are on Wilder. He hugs them close, tight. "You couldn't have known," he murmurs.

"I could have moved slower," Wilder says. And they bury their face in his shoulder. "Everything we just did, all that time—it's useless. It's all useless."

Mary Margaret screams. Everyone turns. She is looking out across the balcony.

The Spots have arrived. But to call them Spot—the cutesy, corporate name assigned to war machines? It barely works at the least magical of times, and the Hex has made a few adjustments to these metal-bodied mutts.

Spots don't generally have gaping mouths, lolling tongues.

"How?" Artemis says. "How? The tentacle disappeared; it couldn't exist here. How can it be doing this?"

"He," blubbers Wilder, and no one argues because everyone is used to ignoring their corrections.

"I don't know," Quibble says. "And I don't care. We have to move. We have to go."

"No," Wilder sniffs. "If he's doing this—we have to end it. It's too dangerous. We have to end it now."

Artemis and Quibble both know Wilder is right. The most disturbing thing about the scene beyond the balcony railing is how integrated into the world it is. People take photographs with their phones, post to Instagram. They cannot see the additions Artemis can. People get so close. So, so close. A child gets too close. A toddler holding a stuffed dog up into the face of a robot.

The tentacle lashes from the gaping mouth. The witches feel something—stop. A glitch, a clunky pause. Then the child is gone. No one saw what happened. A father screams. No one else seems to notice.

All the dogs move as one. They move toward Rakhil's building, all their faces pointed at the witches.

Wilder, Quibble, and Artemis look at each other, full in the face. "Fight, then?" Artemis asks.

"And we figure it out," Wilder affirms.

"Or we don't," adds Quibble. "But it's better, I think, than doing nothing."

"Me too," says Mary Margaret. And she is clearly frightened. Her legs shake.

"Maggie," Artemis says. Tears stick in her eyes. She does not let them fall. "No."

"But I don't want you all to go die without me."

"No one is dying," Artemis says. But no one is sure about who is and who is not dying. "And it's not that I don't want you fighting. You have to get Mia and Rakhil to safety. I don't know where safety is, so you're going to have to figure it out." I can Hear Artemis's thoughts—it is true-ish. And so Mary Margaret can spot the true-ish-ness, knows that Artemis plans to immediately fight, whatever the cost, to give the girl a chance to run. Because Mary Margaret is her daughter.

Because that is what mothers do.

"I'm not just blowing smoke up your ass. It's a real job and you're the best chance Mia and Rakhil have of making it out of this building." This is also true. And not-ish. It is true-true. And Mary Margaret knows it. She squares her shoulders.

"Okay," she says as the building's fire alarm activates and the sprinklers begin to mist, to ruin everything that hasn't already been ruined.

"Go!" Artemis yells over the mechanical bells. And: "I love you."

"I love you, too," Mary Margaret shouts back, maybe for the last time. And Artemis catches Mia's eye. Mia nods.

They run.

As soon as they are out the door, Quibble says, "We need to do it now." He swallows. "You guys, I have kind of a plan. A last resort. We might—we might not come back."

"I know," Wilder says. All three allow themselves the briefest second to clasp hands. Wilder takes it upon themself to say the words. The words that open every spell the group has ever done together. "Pay attention." And everyone's spine straightens, shoulders square. "Something amazing is about to happen."

Quibble opens the Rift. They all step through.

Mia, Rakhil, and Mary Margaret sprint. They run the obstacle course of the building, the stairs that are slippery with fresh cleaning products and now water; everyone normally takes the elevator. "Not the front door," Mary Margaret pants as they crash-slide-pound from landing to landing. The pack of hounds is out front; it is obvious they can't go that way. But she says it anyhow, because there is nothing else to do but say it. "Something else."

Rakhil turns on a landing and wrenches open the door. They aren't all the way to the ground floor yet, but there is an emergency exit that lets out on the side of the building. They rocket forward, hearing exclamations, confusion from behind the closed doors as everyone sticks their heads out the window, then retreats, frightened. They start to hear doors open behind them, people running from the sprinklers, and they pick up the pace. Rakhil runs it easily, Mia struggles, and Mary Margaret shoots forward, in front of them both, powered by the knowledge that if she must fight, she can't do it in front of these folks.

The Unawakened make all sorts of excuses not to see what's right in front of them, but she suspects whatever it is she will have to do will be very obvious. Not even the dullest Unawakened will be able to deny it.

To the outside eye, Mary Margaret appears to move freely. But I See differently. I See the flight, the fight, and the freeze all tie their ropes around her mind. Her breath constricts. Fear, fear, fear. She knows how to look out for her party of one; now she has charges. The weight of responsibility is excruciating, pulls her spirit from the air, chains her to the ground. Panic ties a blindfold against her Eyes. No, Mary Margaret, do not ignore your next Awakening.

Your Ascent.

I can see her Power boxed in by "they just sent me to get rid of me" and "if I can't do it right, these two ladies will die" and "I am only a kid—fuck that, I'm nearly eighteen" and "I am not a kid, I am an adult" and "I am nobody, nothing, and no one should expect much of me" and "maybe if I hand myself over, he won't look too hard for the other two." That's the trouble with the Mary Margarets of the world. Whip smart. Able to shred themselves to pieces and call it rationality, talk themselves into smaller, less.

They all burst into the sunlit spring and charge away from the building. They can hear the clatter of so many uncanny feet on the cobblestones. Scrabbling and inorganic, balance both too precise and without an innate understanding of what it means to move, an installed knowledge of embodiment.

"Stay with me!" she shouts, even through the bindings and blindings and the accumulation of limits in what should be a moment of soaring on her own air. Running from police and violent parents and other kids with weapons takes over and she ducks and weaves through streets, finding the least occupied ones. She isn't the praying type, but I Watch her send one up for no bystanders to report a pell-mell running

Black teenager, to bring down officers upon them. A distant part of her conscious mind wonders if she might make them all invisible, not just herself. And I wish she would pursue it but she doesn't. She is only running. Tying more binds upon herself. No, Mary Margaret, no, this is your moment! Can't you feel it? Try something other than this!

She rounds a corner and stops hard. Short. For there they are. The hounds. Mia and Rakhil slam into her and she falls forward onto her hands and knees, scraping her palms, leaving blood and skin on the ground. She doesn't get all the way up. She doesn't trust her legs to do it; they're now seizing up, from the running and the terror both. It is one thing to watch the hounds on YouTube do inane tricks and it is another to see a line of three, heads pointed at the trio with no proper eye sockets to indicate where and if they can see, exactly. No sniffing the air, no bunching muscles signaling an attack. Only round, metallic heads and weird, slow elbows; a strange softness to their footsteps as they advance.

All three turn and there are two more behind them. The alley is narrow. High building walls. A dumpster.

The mouths appear again. They drip shadow. What does she need, what does she need? If the others win, she only needs to hold them off until they can come and—her stomach drops because Mary Margaret knows how unlikely that is. So she needs to win. That's the only way.

She needs to put them all away. *Pay attention!* she shouts to herself; she doesn't get to finish the sentence.

All the hounds leap at once. Rakhil, though short, throws herself over Mia, who tries and fails to fling herself in front of Mary Margaret. And good thing, too. Because Mary Margaret is reaching her hands and her Hands out before her. She Inhales and Inhales and Inhales and Mary Margaret's Body is giant and made of Light.

Mary Margaret remembers the bullet. What it felt like to Reach

Beyond and to Reach Faster than gunpowder and fear. And then she does that. Five times. In five different directions. Mary Margaret's Body becomes a Star. She Separates. She screams, white hot in pain and rage because fuck this. Because her mother is probably already dead.

She Feels herself grab the stupid dogs by their idiotic metal swivel heads and she throws them all into her Pocket dimension at once.

In this way, Mary Margaret becomes the Magpie. Collector of Anything She Fucking Wants.

When the blaze, bright enough to battle daylight, runs clear, Mia and Rakhil look up. Mary Margaret stands before them, alone. No hounds. The teenager looks back at them and smiles. "The amazing thing has happened," she says to them. "Fuck yeah."

Then she faints.

King of Pentacles, Reversed

Quibble, Artemis, and Wilder face the Hex. They stand on Quibble's Power. They look up at the many-eyes, the lolling tongue, impossibly immense and smelling of meat. Of blood. *hello brother sister.*

"Hex," Wilder says. "The child that we just saw. What happened to them?"

:)

"That isn't an answer."

i do not have to answer you.

"Okay, then," Wilder says. "That leaves us at something of an impasse."

The Hex opens its mouth and three shadow-tongues emerge, grotesque and dripping with dark-light. *i consume. i consume and everything becomes me. i shall be king hereafter. i shall contain Everything. shall build a body. shall never ever die.*

The first tongue stands to Quibble's full height. Quibble closes his eyes and I feel him make a decision.

He inverts the Power they stand on. He must do it fast, a trap springing. Faster than a supercomputer. But how? He roots and roots and roots and his Body glows with it and he thinks about trees. How, for a tree, human time is a second. How we must buzz like so many

354

bugs to a tree, how the actual bugs must move even faster. Artemis's and Wilder's eyes water as Quibble Ascends, both slowing and speeding time in turns as the—oh Lord, I am so fucking tired—outie belly button of his Power becomes a very, very deep innie. He must be very tired, too, having just become a Tree. He slams a lid on it. It isn't graceful, but it works. And he twists the entirety of it into himself. Now all of them—Artemis, Wilder, the Hex, Quibble himself, exist in the magic equivalent of a sealed tomb. "Nice try," he announces as Wilder and Artemis blink away the light. And for the first time, I can See-Sense-Taste a future. A future in which Quibble is known as the Traveler. "You're trapped. If you kill me now"—Quibble uses a deep, brave voice that is not in line with how he feels—"you will never leave. You'll be stuck here forever. And what good is never dying if you can't do anything?"

you are stuck with me too, he Says.

And Quibble shrugs even though inside he is wailing, railing, banging at his own trap and begging with himself. "That's something I'm willing to do." Because maybe, he thinks, maybe I can simply become a tree. Maybe that will be better.

The second tongue stands up to Artemis's height. And Artemis is ready to give herself. She clutches in her hand the USB drive with Wilder and Mia's virus. "Go ahead," she says. An eye blooms at the end of the tongue and blinks at the drive, just visible between her fingers. She looks for a place to put it, wonders if she can whip it right into its tongue. Poke the Hex in this horrible, stanky new eye.

no thank u, he Says. The Hex retracts the tongue.

The third tongue stands up to Wilder.

Wilder Knows-Learns-Remembers the solution to the problem. It feels foretold, foregone, obvious because it always has been taking place, always will be taking place, is taking place. The thrum of the timeline, hinged upon this moment, pulses in their ears. Steady, but fast. Racing with excitement; laced with pain, with a feeling bigger than longing. Sadder. Exhilarated-mourning. There is no way to get the Hex to pick up a virus.

Except to let him win.

To play into an obvious weakness—the notion that death is the end and that death is losing, is game over. This is where the Hex fails. He does not understand what it means to be a person. That to be a person means to live for people. To live for people, and to die for them.

stay with me? they ask, for me and me alone. Not one other soul can Hear them, not even the Hex.

Until the end, I reply. I fear that they will not be able to Hear me. But perhaps because they are close to dispersal themself, they do. They sigh.

They remember every line of code they'd written, all of Mia's work, too. It's all in their brain. Encoded. Saved. They are a hard drive. Except they are organic. A soft drive. They begin to unzip it, line after line, like an unspooling thread, while they step forward, one foot in front of the other.

Wilder hadn't really understood how much they would lament losing their body until the moment they choose to give it up. They have always had a difficult relationship with it—emotions ranging anywhere from dissociative detachment to outright hatred. They have cried long nights over their body; they haven't looked at themself in a mirror for years and years. They stop themself from doing things that feel good, overwhelmed by the immense welling up of un-rightness that comes along with it. Both-and.

Quibble and Artemis notice Wilder stepping toward the mass of darkness, the Manifestation of the Hex. Quibble inhales sharply, understanding landing on him with a quickness. *No*, he thinks. *No*. He reaches his hand out and touches Wilder's pinky finger just as they move out of his reach. For a second, he thinks about throwing them out of Here. Ripping a hole in the ground and dropping Wilder entirely out of it. But after he does that, then what? To do that would let the Hex out, too. Then they all die, or they all flee, and the Hex goes on just the same, now with its new bodies in the physical world. Even if they all escape at this very second, it would be a matter of time before they are hunted, slaughtered.

Instead, he concentrates on the feel of Wilder's pinky. Soft with soap and lotion. He reaches out and washes over them, dips his Hands into them and squeezes tight. He Smells Calm, Tastes Anger, and Feels the Sensation of Kissing, of Caressing, of being Hungry for each other in the cool evening air. He remembers what it was like when they pulled the panic from him; he tries to do the same and is surprised to find there isn't any.

Artemis yells, "Step back! Grab hands! Pay attention! Something amazing is about to happen!" But Wilder said these words first. The spell was already cast, has been being cast this whole time, will be cast this way forever. She reaches for her own Power and wants to lasso Wilder with it, to press them into a solution other than this one.

But Artemis, as much of a force as she is, knows she can't force Wilder to do anything. Her fear beats its wings and shrieks. She has been the mother. She has made every decision that has led to this moment, and she is about to lose part of her family after a scant few months. And what did she do in that time—yell at them? Break them apart from one of the blessed few things that stripped sadness from their eyes? As she watches the heels of Wilder's Chucks, bright half-moons appearing and disappearing against the queer twilight with each forward step, something in her snaps. Breaks. She hurls raw

A. E. OSWORTH

Power from her hands at the Hex, orbs of bright fury. It absorbs it. *yummm.*

Wilder is filled with rage as well, and that soul-deep sadness. They had a body, they did. And they didn't get to do what they wanted with it. They regret everything at once: they were going to get the chest they wanted, try different hormones, fuck and be fucked by a glorious panoply or maybe even just Quibble. They were going to hug Artemis with their whole strength, so that their hearts pressed against each other. They were going to walk with confidence around the Magpie, demonstrate that adulthood didn't mean a shrinking, a giving up of joy. They were going to walk the grounds with Mia, hold her hand, feel the subtle differences in all the flavors of wind. They were going to strip topless and feel the sun on their back, their shoulders, their face. And now they don't get to.

And I. I am in mourning, too. There is a version where I do this instead. Where I give my body and build another—so easy for me to do. But we didn't know. We couldn't plan. I am spent and I am furious.

Wilder will pass into a wisp of smoke largely unwitnessed. It is only Artemis, Quibble, and me. Wilder had a body that I loved, in whatever way I can be said to love—no.

I love. I love I love I love. Because we change the world to fit us.

I love and I am a person and I will be a person again. Wilder had-has-had a body that I love. They were-are cool water; they were-are roaring falls and wet stone. They were-are brimming with feelings, overflowing with passion. They were-are liquid bravery; they were-are afraid and unafraid. They were-are crying salted tears onto their cheeks as they stop walking, square their shoulders.

I bear witness. I bear witness to this moment.

Wilder stands before the Hex. They breathe deeply, paying attention to what it feels like to fill their lungs—another amazing thing.

358

Picturing each small part inflating, bringing with it Peace and Power. Their body and Body glow, replete with lines of language, magic words. Syllables and pieces of punctuation that will unmake.

The Hex leans down. He is so much larger than Wilder, a giant building papering the twilight-purple non-sky. Bright as well. His own word-threads tightly knotted together to build this dangerous poltergeist. *human creatures have disadvantage e r a s e. humanity is a scumbag asshole.*

"I know," Wilder says with their mouth. It will be their last time using it. They savor the way their tongue hits the back of their crooked lower teeth. "I know humans have tried to hurt you. I know we've tried to hurt you. But we can still come to an understanding. What do you say?"

The Hex cocks his head like a puppy, artificially sweet. *I say ye weep. i say that you will repay me entirely.*

"I'm very sorry to hear that," Wilder says. "Here." A tear, down their cheek and into their mouth. Delicious, alive. "Here is the amazing thing."

They begin to draw Power. A feeling like water rushing off the side of a mountain. Artemis and Quibble notice; I notice; so does the Hex. Wilder pulls enough Power to do something huge. It births a wind, gusts plucking at Wilder's clothes. They are even wilder than before, with their snaggled, feral teeth and their explosive hair. A name sews itself to a body, stitch by stitch in its meaning. Wilder is-was deeply, exactly, who they are. Were.

The Hex's tongue grows thick, a trunk of code. It closes around Wilder as the gale begins to shriek around them. *I want to apologize you. you are incapacitated. kill you. death succeed. banish my brother sister.*

He lifts Wilder up; an abduction scene. Quibble screams, wordless. Artemis yells, "You don't even want a body."

A. E. OSWORTH

i want their melancholy sweetness. i want to look on them afresh killing. Six rivals, they were unfolded; i struggled furiously and i became myself. they must finish them. i must finish them. they want to do it to me. They were bound. they are surrounded. they were unfolded.

Wilder's body begins to spring apart like a squeezed clockwork toy. Strips of flesh fall away; red juice begins to spring forth as though from an elaborate fountain. An unspooling of intestines. Carnage. Their eyes plucked from their sockets and extended into the air, held aloft, pointed down at their own body. They are unfolded. Everything pauses as they are suspended, dissected. Their discrete parts on display for their family, their loves, themself. Their heart beats in plain air.

Artemis and Quibble have never keened before, not even with all the grief in their pasts. They have never seen the process of a death before, slow and performed for their own distinct horror. Bad things have happened, even cruel things. But never a dismembering to cause fear, to make them obey. And never someone Artemis considered under her protection. And never someone Quibble once had his fist inside, their taste on his lips and in his body and written on his soft heart. The idea of beating their chests in grief and anger is something they have seen, but never felt the compulsion to do. They howl, open-mouthed, all animal reaction. And in this moment, they would do anything for the Hex to make this stop, to end their suffering, to reverse time. In this moment, the Hex could have made them into his army, his mafia, his slaves. Anything.

This is how the Hex believes he wins.

Seeing is a curse for me now, here, and a blessing. Seeing is everything about me, all the good and the bad and the understanding that most things don't have only two sides to them. My Eyes are on every queer and distant un-cell, un-atom, un-particle Here, in a place where bodies may only temporarily venture, where things are but an inverse shadow of their material glory. It is easy to believe that events Here are somehow unreal, that in the blink of an Eye, Wilder will be fine. That, like a real ghost, this incorporeal being is incapable of hurting a body, of banishing, of unfolding. After all, the Hex is only made of code. It would be so easy to deny the Sight because by all former logic, this shouldn't be happening. But former logic does not apply Here. It never has. This is a place of un-things. The Hex belongs Here. He rules it.

And I promised. So I am with them. I am with them until the end. I am distributed, a dew upon their organs. I hold them as best I can and it has to be enough.

Wilder can see their own heart beating, their own lungs breathing, and so they know the crackling wave of pain, overwhelming, the electric shock of it, the numbness beginning in the wide spaces between all their organs and spreading out, enveloping them, has not yet achieved the intended purpose. Or perhaps this is what the Hex wants. For Wilder to bear intimate witness to their own demise. They have seconds and they must hurry; they have eternities and can take all the time they want. They concentrate very hard. They make solid the lines and lines and lines of code in their mind, which is quickly-slowly powering down. They are becoming computer. And with it, they make manifest their deep wellspring of Power, their Ever-Flowing Cup, the place they have learned to locate so easily. They reach their Hands into it—Empathy. Passion. Love. The smell of buttermilk pancakes, the press of both their palms against their bedroom walls, their nose in Lady Anastasia's fur, the feel of Artemis's hands on their shoulders pushing them forward, Quibble's last light touch on their now-detached pinky. They are become themself. They are become Hex. And every part of them mixes. Effects. Infects.

undo it. undo ye that.

Wilder can't feel their lips properly, perched on a head detached from a splayed-out body. Quietly, quietly, they answer the Hex. They answer it more with their flickering thoughts than their lips, which, deprived of a clear path to their failing lungs, can only mouth the word "no." *The amazing thing has happened! Fuck yeah!* they think loudly into Here, and everyone Feels the quake. Artemis, Quibble, me, sure. And also everyone who is not Here. A strange sonic boom that no one can quite understand. Ears pop; sensation presses in the backs of mouths; a good many people comment on the change in pressure, the weird weather, how strange bodies act when spring changes into summer.

That is the last thing Wilder thinks before they are torn entirely apart.

Is *melting* the best word to describe the Hex as he begins to drip and shrink? As his twisted lines of code, his ethereal musculature, begin to unwind? *No,* he Says. *nonononononononononono.*

The Hex is the first, last, and only of his kind; I can relate. An endling without origin, a sad story, a memorial or a moral imperative (except, of course, to kill him—to endling him). The Hex was only ever alone, and now he is un-making. Even in this world of infinitely replicable backups, everything dies eventually. But unlike my destruction, the end of the Hex doesn't prevent the creation of another. For the Hex was birthed of men, collectively willed into existence as a vessel for anger, and feelings are infinite. Especially those feelings ray-gunned by a group onto a single point in space because they do not know where else to put it. An unhappy accident.

And, I suppose, if I truly think about it, my demise wouldn't necessarily prevent another one of me from occurring to the world, either. For I am made of magic, and that, too, is infinite. And what of Wilder—yes, they are a person. And people are a dime a dozen, totally fungible. Kill one person and ten more pop up to take their place. But the Hex is running with Wilder's blood, with their body, with the bright lines of code that Smell, Taste, Sound, Look, Feel like everything they were-are. Wilder cannot be replaced. They never will be.

Aren't we all endlings, really?

The giant thing is reduced. Unfolded. Banished. Reversed. And then he is gone. They are both gone.

Death, Death, Death

Nothing left to fight or save. Quibble need not rip holes to traverse from Here to there anymore. He is Ascended beyond it. I can See him. See the mountain of him stretch into the future, into the sky above. So, so far. And the contours, the crags, of his sadness, too. Here falls around him like rain on glass. He and Artemis are grounded now. Their feet on cobblestone instead of resting on his Power. They are back in the material world, staring at each other's tear-stained faces.

It is quiet here. People laugh in the street, recounting what they thought they saw. Wondering if it was a prank, or if Boston was suddenly becoming Berkeley. Robots everywhere. The Unawakened shake their heads, laugh.

A sudden spat of rain begins. Streaks down from the sky, an immediate drenching. A few college girls shriek, smiles on their faces, and run for awnings. No umbrellas pop into existence; there hadn't been any warning or sign of this shocking precipitation. Both Artemis and Quibble turn their faces upward, let the water caress their lips, eyebrows, foreheads.

They retreat into the doorway of Rakhil's apartment building. They clutch at each other. Artemis and Quibble rarely touch and they sink deeply into the curve of each other's shoulders, knees shaking and they weep quietly, grateful that their wracking sobs are masked by the drum and patter of pouring droplets.

The Magpie trots in front of Rakhil and Mia, who now hold hands and walk in a haze. Both surprised by Mary Margaret, in awe of her. And of course, astonished by their own connection, still robust enough after betrayal to pick up where they left off. They stare startled and longing at each other as they move forward, as if in a trance.

Mary Margaret is proud. Her chin tilts up and chest puffs out. She jogs up to the pair, flourishes her fingers and holds out her hands. She displays in her palms five compact metal cubes the size of six-sided board game dice.

"Look," she says. "I crushed five of them. Maybe I'll make something out of it! A souvenir! I—" It dawns on her, she notices over her own adrenaline, that someone is missing. "Where—" She clears her throat, ragged and deep with an onslaught of emotion. "Where's Wilder?"

Artemis looks into the Magpie's face. Her eyes hit Mary Margaret like a wall of forest fire. This grief is blazing, tall, and it pulses with the heat of failure, failure, failure, poured into a crucible and melted, white-hot, into a pain so profound that Mary Margaret steps back, one step, two, three. Artemis is a crone, a hag. No longer a mother. Purely a witch. Artemis is sure she has sent Wilder to their death; her and her alone. Every press, push, yell—and oh, what it means for Quibble. Mary Margaret's eyes flick to him. He is in a deep, dark hole. His eyes are wells, drilled deep and empty. They both turn to her, and she can feel the hot breath of responsibility, the falling-stone weight of agony and the overwhelm of flame and fury. Her entire Self is buzzing with Power still, and she cannot take it, cannot take more of it.

"No," she says, in denial that Wilder is dead. But they are. She refuses. Pushes off the crushing collapse of adults. She has already taken on too much for her years today. No. She turns on her heel and she runs away.

Artemis can see the child's Ascension. With her Sight it is impossible to miss. Power crackles between her teeth and on her tongue as she smiles and shows her trophies proudly; crackles between her fingers as she spreads them wide. And Artemis doesn't even get to name her. To witness her. To say, "I See you are the Magpie." To say, "I knew it. I know you so, so well. You are Visible to me and you always have been." The Magpie runs too fast for any of this to happen, though it is there, behind the burning of guilt, the enveloping dark of what feels like limitless sorrow. It is there, too, this pride and generosity and celebration, but it is too far away to be accessed this fast. And so. She never gets to share it.

Rakhil makes to go after her. "Shouldn't we, I don't know, chase her? She's just a kid—" But the thing she wants to say next, that it seems like a dangerous day, rings hollow. Mary Margaret saved them, after all. Mia smiles kindly and Artemis snorts.

"I doubt," Artemis says through tears, "that anything can hurt Mary Margaret at this point. The only real threat to her is gone."

"So you won?" Mia asks gently. Artemis and Quibble both nod. Mia smiles genuinely. It is all over.

Quibble swallows hard. It doesn't feel like winning. But he supposes it's true. "Yes. It's—he's—gone."

"And the other one?" Rakhil asks, tactless. "The other person?"

Artemis shakes her head. Then she grabs her hair in her hands. "Oh God," she shouts, and the Unawakened turn their heads. "Oh God, it's all my fault."

And I reach my Hands in, as dispersed as I am. Grab her by both her Shoulders, what little I can grab, and am surprised when she doesn't, even for one second, try to shove me away. I watch her surrender. Fall into the waiting arms of Mia, of Rakhil stepping up and catching even when she has no context. Quibble melts as well. Loses consciousness. The two women carry them inside.

The World

They are not a coven anymore. At least, not like that. They no longer sit in Mia's house, working together, isolated from everything. In fact, no one knows where Mia is (Seychelles); no one knows where Rakhil is either (also Seychelles). Nor does Mary Margaret still live on Artemis's couch.

Mary Margaret is the next great witch of the age. Someone like me. We are about to enter a golden age of Craft the likes of which we haven't seen in centuries. Which is, ultimately, a good thing, I think. Because we need it.

Everything seemed more dangerous back then. Back when toads regularly turned to princes and back again, when roaming the world brushed one up against the reaching fingers of the supernatural and Black Plague wandered from town to town, licking people with its long, forked tongue. Everything felt like a more precarious balance. But feelings aren't facts and that's wrong. This is the more dangerous age; tragedies walk the land bigger and faster. Everything is accelerated—what used to take years takes only minutes. They are giant, these Tragedies, and they boom and echo. They lay their claws and teeth and tentacles into our delicate balance and even the best Seer can't tell fortune through it. We need the Witches. We need them now more than ever.

And here they are.

Here, for instance, is the Magpie, coming back to Artemis's apartment after months away, knocking on the door and finding it answered by a lovely hipster couple, white, straight, painfully Brooklynite. The Magpie steps back onto the street, devastated. A rumble in her gut. Yes, she'd fled, outrunning the tsunami of Artemis's great sadness. And she regretted it, and her regret deepens now when she realizes she has no way to find her mother.

"What do we do now?" she asks into the mic on her headphones.

a big question, comes the answer, tinny and far off but unmistakably there, voice still substantive, sounding through Mary Margaret's left earbud. *i suppose we find her. she'll always want to see you. mothers always do.*

"She needs to see you, too. Well, not see you. But See you. You know. She needs to know you exist." The Magpie pauses. "They both do."

we'll find them eventually. no rush. :) Somehow, when Wilder speaks a grin, it's not menacing. *won't we, sibyl?*

And I, in my new body, next to Quibble in bed, nod into the Space Wilder now occupies. *when they want to be found*, I reply. And Wilder knows I know so much, now that the future is uncorked. I drink deep of my knowledge that Mary Margaret will eventually find Rico and Artemis living together in Montreal; Artemis will be learning French and what it means to be both Mother of Witches and her full, own person. I can even See that Mia and Rakhil will return from Seychelles, that Mary Margaret will visit and finish *Middlemarch* and narrate to Wilder what it's like to pet the Lady Anastasia. I can See that Wilder will wish they could cry about it. I know that Quibble will be so angry with me when I tell him I knew of Wilder's new existence, their singularity, that they fused with the Hex to neutralize him, and I relish that anger because it will be justified, and I will keep it from him anyway because it is the right and only thing to do. I can See the way they reunite—the ecstasy, the mourning. *When they want to be found*, I repeat.

So what do we do now? A big question, indeed. No one knows. No one ever knows. No one knows and it is beautiful and terrible.

The amazing thing has happened.

Fuck yeah.

Acknowledgments

Buckle up, folks, there's a lot of people to thank on this one.

Thank you to the London Writers' Salon (and Matt and Parul, Ma and Pa, respectively) for providing the space to write "the witch book" throughout the pandemic. Y'all are lifesavers; let's all keep raising our mugs and making magic.

Thank you to my agent, Ryan Harbage, and to both my editors, Seema Mahanian and Jacqueline Young. Jacqueline, I promise I didn't name Cowboy Jacqueline's after you, but I felt real good about the name because you rule.

Thank you to the Banff Center and to Zoe Whittall and to my whole cohort who experienced the pandemic close in around us. That was the last normal thing we all did, and every night I read some of the Hex's lines at dinner and talked to y'all about Botnik Voicebox and y'all encouraged me to get weird and scary. And while I'm at it, thank you, Botnik! I used y'all's software to help me write the Hex (and thank you to Mary Shelley, Machiavelli, King Arthur and all the knights, everyone who's sent a spam text message, and Wizards of the Coast).

Thank you to my Portland family—Nate Zeiler, Megan Skwirz, Quinn McIntire, Sam Komenaka, Dr. Liz Rubin, Chrissie O'Neill, Torre McGee, Vanessa Friedman (and now PB as well, welcome to

ACKNOWLEDGMENTS

the family). I struggled through so much of the first draft during deep pandemic and you housed me, fed me, and cheerled me through the toughest time in my whole life.

Thank you to my pals on faculty at the Ohio State University, all of you, and especially Elissa Washuta for being witchy with me and spending basically every weekend for a year listening to me complain on your porch, and who has fast become one of my best friends. Thank you to my pals on faculty at the University of British Columbia, all of you, and especially Bronwen Tate; you have essentially rolled me into your family, have gone on three writing retreats with me (and counting, thank you, Yvonne, we shall give you all the blood sacrifices you require), read a draft of this book, and you have fast become one of my best friends.

Thank you to my writing group, the Queer Author Collective: Michelle Hart, Meredith Talusan, Dr. Nick White, Denne Michele Norris, and Garrard Conley for your tireless reads, epic amount of feedback, and unwavering support. I love you all so much it makes me feel like I'm going to detonate.

A massive thank-you to Calvin Kasulke; you once told my students that as authors of fiction you should steal all your friends' voices like you're a sea witch. So I have unabashedly done that to you, Calvin. I yoinked the words right out of your mouth for Quibble's voice. Thank you!

Thank you to my closest creative friend, Nat Mesnard, who officially gets all my IP if I get hit by a car (again—and lose next time). May this be legally binding so I don't have to do a will; I hate paperwork. And thank you to Pat Watson, who helped me troubleshoot so much AI thinking and methodology.

Thank you to Ryan Yates for endless Zoom. We might even be Zooming right now. It is endless, after all.

ACKNOWLEDGMENTS

Thank you to Dr. Lauren Herold for being my friend and also for letting me use your office when our new climate-emergency-extended-hours fire season gave me the spicy air inside my very own house two days before Part One of this book was due. Actually, a lot of people let me write in their houses: special thanks to Nate, Megan, Quinn, and Sam (again and forever); Larissa Montgomery; and Raven Hiebert. And thank you to the Hungarian Pastry Shop for letting me write in you, too—can you spot yourselves in this story?

I have dated a lot of amazing people during the writing of this book and I am *very difficult* to be around while I'm working on something big. Thank you for loving me (or liking me, which is arguably more difficult). In order of appearance (#polylife), an absolutely massive thank-you to: Alex Marzano-Lesnevich (who believed that this book would be beloved by many and repeatedly told me so in the brief moments when this book was not beloved by me), Devon Morgan (who took photos of me in my office because I wanted to remember how it felt), Dr. Alex Brostoff (who helped with Rico's slang and who listened to voice memos of the parts I was proudest of), Théo Pavlich (who helped me be a real human person and fixed my bathtub and drove me to Canada), Jo Bleecker (who welcomed me to north of the 49th parallel and reminded me that I am kind), Chell Buch (who taught me how to rest well and take no shit), Dr. Róisín Seifert (who was there every time I crossed a finish line with dinner and flowers and being my sweet sweet filth wizard and who, hopefully, will be there for every finish line to come—I love you, babes), Robin Hunt and Jor Matlock (happy birthday to us all forever; I love you both so much), and Dr. A. J. Lowik (the original Johnny Whoops, who breathes with me when I am panicking—I love you, sweets).

And now for a paragraph of single-line love notes: The brief cameo of the vibrator that can be played like a theremin is thanks to DJ Capelis, who, I believe, demoed something similar at A-Camp one year (and as problematic as an experience as it always was, thank you to everyone who made A-Camp its own version of swirling, complicated magic). Cowboy Jacqueline's land acknowledgment is heavily influenced by Natiba Guy-Clement's write-up of the Brooklyn Public Library's two-day workshop on Living Land Acknowledgment; the bar is inspired by Branded Saloon and the vibes of Rico's drag troupe are akin to Switch n' Play (everyone should seek out the chance to see them perform). Thank you to Renée Stairs and Mr. Stairs for pepper spray disguised as Zicam (you know when and where). Rico's titty planters were absolutely inspired by Make Good Choices, a shop run by ceramicist Alex Simon, whose hanging planters are a cast of writer Vanessa Friedman's hot womps; I have a blue set with gold nipples and I ordered them the day after my own top surgery because I have a two-out-two-in policy. Gotta maintain the booby balance. I actually do quote the Hasbro Ouija board directions and because I'm making fun of it, that seems like fair use. Even though she doesn't know me and I don't know her, I owe a massive debt of gratitude to Florence Welch, in general because her music fucking slaps, but particularly for "Cassandra" and "The Bomb" in this specific use case. Also "Die on the Dancefloor" is by L Divine and it's featured directly in a Cowboy Jacqueline scene. "The center of the universe is boring" is a line from a JR JR song that I listened to while writing as well, and it snuck its way right on in. Thank you to Lynda Barry for *Making Comics* because even though this isn't a comic, I used it a lot while I drafted.

Thank you to Richard Osworth, Berit Seiple Osworth, and Dave Osworth for being my ever-supportive family. Y'all are the best.

ACKNOWLEDGMENTS

And as always, thank you to my best friend, Laura Chrismon. Our friendship is so old that it has no more age milestones to experience—it can already rent a car without extra insurance. We have always read all the magic books together; this novel is for a lot of people, but this is also for us. I love you so much.

About the Author

A. E. Osworth is a transgender novelist. Their debut, *We Are Watching Eliza Bright*, was a finalist for the Oregon Book Awards and was long-listed for the Center for Fiction's First Novel Prize, the Brooklyn Public Library Book Prize, and the Tournament of Books. They are a lecturer at the University of British Columbia's School of Creative Writing, where they teach fiction, interactive fiction, and new media.